Johnny McCarthy

A Coal Miner's Son

Books by Dwight Norris

The Gentleman Host

My Name Is Inferno

Johnny McCarthy

A Coal Miner's Son

A Novel

Dwight Norris

Johnny McCarthy
A Coal Miner's Son

Copyright © 2014 by Dwight Norris

Published by Dwight Norris
Apple Valley, CA 92307

Printed in the United States of America

This book is an historical novel. While every attempt has been made to be historically accurate and culturally authentic, the story of Johnny McCarthy and his family is fiction.

ISBN 13: 978-1503271692
ISBN 10: 1503271692

ACKNOWLEDGMENTS

No book is ever completed without the encouragement and feedback of one's circle of influence. For me that includes many friends and fellow members of the California Writers Club, High Desert Branch. The critique group known as the Wordsmiths was particularly helpful in evaluating early chapters. My good friend and astute story consultant, Bob Isbill, gave me insight into balanced story structure and content. Loralie Kay, a good friend and member of the HDCWC and the Wordsmiths was kind enough to read every chapter of the rough draft and offer helpful observations. A special thanks to my brother Bruce Norris, who took me on a trip to southern West Virginia where we walked the streets of Matewan and saw the bullet holes from the shootout on May 19th, 1920, and stood on the courthouse steps in Welch, the site of the assassination of Sid Hatfield and Ed Chambers. A special thanks to Judi Isbill who read voraciously through the chapters as they were being completed and would frequently say, "Hurry up Dwight, I have to see what happens next!" And appreciation to a new friend, Wendi Smith, who devoured the book quickly with great gusto. Kudos to Roberta Smith for cover design and editing expertise. Thanks to everyone who had a special interest in this book and offered encouragement for its completion.

DEDICATION

This book is dedicated to my grandfather, Willie Norris, who was born November 8, 1893, and who died August 12, 1954, at the age of 60. He is pictured above wearing the hat. To his right are my father and mother, Paul and Virginia Norris. The little guy in front is the author.

My grandfather worked as a blacksmith for the B&O Railroad, first in Grafton, then in Clarksburg, West Virginia. He hand-forged the parts that kept the railroad hauling coal. Though he didn't work in the mines, he died of lung cancer, known in those days as Black Lung Disease, that claimed the lives of so many miners in the early to mid-twentieth century.

My grandfather was known for his strength and toughness, and while I don't doubt his reputation, he was always kind and gentle to me.

Chapter 1

The rats was never wrong.

Johnny felt the rumble deep underground. The trembling started at his feet, worked its way up his legs and hips, even to his shoulders. There was a faint noise too, like distant thunder on a cloudy day, but it was all around—to the sides, above, and below.

Rats scurried up the tunnel towards higher ground. The excavation of the mine at this depth brought it close to the bedrock of the Tug Fork, and a collapse at this level could result in the flooding of river water up to your neck and even the total filling of chambers. When rats made for higher ground, miners was wise to follow.

A chunk of shale dropped out of the roof and crashed with a thud, filling the chamber with dust and crushing the carbide lamp ten feet away. It seemed to Johnny that the whole mountain was coming down. The only light remaining shone out of the portable lamp mounted on the front of his mining cap. But what about Gilbert's lamp? He wore a light on his cap too.

Just then more chunks of rock dropped out of the ceiling, creating a chest-high pile of rubble in front of him and off to the side. So far, the chamber was still dry, and there was headroom to move about. To breathe in was to choke on the dust-filled air.

"Gilbert, can you hear me?"

Johnny searched for his buddee, his fourteen-year-old assistant.

"Gilbert!" he shouted.

He heard a faint voice in the distance, not far away, but muffled in the collapse. Johnny made his way to where the cry was coming from. Rocks small enough to lift he tossed behind him—others he crawled over. Headroom was still enough to get through.

"Gilbert!" he cried out again.

The return call sounded closer this time. Johnny knew that some cave-ins resulted in a chamber sealed off from air and light. In that event, the miners was trapped sometimes for days, suffocating or starving to death before rescuers could get to them. He knew of one time when miners slaughtered the mule that was trapped with them and ate its flesh piece by piece to survive 'til they was rescued.

Johnny figured their depth to be about five hundred and fifty feet. Because of his ability to crawl over the rubble, he had hope this was not a collapse that entombed them, but a pile of debris they could go around.

"Gilbert, where are you?"

Now he heard sobbing just ahead, but still muffled. Then loud cries, though still strangely subdued.

"Gilbert!"

The howl that come from his buddee was now in earnest, desperate even, and Johnny knew that his young apprentice was in a panic. He'd been in the mines for only a couple months, and this was his first collapse.

"Gilbert, it's all right, my lad. We gonna be okay!"

Groans was just ahead now, and Johnny carefully felt his way over a jagged pile of rocks. On the other side, Johnny could see that Gilbert was pinned to the chamber floor, his right leg covered with medium-sized rocks with a good-sized slab leaning on his left shoulder and rib cage.

Johnny carefully lifted the rocks from his leg and looked for injury. The bone in the boy's leg was messed up—not sticking through the skin, but definitely displaced and needing to be set. His foot was crushed flat and didn't look like what a foot and ankle should look like. The larger rock sitting on Gilbert's upper body he could not budge. He found a timber that had broken off the support rigging of the tunnel and used it like a crowbar. With several big efforts, Johnny slid the rock away from the boy's body and off to the side.

"Listen to me, Gilbert," Johnny said. "Your leg is busted and you ain't gonna be able to walk out of here. I'm gonna get us some help."

"Don't leave me!" Gilbert said. "Please don't leave me here!"

"I ain't going nowhere, but I gotta signal for help."

Johnny grabbed a small pickax from his tool belt and began tapping on the rock wall to the rib side of the rubble. His papa had always told him if he was ever in a cave-in to tap on the wall. Tells rescuers you're still alive. And don't ever stop tapping. Raises the need to get to you right now and they'll work harder to get you out while you're still breathing.

"Oh, I can't move," Gilbert said.

"Don't *try* to move. We just gotta be patient 'til the rescuers get here."

"You got some water?" Gilbert asked.

"I'll find my canteen," Johnny said.

He crawled over the top of the rubble back to the other side. With the light from his headlamp he could see his canteen lying intact on the rock floor near the opposite wall of the chamber. Johnny could tell just by crawling over the pile and back he used up oxygen he didn't have to spare. He wondered how long they would have air to breathe.

"I gotta keep tapping," Johnny said.

Gilbert's headlamp had been destroyed in the collapse. The only light in the entire pocket of rock they was in was the portable carbide lamp attached to Johnny's cap, and he knew it wouldn't last forever. He could add water to it from his canteen, and he could even slow the drip into the lower chamber where the calcium carbide was stored. But when the lower chamber run out, all he'd have would be useless slaked lime that wouldn't help him see any better than a blind mule.

Johnny knew he needed to survey the cavity while he still could. He knew that after a cave-in, it's easy to lose sense of direction and not know which way to go. It's hard to remember where the openings was and where the passageways led. As he turned his head and splashed light against the walls, he could see they was entombed for sure. No openings he could see. No passageways to crawl through. No light streaking in from any cracks or crevices.

"You got some more water, Johnny?"

He gave Gilbert a couple more swallows of water, and turned down the dial on his headlamp so less water would flow into the carbide chamber. The light dimmed, but was enough so he could keep tapping against the wall and see what he was doing. Papa said you gotta keep tapping. Always keep tapping. No tapping back yet. They be coming soon. They be answering soon, letting him know they was excavating the cave-in and pulling them out.

The silence was eerie. Not even the squeak of a rat. They had all run up out of here to avoid the collapse, so wasn't none of them around. Smart little bastards, they was. Only himself and Gilbert left. Only noise was breathing and tapping, and no tapping coming from the other side.

Time staggered forward. The light seemed to be getting lower. Johnny took off his cap and looked at his headlamp. The calcium carbide in the lower chamber was almost run out. The acetylene gas it produced was a very small amount, and the flame was less than a single candle on a birthday cake. Johnny knew there was only moments left of any light at all.

He scrambled over in the direction of the far wall, some twenty feet away, and noticed a pile of fresh-fallen rock. The way it puckered out from the rib, it seemed to Johnny that the small rocks might have been spit out of a monkey-head, a small sideways passage that led to a chute, which would lead to the gangway. That would be the ticket out. The rocks was small enough to move. No guarantees, but just maybe. Sweat dripped into Johnny's eyes and stung.

Just then, total darkness.

"What happened?" Gilbert screamed. "Where am I? Johnny? Are you here?"

"I'm here, Gilbert. I'm right here" he said, feeling his way back to Gilbert's side. "You doze off?"

"Yeah, I guess so. When I opened my eyes, it was darker than ever. Didn't know where I was."

"You just stay put," Johnny said. "I'm gonna do some more tapping. They gotta be getting close to us now."

And tap he did.

Tap, tap, tap for ten seconds—listen for twenty.

Tap, tap, tap. Tap, tap, tap.

Papa always said keep tapping, and he knew what he was talking about. Worked in the Ballingarry Mines in Tipperary County twenty-five years. Not as big a mountains as the Appalachians in West Virginia, but big just the same. Papa had been down five, six hundred feet. Been in some cave-ins, some flooding for sure.

Tap, tap, tap.

"Johnny, how come they ain't answering us?" Gilbert wanted to know. "Where they at?"

"They on their way, for sure. Just gotta be patient."

Johnny continued to tap.

Tap, tap, tap.

The darkness was bulky, like the black velvet hood over the head of a convict about to be hanged.

"Aaahhhh!"

Gilbert's scream racked Johnny to the bones.

"What's the matter, Gilbert?"

Johnny reached across his body and touched the hairy rump of a large rat. He let his hand slide down to the base of the tail and grabbed on. He swung the rat overhead and slammed it hard into the rock floor.

"You okay, Gilbert?"

Gilbert was sobbing. Johnny reached for his face and felt the warm, slippery liquid pooling on the surface and running down. The rat had come in darkness and in silence, and slashed through the fleshy cheek of the young man. Johnny knowed they had to get out of this tomb.

Be patient and keep tapping. The words resounded in his head. Words Papa would say. But Papa also said, "God helps them that helps themselves." This seemed like one of them times. Johnny felt his way to the other side of the rock pile where the smaller rocks puckered out from the wall. He reached into the front of his overalls and pulled out the leather cord around his neck with the Blarney Stone at the end of it. The one Papa gave him. He felt it in his fingers and brought it to his lips.

"In the name of St. Patrick," he prayed, "get us out of this hole in the ground, and let us live to work another day."

He kissed the stone, and started tossing rocks.

Chapter 2

Johnny worked by touch. The first rocks was about the size of softballs, and he could toss them off to his right. Sometimes, a bigger rock had to be moved. He closed his eyes to lift one of them, but soon realized it didn't matter if his eyes was open or closed. His darkness was the same.

Johnny thought of his beloved wife, Kate. Stood by him all these years—good times and bad. What would become of her without him? And their precious new baby daughter, Elsie. And their son, Corey, same age as his assistant buried in the hole right now.

"How's it coming, Johnny?" Gilbert called out.

"Getting on okay. Have to see where this takes us. Hear any tapping over there?"

"Nope, nothing happening over here," Gilbert said.

Johnny's excavation was slow, but it moved him forward. He could feel that he had reached the rib of the wall on the far side, and he was still taking out rocks. That meant he was moving into the wall. There *was* an opening, but filled with rocks. He felt hope, but would save his encouragement for Gilbert when he could know more for sure.

"You need to get me out of here, Johnny!" Gilbert yelped.

The urgency and panic of his voice worried Johnny, but he felt the best thing he could do was keep working on their escape. He reached in and pulled out more rocks. Now he had to crawl in and stick his head and upper body into the opening. He was going into a small tunnel. He could feel each side of the round structure with his hands. It was not just a pile of rocks with no shape. It was round like a pipe but big enough for a man's body and he kept moving into its depths. It was part of the structure of the mountain, not bits and pieces thrown together by the force of a collapse.

"Johnny!" Gilbert yelled. "I want to see my mama!"

Strange, Johnny thought. He could have sworn Gilbert's mama had passed last year of consumption. He guessed he could be wrong.

"I'm working on it, Gilbert," Johnny called out. "We're getting there."

Johnny was lying on his belly, fully extended now into the opening. He wished he could measure his progress by seeing with his eyes, but the feel of his hands would have to do. The rocks was about the same at this part of the tunnel, same size, same feel, but this time something told him to push on them instead of pulling them out and crawling backwards. His instinct was right. The rocks gave way and fell out into open space, still dark as the coal they was pulling out of the mountain. But the air felt different—not stale and stuffy, but cooler. Johnny knew he was on to something. He cleared out the last few rocks.

"Gilbert, we got a way to go here," he called out.

Gilbert was moaning and screaming.

"Mama!" he shouted.

Johnny scrambled back out of the monkey-head and over the pile of rubble to be at Gilbert's side. The boy's skin was cold and clammy.

"Mama!" he called out again. "I want to see my mama!"

"All right, listen to me," Johnny said. "I'm gonna take my belt off and wrap it under your shoulders and pull you through the little tunnel."

"Okay, Johnny."

"Now listen," he said. "This is gonna hurt real bad, but it's the only way to get you out of here, you understand?"

"All right, Johnny. Just get me back to my mama!"

Johnny hooked up his belt, which was now a tugging strap. As Johnny started to move him, Gilbert howled. He could only imagine the pain the boy felt. Who knew how bad his injuries was?

"*Aahhh!*" he screamed again.

Johnny found his way around the rock pile towards the monkey-head. He knew he was hurting Gilbert, but he could tell the boy tried to settle down and bear up under the pain. His yells became groans and whimpers.

"Where's my mama?" he cried. "I wanna see my mama!"

Johnny couldn't believe he was scrambling like this in the pitch blackness of a hole in a mountain five hundred feet below the surface. The silence was suffocating. He held his hand up in front of his face. Nothing. He had no hope, except the coolness of the air hitting him in the face. And the desire to get back to his family. Would Papa be moving on like this, or would he have stayed patient and kept tapping on the wall?

The opening of the monkey-head was not wide enough to fit both of them side by side. Johnny had to get in first, then pull Gilbert from behind. His buddee was lying on his back, and Johnny could move him only a foot or so at a time. After half a dozen pulls, he found he did better if he rested a few seconds.

Johnny was grateful the way was pretty clear. The rock floor of the monkey-head was flat and fairly even, unblocked by debris, although at a slight upward slope. He couldn't tell how long he'd been working in this tiny tunnel. Seemed like hours, but Johnny knew it was probably only a little part of that.

As he struggled pulling Gilbert forward, he kept feeling the sides of the monkey-head, for when it came onto a larger tunnel, a chute that led to the gangway. To Johnny, getting to the gangway was almost as good as getting home. He knew the gangway was Main Street in a mine, the roadway where mules was pulling carts loaded with coal, and nippers and spraggers was working, and mule drivers. That's where the help was that he needed to get Gilbert the rest of the way out of the hole.

Only the cool air kept giving Johnny hope. Only the cool air led him to believe this little tunnel deep in the mountain wasn't a tomb. Only the cool air led somewhere, and he held onto that belief.

Gilbert continued to moan, but now uttered words Johnny couldn't understand. Just then, to the left, the chute he had hoped for. Wider and bigger, with a higher ceiling, and clear with a smooth, even floor. Johnny noticed the pea-soup thickness of the dark begin to thin. The air seemed to be a dim gray, and he could see the form of his hand before his eyes. Now the air was not just cooler, but fresher. It was the lifeline he needed. Johnny was able to stand now on bended knees for more leverage and pull Gilbert up next to him with each new stroke.

"We gonna make it now, Gilbert. We getting on out of here. They be waiting for us. You gonna be sitting at that table eating Mama's cooking right soon."

Johnny did not want to take the time to think about how tired he felt or how much pain he was in. He did not want to go there in his mind. And he did not want to rest. He wanted to rise up out of the catacombs to feel the wind blowing on his face and the fresh air in his lungs, and to see the green trees and glow of Kate's smiling face. He wanted to work tirelessly like the mule that pulled his coal to the surface and be done for the day.

Rats squeaked in the gray light and pairs of eyes like red glowing bb's stared from the distance.

The floor of the tunnel continued in an upward slope, but as he pulled Gilbert along, Johnny begun to bump his head on the ceiling. He was pretty sure the ceiling was level, but with the ongoing slope of the floor, less clearance was available. In twenty feet, he could no longer stand, even on bended knee. His necessary crouch took away the leverage of his pull, and the work became difficult again.

He released his hold on the tug belt, and crawled on hands and knees forward as the clearance continued to shrink. His slow creep ended with the near joining of ceiling and floor, closing them into the chute. The only glint of hope, and the source of fresh air, was a three-inch crevice, a sliver of light and air that promised life on the other side.

Johnny heard sounds and squinted through the opening. His view was sideways onto the gangway. He saw the legs of a mule up to its haunches, with the harness strapped on and going back to the loaded coal car. He saw the mule driver up to his chest walk past, and heard a muffled conversation. Mule driver talking to a nipper maybe, telling him to open the ventilation doors and let him pass through.

Johnny was excited, and shouted out. His voice was swallowed up in the mountain. He yelled louder, trying to throw his voice through the gap. His effort got him nothing, but he didn't crawl this far to die on the other side of life. The floor of the chute seemed to be granite, but the ceiling, coal. He could carve that out. He could chip that away if he had his pickax. *Damn!* Why didn't he bring it? Many reasons, he knew. No time to second-guess himself now. He scurried back down to Gilbert and put his hand on his face. Cold and clammy. Maybe in shock.

"All right, Gilbert. Listen to me now. We real close to getting out of here, but I gotta go back and get my tool belt. The tunnels are open all the way, so it shouldn't take me too long. You stay right here, and I'll be back and bust us out, okay?"

"I *will* be back, Gilbert. You can be sure of that!"

Chapter 3

Johnny turned, and descended into the blackness. He felt excited, but afraid at the same time. Excited because he was sure he could break out of the chute into the gangway. Afraid because to go back to the site of the collapse, to flag his way through that tiny monkey-head in thick blackness, made no sense. Why would anybody go back to death and strangling darkness and collapse? It seemed wrong to do it, but he knew he had to.

Moving down the chute was easy enough. Room to move about. Easier to move himself than drag somebody with him. When he crawled from the chute into the monkey-head is when it hit him. Closed in, panicky, nauseous. The monkey-head was so narrow there was no room for losing your way. Forward was all there was, but every inch was pushing a stone wall. Fear threatened to grab him by the neck and choke him out. The darkness crawled down his throat and gagged him.

Johnny kept inching forward, but shouldn't he be in the chamber by now? How long was this monkey-head? It did not feel familiar. How much time should this take? What, a couple hundred yards between the chute and the monkey-head? Or was it longer? Could he have found a different little tunnel that leads to nowhere? And how long has it been since he left Gilbert lying on the edge of life? Keep moving forward is all he could tell himself. Inch by inch. Keep moving.

Finally, the tight little tunnel opened up and he reached into the chamber. A look around would have helped but touch was all he had. He pulled his body to the right, the same area he dragged Gilbert through to get to the monkey-head. But the way was not clear. Rocks blocked his movement. This was the way he took, wasn't it? Had there been another collapse, or had he chosen the wrong way?

He felt his way to the other side but ran into the rocks he had thrown out to clear the monkey-head. He lifted himself over the pile, moving towards the rib on the other side of the chamber. This is where he had tapped on the wall, wasn't it? Or was it over there at some other unseen spot in this hell-hole? Why couldn't he just see where it was? He felt like screaming, like tearing up the whole damn mountain with his hands and walking out into the fresh air.

He calmed himself and looked deep inside. He remembered Papa said always do all you can to help yourself, and when that's not enough, ask for the rest. It'll be there for you.

Well God, if you out there somewhere, and if you created everything like the Good Book says, then you know where I am. And you know I need to get out of here, and I need to get Gilbert out of here. So if you could do something to make that happen, I sure would appreciate it.

Johnny sat there in the silence. Now what? He shifted over to his hands and knees and drug his body to the left. He could feel a large pile of rocks at his left hand, but a clear pathway ahead along the right rib of the chamber. In about ten feet, he felt something on the rock floor. His tool belt. And with his left hand just a few inches away, the pickax he used for tapping.

Is it that simple? he wondered. Thank you, God! He threaded the handle of the pickax through the leather loop and strapped the belt around his waist. He crawled over the pile of rubble, coming down on the opposite wall near the opening of the monkey-head. He lunged into it very excited. No time to stop. No time to slow down. Tell Gilbert the good news, and get them out.

Darkness still swallowed him up, but Johnny made short work of the monkey-head, and was happy to make his way into the larger chute leading to the gangway. Already the air tugged at his lungs and drew him up the slope. Soon he could stand, but not straight up, so it was easier to stay on his knees. Soon he could see the movement of his bloodied hands on the granite floor. Soon he would be out of the chute, up the gangway, and out of the mountain. Gilbert and him would be home.

As he moved up the slope, he could see the sliver of light leaking through the crevice at the end of the chute. Johnny knew that most of that light was from the lamps in the gangway, but even natural light had a way of seeping in. Kind of like water. It leaked through any opening no matter how small. No keeping it out. And he heard the squeaking of rats. Lots of rats.

The slope continued upward and the roof stayed straight across, so the headway was less. The streak of light lay just ahead. His eyes was fixed on the thin slot in the rock. To his left, though, out of the corner of his eye, dark gray movement. Nervous movement as if they wasn't wanting to be seen. He looked directly at it, and gasped.

"Aahhh!"

"Oh my God! *Aaahhhh!"*

The rats scurried away. Left was the gnarled, misshapen face and form of Gilbert Dugan. Strips of cloth had been torn from his legs and arms. Fabric left behind was mostly crimson stained. His eyes had been harvested from their sockets and the only flesh left on his face and skull was the patch on his forehead and the scalp that rooted the hair to his head.

"Aaahhhh!"

Johnny whipped the pickax out of his belt and swung wildly at a couple rats perched nearby. Disgusting bastards! He picked up a rock the size of a baseball and hurled it at a dirty old rat sitting upright on its haunches. A yelp told him it was a direct hit.

Johnny grabbed hold of the belt he had fastened around Gilbert's shoulders. Before he pulled him to the wall holding the seam between coal and granite, he noticed Gilbert's position was one of dignity and peace. Seemed strange to think of it that way. What it meant to him was that Gilbert gave up the ghost before the rats got to him. Gilbert died thinking of his mama, and was truly about to join her at the table prepared in the presence of his enemies. That's what

Johnny chose to believe and that's what he did believe. He retched and vomited on the barefaced rock floor.

He swung his pickax from the ground up, and sliced off chunks of coal from the top of the chute and tossed them aside. He hit the ceiling as hard as he could, fueled by rage. Chunks of coal flew through the air and opened up the gap between floor and ceiling. He slipped his pickax back on his tool belt, and reached for Gilbert's remains.

Out in the gangway, Johnny carried Gilbert's body over his shoulder. When he walked out to the main coal car area, Max, an operations supervisor walked up, along with a foreman Johnny did not know. Jim Mullins, a friend and neighbor, stood off to the side.

"What you doing over here, McCarthy?" Max barked.

"Had a cave-in down at level five. Tunneled out."

"What you got on your shoulder?"

"My buddee, Gilbert," Johnny said. "He died in the collapse. How come nobody come for the rescue?"

"We was busy trying to hit full coal," the foreman said.

"Got it, too!" Max said with a grin.

"I was tapping on the wall of the chamber for hours," Johnny said.

"Tapping? We ain't got no time to listen for tapping," the foreman said. "Too busy hitting our quota."

"Lay him over there on the side," Max said. "We'll coffin his body tomorrow."

Johnny turned and lay Gilbert's body down on the stone floor where the supervisor said. How could he leave him behind after all this? What about them damn rats? Well, this ain't really Gilbert, he told himself. He already in a better place.

Johnny and his friend Jim walked down the gangway to the lift. They stepped into the steel frame, and pushed the lever to UP.

"God-damned bastards!" Jim said.

Chapter 4

Kate ran up to her husband and threw her arms around him. As filthy as he was, Johnny knew she didn't care. She reached up and wiped some smudge off his face.

"You okay?" she asked.

Johnny just smiled and showed his white teeth through that black face. Miners and neighbors gathered 'round.

"That a boy, Johnny!"

"Way to go, man. Glad you're all right!"

Hands patted him on his back and shoulders. Johnny just wanted to go home.

"Wasn't Gilbert Dugan with you?" a woman's voice called out.

Johnny stopped and turned, and looked in her direction.

"Where's Gilbert?"

Johnny turned his back and headed for home.

"Wasn't my Gilbert with you? Where he at?" the woman cried out. "What happened to Gilbert?"

Johnny turned and faced her. "Got killed in the cave-in," Johnny said. "Body's down there right off the gangway. They coffin his body in the morning."

Johnny heard a low murmur from the crowd.

"That's it?" the woman sobbed. "My Gilbert gets left for tomorrow?"

Kate tugged at Johnny's shirt.

"Let's get home," she said. "I'll heat some water for your bath."

As Johnny and Kate approached the wood shack, their son Corey came bursting out the front door.

"Pa, you okay?" he cried.

Johnny put his arms around his only son. He felt a tear run down his cheek and knew it must be black.

"I'm okay, son. I'm okay," he said. "How you doing?"

"I'm good Pa. Can't get hurt in the breaker building. You just sit there and sort rocks."

"The heck you can't," Johnny said. "Boys lose fingers and hands and arms in that God-forsaken place. You know that."

"Seems pretty easy to me, Pa. I must be the oldest boy there. When can I go down in the mine and work like a real man?"

Johnny glanced at Kate and turned to face his son.

"Corey, what happened in the mine today is why I don't want you to *ever* work down the hole. We had a collapse today, and a boy just your age was crushed."

"Aw Pa, I'd be careful. Besides, I just want to run the mules around and take care of them!"

"Oh, and you think you'd be safe doing that, huh? Some of them get pretty mean 'cause they don't like staying down the hole any more than a man does."

"Aw Pa!"

"Listen, tomorrow morning, before you go to the breaker house, I want you to take that bucket and go to the culm banks and bring us back some coal."

"Aw Pa. Why do I have to do that?"

"'Cause it's free coal, and we need it."

"Did they have culm banks in Ireland?"

"Yep. All coal mines have piles of waste. You know that from the breaker house. By the time they dump it all out, there's slate, rock, and little bits of coal that slipped through."

"Did they have mountains of it like we do?"

"Not quite as much," Johnny said. "And that reminds me, when you sifting through picking out the coal, don't climb too high up on the pile. That stuff can shift and bury you alive."

"Did you go to the culm banks for Papa when you was a boy?"

"Yep, but in Ireland they called it duff."

Kate walked up and tapped her son on the shoulder.

"I need some help, young man. I want you to fill the big pot with water, well, about halfway up. And stock the stove with wood. And make sure the tub is clean. We gotta get your pa a good bath."

"Yes ma'am."

"And how's our baby girl doing today?" Johnny asked.

"Two months old today, Pa. Did you know?"

"Of course!" Johnny winked. "She eatin' any better?"

Corey ran outside to the pump, and Kate bent down to lift her baby out of a makeshift box. Mama wore a flowered pink pajama top like a man's shirt and cradling little Elsie in one arm, turned towards Johnny and with her free hand lifted the hem of her top revealing a massive teat about to burst. She squeezed it and sent a stream of milk towards Johnny half-way across the room.

Johnny smiled wide.

"You'll have to help me with that later, big boy," Kate said.

Corey walked back through the door, lugging the pot of water. Johnny sat on a scrappy old wooden chair and watched his wife lovingly insert her large nipple into their baby's mouth. As Elsie sucked, Kate gave Johnny that look that no man can mistake. He felt himself getting hard in his grimy trousers. Johnny knew he was a lucky man. He couldn't wait 'til Kate was all healed up. She got pretty tore up in child birth. Female stuff. He watched his son stoke the fire, boil the cool well-water, and wipe out the round steel tub. Corey was a good boy, and Johnny felt grateful for every member of his loving family.

Corey was ready to set up the tub in the middle of the floor. Johnny pitched in and helped position the tub and pour in some of the steaming water. That was in his best interest because he might be black now with coal dust, but he knew his ass was lily white under all that grime, not to mention soft and tender, and if he scorched that ass with boiling hot water, it might never be the same. So, he estimated the level of heat by sticking in his pinky finger, then added a pitcher of cool water from the bucket. When he felt it was just right, he pulled off his boots and socks, dropped his trousers, threw off his shirt, and plunged into the tub.

"Did Papa take baths like this in Ireland?" Corey asked.

"Pretty much," Johnny said. "But we only had one tub full of water each night, and I was the youngest of five kids, so you know what that meant."

"What?"

"That meant that Papa got his bath first 'cause he worked all day, then the oldest kid, your Uncle Sean, then all the way down to me."

"You mean in the same water?"

"Yep, by the time I got into the tub, the water was cold and black."

"That's awful!"

"It was okay as long as you didn't drink it."

"Oh, that's terrible!" Corey said.

In the tub, Johnny folded his knees up against his chest, and plan as they would, water spilled over the top of the tub all around and soaked the wood floor below. Sometimes he'd just sit on the rim of the tub and avoid all the problems. Kate threw him a rag and a bar of soap, and the work began. Corey pulled out his harmonica and played *Oh Susanna* while Kate hummed along and fixed a pot of lima beans with a few scraps of ham on the stove top. Elsie snoozed in the rough hewn box that was her crib, and Johnny washed to the lively tune.

Just then, *Bam Bam Bam* on the front of the house. The knocking was so hard it wasn't on the flimsy door. Johnny knew the door couldn't take that kind of force. The pounding was on the wall of the house. Kate, Johnny, and Corey all looked at each other in alarm. It was dark outside now. Who would come to the house in such a way?

"McCarthy?" a man's voice called out. "McCarthy!"

Johnny recognized this as Big Jake, the mining company's foreman. Johnny stood up in the tub, half the coal dust streaking off his body, and motioned for the towel from Kate. Just then, the door pushed open, and Jake filled the doorway.

"What are you doing?" Johnny protested.

"What do you mean, what am I doing?" Jake answered.

"This is my house..."

"This is *company* housing, know what I mean?"

"But..."

"But nothing," Jake said. "You people was dirt floor hillbillies, and now you got a floor, ain't you. And I got to talk to you about mining business, and if I got to talk to you about mining business, I will come to your company housing that is owned by the mining company and talk to you, you understand?"

Jake was yelling now, and Johnny was fidgeting with his towel. Elsie whimpered, and Kate walked over to pick her up.

Jake noticed some daisies in a vase sitting on the eating table. "What the hell you got here?" he said. He walked over and picked up the vase that held four daisies and a little water. Kate rushed over and snatched it out of his hands.

"This belongs to me," Kate said. "And not that it's any of your business, but my father was a very fine glass blower in the old country and he gave this to my mother, and now it's mine."

Kate strutted over to the corner of the house where her bed was set and began breast feeding Baby Elsie. Jake's face spread out with a sly grin.

"So, what's this about?" Johnny wanted to know.

"You was involved in a mine accident today, wasn't you?"

"Yeah, there was a cave-in. What happened was..."

"I don't give a shit what happened, but about your buddee, what exactly did he do for you?"

"Well, he was just getting started," Johnny said. "Did they bring his body up yet?"

"I'm asking the questions here. I gotta replace the son-of-a-bitch. What did he do to help you?"

"Well, he knocked down loose rock, put up extra timbers for the roof, you know, stuff like that. He was a hard worker."

"Look, I don't need no damn memorial. I just need to know what he did."

Jake glanced over at the eating table again. Sitting on one of the chairs was parts of the Charleston Gazette. He walked over and picked it up.

"What the hell you doing with a newspaper?"

"I pick one up when I can," Johnny said. "Like to keep up on what's going on."

"I been in a lot of these houses and I ain't never seen no newspapers, not for reading, anyway. How you learn to read?"

"In Ireland my papa used to read to us every night from the Bible," Johnny said. "Then he'd have us read some of it too. Helped us learn to read, and taught us right from wrong at the same time."

"The Bible!" Jake smirked, shaking his head.

"What family Gilbert got left?" Johnny asked.

"What do you care?"

"What do I care? I pulled him out of the hole!"

Jake took a step towards the tub and pointed a finger at Johnny.

"Something wrong with you, mister. Something wrong with this whole family. You need to learn some respect!"

He looked around the room, and stomped out the door.

Chapter 5

Corey trudged down Mate Street in Matewan, West Virginia, towards the colliery. He walked with dozens of other boys along with scores of mine workers in the pre-dawn hours. Work started in twenty minutes, and everyone in town would know when the six o'clock whistle sounded. He heard low-pitched murmurs and curses, but not much enthusiasm. Not 'til Pete caught up.

"Hey Corey, wait up!"

"Pete, what's going on?"

"Oh, not much. We gonna play some ball today?"

"Sounds good to me. You bring a ball?"

"I brought some tape. We *make* a ball."

Corey liked Pete. He was ten and he was funny. He didn't take shit from nobody, even the bosses. Corey felt bad that Pete had already lost two fingers on his left hand from trying to clean the gears while the machinery was still running. On that day Pete wanted to hurry up and get out to play ball. But even with just one good hand, he could throw like nobody's business.

"Load up, you guys!" Old Man Morgan was barking out orders already. "Find a seat about where you was yesterday and get ready."

They turned the lights on, and everybody found a seat. Pete sat over to Corey's right. Once the machinery was turned on to vibrate the chutes and keep the rock and everything moving down, it made a racket and you couldn't hear your friend talking very easy, but there was still some comfort in knowing he was right there. Helped you get through the day.

Old Man Morgan had to yell to be heard. Corey thought maybe that's why he was so mean. He walked around with a broom handle looking for a boy to whack. Most of them ignored him, like he wasn't even there. That way they didn't have to strain to hear him, and they just lived in their own little world.

The six o'clock whistle pierced the crisp morning air. Time to get to work.

The chutes was set up to be steep and Corey sat on his bench near the top because he'd been doing this job for a long time. He shifted the rock and coal around with his feet. His job was to pick out the slate and rock and anything that wasn't coal to keep the good stuff moving down the chute. The boys at the bottom got the easier part— mostly coal.

"Listen up!" Old Man Morgan called out. "We turning on the machinery in a minute, but I want you to hear me before we get all that noise going on."

A loud fart exploded and just hung right there in the pure mountain air. Laughter and giggles followed.

"Who did that?" Morgan yelled. "You boys think that's funny, but I'll show you what's funny. Your production ain't been worth a shit! We not clearing enough coal out of here, and what we do clear ain't clean enough! Got too much slate and shit mixed in!"

Morgan was about to continue his tirade when the machinery turned on. Corey and all the boys laughed because the noise drowned out the little dictator. But he wasn't done yet. He ran up the side stairway to the top of the chutes where the coal cars was about to dump. He frantically signaled his foreman to cut the power and get things quiet again. He tried to calm back down.

Morgan was the living and breathing example of the slogan, *once a man, twice a boy.* He started out in the colliery forty some years ago as a boy. Then he worked in the mines as a man 'til he got beat up enough to have to come back to the colliery as a boss. Once a man, twice a boy.

"So you boys think that's funny too, huh? Well, here's what's funny. You ain't going outside to play today. You will take fifteen minutes to eat your lunch, and you'll eat it right where you sit!"

Corey and Pete glanced at each other.

"And if we don't get better production today, we gonna keep eating our lunch in here 'til we get it right. You decide. It be a long day 'til six o'clock. And another thing. You tell your families they need to stop using that backhouse down by the river, over behind Stone Mountain Camp. It's too close to the river, so it's closed."

"What should we use?" a tiny voice called out.

"What should you use?" Morgan repeated. "I don't care what you use. You can shit your pants for all I care. Use any other backhouse you can find!"

The machinery cranked up, the cars tilted, and rock, coal, and slate began the downward slide. A cloud of dirt and coal dust flew up into the air and settled over the boys. Corey shoved a wad of tobacco in his mouth so the dust wouldn't stick inside, and pulled his kerchief over everything below his eyes. He hunched over and did his job like he always did. It didn't take much intelligence to see the difference between rock and coal. If it wasn't coal, you tossed it aside. Whatever you missed was caught by the guy behind you. That's the way it worked. For twelve hours, six days a week, you did that.

Corey couldn't help but think about working in the mine. He liked animals, and he knew he could handle a mule. It would be like having a pet with you all the time. Up and down the tunnels, walking through, talking to men passing by, feeding the mules, hooking them up. That would be better than sitting on your ass all day with your hobnailed boots buried in coal and your back hunched.

A ruckus started in the back of the room. Corey heard Old Man Morgan yelling at a boy something about working his first day in the colliery. The boy wore gloves. Oh God, Corey thought, you don't get caught wearing gloves. Morgan was yelling louder now, and Corey shifted around to see the action. He saw Morgan raising his broomstick and slamming down on the boy's knuckles.

Oh shit, here we go. Corey learned when he first started they didn't want you wearing gloves because they said you couldn't really feel the difference between the coal and the slate and the rock. Seems like you could see it, but they knew what they wanted. Problem was, when you first start handling coal with your bare hands, your fingers dried out, swelled up, cracked, and bled. They called them red tips. You eventually got used to it and healed up, but the first few weeks was tough. This new boy looked really young, maybe eight or nine, and he was gonna learn the hard way.

The morning dragged on with Old Man Morgan walking between the rows of breaker boys, looking for laggers and slackers. Every now and then he'd whack a boy across the back or the knuckles. Some would cry out—the older boys usually would not. But one thing was sure. All the boys hated Old Man Morgan, but not too many had the guts to do nothing about it.

Pete had a knack for keeping one eye on the coal, and one eye on Morgan. Never did he lose track of where Morgan was. On this day, because the old man had been so pissy, Pete decided to get him back. Corey saw him gazing over his shoulder looking right at the man. Then he'd look back down at the coal. Then, at the man. Suddenly he stood up and with a beautiful sidearm sweep flung a flat rock the size of half a sandwich right at Morgan. It looked like it was gonna be a direct hit, but whizzed harmlessly past his head and bounced off the floor by the side wall.

The old man twitched around like he felt something and started scanning the boys. He peered over in the section where Corey and Pete was sitting. Pete had his head down like a hard working coal-sorter long before the stone would have struck its target, but Corey was taking it all in. Morgan started marching up the row right next to where Pete sat. Corey could see that Pete had several good size flat rocks set out on the side that should have been tossed into the throwaway bin. His eyes got big like a silver dollar he saw once, but he couldn't figure out how to warn Pete. As Morgan came upon him, a light bulb hanging up behind the boss's head cast a shadow in the chute where Pete sat. Pete quickly knocked those rocks into the chute like he knowed what was coming.

"What you just do, boy?" Morgan shouted.

Pete looked up at the man.

"Why these rocks sitting here in the chute when you know they need to be tossed out?"

Pete shrugged his shoulders, like he was puzzled or something. He tossed them into the bin to his left.

"Don't you let me catch you doing something you be sorry for!"

Morgan kept creeping up and down the rows, no longer scanning, but focusing on each boy one at a time. A buzzer sounded—lunch time.

The machinery was quieted, and each boy grabbed his lunch pail. Corey pulled out an apple, a chicken leg, a chunk of bread, and a piece of cake. Pete found some oatmeal at the bottom of a peach jar. Corey split what he had with Pete, right down the middle.

"You know, you hit Old Man Morgan with a rock and there's gonna be hell to pay."

"He ain't gonna see who did it."

"You better hope!"

The short lunch break was over in a blink, and the boys was back sorting through the shit. Mornings in the colliery was hard, but Corey felt the afternoons was twice as hard. Now the stiffness of hunched backs cried out. The pain and soreness of burning fingers was multiplied, and boredom made the day long.

After about an hour and a half, Pete started looking around. He knew where all the boys was, all the bosses, and all the rocks worth throwing. Old Man Morgan was off to the right side of the plant, just like before. Pete looked over at Corey and grinned, showing in his palm the missile he was about to launch. Corey grinned back and shook his head. He had no love for Morgan, but didn't want to see Pete get punished. Just then the old man turned to his right to spit and Pete, with lightning feet, spun around and launched his second missile at Morgan. This one also missed, but clunked on the floor and ricocheted off the wall, landing at Morgan's feet. Now the old man had no doubt somebody was trying to nail him. He looked over the assembly of boys before him. The fierceness on his face deepened. Corey imagined he must be boiling inside. Morgan looked determined to make somebody pay. He walked up to a young boy on the left side of the colliery whom he accused of not working fast enough.

"You think you can take all day?" Morgan screamed. "You think you can do this any way you want?"

"No sir."

"You can't work faster than that, boy? I'll show you how fast you can move."

Old Man Morgan knocked off the boy's cap and hit him with the hard swing of the broomstick across the upper back. The boy yelped. Then he swung the broomstick again and hit him square in the middle of the back, then again on the arm, and once in the back of the head in the hairline. The boy was crying hard now, and all the boys in the colliery was staring right at the old man. He must have known he was over the line because he grabbed the boy by the back of the shirt and dragged him off the bench and out the building. Corey felt like throwing up.

The afternoon dragged on and the boys settled back into their work—four o'clock, five o'clock, now nearly six. Corey could see out of the corner of his eye that Pete was getting restless again. Instead of picking up a rock and tossing it aside, he was looking at it, sizing it up for the fit in his hand, weighing it. Old Man Morgan stood to the left side, near where he attacked his last victim. Corey knew this was a better angle for Pete. He could likely deliver with more force and be right on target. Morgan turned his head to the rear of the room, giving Pete all the time he needed. His slingshot arm delivered a curving shot directly to the ear of the old man. He went down with a yawp, and blood began to gush.

Corey felt there was something about this action, something about it being so simple and powerful that it spoke to justice. The boys on the benches all together rose up with loud voices and charged out the colliery doors. As the room cleared, Old Man Morgan set his sights on Pete. He grabbed him by the shirt and started beating him with his stick. Corey tackled Morgan and was joined by two other boys, who pinned him to the floor while Pete fled out into the street. When the building was empty save for those on the floor, Corey and the other two boys looked the old man in the eye, and marched out the door.

Chapter 6

The next day was Friday, payday, and Johnny stepped up to the paymaster's table to get a statement of his account. It had been a good week with good clean seams of coal, except for that cave-in, which ruined the day. Not much coal mined that day. Otherwise, full coal most days.

Johnny would be paid 50¢ per ton of coal he brought up from the earth. It didn't sound like much, but if he hit the right seams and worked fast, he could do all right and his family could get what they needed.

But now, Johnny and the other miners was subject to the operators renting tools and equipment to the miners. Some of them had tools that was old and not sturdy enough to hold up to the rigors of mining, so the company supplied picks and shovels and other tools—for a fee. And the lanterns. The lanterns had to be special issue calcium carbide—no open flame—they said, to cut down on explosions that happened sometimes with the methane gas. Firedamp, some called it, could kill a lot of people all at once.

"Johnny McCarthy," he said as he approached the table.

The paymaster pulled out an envelope.

"Sign here," he ordered.

Johnny took the envelope from the paymaster's hand and walked out onto the street. He opened the envelope and looked at the paperwork.

Stone Mountain Coal Company
Statement of Wages

McCarthy   April 2, 1920

22 Tons of Coal @ 50¢ = $11

Deduct:
- Full tool belt: 18¢
- Sledge hammer: 40¢
- Pickax: 25¢
- Hand-pick: 20¢
- Lantern and cap-lamp (fully charged): 40¢
- Gas mask: 25¢
- Company housing: $2

Full pay: $7.32

"Hmm," Johnny was almost speechless.

His friends started swarming around him, looking at their statements.

"Holy Christ!" said Jim, a strapping German. "It's a wonder they don't charge you for breathing!"

"With the gas mask, I guess they do!" Sean, an Irishman said.

"What are we supposed to do with this?" another said.

Johnny dug further into the envelope and found the scrip that stood up for the net pay. They was little coupons marked for the company store down on Mate Street. Some of his friends wanted cash, but Johnny knew they never had a chance to get to Charleston or one of the other big cities where they could spend cash anyway. So this was okay with him. The company store was right there, and would provide his family what they needed.

Johnny walked into his house with a smile on his face, and placed the scrip into his wife's hands.

"How's baby girl?" he asked.

"Looking like a happy little baby!" she said.

Kate put water on the stove and washed out the tub.

"Where's Corey?" Johnny asked.

"Not home yet."

"It's almost seven o'clock. Should have been home by now," Johnny said. "I'll run down to the colliery. Get the bath later."

. . . .

Johnny walked down Shamrock Road on the way out of the Stone Mountain Housing Company. Ahead was a gang of sooty-faced little ragamuffins playing tag. Johnny wondered if there would ever be anything more than this for his son.

Johnny walked up to the colliery and the building was all closed up, but a light was on at the back. He banged on the door.

"Anybody here? Hey! Anybody here?"

The door squeaked open slowly. Old Man Morgan stood in the opening.

"What you want?" he asked.

"Looking for my son, Corey."

Morgan stared Johnny in the face.

"Let him in," a voice from inside called out.

Johnny recognized the voice as Jake's. He entered to find Corey standing up against the back wall, with Jake to one side of him, and Max, an operations supervisor, on the other. Corey's hair was mussed up, and blood was dripping from his lower lip. Johnny felt a jolt of adrenalin and noticed he was clenching his fist.

"What's going on here?" Johnny asked.

"Seems yesterday, at the end of the shift, your son tackled Mr. Morgan here to the ground," Jake said. "We can't have assaults on mining company management. We just trying to straighten this out."

"Is that true?" Johnny asked.

Corey hung his head. Johnny looked at all the men.

"Sorry for all the trouble, Mr. Morgan," Johnny said. "Did you apologize to Mr. Morgan, Corey?"

Corey looked at his father, then silently hung his head.

"I'm real sorry about this, Mr. Morgan. Jake, Max, I'll see to it this never happens again."

"Yeah, you best see to it," Max said, "that is if you want to keep your jobs. We here to mine coal, not be fighting."

Jake stepped up to Corey and grabbed the front of his shirt.

"You understand what's expected of you now, boy?"

Corey looked the big man in the eye, tears welling up, his lip trembling. Jake shoved Corey in the direction of his father.

"Get out of my sight now," Max said. "You making me sick."

Johnny grabbed Corey by the arm and walked towards the door.

"Sorry for all the trouble, men. Things will be different now. You'll see."

. . . .

Johnny and Corey walked towards company housing.

"I can't believe you would attack old Mr. Morgan! What'd he ever do to you? He spent more than forty years of his life working in the mines, providing for his family. Goes to church whenever they can get a service together. Even brings the lesson on Wednesday nights sometimes. He is a fine man and everybody in these parts knows it. There ain't a mean bone in his body…"

It was a bright moonlit night, and it seemed the second them words was out of Johnny's mouth, Corey bolted into the woods that cut behind company housing.

Chapter 7

"Where is he?" Kate asked.

Johnny hung his head and walked over to his chair. "Where he *at*?"

"He was down at the colliery talking to his bosses."

"Talking to his bosses?"

"Yeah, seems he knocked Mr. Morgan to the ground?"

"Corey?"

"Yeah, he's getting pretty big, you know."

"But why would he do such a thing?"

"Got a wild hair, I guess. Needs to be more respectful."

"That don't sound like Corey. So where is he now?"

"He run off."

"What do you mean, run off?"

"We was walking back to the house, and we was talking, and he just run off into the woods."

"Run off into the woods? What did you say to him?"

"We was talking about respect, and how he can't go attacking one of his bosses like that."

"But what happened? Why'd he go and do something like that?"

Johnny shrugged his shoulders and stuck out his lips.

"Beats me."

"You didn't ask him?"

"What difference it make? He got no business attacking a grown man, especially one of his bosses."

Johnny reached down and started pulling off his boots.

"What you taking your boots off for? You get out there and you find him!"

"Find him? It's dark out. I don't know where he's at!"

"Well, you best find him. That's your son out there!"

"Woman, I got to get up before daylight and work in the mines! I can't traipse around the woods all night!"

"Well, I can't do it. I got a baby to take care of."

"I don't know where he's at, but he knows where I'm at. Let him come to me."

"Well, something happened where he don't *want* to come to you. That's what I think."

"He just got to learn some respect, that's all."

"Oh, like Mr. Jake tell you, you gotta learn some respect?"

"Get my bath water together, woman. I gotta take a bath."

"Get your own bath water together. I gotta take care of my baby."

Johnny stared hard in her direction. Many thoughts ran through his head. What to do with a cantankerous woman? Years ago, right before they got married, Papa told him you beat a woman real good on her wedding night, she never give you any trouble. He couldn't do it at the time, but nights like this make him wonder if he should have.

He stumbled around the stove sticking some wood in the burner. No scraps of coal around tonight, just a little wood and some shavings. Corey's fault. He knew he should have went out to the culm bank. Mountains of shit out there. Always some bits of coal to be had. He struck a match and got the fire going. Got some water from the pump outside for the stove. Grabbed the tub and wiped it out.

"What we got for dinner tonight?"

Johnny looked over at Kate.

"What we got for *dinner* tonight?"

She stared back at him, her face unyielding. She adjusted her body weight and continued feeding her baby.

Johnny rummaged around the ice box—a piece of chicken wrapped in wax paper, a scrap of bread, a jar of okra. Cold night on a warm spring day.

Chapter 8

Kate fed the baby, bathed a makeshift bath, and pulled herself together. She kept a hard face on while she packed Johnny's lunch—couple apples, a hardboiled egg, and a heel of bread—food she'd stashed earlier in the week. She helped him get off to work, but now couldn't stop crying. Her son out in the woods—all night! Just fourteen years ago she was nursing *him,* and now no telling where he was. Ain't right, no way.

She had to pull herself together, get down to the company store. They almost out of food. Pay come in at just the right time. She wrapped Elsie in a soft cotton cloth for a diaper, and little pajamas she fashioned out of an old flannel shirt—nice and soft and comfy. She then wrapped a little blanket around the whole package, more to seal the tiny bundle together than keep her warm. It was a nice enough day.

Kate had to walk with her baby out of the company housing area, down a dirt road, and then on over to Mate Street. The company store was down by the end of the street, more than a quarter mile all told. So how to carry her baby and still keep her hands free? She grabbed an old sheet, folded it length-wise, and wrapped it around Elsie's back and threaded it over her shoulder and behind her own back, tying it in a sturdy knot right by her neck. *Perfect!* Almost good as a kangaroo. Now she could take stuff off the shelf and still know her baby was safe.

Kate's friend, Emma, was pumping water out by the community pump.

"Hey Emma, you want to go down to the company store with me?"

"I would," Emma said, "but Sarah's really sick. I gotta get some water and hurry back."

. . . .

Foreman Jake walked along Mate Street in the direction of the colliery. Coming towards him was Doug Tanner, a detective sergeant with the Baldwin-Felts Detective Agency.

"Hey, what brings you to town, Mr. Tanner?"

"Well, the train brought me in," Tanner said, "but I know that's not what you meant."

"Yeah, you right about that. Good to see you. What's going on?"

"Oh, the usual," Tanner said. "Keeping the miners in line. Regulating a little bit."

"You got any evictions this time?" Jake asked.

"Yeah, a couple. You know, them widows just can't pay the rent."

"I hear that," Jake said. "You know, some of the women around here is pretty good lookers, know what I mean?"

"I figured you'd be too busy to notice the women around here," Tanner said.

"Oh, I'm busy all right," Jake said. "But there ain't no other women around here except in company housing. I can't get into Charleston that often."

"There ain't no whores down by the saloon?"

"Nah, not really, but I'm gonna get me some before too long," Jake said. "That's what *I* say."

"You mean with these women?" Tanner asked.

"Yeah!"

"You're better off not to," the detective said.

Just then, coming up from behind, the police chief.

"My name's Sid Hatfield," he said. "I'm police chief of Matewan."

"Howdy, Doug Tanner with Baldwin Felts. You got a nice town here."

"You been here before, ain't you?"

"A couple times."

"I thought so. You here to evict anybody today?"

"Well, might not be today, but in the next *couple* days."

"Before you do anything like that," Hatfield said, "you get me the paperwork."

"But this is the mining operators' business," Tanner said. "This here town is run by the company."

"This is *my* town," Hatfield said. "I'm the law here, and I want to see that things is done proper."

"Well, it's certainly nice to meet you, Mr. Police Chief," Tanner said. He stood up straight, smiled, tipped his hat, and spun around on his heel to walk away. Then he stopped short and turned towards Jake.

"You remember what I said, man. Think about it."

. . . .

Kate made her way through the front door of the company store and picked up a hand basket. She needed the usual foodstuffs and supplies—gallon of milk, dozen eggs, or two if she could afford it. Elsie was content, snug up against her mama's body.

Kate walked over to a table and picked up a pound of apples. Then some bread, and some coffee. Pound of butter would be good. Some meat. Gotta get some meat. Steak not bad. Hmm, chicken a little cheaper. Potatoes would be good. Potatoes only in bushel size. No way she could carry a bushel of potatoes, and everything else too.

Oh, there's those new cookies from that company back east, *Oreos* they called them. Hmm, they sure good. Nice to have around. Sixteen cents a pound. She put them in the basket and walked up to the register. As she placed her items on the counter, she noticed a basket sitting right there filled with Hershey Bars—three cents apiece. Chocolate? Just solid chocolate? That have to be good. She placed three of them on the counter. The clerk was about to ring up her purchase.

"You got any fish?"

"Tuna in a can, over on that table."

"No, I mean *fresh* fish."

"Everybody asking for fresh fish. No, we ain't got no fresh fish."

"Oh, I just remembered, I need a block of ice too."

"Jimmy, go get the lady a block of ice," the clerk said to his assistant.

The clerk continued to punch keys on the cash register.

"Okay, that come to $8.76."

Kate laid the scrip on the counter.

"This only $7.32," the clerk said. "You short almost a dollar and a half."

The words stung.

"But this is about what I get every week," she said.

"You short a dollar and a half."

"How much is the butter?"

"Seventy-five cents a pound."

"Wasn't it less than that last week?"

"Yeah, it was seventy-one cents last week."

Kate's mouth dropped open.

"Hey, this is a store, and prices go up sometimes. What you want me to tell you? Prices on *everything* go up. You want credit?"

"No!" Kate said. She knew how Johnny felt about getting in debt to the company store.

Elsie began to stir, and Kate thought of what to do.

"You want to take out the milk?" the clerk asked.

"No, I gotta have the milk. Take out the *Oreos,* and take out the chicken."

"Okay, you still eight cents over."

"Take out the Hershey Bars." Her voice trailed off and the clerk punched at the cash register.

"Okay, that do it!"

Her groceries was loaded into two heavy-duty brown paper bags, with the block of ice wrapped in brown paper and placed at the bottom of a bag. The bags weighed a lot, but Kate cradled one in each arm, balanced it all out while protecting her baby, and waddled out the door.

She walked eastbound, along Mate Street, with the sun higher in the sky now, blasting into her eyes. The weight of the bags caused them to shift in her arms and every few steps she had to stop and re-grip them. She trudged along almost blindly, wondering how much farther she had to go, knowing she'd been walking for only a minute or two.

Elsie was fussing now. Kate hiked the bags up higher in her grasp, and took her next step, striking the end of a small log that lay in the pathway alongside the road. She fell headlong in the dirt. Mindful of her baby, she turned slightly to the side on the way down to protect her in the fall. The groceries was strewn out on the roadside, and the block of ice came loose from its wrapping and was coated in dirt.

"Let me help you with that, ma'am."

Kate had heard that voice before. He put his hand under her arm and helped her up. As she came upright, she looked into the face of Big Jake, and jerked away.

"You the fellow that was at my house the other night."

"Yes ma'am, just on company business."

"I don't need your help!"

"Well you need somebody's help," he said. "This here ice is just gonna melt."

Kate comforted Elsie the best she could and rearranged the groceries in the one bag. Jake picked up the bag with the ice and put everything back together. Elsie had shifted around to Kate's right hip, with the bag of groceries on the other. When she was ready to go, she looked at Jake.

"I'll just help you with this, ma'am. There's no sense wasting this ice and the rest of this food."

Kate knew she couldn't get home with everything by herself. She turned and started walking as fast as she could. Jake followed along behind.

"Since I know where you live, ma'am, I could bring this food along later, but this ice wouldn't make it."

Kate's legs was burning, but she wanted to be done with Jake as soon as possible.

"Sure a nice day today, ain't it?" Jake said.

Kate increased her pace. As they neared the house, she noticed Jake running out of things to say.

"I hope Corey's feeling better right soon," he said.

Kate whipped around in front of the porch. "What'd you say?" she asked.

"Well, he wasn't at work the last couple days, so I just figured he sick."

"Don't ever come to my house again!"

"Yes ma'am," Jake said. "Now you can get back to nursing your baby."

Kate glared, and Jake winked.

Chapter 9

The closing whistle for the mine sounded. Johnny started walking down towards Mate Street.

"Hey buddy, let's go down to the saloon, get a couple drinks," Jim Mullins said.

"Ah, I don't know. I should probably get home," Johnny said.

"Come on. Take a little break, man. You earned it."

Jim had become one of Johnny's best friends. Johnny knowed he was a good family man and always took care of his wife and kids best he could. But he also knowed that Jim held a lot of anger towards the coal company, what with all them evictions, cheating miners on their pay, and that one time when his wife got sick and they couldn't find the company doc for three days. Johnny didn't like to get into head-buttin' talks with him, but maybe this one time it wouldn't go that way.

....

The sign above the door read, *The Gottmore Saloon*. Funny, since prohibition started earlier this year, Johnny thought, they don't got more, they got less. Mostly moonshine from the hills and hollers. No beer and no whiskey. Just as well. The taste of moonshine was a bit stiff, and Johnny would not drink too much of it. He and Jim found a seat at a table just off the bar where two glasses of moonshine was put in front of them.

"Too bad about that Dugan boy," Jim said. "What actually killed him?"

"Oh, he was messed up, man. You didn't get a close look, but his foot was crushed. Broken leg. Also that rock that was laying across his chest and shoulder. Might have messed up his breathing."

"Sad for his aunt," said Jim. "What was it, two months ago that she lost her husband in that explosion?"

"Yep, right at two months. That's what got Gilbert working in the hole."

"Man, she lose her husband, and now she lose her nephew," Jim said. "Guess they be throwing her out next, after they auction off any tools he got. Kind of stinks the way they treat miners and their families."

"I guess they just doing the best they can. Keep things running smooth so they can keep paying us."

"You kidding me? Jim said. "If you think about it, they treat mules better than the miners."

All the seats was filling up and workers was standing around in circles, nursing their glasses and letting off steam. A couple of men in three-piece suits and dress hats worked their way through the room.

"What you mean?" Johnny asked.

"Because a man die, they replace him. But if a mule die, it's a big deal. Ain't so easy to replace a good mule."

Johnny shrugged his shoulders and kept looking in his glass.

"You know," said Jim, "Ed Chambers and a couple of his friends went to Charleston to talk to the union officials. He gonna find out what it's all about. You gotta come to that next meeting."

Johnny took another swig from his glass. All the voices in the room was getting loud, and Jim and Johnny almost had to yell to be heard.

"You join the union if they get it down here?" Jim asked.

"I don't know," Johnny said. "Up north they got the union, and the first thing they did was strike, and get people killed."

"You mean Paint Creek?"

"Yeah! What the hell?"

"Well, they was trying to get the wages up!" Jim said.

"Yeah, but I heard that even after they got the union at Paint Creek, the miners was still making less than the other union miners right up the river!"

"That's why they did the strike!"

"Yeah, I know, but all it led to was shootings and killings," said Johnny. "Like at the Holly Grove settlement, the sheriff and a bunch of them detectives that the mining company hired put more than a hundred machine gun bullets through the wood shack of that miner, uh, Estep was his name. Killed him. Then a bunch of miners attack Mucklow and kill a bunch of people, and back and forth it goes. Ain't no way to live!"

"So you think going down the hole and getting blowed up by firedamp is okay?" Jim said. "You think it's okay that you can't see a decent doc when you need one? Or you get cheated at the scales?"

Johnny shrugged his shoulders.

"You think it's okay to leave a dead boy's body down in the mines when you know what the rats is gonna do to him overnight?"

Johnny bristled, and almost grabbed Jim by the shirt.

Just then the thunderous roar of gunfire erupted in the small saloon. The taste of gun smoke crawled across their tongues. Johnny looked up and saw those two three-piece suit guys standing on the bar, guns smoking and pointing to the ceiling. The room went dead silent.

"Way to go, boys," the biggest of the two said. "Everybody know who we are?"

"Yeah, we know who you are," an old man called out in the back.

"Who said that?" the other man on the bar said.

"I did." The man stepped forward and the room cleared around him.

"And what might your name be, old man?"

"Harold, Harold Baker."

"Harold Baker. Well, Harold Baker, do you know how to dance?"

"Reckon I do."

"Good, we got a harmonica player in the room?"

The two on the bar looked around.

"I said, we got a *harmonica* player in the room?"

A man signaled from down front.

"All right, Mr. Harmonica Player, I want you to play us a tune, you hear? And Mr. uh what was it…uh Mr. Baker, I want you to show us some of that Appalachian Shuffle or whatever you call it. Okay? Let's go!"

The harmonica player obliged with a lively tune, and Mr. Baker shuffled his feet in the tradition of the West Virginia mountain people. The men on the bar both fired shots near Mr. Baker's feet. The dancing and the playing stopped.

"Keep going," the biggest of the two said.

"You making fun?" Mr. Baker asked.

"We just *having* a little fun."

"If you making fun, I ain't dancing no more," Mr. Baker said. "You can shoot me dead between the eyes if you want to. I ain't helping you make fun of my momma or my pappy."

Every eye was on the men on the bar. One of them fired another shot into the ceiling.

"All right you hillbillies, listen to me!" he said. "I am Sergeant Douglas Tanner of the Baldwin-Felts Detective Agency, and this here is Detective Otis Borchard. We walking around while you all are drinking it up, getting drunk the night before your big day off. And we hear all this talk about unions. Union this, and union that! We here to tell you they ain't gonna be no unions in Matewan. They ain't gonna be no unions in Mingo County. They ain't gonna be no unions in southern West Virginia, do you understand me?"

The room fell dead silent and all eyes was on the detectives.

"There are two of us here right now. But by early next week, there be a dozen of us in town. And if need be, in case there was something like a union meeting, or a strike, we could have hundreds of detectives here, enforcing the law. We got too much fire power for you to ever win out over us or the mining company. You get me?"

"You got enough fire power to get out of here tonight?" a voice called out.

"What do *you* think?" the detective answered.

"We think you got a problem," another voice yelled, "unless you want to shoot unarmed men in cold blood!"

"And there be a noose waiting for you for that!" another called out.

The detectives started looking at each other and moving about nervously. Then all the men in the saloon started moving around, some coming near the bar, some arguing with each other. Several men grabbed the detectives around the ankles and brought them down with a thud. Men started swinging at each other. One man got in Johnny's face for no reason at all, and shoved him back. Then he cocked his right hand and started to swing.

Johnny stuck out his left arm in a guard position, lowered himself with bended knee, and shuffled in close. He exploded with a right uppercut to the midsection, knocking the wind out of the man, and finishing him with a right cross to the jaw.

Right then Sid Hatfield and two of his deputies walked in and fired a couple shots into the ceiling. All fighting stopped. Hatfield cleared the saloon and ordered the miners to go home. The detectives he took into custody for their own protection, he said, but Johnny thought of some charges that could probably stick. Johnny and Jim walked down Mate Street together.

"I didn't know you could fight like that," Jim said.

"Why you say that?"

"They beat on your son, you didn't do nothing. I figured you was afraid."

"That's different. I gotta keep my job!"

"They take a broomstick to *my* son, I shove it up their ass!"

Chapter 10

Beams of sunlight broke through the cracks in the plank walls, and the cries of roosters pierced the still, quiet air. Johnny swung off his bunk, slipped on a pair of trousers, and walked out into the open area to the common well. He pumped a bucketful of water before a line formed, got back, and started heating it on the stove.

"What you doing getting up so early on your day off?" Kate asked.

"I'm gonna fix some breakfast. We got any bacon to go with them eggs?"

"No."

"What kind of meat we got?"

"We ain't got no meat," Kate said.

"You went to the store, didn't you?"

"Yeah, got what I could with the scrip you gave me."

Johnny looked at his wife.

"I ain't complaining," Kate said. "Just that there wasn't enough for everything I was gonna get. But we got some bread, some eggs, some flour, and a pound of butter. And some apples."

"We got potatoes or any vegetables?"

"Yeah, we got a couple potatoes left, and we got okra," Kate said.

"But no steak."

"Nope."

"I know we can get some tomatoes," Johnny said.

"Yeah, and maybe some green onions."

"But if we only had some steak," Johnny said. "You did all right, though. I ain't blaming you. But you know, I had a pretty good week. Lost most the day on that cave-in, but I hit full coal all the other days…besides, we got a cent and a half raise just two weeks ago."

"What they tell me at the store is that prices go up. Go up on everything."

"Yeah, seems every time we get a raise, prices go up. Any time a mule dies, prices go up. Any time they feel like it, prices go up. How we supposed to keep up with that?"

Kate gave Johnny a weary grin, and kissed him on the cheek.

"Maybe we need to get some chickens like Sam and Emma down the way," Kate said. "That way we have chicken and eggs any time we want."

"That sounds like a good idea," Johnny said.

Kate mixed up some flour with a little milk and a pinch of salt, and set some biscuits to baking in the oven. Then she broke open some eggs in the cast iron skillet and cooked them on the stove.

"Ain't nothing like the smell of your biscuits first thing in the morning," Johnny said. "Fills up the whole damn house."

Johnny and Kate put some butter on top of their biscuits and cut up some apples. Before Johnny finished, Kate started bathing Baby Elsie.

"We going to the tent service today?" Kate asked. "Brother Joseph bringing the lesson."

"Company preacher," Johnny said. "I already got his message. Tell us how we got to be thankful for the coal operators. And I am, but I ain't gotta hear it again."

"Yep."

"No, not me," Johnny said, hanging his head.

"What you doing?"

"I'm going in the woods," he said. "Gonna look for Corey."

. . . .

Johnny set out from the stand of trees at the back of company housing, same place where Corey run off into the woods. Soon he was away from all signs of their little ramshackle shantytown, and not even sounds of pots and pans could be heard, nor the shout of a child.

The bushes grew thicker as he trudged northbound, and the ground sloped upward into the mountain. His footing was uneven and he could feel that he was walking around the side of Stone Mountain. With no cleared pathways to make his trek easy, he kept crunching through ever thickening and stiffening brush. Just ahead, the undergrowth was a dense thicket of trees and brambles. Johnny thought the only thing could live and move in that thickness was snakes and rabbits. Some logs and timbers formed a pile for cover. Just then, the strong smell of cucumbers came to him. One thing Johnny knew for sure was a nest of copperheads smelt like cucumbers, and he wanted no part of that. He crashed through the brush to his left and headed down the mountain. His movement became a blur as branches lashed his face and upper body. He descended faster and faster until he lost his footing and began to tumble down the mountain. He snapped shoots and saplings as he came down hard, but then saw where he could spread out his arms and legs and get steady on his belly.

He was not near a beaten down pathway, but a seam in the vegetation because of the way it grew, the way it sought the sunlight and rain from the sky. He slipped swiftly to a lower level under his own control. Giant oaks, white birch, and maples dotted the landscape and claimed space around their trunks.

Johnny figured he'd dropped down three hundred feet when he came to a northbound pathway wide enough for two horses shoulder to shoulder. He hoped Corey was lucky enough to have found this route so he could move freely into a more open land mass. He hoped his son was safe, not snake-bit, not bear-mauled, not injured in a fall. Hell, he hoped his son was alive.

Johnny kept an eye on the sun overhead. He hoped to find a clue to Corey's whereabouts this very day, but if not, he wanted to at least get back home before dark. When the sun began to dip in the western sky, Johnny would have to turn around.

He figured he had walked some two and a half hours, and that the sun had another hour and a half before striking the high point in the sky. He kept stepping fast along the pathway and meant to get the most out of his day. The path had served him well, and allowed him to cover a goodly distance. After another hour, Johnny felt he'd covered four or five miles. He was advancing quickly alongside the mountain.

He arrived at an open area where a dirt road crossed his path. Westbound, the road led down the mountain toward what Johnny felt sure was the Tug Fork River. Eastbound, it led into a holler, a soft valley sitting between two medium-sized hills. Johnny knew it was a good place for a small number of people to settle because the hills offered shelter from the winds and gave them a little piece of land that nobody else could wander onto. The lush greenery could be cleared as needed or used for the berries and seeds it produced. Made Johnny feel good to find a holler like this so close to Matewan.

He walked along the road that led into the valley and heard voices ahead. People live here. He hoped they wouldn't be hostile to a man walking into their abode. He was unarmed, after all, and they was sure to have rifles and shotguns. Maybe they had seen Corey. Maybe Corey was even staying with them.

He began to hear fiddles and a banjo, and a harmonica holding its own. As he got close, he saw an old man dancing to the music, looking like he was moving on down the road but staying right where he was. Others standing around clapping their hands and moving to the rhythms. Shacks was built around the outside of the open space with some canvas lean-to's mixed in.

"Hello!" Johnny called out. He thought he smelled fresh coffee.

The men, ten or so in all, walked in his direction. The two that led the way was armed—one with a deer rifle, the other, a twelve-gauge shotgun.

"What you want?" one of them answered.

"I'm from down the river, in Matewan," Johnny said. "Coal miner. Looking for my son. He run off."

"How old he be?" the man with the shotgun asked.

"He's fourteen."

"What's your name?"

"Johnny, Johnny McCarthy."

They stood there looking at Johnny, as if sizing him up to figure out if he was dangerous or not.

"Come on up and set a spell," the other man said. His dark gray beard hung down to his belly.

Johnny followed them up the steps to what looked like a general store, but he couldn't imagine they used it to sell goods like the company store in Matewan. It seemed to him more like a storehouse where they kept whatever foodstuffs and supplies they got together, and just shared it with their little group. They sat down on the porch. The man with the shotgun leaned it up against the front wall.

"My name's Leonard. This here's Conan," he pointed to the bearded man.

"You want some coffee, or you want some moonshine?"

"Coffee's all I need," Johnny said.

Women scooted little children along, like they knew they had a stranger in their midst.

"So you been working in the black hole a long time?"

"Coming up on twenty years now," Johnny said. "Papa worked the mines before me in Ireland."

"Whoa! You a lifer in the mines, ain't you."

"It's all I know," Johnny said. "You ever worked the mines?"

"Long time ago," Leonard said. "Father died of the Black Lung Disease. Brother killed in a methane explosion. Got my ass out of there."

"You want something to eat?" Conan asked. "We got some potatoes, some greens, and some fish."

"Some fish?" Johnny said. "Where you get some fish?"

"Out of the water," Leonard said with a grin on his face.

"Yeah, I would like that a lot," Johnny said. "I could sure use some food."

"What your son look like?" Conan asked.

"He about yea tall," Johnny said. "He only fourteen, but he got most of the growth of a man. He wearing coal miner's clothes. You think you seen him?"

"Yeah, we seen him," Leonard said.

"You seen him?"

"Yeah, he be here with us for one night."

"Where he now?"

"He wanted to get far away from Matewan. Heading towards Charleston. No holding him back."

"He hop the train?"

"Don't know for sure," Leonard said. "Could have just down the way in Red Jacket."

Johnny stared downward, deep in thought. After a long time, he looked at the plate that was set before him.

"What kind of fish is this?" he asked.

"It's bass, smallmouth bass," the old man said. "And them's turnip greens."

"It's good," Johnny said. "I ain't ate fish in a long time."

"Show you how to catch them in the morning," Conan said.

"Oh, I can't stay the night. I gotta get home before dark."

"You ain't gonna make it back to Matewan before dark."

"But I got to," Johnny said. "I gotta work tomorrow, and my wife will worry."

"You a good twelve miles from Matewan," Leonard said. "And the sun's already starting to dip."

"Twelve miles? I thought I was about five, six at the most."

"It's late afternoon now," Conan said. "You covered more ground than you thought."

"Well, that's okay," Johnny said. "If I'm still walking in the dark, I'm sure I can find it."

"Oh, you don't want to be out here in the woods after dark," Leonard said.

"Worst problem is the bears," Conan said. "Bad enough to meet a bear in the sunshine. A bear find you in the dark, you ain't got no chance at all."

Chapter 11

Elsie fussed until she got all the way worked up, and then she wailed and wailed so that nobody but a dead person could have laid there any longer. Kate felt there was nothing really wrong with her—just ornery, but this alone made her get up and take care of business. She saw that her baby was wet. Nothing unusual. She took off the makeshift cloth diaper and saw some redness on her baby. Little gamey in the hooch. She washed her down and rubbed on a little goose grease in the right spots and got Elsie to settle down. Then she got her to smile, even coo.

The starting whistle sounded down at the mine. Men from all over Matewan was reporting for work, or was already in the hole. But where was Johnny? Kate felt a bunch of emotions about Johnny. The past week had not been good between them. She hated it when Johnny and Corey fought. She didn't know all of what happened between them, but suspected there was more to it than she knew. A young man had to find his way. He had to make mistakes and be allowed some leeway. She didn't even know if he'd done anything wrong, but the rift between him and his father showed her that *something* was going on. Corey was a good son, and Johnny was a good father. Sometimes, even a good son and a good father have a falling out. She wanted the wound healed, but knew it could take some time.

Kate stepped outside to the community pump to get some water. Emma walked up carrying her bucket, little Sarah in tow.

"Hey Emma, Sarah feeling better today?"

"Yeah, she's doing pretty good."

"Wish you didn't have so far to walk for your water," Kate said.

"Oh well. Is what it is."

"I'm gonna fix some eggs and bread for breakfast," Kate said. "You wanna come in?"

You sure?" Emma said. "We all on a tight string around here. Not much to spare."

"Yeah, it's okay. Johnny wasn't here last night, so we got some extra this morning."

"What you mean he wasn't here?"

"He went off in the woods looking for Corey. Didn't come home last night."

"Do you think he's all right?" Emma asked. "I guess that's a silly question. How would you know?"

They walked into Kate's house. Little Sarah was drawn to baby Elsie, as usual, and the two mothers talked by the stove.

"I figure he either found him," Kate said, "and he's having to take care of something about that. Or he got hurt."

"Or he got *lost*?" Emma asked.

"No, I don't think he got lost. Ain't his way to get lost. He find his way one way or the other."

Kate passed Emma a plate of eggs.

"He like coal mining?"

"It's all he know," Kate said. "The family do this work way back in Ireland. His father killed in the mines. Grandfather killed in the mines. Johnny trying *not* to get killed in the mines."

"Ain't an easy life," Emma said.

"Even worse in Ireland," Kate said. "Back in the 1800s, they put the women down in the mines, put them in a harness to pull them coal carts. After a while, most of them never stand up straight again! Back all hunched and everything."

"You mean they work them like a mule?"

"That's about right. I never seen nothing like it here."

"That's true," said Emma. "Here they think it's unlucky for a woman to be in the mine."

"Don't know what they do in Ireland now," Kate said. "Here they just super..., supersti...oh, whatever the word is. Unlucky, I guess."

"Yeah, well I gotta get going," Emma said. "Get me some water, and stop by the company store. Few of us going. You wanna come?"

"No, I just stick around here. I ain't got no more scrip to spend anyway."

"All right. Don't worry too much," Emma said. "Johnny be all right. He thinking about you right now. I can just feel it."

Chapter 12

Johnny washed his face in a trough outside the cabin where he slept. The cool water felt good and woke him up right fast. Roosters crowed, and people came to life in the little holler. As he shook water off his face and out of his hair, Leonard appeared holding a little towel.

"Thanks," said Johnny. "Perfect timing."

Leonard cradled the 12-gauge in his right arm, about where it was yesterday when Johnny first laid eyes on him.

"Let me show you something over yonder," Leonard said. "Then we get over to the store and get some breakfast."

"You always walk around with that shotgun?" Johnny asked.

"Got to be ready at all times," he said. "It ain't that we got that many outsiders. But you never know when you come across a nice plump cottontail for dinner. Got to be ready."

They walked farther towards the back of the little valley. After getting past some tangled oleander, the dirt showed fruits Johnny did not expect to see. Half-grown corn stood in tight little rows, bean plants on stringers, long furrows of potatoes, celery, green onions, and who knows what all. Women and children already tending to the bounty.

"Wow!" Johnny said. "I didn't know you had all this!"

"See, that way, we take care of ourselves," Leonard explained. "Don't need no outside help."

"How long you been set up like this?"

"We been in this holler about six months, but this our first garden. We been saving seeds and this our first crop. When we harvest, we hold back even more seeds, and we really be ready."

The two men started moving back to the store.

"How many people you got in this holler?" Johnny asked.

"About eight main families, along with some stragglers," Leonard said. "We got some orphans, and we got a couple of widows from your coal mine down there in Matewan."

"Widows! Who?"

"A woman named Mabel, and another one called Charlotte. Both their husbands was killed in the mine, and after a short time, you know, they just evict them from the housing and they wander off."

"I think I remember Charlotte," Johnny said.

The men climbed the steps to the porch of the store and sat at a table near the pot-bellied stove. Johnny could smell the boiling black coffee before he could see it. A woman soon stepped up holding the pot in her hand, and Conan joined them at the table.

"This here's gonna be a good breakfast," Leonard said. "This my wife, Louise."

"Oh, hello," Johnny said. He was caught by surprise. He didn't expect Leonard to be introducing his wife, but stood up awkwardly to pay his respects. Leonard and Conan looked amused.

As they sipped their coffee, Leonard's wife came back to the table cradling a steaming pot wrapped in a towel. A wooden bowl sat in front of each of the men. Louise served her man first by scooping out a glob with a long-handled spoon and slinging it towards the bowl. Most of the flying glob landed in the bowl, the rest on the table. Before she could set Conan's blob flying through the air, Leonard started wiping up the table with his bare fingers and licking them clean.

What was this stuff? Oatmeal? Farina? Cream of wheat? Homemade, whatever it was.

Conan's blick was a half and half job, and he too started cleaning up the extra. Now it was Johnny' turn. *Scoop! Wham!* Dead center shot!

"See?" said Louise. "That's why I serve these two characters first. Gets me warmed up for our guest. How you like your eggs?"

"Um, over easy would be great!"

"You two guys, the usual?"

They nodded.

"Thanks Sweetie," Leonard said as he grabbed a piece of her ass.

"So you folks have family in West Virginia?" Johnny asked.

"Yeah, I got some in Clarksburg," Leonard said. "Louise got some in Grafton."

"And I got some around Morgantown," Conan said.

"You see them much?" Johnny asked.

"Hell no! Don't need to see them," Leonard said. "We do all right by ourselves."

"Ain't nobody gonna do nothing for you," Conan said.

"But don't you like to see them once in a while?" Johnny asked.

"For what?" Leonard said. "Anything you gotta do, you gotta do yourself, so just might as well get on with it."

Louise came back to the table with an awful lot of food. For Johnny's plate—fried potatoes, thick strips of bacon, chunks of ham, at least three eggs, and if not over easy, she sure tried a few times. Biscuits, butter, jam. Johnny couldn't remember when he'd seen so much food on one plate.

"This is unbelievable!" Johnny said. "Leonard, Louise, Conan, thank you so much. Delicious!"

"We glad you like it," Leonard said. "You gonna need a good breakfast in you for our fishing trip."

"You know, I don't want to put you folks out," Johnny said, as he cleaned his plate. "I got a long trip ahead of me just to get home."

"Nah, we want to send you home with a bunch of fish on a rope, and we want to show you how to catch them."

Johnny sat beside two armed hillbillies in an out-of-the-way neighborhood of their own holler. They ain't seen a badge representing the law in a fortnight of Sundays. The more he thought about it, the more his skin began to itch. They came across all friendly and everything, but the likelihood of them letting him just walk off now was about like the company store having a half-off sale. So he decided he would have to go along with things for now, and hope everything worked out okay.

"You fish lately?" Conan asked.

"No, it been a while."

"You fish when you was a boy?" Leonard asked.

"Yeah, in Ireland," he said. "In the lakes and ponds."

"Yeah, well right here, we got mostly the big river, and lots of little creeks" Leonard said.

The men started walking out of the holler, westbound on the dirt road.

"When you fished them lakes and ponds," Conan asked, "did you pull some fish out of there?"

"Yeah, we always got some."

"How you get them?"

"We fished on the bottom," Johnny said. "You know, we put some meat or fish scraps on the hook, and sunk it on down. We got catfish or other fish that ate off the bottom."

"Did you use a boat?"

"Sometimes we go with somebody on a little boat," Johnny said. "Sometimes on a dock, sometimes on the shore."

"Did you use a pole?"

"No, never had a pole."

"That's okay, lots of ways to catch a fish," Leonard said. "but we gonna show you something new. We could fish the bottom at the river, but the river moving so fast it's hard to keep the hook in the same place."

"Yeah."

"And sometimes you catch big fish on the bottom of the river," Conan said, "but around here, catch more fish on top."

"Okay, but how you do that?"

"Well, we got hooks and we got line," Leonard said. "But this is the key."

He held up a cork in his hand. "Moonshine jug cork," he said. "and we take this ice pick and make a hole in the cork. Then we run the line down the middle of the cork, maybe three feet out, and on the other side of the cork we bend these soft lead balls around the line. They like tiny little bb's. Just enough weight. Then we tie this hook to the end of the line."

"Very small hook," said Johnny.

"Yep, you can bring in a bigger fish with a smaller hook, but you can't bring in a smaller fish with a bigger hook."

"How you tie it?" asked Johnny.

"Special knot," said Conan. "Put line through the eye of the hook, wrap back around and make a loop, twist around the line three or four times, then thread back through the loop and pull tight. Best knot."

Johnny could see the river up ahead and down the slope.

"What you use for bait?"

"We like these the best," said Leonard.

He pulled a handful of earthworms out of a pouch.

"These come from the garden," he said. "They not night crawlers, big and tough, but smaller. Fish like them better. We put the hook through here, what we call the collar, this band around the neck. It's tougher. Worm stay on the hook longer."

"We used meat, or fish scraps," Johnny said, "Anything that would stay on the hook."

"That's okay for bottom fishing, but this is top fishing. The worm is alive and moves in the water like it's just floating down the stream. Fish love that and *bam!*"

"So you just throw it out there?"

"You can. That's okay," said Leonard. "But we look for a good pole."

Johnny could see they was about a hundred feet from the river bank.

"Over here," said Conan. "Look at this stand of shagbark hickory sapling. We find one six, maybe seven feet tall. Here."

Conan pulled out a large buck knife, the kind you would use to skin a deer, and cut the sapling off at the base. He trimmed the little sprouts and branches that was starting to spring off the main stem, and left the smooth bark for a good grip. He held it up and flicked it in the air.

"See, this is just right," Conan said. "It's not too stiff. It has just enough give. You tie ten or twelve feet of line to the narrow end of the pole and flick that cork out there. You can put it out beyond a rock, and float it right in there over a deep pool. This is the way to go, man."

The men hurried to the river bank and worked on setting up their rigs. Conan cut a couple more sapling shafts and each man worked on setting up his own pole. Johnny felt excitement at learning a new way to fish, almost like he was a kid again. When Leonard and Conan was ready, they checked on Johnny's gear to see if he was ready too. Johnny no longer felt they would knife him, shoot him, or drown him in the river.

Leonard cast his line first, but Johnny and Conan was close behind. *Bam!* Leonard's cork was yanked down under the water, then Johnny's, then Conan's, just in the order they was cast. Leonard brought his fish to the bank with his hickory pole bending hard in the middle, but Johnny's and Conan's got away.

"Oh, that was a great hit!" Johnny said. "He got my worm. You got another one?"

Johnny saw many fish get pulled from the dark pools along the banks of the river that day. They was stout, proud-lookin' fish, with markings to help them blend in with the sand and the rocks. Smallmouth bass, they said they was. Johnny never saw nothing like it. Time passed without notice. He looked overhead.

"Sun straight up in the sky," he said. "I gotta start for home."

"Okay," Leonard said. "Let's set you up with a stringer of fish."

"You don't mind if I take some fish?"

"You caught your share," Conan said.

The two men set Johnny up with a nice bunch of fish on a rope, threaded through their gills, with a hard knot at the end. Johnny took the rope and shook each of their hands, looking them straight in the eye. He was about to head off down the path.

"Wait a minute," said Leonard.

Conan sorted through a large sack and pulled out a giant, store-sized pickle jar.

"You gotta put your fish in here," Conan said.

"Why, it's easier to just hold them by this rope," Johnny said.

"Remember what we told you about them bears in the woods?" Leonard said. "You walk through the woods carrying them fish like that, you ain't gonna make it home with no fish! You might not make it home at all!"

"I thought the trouble was just at night!"

"Bears are where they find you, man. Bears are where they find you."

Chapter 13

K ate was sure Johnny would be home today and decided to clean up the house. She heated a bucket of water and washed down all the horizontal surfaces with a brush and a rag. This took more work than she expected. Homes can sure get dirty with the coal dust and four people living in them.

Four people. That's what it used to be when Corey was still home. She missed her son more than she could explain. Who would have thought at fourteen he would run away? He's too young. She knew she wasn't ready to give him up, and didn't believe it was good for him to be away from home. Where could he be, and what is he doing? Who's taking care of him? How is he getting along? Does he know how much we love him?

She hoped that Johnny would come home with Corey by his side, or at least knowing where he is and that he's okay. This more than anything else in her life she wanted fixed right now, but she didn't know how to do it. And what if Johnny didn't come home today? Oh, she couldn't bear to think about that.

Kate pulled out her last bar of White King Bleaching Soap and cut off a piece for the top of the stove. Some hot water, hard scrubbing with the stiff-bristle scrub brush, and before long it sparkled. Kate heard there was a new product out now called Ivory Soap Flakes, but they couldn't afford two kinds of soap in one house, so White King would have to do.

Next she wiped a damp rag on the straight up surfaces—the walls, sides of the stove, chairs, and beds. Cockroaches darted away from around the stove. Then she took the broom to the floor. Elsie kept on slumbering, so Kate made good use of the time. She opened the door and swept out the dirt, blowing a big cloud of dust out onto the porch.

Next, Kate wanted to wet-mop the floor. The floor was made of planks of wood, but once every few weeks it freshened up the whole house to swab it down with a wet mop. But she had to set up a new one. She took the mop nail, fashioned on the anvil by the local blacksmith, and stood it on its end, a flat base several inches wide. In this position, the shaft of the nail stood five or six inches high with a sharp point at the top. Kate took clean old pieces of cloth that was just cut the other day and pushed them over the sharp end of the nail. When enough of the pieces was in place, she capped it with a piece of leather, then placed the nail horizontally in a frame at the end of the mop handle. With hot water, soap, and the bathing tub, she was ready to do the job.

As she mopped, Kate wondered where Johnny was and how he'd spent the past two days. She didn't know what she would do if something bad happened to him. First, she is separated from her son without understanding why, and not knowing where he is and if he's okay. It would be just more than she could bear if Johnny was taken away too. Please, let it not be that, she prayed silently in her heart. She knew she could not bear nothing like that.

Kate worked out a slick way of twisting the mop with her wrists so extra water was pressed out from it. This allowed her to move quickly over the planks without soaking them too much, making them hard to dry out and end up warping. The extra water that was squeezed out she could easily spread out over a dry board. As she was finishing up, Elsie began to stir. Kate finished the floor and put the mop aside. She'd rather tend to her daughter anyway.

What a beautiful baby God had blessed her with. It took so long for their second child, she and Johnny thought it would never happen. The sparkle, the innocence, the joy on her face when Kate kissed her and rubbed their noses together. She knew she must have felt the same sense of joy when Corey was a baby, but he was on his way to manhood now, and no longer needed her like a baby does. Their relationship went beyond trust, and Kate knew she was the whole world to Elsie.

With Elsie fed, bathed, and changed, Kate turned her attention to laundry. She set the washboard in the family tub and grabbed the pot from the top of the stove. With another chunk of White King and steaming hot water, Kate scrubbed cloths used for diapers, and the two shirts and trousers Johnny wore, along with some socks and a dress or two of her own. A good rinse job and then out on the line in the sunshine and the breeze, and it was done.

Kate lay Elsie in a basket on the porch. She decided to take on one more chore—split some wood. With the wood stove and the need for hot water, cooking, and warming the house in the early morning, wood would never go unused. Kate was not without skills with the ax. She had wielded the ax before and actually enjoyed the muscle stretch she got to her back and sides, and the workout for her arms. Johnny had carved his initials at the end of the handle, *JM,* because he was proud to have this house and to own his own ax. And Kate was proud of her husband. *Split!* Little pieces of splintered logs flew off to the sides. The noise startled Elsie, so Kate hummed a tune from the old country. It made Kate happy to know that in West Virginia, Elsie would never be asked to go down into the mines. At least she didn't think so. This was a comfort.

Elsie still fussed, so Kate cut short the wood splitting and lay the ax head-downward on the porch next to the front door. She carried Elsie into the house, cradled her in her arms, and comforted her with her breasts. So fulfilling. So satisfying.

All at once, heavy steps on the front porch.

Kate sat straight up on the bed, dead silent. Elsie began to whimper and Kate placed her hand gently over her baby's mouth. Kate's heart pumped hard, like a man running from a charging bear. Something not right here. Oh God, please help.

The seconds passed by like syrup flowing out of a maple tree on a winter day. Time was frozen, or at best, real slow. Somebody out there, no doubt, but now not making any sound. On purpose, but why? Kate tried to close the buttons on the front of her shirt.

Bam! Bam! Bam! The pounding on the front of the house.
Bam! Bam! Bam!

"If you home, come to the door!" the voice demanded.

Kate bristled and Elsie began to cry.

Kablaam! The front door flew open and there stood Big Jake.

"Where he at?"

"Where who at?"

"Who you think I'm talking about, woman? Your husband ain't in the mine today. Where he at?"

"Get out of my house!"

"I told you before, this ain't your house," Jake said. "This a *company* house. And being a foreman for the company, I can come in here any time I want."

"Johnny will talk to you about this when he gets home."

"So he not even around? Jake said. "Where he go?"

"He went into the woods and look for our son."

"Look for your son? He got responsibilities, you know. He trying to lose his job?"

"He'll talk to you later. Now get out!"

"Woman, you more irritating every time I see you," Jake said. "You need a lesson of respect."

"Get out of here!" Kate yelled.

Jake took a step towards Kate on the bed. She clutched Baby Elsie to her bosom.

Jake unfastened the straps over his shoulders and dropped his overalls below his waist. He reached down and grabbed himself.

"Bet you ain't never seen nothing like this," he said.

Kate screamed, and then realized how upset she had made Elsie. She tried to pat her baby and comfort her, but it was too late. Elsie had been startled and scared, and howled that out-of-control helpless cry that was driven by fear. She held her baby close over her chest.

Jake grabbed Kate by the arm, but she pulled back trying to protect her baby. Jake's face showed rage and he grabbed once more for Kate's arm. Again, she screeched and pulled back. Jake looked like something snapped inside his head and he ripped the baby out of her mother's arms and flung her against the wall. Elsie's cries went silent, and Jake threw himself on top of Kate. He put one big hand around her throat and ripped at her clothes with the other. He penetrated and grunted like a mudding pig until he spewed his seed all over Kate, inside and out. Kate screamed in pain and dry-heaved until she vomited on the floor.

"You filthy pig!" Jake blurted out, slapping Kate across the face.

"My baby! Where's my baby?"

Jake got up and tinkered with his britches. Kate could barely see, and stumbled across the floor, searching for Elsie. Jake saw where the baby lay and walked over and picked up her lifeless body just before Kate got there. He held her upside down by one leg, and grabbed Kate by the shirt.

"I take care of this," Jake said, "and if you know what's good for you, you keep your mouth shut! Your husband lose his job for any more trouble."

"I want my baby!"

"I take care of this!" Jake yelled as he shoved Kate to the floor.

He tucked Elsie under his arm, turned, looked both ways, and bolted out the front door. Kate ran through the doorway, and saw Jake walking as fast as he could down the old path that led to the abandoned backhouse. The one with the muck, and the dung beetles. The one too close to the river.

"Oh my God!" Kate bawled.

She grabbed the ax off the porch and took off after Jake. He didn't seem to know he was being followed and once behind the cover of thick brush and saplings, carried Elsie again by one leg, dangling her like so much trash. Kate ran forward, gaining on the big man, trying to stay quiet so she could come upon him in surprise.

The pit lay just ahead—the stench told the tale. The commode sat over the pit between two wooden walls, but most of the hole was off to the side and open to the air. The stink cut through all senses and coated the tongue, and the throat, and inside the nose. But closer yet, Kate could hear the clicking dance of the swarming beetles, as their hard outer shells smacked up against each other.

Jake stood at the edge of the pit swinging Baby Elsie by the leg, ready to toss her into the muck. Kate quickly crept up behind him and wielded the ax handle like a baseball bat, clocking him with the heel of the ax on the back of the head with a full, free-flowing swing. She felt his skull give way as it caved in under the force of the blow. The big man's hand went limp and he dropped the body of Baby Elsie on the edge of the pit. He fell headlong into the shit like a tree falls in the forest. Only his legs stuck out of the slime like two pointy skewers sticking out of a pig's ass. The rolling beetles looked like a boiling pot of Irish stew and the sucking sounds of the sticky froth trumpeted that Big Jake would soon be swallowed up in the bowels of the earth. Never again would he lift a hand to hurt another man, woman, or child.

Kate tossed the ax aside, and cradled the body of her baby girl.

Chapter 14

Johnny made good time along the same trail he followed north to the area of the holler—good time considering in addition to carrying a small knapsack, he now juggled a huge pickle jar filled with smallmouth bass. He wondered how important it was that he do this. What if it was a joke and Leonard and Conan was laughing his entire trip home? He never saw no bears around Matewan, and sure enough none on his journey north. Better safe than sorry, he thought.

He stayed on the lower pathway as he got close to Matewan. He was anxious to see Kate, but saw no reason to climb up the mountain some three hundred feet to fight through the thicket that he found behind company housing, what with the copperheads and all. Besides, by staying on the current pathway, Johnny figured he would enter town at the north end on Mate Street, right where the company store was sitting. He was happy with the fish they caught, but he wanted steak, and it was steak he would bring home to his wife.

He had time to think about his family situation. He missed Corey terrible and wanted him back with the family. He didn't understand why he run off, but after covering the distance he did, he respected his determination to get out of there. Maybe there was reasons he didn't know. Maybe they would make sense when he understood. Pretty gutsy thing for him to take off like that. But he still wanted him back with the family, and he felt that would happen soon. Somehow they would get their son back.

And Kate. He knew how lucky he was to have a woman like Kate. She was a hard worker and devoted to her family. Yeah, things had been a little rough lately, but only because the family was suffering. She didn't like not having Corey at home any more than he did. He knew that she loved him and both their children. And he liked who she was. Always did. She had a kind and good heart. Not a mean bone in her body. When he got home, they would get their family back together and life would be good again.

And what do you say about Baby Elsie? A package of joy sent straight from heaven. What a special baby girl. Johnny remembered so many times looking her right in the face, and their eyes would connect, and her face would light up, and well, just remembering it brought tears to his eyes. She was his little princess butterball. And he would see to it that she had a good life. He knew that she would never spend one day down in the mine, like girls in the old country. It was a new place and a new time.

Just up ahead, in the tail end of the woods, a little meadow with daisies and yellow butterflies flittering around. He picked a handful—they was her favorite, after all—and stuffed them in his knapsack, trying not to smash them too much.

Johnny broke through the last of the woods and the company store lay right ahead. He walked the last few steps through the front door, excited to show what he got.

"Hey," he said to the clerk. "Who's managing today?"

"That be Gus. You wanna talk to him?"

Gus was a tall man with a shiny bald head. Remnants of hair decorated the sides of his skull.

"Want some fish?" Johnny asked.

"Fish? We don't sell no fish."

"People want fish sometimes," Johnny said. "You could sell this."

"What kind is it?"

"Smallmouth bass, from the river."

"All right, you can leave them here if you want," Gus said.

"Leave them here? I want to trade for some steak," Johnny said.

"Trade for some steak? This a store, not some farmer's market."

"Look, I know people want fish sometimes. You could sell this and make money."

"Let me see them."

Johnny opened the jar and pulled out the rope.

"You catch these?"

"Yep."

"When you catch these?"

"Today," Johnny said. "This morning."

"How much steak you want?"

"Weight for weight. Pound for pound."

"Ain't no way fish is worth the same as steak," Gus said. "Let's see what we got here."

Gus lay the stringer in a produce scale.

"Right at eleven and a half pounds," Gus said. "I'll give you one pound of steak for these fish."

"One pound?" Johnny said. "You gotta do better than that!"

"I don't gotta do nothing!" Gus said. "When you say these fish was caught?"

"Today."

"Well, look at this."

Gus held the stringer up and some of the fish was bent to the side. "They stiff," Gus said.

"That's only because they was in this pickle jar for a while."

"Why was they in the pickle jar?"

"Cause I was walking with them in the woods, and didn't want to have no bears chasing me down."

Gus looked at Johnny and busted out laughing. "Look," Gus said. "If these was fresher, like they was caught an hour ago, I could do better for you, but a pound of steak is all I can do."

"Come on, man. I need more than that."

"You know, I got other things to do," Gus said, "And you starting to bust my britches. I give you *half* a pound of steak for these fish. That's it. Take it or leave it. Yes or no."

Johnny walked down Mate Street wearing a big smile and carrying his steak. Kate gonna be real happy. He knew she could do a lot with half a pound of steak. He couldn't wait to show her and see Baby Elsie.

Chapter 15

Johnny neared the Stone Mountain Coal Camp and the little house he shared with his wife and baby girl. The sun was setting, and as he approached what had been home for the last five years, he felt a sense of loneliness. It was almost like there was an emptiness, a fog of sadness over the house. There was no sounds, no signs of anything happening.

Johnny ran up the steps and over the porch as he hurried into the house. Inside was very dark.

"Kate, where are you?"

He hurried to a table near the kitchen and struck a match to light the kerosene lamp.

"Kate!"

He saw her in the corner, lying on the bed with her back towards him.

"Kate, you okay?"

He walked over and knelt down, putting his hand on her shoulder.

"Sweetie, you okay?"

Without turning, Kate let out a low-pitched whimper that grew to an enraged wail. Johnny didn't know what this was about, but he knew it was deadly serious. He put his arms around her.

"Sweetie, it's okay," he said, patting her arm.

"No, it's not okay," she said, "and it will never be okay."

"Kate, what..."

She began crying hysterically, wailing from deep in her gut. Johnny gently but firmly turned her over, and saw Baby Elsie.

"What's the matter?" he said. "Why is she..."

Kate cried harder and harder, gagging and choking.

"What's the matter with her?" Johnny asked. "What..."

He looked at Kate's face and saw bruising and redness on her neck. He grabbed onto both her arms.

"What happened?" he shouted.

Kate covered her face with both hands and continued to cry. Johnny reached for Baby Elsie, wrapped in a blanket, stiff and lifeless in his arms. He pulled back the blanket and looked into the still face of his baby daughter. He fell to the floor, clutching the physical form of Elsie close to his heart and cried. And Kate cried, and they both cried as the sun disappeared beneath the western horizon, and darkness enveloped their house.

After a while, a knock on the door.

"Johnny, Kate?" the voice called out. "Is everything all right?" It was Jim. Johnny opened the door, and his wife Stella stood by his side.

"What's the matter, man?" Jim asked. "We couldn't help but hear the trouble."

"Come in," Johnny said. "Our baby…"

Stella rushed to Kate's side and Jim put his arm on Johnny's shoulder.

"Oh my God, what happened?" Jim asked.

Johnny turned, looking towards Kate.

"I had bathed her, fed her, dressed her," Kate said. "Then I held her in my arms and was walking across the floor, and I tripped over the mop. I fell straight ahead on my face, and as I tried to break the fall, she flew out of my arms and hit her head."

"Oh dear God," Stella said softly.

"And just like that she was taken from us?" Johnny asked.

Kate broke out in tears again, and fell into Johnny' arms. Stella took Baby Elsie and cradled the poor child.

"What can I do for you, man?" Jim said.

He put his arm around Johnny's back and the two walked outside.

"What can I do for you?" Jim asked again. "I'll tell them tomorrow why you're not working."

"I will work," Johnny said.

"How can you work?" Jim said. "You need to stay home, be with your wife."

"Maybe Stella, and Emma, and some of the other friends can come to help Kate. I need to work."

"You can't work, man. Stay home with your wife!"

"If I load no coal, I make no money," Johnny said. "My family needs the money, so I will work."

"Big Jake saw that you wasn't at work today," Jim said. "Said he was gonna go looking for you."

"He said that?" Johnny said.

"Yep, that's what I heard him say. Did he come over here?"

"I don't think so. I wasn't here."

"Where'd you go?"

"Back up yonder," Johnny said. "Went north quite a ways looking for Corey."

"Find him?"

"Found some people living in this holler say they saw him," Johnny said. "Least I know he was okay when he passed through."

"I am so sorry about this, Johnny."

"I know," he said. "I can't even believe this."

"Really, don't feel like you gotta work tomorrow," Jim said. "We'll see that you get enough to eat."

"Probably better for me if I do work," Johnny said. "Better to stay busy through something like this, you know?"

Chapter 16

Morning broke early on Johnny McCarthy. He started the fire in the wood stove, made some coffee, fixed his own breakfast, and stuffed his lunch pail full of bread and eggs, along with an apple. The kerosene lamp shone a dim light on the box that Elsie used to sleep in. It still held her body, but now was draped in a white sheet with a ghostly presence. Once a crib, now a coffin.

Kate went silent after the emotional upheaval of last night. Johnny did not want to disturb her rest. God knew she needed it. But he wished he had more answers. When she fell on the floor, Elsie was dead, just like that? Did she struggle? Did she suffer? Or was she dead right off like when a blue jay flies into a window pane? He couldn't imagine it. Having a beautiful baby like Elsie one minute, and the next, a baby that never smile again. It's too hard for the mind. One thing he wished, though, that he never looked into Baby Elsie's face like he did last night—look into the face of his baby girl who was dead. He could not get the look of that baby's face out of his mind. No how, no way. He close his eyes, he see it. He open his eyes wide and look up at the sky, he see it. He cry, he see it. What a sad, sad memory to carry in his head.

Johnny trudged down Mate Street with dozens of men when Jim caught up to him.

"How you doing?" Jim asked him.

Johnny looked at him in appreciation, but couldn't bring himself to say nothing. As they kept walking with miners all around them, Johnny noticed the armed men on horseback here and there, strung out down the street.

"What are those guys doing here?" Johnny asked.

"You know," Jim said. "Strong-arm work."

The men approached the portal and reached for the clipboard to sign in. Operations supervisor Max stood by where Big Jake could usually be seen.

"Where's Jake today?" Johnny asked.

"You seen him?" Max answered.

Johnny just shrugged his shoulders. Lots of things he couldn't figure out. He supposed to know where Big Jake is too?

"You partnering with him today?" Max asked Jim.

Jim nodded.

"You get in the cage and take it down to level three," Max said. "Then you get out, walk along the gangway, and take the next cage down to level six."

"Level six?" Johnny asked. "Ain't that level all cleaned out?"

"Nope," Max said. "Just walk to the right when you come out of the cage, about a hundred feet down a bit of a slope, and you find tunnel eighteen on the right hand side. Couple of good seams in there."

"There cars down there for the coal?" Jim asked.

"Yep. And don't forget your tools."

Johnny and Jim descended into the earth with drills, two canisters of black powder, pickaxes, shovels, couple of lanterns, a tamping rod, fuses, matches in a water-tight case, a folding ladder, and the calcium carbide lights on their caps.

"We be over a thousand feet down at level six," Johnny said.

"Yep, cause you didn't come to work yesterday. Their way of getting back at you."

"Yeah, but why are *you* here?"

"Make sure you get back home."

Johnny pursed his lips and felt grateful he had a friend who cared enough to go with him into the yawning chasm. The deepness of the hole swallowed them up like the depths of hell. They walked out the second cage at level six and foot-slogged down the gangway towards the tunnel on the right. As they got close, Johnny could feel the roof pressing down on them, all the mountain's weight pulling towards the center of the earth, with the two of them caught in the gap.

The tunnel groaned and creaked under the strain. Here and there a rat squeaked through the ringing silence, and a pair of beady red eyes peered from the distance.

As they walked, tools in arms, the slope of the gangway kicked in. And there, ahead of them, beside them, beneath them, and all around them, the water.

"Water!" Johnny said.

"They really sticking it to you," Jim said.

"How we supposed to work in the water?" Johnny said.

"Don't suppose they care so much."

"We ain't making full coal today!" Johnny said.

"No, we ain't making no quotas at all."

The slope kept on and water poured over the top of Johnny's gumboots. Then into Jim's.

"Forty-eight degree water sure is cold," said Jim. "But as long as we got some coal cars, we be all right."

They made their turn into tunnel eighteen. The railings underfoot was still there and four coal cars stood empty up ahead. The water level settled right at just above the knees. The men stood silently in the darkness, the only sounds the hissing of gas, and the trickling of water. Johnny shined his lantern overhead, and there above them in the middle of the roof and coming downward to the side walls, what looked like a rich seam of black coal.

"There we go," said Jim. "We load some cars with that."

Johnny took out his long-handled augur drill and extended several sections upward to the top of the tunnel. He got some traction and with a few quick turns bored a hole in the surface of the span over their heads. Then with a larger bit he dug deeper and wider, making a hole big enough to hold a squib charge of black powder. Jim set up the ladder.

"Here, I do this part," he said.

Jim stepped up the ladder, stuck in the blasting cap, sealed it with clay and set it up with a fuse. He struck the match and the men backed out towards the gangway.

Kablaam!

Black rock showered down in the passageway over the water, into the cars, against the walls, and back towards the miners. It was a good blast, releasing so much of the black gold along with some slack, yet without causing a cave-in. The men stood in the water and waited until the dust settled so they could breathe cleaner and survey the scene ahead of them.

"Let's get this coal in the car," said Jim.

"Yeah, look at this lump coal floating right here," said Johnny.

"Yeah, just grab it and throw it in. There's more down here, though."

Jim kneeled down and reached for all the coal he could get resting on the floor and beneath the surface. His face dipped into the black water as he stretched out his arms and pulled up all that was within his reach. Johnny and Jim had been around the coal business long enough to know that coal with sulfur, shale, and rock sank to the bottom. Only the purest floated on the top.

"Yeah, they pay us for that too," Johnny said. "They grind it up anyway. Sort it out."

When they was hungry, Johnny and Jim sat up on the edge of the coal cars and opened their growlers. Jim had brought some sandwiches, cake, and an apple. Johnny had his eggs. It was odd for them to be eating on the side of a coal car, like they was sitting on a boat or something. One thing about all the water is it kept the rats away, and the miners didn't have to be so on guard or worry that one of the long-tailed bastards would make off with their food. As far as they knew, not one rat even broke the water looking for something to eat. They was probably high in the crevices or deep in the holes that was above the water level. Johnny figured they had plenty stored away to eat, and wouldn't act hungry 'til the tunnel was dry and a careless miner set his lunch pail down and turned his back.

The day passed slowly for the two friends, working in the cold, dark bowels of the earth. They set off two more blasts through the afternoon to be sure they could fill some of the cars that was sitting there. Between the two of them, they filled nearly three of the four cars and marked them with chalk. They figured they pulled out maybe four and a half—five tons. Not close to the five or six tons they could each have loaded under better conditions, but not bad considering.

Johnny was happy to get through the workday and make some money, but now it was time to get back to the life that had become so hellish, to return to the truth of his dead baby girl, and the happenings that got them there. As they rose up in the cages, Johnny's mind became cluttered with questions. What time of day did Elsie die? How did it happen again? Did she suffer? Both men was soaking wet and black from head to toe, with the only white flashing when they blinked their eyes or opened their mouths. But Johnny had streaks flowing down his black face, streaks of tears running off his soot, tears from the loss of his precious baby girl.

Chapter 17

Johnny and Jim shuffled up to the little house on Shamrock Road, the one that held the body of Johnny's baby girl. He saw that friends stood around on the porch talking quietly. As they came up to the front door, it seemed to Johnny that many of the friends didn't recognize them.

"Johnny!" Gino said. "You so black from soot I didn't even knowed it was you. I thought you was a couple of them niggers that's been moving in here lately."

Johnny lowered his eyes and stepped into the house. He found Kate sitting next to the box that had become Baby Elsie's coffin. Johnny saw that Kate and her friends had lined the box with a tarp and filled the bottom with ice. A white sheet with pillows and a touch of lace dressed it up real nice. Kate's eyes rose to meet her husband's, and then quickly turned down to the floor. Johnny never looked upon a sadder, more desperate scene in his life. Kate could not speak, and neither could Johnny. Stella walked over and greeted her husband.

"We'll get everybody out of here so you can get cleaned up, and be with your wife," Jim said.

"Yeah," said Stella, "and after you get out of the tub, just throw them clothes out on the porch and I'll come over after a while and fix them up for you."

Johnny smiled and nodded. Everybody looked so helpless as they left, like they wished they could do or say something that would make a difference, but was just at a loss. He noticed that no one could even shake his hand or hug him, so filthy was he from soot and the black water.

After closing the door, Johnny stepped out of his boots and stripped off his shirt and trousers, as well as socks and undergarments. All of it was soaked to where it was clingy and grimy. He was happily surprised to find that some of his friends had stocked the stove and already heated a large bucket of water. He poured it in the tub and tested it with his pinky. Kate, a bit hunched over and limping where you couldn't help but notice, brought some cooler water to balance it out.

"You okay?" Johnny asked.

Kate just nodded. Johnny sat on the edge of the tub and Kate handed him a bar of White King and a cloth for washing.

"Thank you, Sweetheart," Johnny said. "Glad you had so many friends to help you today."

Kate wouldn't look him directly in the eye. And she wouldn't speak. She must be too broke up about all this, he thought. She soaped up the cloth and walked around to his back and scrubbed.

"I can't believe our baby girl is gone!" Johnny said as he broke out crying.

Kate moved around to the other side and threw her arms around him. She looked like she had been crying all day, and kept on now as she held onto her husband. When the tears run dry, Johnny toweled off and got something to eat. Then he lay down with his wife in his arms.

"I don't understand why this happened," he said. "Why does God let something like this happen? She had the best ma in the world. She had a pa who loved her. We would of gived her a good life."

Johnny kept on until his words dropped off in a deep slumber.

Chapter 18

Johnny fell asleep with his wife in his arms, but woke up without her. As wakening thoughts began to run through his brain and he could feel she wasn't there, he jerked from his side to his back and looked around the house. There she was, her head resting on the edge of Elsie's coffin with her arm draped over, reaching out to her little girl.

Johnny leapt up and hurried to her side, placing one arm around her shoulder, stroking her hair with the other hand. He heard some hollering outside. Johnny threw on some trousers and walked out on the porch. The sun was just streaking over the peaks to the east. He could see two of them Baldwin detectives on horseback down the row, and two on foot. They looked like they was paying attention to a building five or six houses down. He stepped into some boots, grabbed a shirt, and made his way down towards the action. Jim came walking out three houses down.

"They sure starting early," Jim said.

"Yep," said Johnny. "They either want to get back on the nine o'clock train or they wanting to do this before anybody wakes up."

The two detectives on horseback stood back as if on guard in front of the little house, while the two detectives on foot walked up to the door. All was armed with side pistols, and the mounted detectives cradled rifles as well.

"Ain't that Mrs. West's house?" Jim asked.

"Yep," Johnny said. "Gilbert's aunt."

Before Mrs. West could answer the door, Sid Hatfield and one of his deputies walked up to the house and talked to the detective sergeant in charge. Johnny and Jim moved close enough to hear what was said.

"Morning Chief," Detective Tanner said.

Hatfield was all business. "What you doing out here so early?" he asked.

"We getting this done so we can get back out of town," Tanner said.

"I told you I wanted a list of names and any paperwork you got from the county."

"Well, this here one is West," the detective said. "And I got the eviction notice from the mining company, and the contract."

Hatfield took the paperwork in hand.

"Right here," the detective said, pointing to the yellow dog clause. "You know this ain't no month to month lease, or year to year lease, or nothing like that."

"But her nephew was just killed a week ago," Hatfield said.

"We been through this before," the detective said. "This lease is based on an employer-employee relationship, and there ain't no employee of the mining company living in this house. So they taking it back."

Mrs. West stood in her doorway, crying. Miners and their families gathered in the roadway, some carrying rifles.

"Why don't you give her a little time to get her stuff together?" Hatfield said.

"She got five minutes," Tanner said.

Hatfield walked up to Mrs. West on the porch and looked like he was explaining the situation to her, even comforting her. Then Tanner spoke quietly to his two henchmen on horseback. Straight away they rode to the back of the house and began stomping out her garden. Pie tins that marked the rows shimmered in the rising sun but disappeared under the flurry of hooves.

"What you doing?" someone from the crowd shouted out.

"From now on, no more gardens," Tanner yelled. "It's competition with the company store, so no more gardens!"

A low rumble could be heard from the crowd. While the horses got their exercise, the two other detectives walked up to the front door and knocked again. The woman come to the door and was taken by the arms and led out the house. They seated her on the ground in front of the porch. Then the detectives took all her earthly possessions and tossed them into the street—rocking chair, pot, cast-iron frying pan, clothing, a basket of food items.

When the house was empty, Johnny and Jim watched as the Baldwin-Felts detectives moved on down the street to find other tenants who no longer had their husbands or sons or anyone working in the mines. Most of the neighbors surrounded Mrs. West with assurances that she would be okay, that they was part of the only family she had left in the world, and would help her take the train back to Charleston. Johnny and Jim pressed in and patted her on the back.

"God be with you," Jim said.

"I'm real sorry about all this, Mrs. West," Johnny said.

Mrs. West turned her back on him.

Johnny and Jim tromped back to the McCarthy house. Stella had arrived to comfort Kate, and the two men fixed some eggs and warmed bread, along with some chopped up apples.

"What time is Brother Joseph coming by?" Johnny asked.

"About noon, is what he said," Stella answered.

"You going to the mine today?" Jim asked.

"I gotta dig a grave out yonder," Johnny said. "Reckon I better take today off and mourn my baby girl."

"I'll help you with the grave," said Jim.

In about an hour, the two men was ready to walk east, to the foothills of the mountains, in the place where wisps of white, yellow, and purple flowers grew here and there in the awakening earth. Johnny and Jim walked out on the porch and saw four Baldwin-Felts detectives coming up to the house.

"Morning gentlemen," Detective Tanner said.

The two men turned to face them and nodded their heads.

"Which one of you is Johnny McCarthy?"

Johnny raised his arm.

"McCarthy, we got a foreman missing. Goes by the name of Big Jake. According to our report, you wasn't at work on Monday, so

Big Jake told the operations supervisor that he was going to stop by your house to see where you was at. Did he stop by here?"

"Uh, I don't know, sir. Um, I wasn't here."

"Where *was* you?"

"About twelve miles north of here along the river, looking for my son."

"So you wasn't here. Was your wife here?"

"I think so."

"Well, get her out here so we can talk to her," Tanner said. "We just trying to find out who saw him last. We got no idea where he's at."

"Uh sir, my wife can't talk right now," Johnny said. "You see, we had this accident and our baby girl was killed, and we fixing to bury her today. My wife, she's just too upset to talk to anybody right now."

"You saying your dead baby girl is in this here house right now?"

"Uh, yes sir."

"Well, let me see," Tanner said. "God damn it, this here is an important investigation over a mining company matter!"

"Sir, could you talk to her another day?" Jim said. "This is a really bad day for her."

"I didn't ask you to say nothing!" Tanner said.

The detective sergeant grabbed Jim by the shirt and pushed him back against the front of the house. The two detectives on horseback jumped down, and in a moment all four Baldwin-Felts bad boys was on the front porch. Johnny held out his arms with palms up as if to quiet things down. Then he opened the door.

The four mining company men walked slowly into the small house, their chests sticking out and shoulders back. Their heads was looking all around, taking everything in. Tanner walked over to Baby Elsie's coffin where Kate sat.

"Sorry for your loss, ma'am," Tanner said. "Did Big Jake come by here on Monday?"

Kate burst into tears and heavy sobs, her face dropping into her hands. She stood up best she could and started screaming, "Get out of my house! Get out of my house!"

Johnny grabbed Kate to hold her back. Tanner shook his head in disgust, and the other three lawmen looked at their boss as if to see if there was any action he wanted them to take. The four of them walked slowly out the door, with Tanner looking back at Johnny in contempt. Johnny followed them out the door.

"I'm sorry," Johnny said. "She been dealing with lots of trouble lately. Ain't her best self today. Won't happen again."

Chapter 19

Carolina wrens sang their *tea-kettle* songs from the high branches and red-bellied woodpeckers tapped on hollow-sounding trunks as the overhead sun filtered its light through the trees. A modest northeasterly breeze rustled the newly-sprouted leaves.

Baby Elsie's coffin was sealed up and sat beside the hole in the earth that Johnny and Jim had dug. Johnny looked back and thought a good forty-five to fifty friends and neighbors had come to the gravesite. He stood behind his seated wife, his hands squeezing her shoulders. Brother Joseph led two verses of "Shall We Gather at the River?" Then he started preaching.

"It is with heavy hearts that we gather together today to commit the body of Baby Elsie McCarthy to the ground. She was born February 2nd, 1920 in Matewan, West Virginia, and was killed in a horrible accident on April 5th of this same year, also in Matewan, West Virginia. She is survived by her father, Johnny McCarthy, a mineworker here at the Stone Mountain Camp, her mother Kate McCarthy, a wife and housewife, as well as mother, and her older brother Corey McCarthy, who ain't here today and ain't living with the family at this time."

Johnny shifted his shoulders nervously as he listened to the young preacher.

"Beings that little Elsie McCarthy was just a baby, less than one years old, there ain't no doubt about her place in heaven with God. Since she had not yet reached the age of accountability, which is generally recognized to be around twelve years old, where a person makes up their mind about what to do or what not to do, and definitely knows the difference between right and wrong, there is no doubt that she was sinless in the eyes of God, and could not possibly have any sins marked up against her which would send her straight to hell."

That was a relief to know, Johnny thought. He was hoping the preacher would get to something that would comfort his grieving wife.

"We don't know why God decided to take little Elsie. Some things is a mystery in life. It could be that God needed another angel in heaven. It could be that through God's foreknowledge, He knew that this would be better for Elsie. It could be that there was a better place for Elsie to be than here in the Stone Mountain Coal Camp. We do know that she is in a better place where she will not have to know the hardships of mining life."

Kate shook beneath Johnny's touch, and wept as silently as she could. Johnny felt like he was getting worked up and scanned his eyes over the landscape, watching the red-breasted robins hop along the ground looking for worms, and the scurrying squirrels snatching up acorns.

"Why, who knows but that if Elsie had been allowed to grow up into a little girl or a young lady, all sorts of evil could have befallen her. Things could have happened to her that her mother and father couldn't have protected her from. There are young men traveling the country who look to steal a woman's virtuosity and sometimes ain't nothing can be done to stop it."

With those words Johnny swallowed hard and prayed for this soon to be over. When it was, he took Kate's hand and pulled Jim and Stella off to the side.

"I want to thank you for coming out today," Johnny said. "Means a lot. I just want to say this was a sweet little girl, and we sure loved her. She might of went to a better place, but if God could have seed himself to leave her here with us for just a little while more, she wouldn't have missed out on no love. I can say that for sure.

"So God, if You up there," Johnny said looking up at the sky, "and if You listening, please take care of our little girl, and save her for us for when we get up there too. Amen."

Chapter 20

The last couple days was okay for Johnny in the mines and everything. Good seams and clean work. Well, clean as far as getting things done. Hit full coal three days in a row. Can't do better than that. He couldn't wait to get home.

"You going to the meeting tonight?" Jim asked as he caught up to Johnny.

"Yeah, right after bath and a supper," Johnny said. "Who's speaking?"

"Ed Chambers got back from Charleston. Brought that petition for a union charter. Can't wait to hear what he got to say."

Johnny walked into his house and found Kate asleep on the bed. He bent over and stroked her face. Didn't mean to do that. Big smudge left behind. He started a fire in the stove and put a bucket of water on top. He checked out the tub and started to remove his clothing. Kate rolled over and looked at him.

"Hi Sweetie," he said.

Her gaze stayed fixed on Johnny, but she didn't say nothing. He walked over to her bed and started to reach for her face again, but stopped himself just in time. He showed her his black hands and smiled.

"Don't want to touch you with these!" he said.

He moved over to the stove and tested the water.

"How you feeling today, Sweetie? I'm doing okay. Hit my quota today, about six tons, no problem."

Johnny bathed and dressed, and poured the black water on the ground out back. Then he fixed himself a plate of supper, and one for Kate. Johnny wolfed down his food.

"Come on, Sweetie," he frowned. "You gotta eat more than that. Gotta keep your strength up."

. . . .

Johnny and Jim plodded out the Stone Mountain Coal Camp, down Mate Street through Matewan, across the tracks and down by the river to the Community Church. Four men with rifles formed a circle around the entrance to the meeting place. Lots of men stood around outside, but Johnny and his friend signed their names on the list and went inside to sit down. When the men got settled, Ed Chambers, owner of the hardware store, marched out on stage to loud cheers and applause.

"Okay men, let me take the mystery out of it for you. I spent the last few days in Charleston meeting with officials of the United Mine Workers Association. I met John L. Lewis, new president of the UMW. I met with other leaders like Bill Blizzard, and Fred Mooney. Frank Keeney. They was all there. These are good men and they are determined to see the success of the union in West Virginia."

"Yeah!" one miner called out.

"Wahoo!" from another.

All the miners yelled and clapped their hands.

"So I went there with a petition in hand to get a union charter for all of the Tug River Valley. And I got that charter right here!"

The men yelled, whistled, and cheered. Johnny thought the noise would never die down.

"Now I gotta tell you men that if you sign up for the union, life could get harder before it gets better. They might fire you. They might evict you from company housing. They might try to replace you with scabs!"

Roars of anger came from the crowd.

"But if you a certified miner, you have value to the coal operators because the only thing they care about is getting that coal out of the ground. And ain't nobody better at that than a certified miner!"

The cheers was enthusiastic again.

"So let me ask you, how many of you would like a 27% pay increase?"

Big cheers from all over the room. A guffaw was heard towards the back.

"You know that in the central field the miners went on strike for two months and won a 27% increase. Unheard of. If you making fifty cents a ton and you loading full coal, let's say six tons a day, that's three dollars a day...six days a week, that's eighteen dollars a week, and that's about seventy two dollars a month. You get a 27% raise and you making close to a hundred dollars a month!"

More cheers.

"You in tall cotton!"

"What about safety in the mines?" a miner called out. "Does the union do anything to make us safer?"

"That's a good question," Chambers said. "Nobody survives an explosion. None of us ever forget Monongah, thirteen years ago, when three hundred and sixty-two men died in the worst mining disaster in the country's history. Could that have been prevented? Most likely. One thing the union does is make sure the mines get inspected like they supposed to. We got the West Virginia Department of Mines, but how often they come out and inspect? And we got fire bosses who supposed to inspect every working area for firedamp and ventilation. Well, the union makes sure they do. They also make sure every man down in the hole is trained in safety. Imagine if one laborer makes a mistake with an open flame and kills hundreds of men who knowed better. The union makes a big difference like that."

"Oh brother!" a strident voice was heard to say.

"What about cribbing?" another miner called out. "Can the union do anything about that?"

"Yeah, we all had this happen. We load two thousand pounds in the car, but the car ain't full. They redesign the car so when we fill it up, we actually loaded two thousand five hundred pounds, and we get paid for a ton. Last time I checked, a ton is two thousand pounds."

"Yeah!" one called out.

"That's right," said another.

"So one thing that's been negotiated in the northern districts is that two thousand pounds is two thousand pounds, and two thousand pounds is a ton. And up north they check on that by having two check-weighmen, one a part of the coal operators, and one a part of the union, and it takes both of them to decide any docking penalties."

"That's good," one called out.

Another miner still in his overalls, a man Johnny did not know, stood up and shouted out. "This is bullshit!" he said. "They ain't never gonna let the union in here anyways!"

"Now hold on," Chambers said. "Here's the thing. The time for the union has come. Not just because we need it, but because the coal operators in the north need it too. With cheap labor here in the south, our coal operators undercut the price of the coal in the rest of the country. Now nobody wants that except the coal operators right here. So for the first time I can remember, the whole country is wanting the union to work out here in Mingo County."

"That don't mean shit!" the miner shouted back. "The coal operators down here are the ones that let the union in or not, and they ain't gonna do that no how!"

"Why don't you sit down and shut up!" a miner across the hall called out.

"Why don't you cart your ass over here and make me, son?"

Lots of miners jumped to their feet with more shouting and pushing.

"Whoa, hold on now!" Chambers called out. "Hold on! This is a chance to make a real difference for our families down here in Matewan."

"Bullshit again!" the man in his overalls stood up and shouted. "They ain't gonna do nothing for ya. All they want is your money!"

This time, the men sitting around the troublemaker stood up and grabbed a hold of him. Johnny watched as the men quickly wrestled him out the back door of the church. Yelling and scrapping was going on out there, but then they shut the door.

"Sorry about that, men," Chambers said. "Just to show how wrong this fella is, you can sign up and get your union card tonight, if you want to. The union has decided to waive the sign-up fee, and they have decided to waive the monthly dues until they can negotiate a raise for all of you. So if you want to start on the road to things getting better, this is the next step."

One of the men manning the sign-up tables was a man Johnny had never seen before, but he was glad-handing every miner that came within reach of his table.

"C. E. Lively," he would say. "C. E. Lively."

Johnny watched the multitude of men crowd towards the back tables. They talked of not being able to keep on as things had been. They needed security, protection, and respect. Johnny knew that to sign on the dotted line was an important decision and a commitment to a new path. Johnny didn't believe the things the rabble-rouser was shouting out. But problem was, it was like declaring war on the coal operators, asking to get fired, evicted, and having no income at all. Yeah, there was problems working for the coal company, but at least they had something to eat every day and a roof over their heads. Johnny would think on it, but he couldn't see how things could be so bad he would get right in the face of the coal operators like that. Time would tell, but to his way of thinking, not much ranked higher than that regular paycheck. Papa always said, "Don't bite the hand that feeds you."

Chapter 21

Johnny skipped a stone over the surface of the Tug Fork and watched it run in and out of the little ripples.

"You know," he said, "A lot of our men been union members for a little over two weeks now, and nothing's happened to them."

"Yeah, it's been kind of quiet," Jim said. "But they might be fixin' to crack down real hard."

"Well, they ain't got no raise yet, but ain't nobody been fired neither."

"Yeah, I guess it takes a while for things to happen."

"I notice they been a little quieter," Johnny said, "like they ain't trying to be friendly, or nothing."

"They might be gearing up for trouble. But you been pulling so much coal out of that new seam you broke open, maybe they real happy with you about that."

"Yeah, that seam's the biggest I seen in a long time," Johnny said. "I figure it might be a hundred, hundred and ten feet wide."

"From what I seen, looks pretty pure too. Not much slate or rock mixed in."

"Yeah, so far. Hey, we can talk about work tomorrow," Johnny said. "This our one day off. Let's go catch some fish!"

"Fish?"

"Yeah, I got some line and hooks and stuff at the house. You think Stella will mind staying a bit with Kate?"

"Nope, she probably want to anyway."

Johnny and Jim ran to the house.

"Hi Sweetie," Johnny said. "You doing okay?"

He touched Kate's chin with the back of his fingers. She looked deep into his eyes.

"We gonna go fishing in the river," Jim said. "You mind staying and keeping Kate company for a while?"

"No, that's fine," Stella said, "as long as you bring back some fish."

"We'll bring them to you if you scale them and clean them," Jim said.

Stella made a gagging gesture with her mouth, and laughed.

Johnny grabbed a big pickle jar from behind the stove.

"What we need that for?" Jim asked.

"You'll see."

A quick stop at Mrs. West's trampled out garden to dig up some worms, and Johnny and Jim was off to the south side of Matewan, across the tracks, past the church, and down to the banks of the river.

"I didn't know you knowed how to fish the river," Jim said.

"Couple of hillbillies up in a holler north of here showed me. Here, hold this line."

"We gonna fish with a dropline?"

"No, we gonna cut a couple poles, like from that stand of saplings over there."

Johnny eyed just the right size shafts growing out of the ground. In no time, he set up the line about the same length of the pole tied to the tip, set up the moonshiner's cork, the hook, and some tiny lead weights. Worm on the hook, and they was in business.

Johnny saw Jim flipping his hook into the water, while he set up his own pole. On the third flip, a fish hit his worm, and kept it too.

"Dang," said Jim.

"That's the way it works," Johnny said. "That's why they call it fishing!"

Johnny and Jim worked their way down the river, casting their hooks in every few steps. That way, they was always in new territory with new fish in the area and coming through. They started bringing them onto the bank, so Johnny set up a cord with a nail tied to the end.

They ran the cord through the gill flap and created a stringer so it could hold lots of fish.

"You know, last night after work, I was so tired," Johnny said. "I gotta get me my bath before I eat, and I had so much stuff on my mind I didn't think about chopping no wood for the stove in a long time. We was almost out. So I looked around, and I couldn't find my ax."

"Couldn't find your ax?"

"Nope. I asked Kate about it, but she ain't talked much since Elsie died. She just kind of stares off."

"What you think happened to it?" Jim asked.

"I don't know. You seen any niggers walking through our neighborhood?"

"Nope," Jim said. "They supposed to stay in their own neighborhood."

"Yeah, I know. But just the same, you got to keep your eye out."

"Um hmm."

"Hey, when Stella stays with Kate, does Kate talk to her?"

"No," said Jim, "it's pretty much the same as with you. Sometimes she stares off into the air, and sometimes she look you right in the eye, but she don't say nothing."

Johnny and Jim kept working their way down the river, watching their stringer of fish get fatter and fatter. Johnny noticed deep dark pools near the bank with large rocks on the edges. Seemed like the depth and the darkness near the rocks drew the big fish in. *Bam! Another one for the stringer!*

Just then, a strong odor drifted to Johnny's nostrils, and then Jim's.

"Oh man, what is that smell?" Johnny said.

"Whew! That's a strong stink," said Jim. "Smells like what we had in Bluefield before we come down here. After a firedamp explosion killed about thirty men, we had to go in there and clean up, and I tell you I could never forget what that was about. Miners was torn apart, and we had to scrape pieces of men's bodies off the floor with shovels. The smell was terrible."

"So the smell was blood, or what?"

"The smell was *death*," Jim said, "and you can't never forget it after you smelt it."

"It seems to be getting stronger as we keep going down the river," Johnny said. "You know, up ahead is that abandoned backhouse they built too close to the river. Maybe something died in there."

"Yeah, we be next we keep going over there," Jim said.

"No, we got to check it out."

The two men stopped fishing and kept moving in the direction of the terrible odor. It coated their tongues and made their eyes water. Just when Johnny felt there was no way to keep going any farther, there it was. Sticking out of the ground was a form, almost like a man, or a head and upper torso, but it was maggot-infested and covered in mud. Angry flies buzzed around and even attacked Johnny and Jim. Looking at it and feeling like victims of the piercing odor, Johnny turned to the side and vomited everything that was trying to stick around in his stomach. Jim was right behind. Neither could stop the urge to throw up their entire insides.

"Let's get out of here," Johnny said. "We gotta report this."

Chapter 22

Johnny and Jim stood upriver far enough to avoid most of the smell. Problem was, wind was blowing their way and they couldn't help but pick up traces of that awful stench.

Johnny could see Sid Hatfield with a kerchief over his nose and mouth as he looked down at the corpse. Sid had two officers on the site, and had deputized two others to do the worst of it—wield shovels and move the body. In turn, Johnny saw each of the five men bend over and retch up their guts. Sid Hatfield walked in their direction.

"That's quite a sight," he said.

"Most disgusting thing I ever seen," Johnny said.

"You didn't find nothing else, or see nobody walking around?" Sid asked.

"No, we was just fishing, walking down river when we got whiff of it."

"You see anybody going to the area of the backhouse pit, the one that supposed to be closed?"

"No, I ain't never seen nobody going back there," Johnny said.

Jim just shook his head and shrugged his shoulders.

"Why don't we go for a walk up there, and look around," Sid said.

"Any idea who the poor fellow is?"

"Awful hard to tell, but I think it might be Jake."

"Oh my God," said Johnny. "I wouldn't wish that on nobody!"

"You think he fell into the pit?" Jim asked.

"Looks like it. The reason we had to close this backhouse is it's so close to the water that whatever's in the pit drains into the river and poisons it. It almost becomes like quicksand, and anything that goes in there eventually works its way into the river."

The three men walked the area around the pit. The dung beetles swarmed in threat and defiance.

"Lots of footprints," Sid said. "People still been coming here. Don't know why."

Johnny and Jim stood looking into the pit. The rolling motion of the dark brown beetles could almost put a man in a trance. Sid walked over south of the pit and stooped down in the weeds.

"Look at this!" he said, holding an ax in his hand.

"What the...that's my ax!" Johnny said.

"It is?"

"Yeah, look here."

He showed the police chief his initials carved on the end of the handle.

"I been looking for this," said Johnny.

"Well, I got to hold onto it for now," Hatfield said. "A man died here, and now we find an ax. I got to keep this 'til we know what's going on."

. . . .

Midweek, Johnny heard that Hatfield had the corpse wrapped in canvas and loaded into a pine box. A coroner had to look it over and figure out who it was, and there was no coroner in Matewan. So they shipped the box to Williamson.

After dinner, Johnny, Jim, and a handful of men knocked on the door of Ed Chambers' house in response to an invitation for a private meeting. Johnny knew it was about the union, but he wondered specifically why Mr. Chambers wanted to talk to this little group privately. The men sat around a huge dining room table sipping tea and lemonade served by two Negro maid servants. An elegant crystal chandelier hung directly over the table, shedding light on their note papers.

"Men, thanks for coming tonight," Chambers said. "We had a good meeting at the church a couple weeks ago, and we off to a good start. Now we know that you men ain't joined the union yet, but there's much more to it than we've already talked about.

"There are details we got to address, like our constitutional right to peaceably assemble and engage in free speech. They can't take those rights away because of where we work. We're Americans, and those rights follow us no matter where we work and no matter where we go. Truth is, the mine operators would like to control us as much as they can to get more out of us, but if they treated us with dignity and respect, I believe they'd find we would work out better for them too. We would *want* to come to work and do good for the company, for our families, and out of self-respect, for ourselves too."

"Makes sense," one of the miners said.

"We also need the operators to recognize the union, and accept it. Sometimes they act like it don't exist. As a union, we a legal entity governed by laws with a charter and a set of bylaws that guide us into what we can do and what we can't do. We not just making it up as we go along. We got objectives and rules about how to reach them. So the operators need to take us seriously. This is a big deal!

"Another thing, workers get discharged. Sometimes it's for cause, like maybe the worker can't produce full coal even on a good day. Sometimes it's for joining a union, although none of us has been let go for that, and it's already been about two and a half weeks. But when a man is cut loose, irregardless of the reason, we want the mining company to stop blacklisting those workers. A man fired one place, fine. Didn't work out. But he shouldn't be kept from working everywhere else. Give the man a chance!"

"Yeah, that's right," several voices was heard.

"And one more issue. This company store thing gotta stop!"

"Yeah."

"That's the truth!" many voices was in agreement.

"They don't even pay you money so you got choices about where to shop. They give you this funny money they call scrip, but it's only good at the company store. And at the company store, sometimes they give you credit and sometimes they don't. How many of you, just to get what you need, get further and further in debt to the company store?"

"That's right," someone said.

"That's the way it is, all right," said another.

"I got a question, Mr. Chambers," Johnny said. "If we *did* get paid in cash, where else we supposed to shop around here?"

"Good point," Chambers smiled. "There might be times when you could get into Charleston by train, but even if you couldn't you might be able to save a little money when you had a good week. Stashing some cash is always a good thing to do."

Johnny nodded.

"So these things gotta change," Chambers said. "Now why you suppose I ask you men to this meeting at my house?"

The men all stared right at Mr. Chambers in dead silence. Tension was building. Finally, one had the courage to speak.

"You gonna ask us to do something?" he said.

Mr. Chambers burst into a wide grin, revealing several gold-capped teeth.

"Fair enough," he laughed, "that's good thinking."

His smile and relaxed manner broke the tension and caused everyone to laugh.

"Yes, I'm gonna ask you to do something. I'm gonna ask the dozen of you to take the train into Charleston for more training about the union. Even though you not members yet, we see your leadership qualities. We need young, dedicated men like you who understand how things work, who know about the laws and the bylaws, who understand the objectives and the methods of the union."

"When would we do this?" one of them asked.

"You will take the 8:00 A.M. train tomorrow, so Thursday evening, Friday, and Saturday you will be in Charleston. You stay in the Charleston Hotel on Meeting Street, guests of the union. You return on the train on Sunday. Does everybody understand what we're doing? Does anybody not want to go?"

"Um, sir, what about our wages?" Johnny asked. "Most of us can't go without pay for three days."

"Another good question," Chambers said. "The union will underwrite your wages for this trip to Charleston. In other words, the union will pay you full coal for these three days."

"Oh, man," Johnny said.

"Oh, that's great!" said another.

"So, thank you, gentlemen. I want you to be at the train station by 7:30 A.M., and I will...

Crack!

A single shot from a rifle shattered the peace, darkened the chandelier, and scattered its pieces all over the table and the dozen men.

Chapter 23

Johnny walked up to the train depot with a satchel holding a change of clothes and the other things he would need being away for a couple days. Jim, Gino, Heinrich, and some others was just arriving. Johnny walked up to Mr. Chambers.

"Mr. Chambers, so what was that all about last night with the shooting and everything?"

"That was the end of a very expensive chandelier and the beginning of a very unhappy wife," Chambers said.

"But…"

"I know what you mean. The fact that it was only one shot, and that it was very targeted to a light just means they was watching. It was like a warning. They was telling us they knowed what was going on and they could do something about it if they wanted to."

"Is that sort of thing normal around here?"

"Starting to be."

. . . .

Johnny and his friends sat around a huge wooden table in the dining room of the Charleston Hotel. Chandeliers lit the way and servers set steaming plates in front of them. Johnny couldn't believe the food that was sitting right there—piles of roast beef, mashed potatoes, and green beans with little round onions and red things that was soft. Gravy covered half the beef and potatoes. Steaming dinner rolls was in a large bowl in front of the men, wrapped in what they called a *napkin*, bigger and nicer than most towels he had in his house. Huge chunks of butter was passed around. The forks and the knives and the spoons was shiny and thick, like they couldn't get all swallowed up in your hand. The men had their choice of big glasses of tea with ice, or coffee. You could have sugar and cream, and all the pepper and salt you could sprinkle.

"I never knowed food could smell so good!" Johnny said.

"I ain't never seen so much food on one plate!" Heinrich said.

"Hey Gino," Johnny asked. "You ever take a shit in one of them closet toilets before?"

"Can't say as I have. Felt kind of funny just walking to the end of the hall instead of going outside to a backhouse."

"How come you stay in there so long?"

"He was having a good time." Heinrich said.

Gino tossed a roll in his direction.

"Oh my God!" Jim said. "What's that white stuff there in that little bowl?"

"Don't know. You want some?"

Johnny slid the bowl over to him. Jim helped himself to a big forkful of the unknown and began gasping and choking. "Horseradish!" he said. "Hot as a powder blast!" His eyes was watering something awful. "Fumes coming out my nose!"

"I heard it's dangerous to eat any more after something like that happen to you," Johnny said. "Why don't you slide your plate over here and I'll take care of it for you."

"Yeah, over my dead body!"

. . . .

After dinner, Johnny and the others filed into a large auditorium with theater-style seats and a big stage. They found out it used to be the Rialto Theater until they moved to new digs at the north end of town. The room was big as a cavern, but miners was filling the seats.

"We thought we was the only ones," Johnny said to Jim, "but they must've sent men from all over the Tug River Valley."

An unknown man with a booming voice stood before the assembly, asked everyone to stand, face the flag, and place their hand over their heart.

I pledge allegiance to my Flag, and to the republic for which it stands, one nation, indivisible, with liberty and justice for all.

"Please be seated. Men, welcome to this meeting of the United Mine Workers of America. It is my pleasure to introduce to you the Secretary/Treasurer for the United Mine Workers of America, District 17, Mr. Fred Mooney."

Loud applause and cheers erupted from the audience.

"Thank you men. Thank you," Mooney said, nodding his head and raising his arms.

"Thank you very much. And thank you to Robert who led us in the pledge. Robert has been my assistant for the past three years when it was my privilege to take over as Secretary/Treasurer for District 17 of this great body. And by the way, District 17 covers Virginia, Tennessee, Eastern Kentucky, and Southern West Virginia. I believe most of you are from Eastern Kentucky and Southern West Virginia, do I have that right?"

"Yes sir!" the men yelled.

"And let me see if I understand. You are the men who get in the cages and go down in the hole to extract the black rock from the earth, am I right?"

"Yes sir!" one miner yelled.

"You are the men who *risk your lives* to go down into the earth, sometimes hundreds of feet, sometimes *thousands* of feet beneath the surface, never knowing if you will see the light of day again. Am I right about that?"

"Yes sir!" many of the men yelled.

"You are the men who have already lost friends, loved ones, and family members to the dangers of the mine. Am I right about that?"

The shouts of affirmation came forth louder than ever. Johnny could see that Fred Mooney was a man to be reckoned with.

"And I want to tell you that you are to be respected for the work that you do, that as you go forth into the depths of the earth that you are brave and courageous, and you are worthy of every measure of safety that can be applied to protect your lives, and that you are worth every penny of the wages that you earn!"

Loud cheers from the audience…

"I have been where you are," Mooney said. "I started working in the mines when I was thirteen. I was a trapper boy, you know, the ventilation doors that had to be closed so miners could breathe in their chambers, but had to be opened in time for the mules and the coal cars to roll through. How many of you have worked as a trapper?"

Many hands shot into the air.

"You know what I'm talking about. That's an important job. Or maybe you became a spragger, or a mule driver, and then a buddee to really learn the craft of mining. And then the day comes that you finally become certified as a miner and the whole world is yours, that is if they don't kill you first."

The audience went dead silent.

"Every miner has had the experience of loading a full car of coal and then they cheat you at the scales. They say it was a short ton instead of a long ton. Or they say it had too much rock and shale in it. I guess I could go on and on about the things that are wrong and how we as miners suffer at the hands of the coal operators, but I want you to see more of the big picture as a result of being here in Charleston.

"You miners from Eastern Kentucky and Southern West Virginia have not yet reaped the benefits of the union. We just getting started. Greed prevents the coal operators from doing the right thing. In the strike at Paint Creek and Cabin Creek in Kanawha County, all we asked for as far as the money goes, was 2½¢ more per ton than we was getting. Because that's what other union miners was getting in the area. Would have been about 15¢ per miner per day. But the coal operators couldn't see it.

"Now the strike lasted a little more than a year in 1912 and 1913. About fifty people died from violent deaths, and bankers estimate the strike cost about a hundred million dollars! Imagine that, all because they didn't want to pay 15¢ a day.

"So everybody's talking about the 27% increase that miners got in other parts of the country. That was after a two-month strike. We're gonna ask for a raise of 10%, so if you making 50¢ a ton, you'd be making 55¢. It may not be that easy in West Virginia and Kentucky, and we might have to go on strike so they take us serious, but we willing to do that.

"You know that the UMWA is a national union, representing miners all over the country. But you need to know that West Virginia is a special situation. West Virginia was created as a state by Abraham Lincoln in 1863 as part of the preparation for war. Because of that it has always had a stigma. It's always had a challenge to be recognized as a legitimate state. Wonderful people. Wonderful resources. But marked with a target on its back for exploitation. In addition to that, by 1871 Democrats rewrote the constitution of our beautiful state and weakened the power of the office of the governor, reduced the budget, and made it more difficult for the state to resist the efforts of companies to come in and exploit our people and steal our resources. That's what makes the fight here a little more fierce.

"Now we want you to get a good rest tonight because there will be a lot more presented to you over the next two days. I want to let you in on a surprise. You've all heard of Mother Jones and what a powerhouse she is in the labor movement. Well, she arrives by train tomorrow from Philadelphia, and she'll be speaking to this group in the afternoon.

Chapter 24

On Friday, the second day of instruction in Charleston, Johnny was late to some of the presentations. but for this last one of the day, he had heard so much about the speaker he didn't want to miss a thing.

Johnny listened to the younger man with the booming voice introduce Mother Jones. She sat in a chair off to the side on the big stage. There she was, all dressed up in black, short and stocky, with hair as white as the lace around her neck. Black dress, black hat, black boots. She looked intently at the emcee, and then scanned the audience back and forth with her eyes, waiting her turn.

Finally...

"Gentlemen," he said, "a warm welcome please for Mother Jones!"

It seemed to Johnny that many of the men must have heard this woman before, because with no prodding, the entire audience rose to their feet in wild cheers and applause. At last, the speaker they had been waiting for.

Thank you men for coming to listen to me today. I am humbled by your presence, and for the sacrifice that you make. One time recently in Scranton, Pennsylvania, they introduced me as a humanitarian. I'm not a humanitarian. I'm a hell-raiser!

Whoa, thought Johnny. This woman is bold, to come right out and say that. She was a woman of action. She wanted results.

The first thing is to raise hell, says I. That's always the first thing to do when you're faced with an injustice and you feel powerless. That's what I do in my fight for the working class.

Johnny's eyes, mind, and thoughts was riveted to the stage. He couldn't help but note how quiet it was in the auditorium. No rustling, no fidgeting. Just the powerful woman speaker.

If there's one thing that gets my hackles up it's the exploitation of children. Some years back, in Kensington, Pennsylvania, seventy five thousand textile workers were on strike, and at least ten thousand of them were children. Most of them weren't even ten years old, but they were missing hands and fingers, and they were stooped over and skinny. I asked the newspaper men why they didn't publish the truth about child labor in Pennsylvania. They said they couldn't because the mill owners had stock in the papers. I said, well I have stock in the children, and I'll arrange some publicity.

Johnny couldn't help but think what a wonderful speaker Mother Jones was. She was filled with passion for the cause. She needed no prompting, no notes. Her zeal just oozed out of her.

I brought some of the children up on the stage and held them up, cut off hands, and fingers, and all. They weren't hard to hold up. They were light in weight. I told the people that Philadelphia mansions were built on the broken bones and quivering hearts of children. City officials stood in open windows of the city hall across the way, and I told them some day the workers will take possession of your city hall and when we do, no child will be sacrificed on the altar of profit. The city officials quickly closed the windows, just as they had closed their eyes and their hearts.

The employment of children is doing more to fill prisons, insane asylums, almshouses, reformatories, slums, and gin shops than all the efforts of reformers are doing to improve society.

I learned in the early part of my career that labor must bear the cross for the sins of others, must be the vicarious sufferer for the wrongs that others do.

There's talk of women getting the vote. There's been marches and demonstrations all over the country. And that's fine, but I have never had the vote, and I have raised hell all over this country. You don't need a vote to raise hell! You need convictions and a voice!

Applause broke out all over the auditorium. Johnny was shocked by the energy of this woman. She moved about the stage like a dancer, though her moves was not dainty or feminine, but bold and strong. She seemed to be moving in all directions at the same time. Her arms waved all together. She could not contain her passion.

As labor, we must stand together. If we don't, there will be no victory for any one of us. My friends, it is solidarity of labor that we want. We do not want to find fault with each other, but to solidify our forces and say to each other, we must be together. Our masters are joined together and we must do the same thing.

Injustice boils in men's hearts as does steel in its cauldron, ready to pour forth, white hot, in the fullness of time.

In spite of oppressors, in spite of false leaders, in spite of labor's own lack of understanding of its needs, the cause of the workers continues onward. Slowly his hours are shortened, giving him leisure to read and to think. Slowly his standard of living rises to include some of the good and beautiful things of the world. Slowly the cause of his children becomes the cause of all. His boy is taken from the breaker, his girl from the mill. Slowly those who create the wealth of the world are permitted to share it. The future is in labor's strong, rough hands.

Johnny realized that Mother Jones moved all over the stage in this large auditorium without carrying a microphone, yet she was heard clearly. When she spoke, her voice naturally carried and made sound you could understand right next to your ear. It was like she was talking right to you. Johnny had been caught up in her message and her passion, and didn't realize until now that this woman had spoken for a long time. His stomach told him that dinner was long overdue.

Yes, I have been threatened as I travel the country. I embarrass mine owners, and mill owners, and factory owners. I undermine their profits and their wealth. But how many of us have to give our lives to pave the way for their wealth? I will pray for the dead and fight like hell for the living!

In a newspaper article, some newspaper man called me a lady. A lady is the last thing on earth that I want to be. No matter what the fight, don't be ladylike! God Almighty made women, and the Rockefeller gang of thieves made the ladies!"

I am not afraid of the pen, or the scaffold, or the sword. I will tell the truth wherever I please. If they want to hang me, let them. And on the scaffold I will shout, freedom for the working class!

Johnny felt a great surge of energy. The men in the audience could not hold back. Every one of them rose quickly to their feet and cheered and applauded for what seemed like half an hour. Mother Jones waved and blew kisses to all of her adopted family. Finally, the auditorium quieted. As men started to rise from their seats, Johnny beat a path to the front. He had to meet this powerful woman. He had to make the acquaintance of Mother Jones. He waited for a few to clear out of the way, but it didn't take him long to greet the female leader of labor.

"Mother Jones," he said, "my name is Johnny McCarthy, and I'm a miner in Matewan, just south of here."

"Pleased to meet you," she said as she started to look around for other men to greet.

"Uh, I just wanted to tell you how much I enjoyed your speech," he said. "My father was from Ireland like you. And his father before him. They both died in the coal mines."

"Where at?" she asked.

"County Tipperary, next to County Cork," Johnny said.

"That's where I'm from, Cork," she said. "That's a pretty rough place for labor. My father got us out of there when I was still a girl."

"Yes ma'am," he said. "Well, I wanted to give you something that my father gave me."

Johnny reached in his pocket and pulled out a leather necklace. "It's a blarney stone," Johnny said. "Part of the Blarney Castle. Supposed to give you strength and luck."

"Oh, I always wanted one of those, but I couldn't take that," she said. "It was a gift from your father, and besides, you're the one working in the mines!"

"I'll be all right," he said. "Your life is at risk too, and besides, you make a bigger difference than I do. We need you. We *all* need you."

"But…"

"Please. It would mean a lot to me for you to wear it."

Mother Jones smiled and gave him a big hug.

"Johnny McCarthy, huh? That's a name I won't forget."

. . . .

Johnny walked out the back of the auditorium, and stepped onto the street.

"Hey, I been saving you seats all day," Jim said. "Where you been?"

"I just been looking around in stores and hotels asking about Corey. Trying to find a place where he might be working."

"He loves mules, don't he? Go find a stable!"

Chapter 25

Saturday morning, the last full day of training, Johnny awoke with fiery memories of Mother Jones' energy on stage, her passion, and her penetrating voice. He couldn't get her out of his head, nor did he want to. From knowing her convictions he felt strengthened, even inspired. But something else was on his mind, too.

"Good breakfast," Jim said. "You ready to walk over?"

"In a minute," Johnny said. "I gotta take care of something, but you go ahead. Save me a seat. I won't be far behind."

Johnny headed down Meeting Street in the opposite direction, into the thick of the downtown area. He hopped a streetcar and rode it to Clendenin Street, then over to Quarrier, and north to the banks of the Elk River. He climbed the steps of the Quarrier Street Bridge and crossed the river. Finally on the north side of the river, he knew this was taking too long, so he turned to face traffic and stuck out his thumb. Before long, a Tin Lizzie rolled up and pulled over.

"Where you going?" the man called out.

"Know where Gordon's Stables is at?" Johnny asked.

"Yep, just a few miles down the road, outside of town," he answered. "Hop in."

Johnny looked at the inside of the Model-T, touching the handles and knobs with his fingers.

"I ain't never been in one of these," Johnny said.

"Where you from?" the man asked.

"Mingo County," Johnny answered. "Coal country."

"You a miner?"

"Yep."

"Sounds like a tough job," the man said.

"It's a living," Johnny said. "What's something like this cost?"

"About three hundred dollars."

"Whooee!" Johnny cried out. "Don't think I'll ever see that much money in one place."

"What you doing at the stables?" the man asked.

"Oh, just looking for somebody. There any other stables around here?"

"Sure, lots of them. Most of them is away from the city, like Gordon's, on the other side of the Elk or the Kanawha. And there's a few just east of the city. By the way, my name's Willie," the driver said as he extended his hand.

"Johnny. Johnny McCarthy."

In a couple minutes, Willie turned the Tin Lizzie down a sweeping driveway lined with stately oaks. It curved around and had a matching roadway on the other side of them trees so somebody could come in or go out that other way. Finally, they rolled up in front of what looked like a king's palace, a building 'bout as big as the hotel they slept in last night.

"Look at that!" Johnny said. "What kind of place is this?"

"This is the Gordon's house," Willie said. "Do you know who Wesley Gordon is?"

"Nope. Never heard of him."

"Mr. Gordon is one of them landowners who leases land to the coal operators."

"You mean he lives here?" Johnny asked.

"Well, this is *one* of his houses. He's also got a house in New York, and one in Florida."

Johnny's mouth dropped open and he stared in silence for a long time. Across the front of the house was a shiny porch with no railings and no rocking chairs. Up and down right next to each other was these big pillars like they was holding up the front of the house, almost like trimmed out tree trunks, the kind he'd seen in pictures in the Gazette.

"You mean this house is for one family, like Mr. Gordon's family, and he got other houses too?"

"Yeah, let's get out and I'll show you around," Willie said. "I run the spread here for Mr. Gordon."

They walked around the east side of the house through a flower garden—roses, daisies, daffodils—bright yellows, reds, and greens. The land continued on around the other side with white fencing, a couple of barns, corrals, and what looked like a bunkhouse.

"Hey, I'm sorry to have to ask," Johnny said, "but do you have a backhouse somewhere close? I really gotta go."

"Let's go through the back door of the house here," Willie said. "They got a commode inside."

"You mean they got a toilet closet just like the hotel?"

"They got more than that. Wait 'til you see."

Willie pushed open the door around back and walked in. He grabbed Johnny by the arm and led him to this room. Not only did they have the commode and that soft white paper. There was a sink in there with soap and clean towels all folded up nice. It even smelt fresh like a flower garden. Johnny never thought he'd be using an inside toilet three days in a row. If Gino stayed a long time in that toilet closet in the hotel, he'd of stayed all day in this one.

"You sure Mr. Gordon ain't gonna mind that I used his inside commode?" Johnny asked as he came out.

"He ain't even here. He's in Philadelphia on business, and then he's going to his New York house."

Johnny walked into an open space larger than his whole house. He got down on his hands and knees and felt the wood that made up the floor.

"What you doing?" Willie asked him.

"Trying to figure out this wood," Johnny said. "We got wood floors in our house, but it don't look like this. Our floors ain't smooth and shiny and all together like this. I ain't never seen nothing like this before. The hotel floors ain't even this good."

Just then, before Johnny's eyes, stood two women's feet wearing fancy black strap leather shoes.

"Mrs. Gordon," Willie jumped in, "this is Johnny McCarthy, a coal miner from Mingo County."

Johnny jumped to his feet and grasped her held out hand.

"How do you do?" she said. "What brings you to Charleston?"

"Oh, well, I was just using your commode, ma'am." Johnny couldn't believe he just said that. Mrs. Gordon giggled. She was an attractive middle-aged woman, but the thing Johnny noticed even more was the woman's perfume. He didn't know what it was, but it stung his eyes and put a bitter taste on his tongue. Sprang off her like a skunk. No wonder her husband was in Philadelphia or New York, or wherever Willie said he was.

"Melissa," Mrs. Gordon said to a colored maid, "get Mr. McCarthy here a glass of lemonade. In fact, let's all walk into the kitchen."

Johnny walked with Mrs. Gordon, Willie, and the colored help into the kitchen, not knowing a lot of what he was seeing. It was like a movie picture that passed by too fast. The kitchen was about the size of his whole house back in the Stone Mountain Coal Camp, maybe bigger. Lots of drawers and shelves, flat surfaces to put things on, two big fancy stoves, and an ice box tall as a man.

When the maid opened the door of the icebox, she reached in and pulled out a pitcher filled with lemonade.

"Where's the block of ice?" Johnny asked.

"This isn't an icebox," Mrs. Gordon said with a smile. "This is a refrigerator. Runs on electricity, like this lamp."

The lamp hung from the ceiling and had a wire attached to the wall. Johnny stared into the refrigerator with all kinds of meats and cheeses and vegetables and apples inside.

"Right now the refrigerator is run by a generator," Willie said. "Once West Virginia Power & Electric gets going, the refrigerator will just get plugged into the wall too."

Johnny sipped the lemonade.

"Cold," he said. "Refrigerator stays cold all the time?"

"Yep."

"With no ice?"

"So, Mr. McCarthy, what brings you to Charleston?" Mrs. Gordon asked again.

"Oh, I was here based on coal mining business."

"Union," she said.

Johnny looked away, but nodded agreement.

"And what brought you out to our house?"

"Well, I was looking for somebody," he said. "My son, actually."

"Your son?"

"Yeah, he run off about a month ago."

"And you think he came to our house?"

"Oh, no ma'am. He did head for Charleston, though. I just figured he might be working in a stable."

"You hire anybody in the last month?" Mrs. Gordon asked Willie.

"No ma'am, been about three months since we hired."

"What makes you think he'd be working in a stable?" Mrs. Gordon asked.

"Aw, he just loves horses," Johnny said. "Actually, I guess its *mules* that he likes."

"Mules?" Willie said. "Only one ranch in all of Charleston that handles mules, and that's Wilson's. Out east of the city. Out past Spring Hill Cemetery."

"What's the best road to take?" Johnny asked.

Willie looked at Mrs. Gordon.

"Just take him out there in the auto," she said. "Mr. McCarthy, I hope your union can help you out, you know, get what you need."

Johnny turned to walk away.

"And Mr. McCarthy, I hope you find your son."

Chapter 26

Johnny couldn't believe his good fortune. Not that Corey was there, but there was a chance, if he was alive, that is. He didn't want to think that way, but he'd already lost one child, and didn't know how he'd handle another loss that big.

"Mighty nice of you to take me over to these stables," Johnny said.

"You can thank Mrs. Gordon for that," Willie said. "Since she cut me loose, I'm happy to do it."

"So tell me about this auto," Johnny said. "How fast one of these things go?"

"Well, if we was on a long and straight country road, we could cover about forty-five miles in one hour."

"Forty-five miles in one hour?"

"Yep. Course, there ain't many country roads that straight for that long."

"And what about starting it up?" Johnny asked. "I saw you just push on a lever to start it, but I read in the Gazette you had to turn a crank on the front end."

"A year or two ago that was true, but that could break your arm," Willie said. "The engine could backfire or kick back against you and crank the handle so that it broke your thumb or your wrist."

"That ever happen to you?"

"No, thank God. But I knowed of it happening to a couple friends of mine. Took a strong man to get an automobile going. No woman be driving it for sure."

"You mean women are allowed to drive these things?"

"Yep. Mrs. Gordon does. Got her own Model-T in the barn."

"Are you telling me for sure?"

"No question about it," Willie said. "She laid down the law. If Mr. Gordon had one, and I had one to run around town with, she was sure as hell gonna have one!"

"Me oh my," said Johnny. "And she can start it?"

"Sure enough. Mr. Ford changed it, put an electric starter in it, and made it a whole lot easier."

"So just because Mrs. Gordon wanted one, Mr. Gordon run right out and got her one?"

"Oh yeah, when Mrs. Gordon puts her foot down, Mr. Gordon comes through and fixes whatever it is."

"But didn't you say these was about three hundred dollars?"

"Yeah, but Mr. Gordon could buy a new one of these any time he wanted to," Willie said. "Buy ten of them if he wanted to."

"He got that much money?" Johnny said.

"More than you could imagine."

"I be happy if I could just find my son."

The Tin Lizzie rolled up to Wilson's Ranch and drove over to a loading area behind the barn. A man who looked like he was in charge was ordering a couple boys around, unloading these bales of hay off the back of a wagon.

"That man over there acting like a foreman?" Willie said. "That's Mr. Wilson, the owner. A real hands-on kind of man."

Johnny hurried over to the wagon.

"Mr. Wilson," he asked, "you got any more boys working here on your ranch? I was looking for my son. He run off a little while ago."

"How old a boy is he?"

"He's fourteen. Brown hair. Pretty big kid for his age."

"Check the corral over there east of the house," Wilson said. "Couple kids working over there. Might fit that description."

Johnny marched over in that direction, squinting his eyes trying to see what the boys looked like. The closer he got, the more he thought the one on the right might be his son.

"Oh my God!" Johnny blurted out. "Oh my God."

He jumped over the rail and held on tight to his son. Corey wasn't returning the embrace, but Johnny was glad to find him anyway.

"Son, son, son," Johnny said as he embraced Corey again. "Your ma and me have missed you so much."

Corey hung his head.

"How *is* Ma?" he asked.

"She been through a rough time," Johnny said. "And she misses you so much. Worried about you all the time."

"I'm okay," Corey said.

"You been working with the mules?"

Corey smiled and nodded.

"You come home, son, and we'll see about getting you working with the mules at the mine."

"Really?"

"Yeah, and son there's something else you need to know," said Johnny. "Your sister, Baby Elsie, well, she was in an accident and she died a few weeks ago."

"What? What happened?"

"Your mom, she was carrying Elsie inside the house, tripped over the mop, and fell. Baby Elsie went flying and hit her head, and just died right there on the spot."

"I can't believe it!" Corey said.

"I know," said Johnny. "It's so hard to believe she's gone, but that's another reason me and your ma need you so much. Your ma is so lonely with both her children gone. She's just sucked up into herself, ain't hardly talking. Won't you come back, son?"

"Yeah, I'll come back. But I'll come back for Ma, not for you."

Corey's remark threw a chill on seeing him, but Johnny was still glad he found his boy.

They said their good-byes, hopped in the Tin Lizzie, and got dropped off in downtown Charleston. They found Meeting Street and came to the auditorium where the miners and speakers had met. It was a little after five o'clock and the men was walking out of the building.

As the crowd cleared, Johnny and Corey walked into the auditorium, and there talking with a few of the other men, stood Jim.

"Jim! Jim!" called Johnny. "Look who I found!"

"Oh, that's wonderful! Wonderful, wonderful," said Jim. "How are you, Corey?"

Corey smiled and nodded.

"Oh, a sheriff come by looking for you," Jim said. "Don't know what he wanted, but he's been hanging around most of the day."

"Wonder if everything's all right back home," Johnny said.

Just then, without warning, strong hands gripped each of Johnny's arms and he was pushed against the wall.

"Hold still!" the deputy said. "You're under arrest for the murder of Jake Moskowitz."

Chapter 27

The Norfolk & Western rolled into the Matewan depot in the late morning. Johnny had spent the night in the Charleston Jail. Corey took his hotel bed and Jim promised to look after him. Johnny hoped Corey would not believe the charges stated by the sheriff's deputy and run off again. He knew he didn't kill nobody, and he found it hard to believe they could prove beyond a shadow of a doubt that he did kill somebody, if he didn't. For sure, he'd be able to straighten this out.

Because the charges was murder, Johnny sat handcuffed to the deputy who arrested him, with another deputy sitting right behind him. Both lawmen was packing a sidearm. Johnny saw Corey and the men from the union meetings walk into the car just forward of theirs. So far, the deputies allowed no contact between the suspect and his friends or his son. The train jerked to a stop and the deputies stood up along with Johnny.

"Could I just have a few words with my son?" Johnny asked.

"No, you're charged with murder," the deputy said. "You come with us."

"But I just wanna…"

The deputies grabbed Johnny by his shirt and arm, and manhandled him off the car. Once on the ground outside, the deputies was on both sides of him and walked right next to the railroad tracks into town and up to the Matewan Police Office.

"Chief, we got your prisoner."

. . . .

Corey walked with Jim away from the train depot, down Mate Street, and on up to the Stone Mountain Coal Camp. Corey could feel

Jim's caring and support as he put his hand on his shoulder and encouraged him about his father.

"This is a big mistake," Jim said. "Your pa had nothing to do with killing nobody. Once they dig into this, they'll know they made a mistake."

"Thanks Mr. Mullins," Corey said. "How's my mama?"

"She'll be real glad to see you, that's for sure. Now you go give her a big hug, okay? And I'm awful glad you're home too."

Corey was surprised when Jim put one arm around his shoulders and patted him on the back. He ran up the front steps to his house on Shamrock Road, across the porch, and through the front door. His mother looked shocked as he burst into the room.

"Corey! Corey! Oh dear God!" she said as she pulled him into her arms.

She held on for a long time and wept as she held her son close. She would not let go nor loosen her hold. Corey found her love and tenderness so touching that his eyes welled up in tears and he was very glad to be in her arms.

"Oh Corey," she said as she finally stepped back a touch and looked him in the eyes. "Oh my son, how have you been? And where was you? And how did you get here? I had no idea that you was coming home."

"Pa went looking for me," he said. "And he found me, and he told me how much you missed me. And he told me…"

As he got to this part, tears began flushing his eyes.

"He told me about Baby Elsie," Corey said.

Mama latched on around his neck again, and spilled her tears onto his shirt. Both cried long and hard, and bonded stronger than if they had never been separated.

"I was…"

Corey put his fingers across her lips.

"You don't have to explain nothing to me," he said. "Pa told me how it happened."

She rested her head on his shoulder.

"Where *is* your pa?" Mama asked. "Didn't he come back with you from Charleston?"

"Yeah, he did," Corey said. "But he didn't ride in the same car with the rest of us."

. . . .

Sid Hatfield waited until the deputies from Kanawha County left his office. Then he walked over to the cell and unlocked the door.

"Here, I ain't gonna cuff you," he said. "But sit down in that chair. We gotta talk."

"Sid, I didn't do nothing," he said. "I ain't killed nobody."

"Now hold on a minute," Hatfield said. "The coroner in Williamson got hold of me after doing the autopsy, and told me that Jake's skull was crushed right in the back of his head. It was actually bashed in like you'd take a sledgehammer to a piece of plywood. His skull just caved in."

"But I didn't do it!"

"Then I find your ax over there in the weeds, like you throwed it over there after hitting him. Even some dried blood on the ax. Then you showed me your own initials carved right there in the end of the handle!"

"That don't mean I *did* it!"

"Then," Sid continued, " I find out there was some bad blood between you and Big Jake, that he had came out to your house and gave you a hard time when that Dugan boy was killed in the cave-in. And another time he got rough with your boy after he attacked Morgan in the colliery."

"Where'd you hear all that?"

"I can't tell you right now," Hatfield said. "But it's true, ain't it?"

"Yeah, those things are true, all right," Johnny said. "But it still don't mean I did it! And why'd you have me arrested in Charleston right in front of my boy?"

"After I talked to the coroner, I knowed we was gonna have to deal with this," Hatfield said. "We got evidence against you we can't just pretend like it don't exist! When I couldn't find you and I find out that you was in Charleston, I gotta figure you might take off to who knows where and not want to come back and face these charges. So I called the sheriff in Charleston and had you arrested."

"But I wish you ain't did this in front of my son!"

"Didn't know nothing about your son," Hatfield said. "Just had to make sure you was coming back. When did you last see Big Jake?"

"The only times I seen Big Jake outside the mine was that night he come to my house after Gilbert died in the cave-in, and I was in the tub and I sure couldn't of did nothing at that time. And the other time was in the colliery when I was looking for my son. And Max, the supervisor, and Mr. Morgan was there too. When's the last time anybody seen him? When did he disappear?"

"The last day he was seen was Monday, April 5th," Hatfield said. "He was at the mine in the morning."

"April 5th, a Monday," Johnny mumbled to himself. "That be almost a month ago. Let me think. April 5th, April 5th."

And then it came to him.

"April 5th!" he said. "I wasn't even here April 5th!"

Just then, Kate hobbled through the door of the police office.

"My husband is right," she said. "He wasn't here, but I was."

Chapter 28

Jim walked out of his house in the Stone Mountain Coal Camp, clear to the downtown area of Matewan. Ed Chambers wanted him and all of the future union members who traveled to Charleston the past few days to stop and chat with him at the hardware store. Jim wondered if there would be no more meetings at his house due to the shot that was fired. He mentioned an unhappy wife, losing that chandelier. Can't blame them, he thought.

Jim walked in the front door of the store and saw that half the store was filled with miners, union members, laborers, and prospects. It was obvious that interest was keen in Matewan over changes that could be brought about by the union. Jim made his way to the front counter of the store where Mr. Chambers talked to several men at the same time. When Chambers saw Jim, he turned towards him for a moment.

"Hey, how you doing?" Chambers said. "How'd you like the conference?"

"Very much, sir," Jim said. "Thank you for sending me."

"Well, I'm glad we did," Chambers said. "Glad we did. We need young blood like you and your friends to help lead the way. Lot of tough issues, here."

"Yes sir."

"By the way, where's your friend, uh Johnny...Johnny McCarthy?"

"Oh, well, he's around somewhere," Jim said. "Might be outside."

"Well, I'll look forward to talking to him," Chambers said. "Don't forget later in the week, Wednesday or Thursday, we gonna have Frank Mooney, who you heard in Charleston, and Bill Blizzard, right here in Matewan."

"Yes sir, looking forward to it."

Jim headed towards the door, but ran into Gino Antonnucci.

"Hey, let's get out of here," Jim said. "Let's head over to Maxwell's Café."

After grabbing a coffee, the two found a little round table on the boardwalk outside.

"Big things happening, huh?" Gino said.

"Yeah, lots of excitement," said Jim. "It's like working's not enough. Now we got all this union stuff going on, people running around. How'd you like the meetings?"

"They was great! And I guess we're not done. More later in the week."

"Yeah," said Jim. "Look at all the strangers in town already. Must be sleeping out in the woods."

"I hear they're coming from Logan County, McDowell, Boone. Lots of different mining camps—War Eagle, Noland, Roderfield. Maybe two or three thousand men."

"Hard to believe!" Jim said.

"Yeah, and they packing firepower, too," said Gino.

"Yeah, but you can tell they hillbillies. They ain't no mine guards, or State Police."

"Yeah, they hillbillies, all right."

Just then, two large Negroes came walking down the boardwalk, blowing on their coffee. The street was filled with men milling around, talking. You could feel buzz in the air. All the outside tables was filled, except Jim and Gino's.

"Uh, excuse us gentlemen," the shorter of the two said. "We sorry to bother you, but would it be okay with you if we sat for a couple minutes and drank our coffee?"

Gino and Jim looked at each other, and after a couple of seconds said, "Yeah, fine, sit down."

"Caleb Jackson," the shorter man said with a smile.

"I'm Matthew Washington," the tall man said.

"You a big man," Jim said, looking straight up in the air.

"Yeah, my daddy was big too," he said.

"I guess he was," Gino said, laughing. "You two miners?"

"Yeah, live in the Stone Mountain Coal Camp." said Caleb.

"Oh yeah? Whereabouts in there?" Jim said.

"The colored section."

"Oh, never been in that part," Gino said.

"Yep."

"How long you been with this company?"

"About a year," Caleb said. "Matthew here, about four months."

"How you like it?"

"Like it just fine," Caleb said.

"Oh yeah?" Jim said. "Mining is hard, hard work. What you like so much about it?"

"Hard work?" Caleb said. "You ever been a slave?"

"No, and you ain't never been a slave neither," Jim said.

"No, but my grandpappy was."

"So what you like so much about the mines?" Jim asked again.

"Lordy, lordy, where do I begin?" Caleb said. "First, let's talk about freedom. I get paid by the coal that I load, so I can work hard or I can slack off. I travel about the mine and sometimes I don't see no supervisor for hours and hours, or even days. I decide my own pay, I can move about, and I decide when to quit for the day. That's what I call freedom."

"But you stuck down in the hole!" Jim said.

"I'm there 'cause I want to be," Caleb said.

"Fair enough," said Gino. "Fair enough. It's still hard work, though. Hardest work I ever done."

"Guess you ain't never picked cotton," Matthew said.

"Pick cotton? You saying picking cotton is harder work than coal mining?"

"Picture this. You standing out there in the middle of this field, cotton as far as you can see. The sun is beating down on your head.

You got your pick sack draped over your shoulder so's you can use both hands."

"You out in the sunshine and the fresh air," Gino said. "Sounds pretty good to me."

"You ever seen a cotton plant out in the field?" Caleb asked.

"Nope," Gino said.

"The cotton don't come in a pretty box like at the store," Caleb explained. "It's in a boll, and the boll is like a sticky, prickly hand full of burrs that holds the cotton, and you got to pluck that cotton ball out of the hand that holds it. That's your job. And the boll's job is to prick your hand and your fingers and make them bleed as they stealing the fruit of the cotton plant. That's the battle that goes on all day long."

Jim and Gino was listening but could think of nothing to say.

"And you can't use no gloves," Caleb went on. "Cause you wouldn't be able to feel the cotton to pull it out, just like when you working in the breaker house, you can't wear no gloves for that."

"So how much you get paid for cotton?" Gino wanted to know.

"Oh, I'm getting to that," Caleb said. "But first, you gotta see the whole picture. Some days you gotta hoe the row. And you gotta sometimes thin out the cotton plants 'cause they overplant. Then, even if they don't overplant, you got to knock down the weeds, and the Johnson grass, and the Jimson weed, and the nut grass, and the cockleburs so it don't choke out the cotton. And you got to hoe two times in the summer for three or four weeks at a time, and the row could be half a mile long and you can't even see the end of it. And they leave you a can of water at the end of the row. And your back feels like it's breaking, and you're sweating to death with a hat on and rags over your neck. I never pick another cotton ball in my life. Do anything but cotton picking."

"So how much you make picking cotton?" Gino asked again.

"Penny a pound," said Caleb.

"Penny a pound!" said Gino. "And how much cotton you pick in a day?"

"Depends. If you get in a rhythm with your hands, and your back's feeling okay, you could pick five hundred pounds. That's the most I ever did, but you can't do that everyday."

"Five bucks for the day," Jim said. "That ain't bad."

"Like I say, you can't do that everyday. Your back's feeling like shit, you lucky to be picking half that, and you feeling like shit all day."

"So you traded King Cotton for King Coal," Jim said.

"Yep," Caleb laughed. "And white gold for black gold!"

"One thing for sure," Jim said. "We all black when we come out of the hole!"

Chapter 29

"**S**weetheart!"

"Have a seat, Mrs. McCarthy," said the police chief.

"Sweetheart, what are you doing here?" Johnny said.

"I got to be here," said Kate. "I got to speak the truth."

"But Sid, she don't know nothing about this."

"Well, let's see what she knows," Hatfield said. "Mrs. McCarthy, tell us what you know about Big Jake's death."

"Johnny went to look for our son, Corey," she said. "He headed out into the woods just like Corey run off."

"When was this?" Hatfield asked.

"It was a Sunday a few weeks ago. It was his day off, and he wanted to try and find Corey. And I was glad he did."

"All right, go ahead."

"And so he didn't come back that night," Kate said. "I figured he found Corey or was dealing with some kind of problem about that, so I wasn't too worried. I was a little scared, but I knew he'd be back the next day."

"And *did* he come back the next day?"

"Yes, he did. Late, late in the day, towards the evening."

"And where did he say he was?"

"Where I was, was…" Johnny started in.

Hatfield raised his hand, motioning for Johnny to be quiet. He then turned his attention back to Kate.

"He told me he went north along the river. Found some hillbillies that lived in this holler. They was friendly, and they fed him. He was gonna come back the same day, but it was late and getting dark, and they told him it was too far to go before dark and too dangerous and he should spend the night with them."

"Is that what happened, Johnny?" Hatfield asked.

"Yeah, pretty much. The next day they taught me how fish the river, and I started back about noon."

"And Mrs. McCarthy, how did you spend that day before Johnny come home?"

"Emma come over with her baby girl in the morning and we ate breakfast together," Kate said. "Then I scrubbed laundry, cleaned the house, gave my baby a bath and changed her. Then I washed the floor and split some wood."

"Split some wood," Hatfield said. "And you split the wood with *your* ax, the one with Johnny' initials carved into the end of the handle?"

"Yes sir, that's what I done."

"So this day was a Monday, almost a month ago" said Hatfield. "Look here at this calendar. This is Sunday, May 2nd. Today. Then all the way back up here, this was Monday April 5th. Was that the day we're talking about?"

"Yes, I think so," Kate said.

Johnny was stunned into silence and stared across the desk at his wife, anxious to hear what else she had to say.

"So then what happened?"

"When I was splitting the wood, my baby got cranky so I picked her up and took her into the house to settle her down for a nap."

"Where is the ax at this time?"

"I left it on the porch with the head down and the handle leaning on the house."

"Then what happened?"

Kate folded her hands in her lap and looked down at them. Her breaths became deeper and her chest started heaving, and tears poured from her eyes. Her face turned a deep crimson. Her voice was silent.

"Kate," Johnny said.

"I lay on the bed and nursed Elsie. I remember it as a very happy time."

"And then what?" Hatfield asked.

Her face was intense, sullen, empty .

"And then there was heavy steps on the porch, and a loud banging on the door, and then quiet listening. I knew it was trouble with the quiet listening. And then he yelled, and I knew right away who it was. And then he kicked in the door, and it was that monster people call Jake."

"Kate!" Johnny said.

"What else?" Hatfield asked.

"He come in and he was angry," Kate said. "He wanted to know where Johnny was and I told him where he went, and he kept asking about my husband and I told him to get out, that he could talk to my husband later about this, and we yelled back and forth at each other, and he said I needed to learn some respect, and my baby was crying real hard and it made him mad and he slapped me and grabbed Baby Elsie and threw her against the wall and her crying stopped right then and she was quiet and I knew something was very wrong with my baby."

It broke Johnny's heart that Kate was sobbing now with tears streaming down her face. Her moaning was from deep in her throat. Her despair nobody could make go away. Johnny staggered to the other side of Hatfield's desk and embraced his wife. Their tears blended in her lap.

"So you're saying that Jake killed your baby," Hatfield said.

"Yep," Kate said, nodding her head.

"Then what happened?"

"I tried to get to my baby to hold her, and he picked her up by the leg, hanging her upside down, like she wasn't even a real baby, and I tried to get to her and he pushed me down on the floor and said he would take care of this, and that I better keep my mouth shut or my husband would lose his job, and he would take care of it."

Johnny cried in Kate's lap.

"Then what?" Hatfield asked.

"Then he tucked my baby under his arm and walked out of my house and started walking away real fast. I went to the doorway and screamed, but he didn't pay no mind. And I saw where he was walking and he was starting out down the trail that led to that backhouse that was closed with the swarming dung beetles, the one by the river, and I knowed that he was gonna throw my baby into that muck with those disgusting bugs and they would eat her and I could not let that happen. So I grabbed the ax and I chased off after him, and I was catching up to him, and he got to the edge of the pit and started swinging my baby by the leg like he was gonna toss her out with the garbage, like she was worthless and nothing, and I ran up and I swung the ax and hit him right on the back of his head, and I felt his head give out, and he dropped my baby right there by the side of the pit and he fell head first into the beetles and the filth and that's where I left him. And I picked up my baby and went back home."

Johnny could see that Kate was drained from telling her story. Her chest heaved and she could barely catch her breath, like all her strength had gone out. Johnny too felt like the life had gone out of him like a balloon runs out of air.

"And you tossed the ax in the weeds?" Hatfield asked.

"Yes, I think so," Kate answered. "I don't rightly remember."

Chapter 30

"Yeah, that's one good thing," said Caleb. "In coal country, you don't like one camp, you just pick up and move to another. Ain't nothing says you gotta stay."

"Yeah, but the only job you get is a coal miner," Matthew said. "You ain't never gonna be a boss over a white man."

"That's okay," said Caleb. "All I want to do is bring the coal up out of the ground. Then they pay you just like a white man. Don't matter if you're colored or not."

Jim and Gino glanced at each other. Gino seemed to enjoy listening to two Negroes talk about their time in the coal mines, just like Jim did.

"Except for Concho," Matthew said. "You ever been there?"

"Up in Fayette County?" Caleb said. "Yeah, I remember that place. They don't really let you work there, or stay there. They don't even want you passing through there, but if you happen to come by the place, you find out real quick."

"What do they do?" Jim asked.

"They not gonna have nothing to do with you," Caleb said. "If you went to the company store, they won't serve you. If you went to the post office, they won't help you. And they sure as hell ain't gonna give you a job."

"Yeah, I remember that place," Matthew said. "It was way up high on the side of the gorge, way up above Arbuckle Creek. So you almost got to go out of your way to get through there."

"And I remember the tipple they used was at the New River at Erskine. They had to get the coal all the way down there."

"Yeah, only a couple hundred people live there," Caleb said, "but they must have a sweet thing going, almost like a bootleg mine, you know, like the overburden was just sitting right there on the top."

"Yeah, like a dog-hole. Not a big operation, but it just keeps spitting out the coal."

"You guys ever mine in any other state?" Gino asked. "Pennsylvania? Ohio?"

"Not me," Caleb said. "I heard they let the Negro vote in West Virginia, the only state that does. So I just figured things was a little better for colored people in West Virginia."

Matthew nodded and leaned over with a flask of mountain dew to add to everyone's coffee. Jim declined and Gino accepted. Just then, Jim's ears perked up as a group of men rushed by in the street saying Johnny's name. Some used his first name, some his last, McCarthy. What's going on?

Down the street he could see a small gathering of men with some pushing and shoving. He could hear some arguing, and once again, the name McCarthy was said, this time yelled with anger.

"Hey, let's go see what the trouble is," Jim said as he slapped Gino on the arm.

The two trotted down the street. Jim heard something from behind and turned to see, to his surprise, Caleb and Matthew following along.

"Hey!" yelled Jim. "Leave him alone!"

Fourteen year old Corey was being faced up to by a couple of men right there in the middle of the street.

"I said leave him alone," Jim yelled again.

"This is the kid of the bastard that murdered Big Jake," said the man. "His name's McCarthy."

"You don't know that Johnny McCarthy killed Big Jake," Jim said.

"Yeah, they arrested him in Charleston and brought him back on the train."

"That don't mean he killed nobody," Jim said.

"You think they arrested him just for the fun of it?"

"I know Johnny. He didn't kill nobody," Gino said. "And even if he did, it don't mean his son had nothing to do with it. He's just a kid. Leave him alone!"

"Yeah, well I say we don't need his kind around here," the man said. "Big Jake was a good man and a good mine operator."

With that, the trouble maker set his feet up there in the dirt street and took a big swing at Jim. The punch sailed overhead, but he felt the breeze as it flew by. Now other men was squaring off, punching and scuffling. It was hard for Jim to focus on any one person, the fight had become so general. The guy who swung and missed was coming again, so Jim beat him to the punch and knocked him to the ground. Where's Corey? With that, he saw him and grabbed him by the arm.

"Here, go sit over there," Jim said, running him to the table the four men just ran away from. "Don't go nowhere. Wait for us here!"

Jim ran back to the tussle and saw that the fight got bigger. Now it looked like at least twenty men was squared off throwing punches. It looked to Jim that it was pretty well-divided between mine workers and mine operators. Jim had to move quickly to avoid getting hit and bust several of his attackers in the mouth. He noticed how Caleb and Matthew was right in the middle of it. Caleb kept knocking men down with short, choppy punches, and once in a while a haymaker. Matthew kept scattering the crowd. He was so big it didn't look like too many men wanted much of a piece of him.

In a few minutes, the fight gradually scattered out. None of Hatfield's officers showed up. No State Police. No Baldwin-Felts detectives. No volunteer militia. It seemed like men just got tired of fighting and drifted off. But Jim still heard Johnny McCarthy's name called out as men walked away.

"Let's shoot the son-of-a-bitch!"

"Let's hang him!"

The trouble-makers disappeared down the street and their voices faded away. Jim thought they didn't seem to want to get nothing done as much as they wanted to stir things up, to call names and yell a little bit.

"You pack a pretty good wallop," Jim said to Caleb. "You done some fighting!"

"We all done some fighting in *this* world," Caleb said. "I don't mind mixing it up a little, but I do not like those guys that ride around on horses at night wearing them white sheets with them hoods over their heads."

"Yeah, they always carrying torches and lighting fires and shit," Matthew said.

"The KKK? You seen those guys around here?"

"Oh yeah! They was out the other night," Caleb said. "Had a little come-to-Jesus meeting where we could see it just off in the woods. Set a cross on fire, made a lot of noise, some shooting."

"I ain't heard of this happening in a long time," Jim said. "You hear about it in the south, but I didn't know they was doing it up here no more."

"The way I figure it," Matthew said, "they just letting us know they there. Trying to keep us in line, you know?"

"Yeah, but sometimes they like to hang a colored man," Caleb said. "They figure that *really* keeps us in line."

"That stinks," said Gino. "If they got to cover their faces up, they just cowards, that's all."

Jim saw Corey walking over and embraced him. He wanted Corey to feel safe and like people was behind him, even though his ma and pa wasn't there. Jim knew that Corey already met the acquaintance of Gino, but he spoke up for Matthew and Caleb so Corey could shake their hands.

"Thanks," Corey said. "You guys can really fight!"

"Sometimes you got to stand your ground," Caleb said.

"I can fight a little," Corey said, "but maybe you could show me how to *really* fight."

Caleb and Jim glanced at each other.

"Your pa could show you," Jim said.

Corey dropped his head towards the ground and shrugged his shoulders.

"Nah, I don't think so."

"What you mean, you don't think so?" Jim said.

"Say, Ma went down to the jail a while ago. See if she could get Pa to come home. I ain't seen her since."

"Come on, let's take a walk down there and see what's going on."

Chapter 31

"That's a sad, sad story," Hatfield said. "And I believe you. Sounds just like them coal operator bastards, and especially Big Jake. But I want you to know it ain't my call."

"What you mean?" Johnny asked him.

"A man died from a blow to the skull with an ax," Hatfield said. "More than that, a *mine operator* died from a blow to the skull with an ax. The County Prosecutor will have to decide whether or not to press charges. In fact, justice may demand that this be settled with a trial. The *people* may demand it."

"How would that work?" Kate asked.

"The county seat is Williamson," Hatfield said. "That's where the County Prosecutor is, that's where the courthouse is, it's where the judges are. So the decisions come out of Williamson. If the County Prosecutor decides there needs to be a trial, it would be there in Williamson."

"But I've already confessed to hitting him with the ax," Kate said.

"Yes, I know," Hatfield said. "The trial would be more about the circumstances around the assault."

"Assault?" Johnny said.

"That's what they'll call it if there's a trial," Hatfield said. "In fact, assault would be the nicest thing they'd call it. I'm afraid they'll want to call it murder."

"But I didn't mean to…"

"I know, I know," said Hatfield. "Remember, I believe you. But I'm just telling you what this will be like if they decide to put you on trial."

"Would we have to have an attorney?" Johnny asked.

"Yep, you'd want an attorney all right, but I know you can't afford to just go out and hire one. In a situation like this the court will appoint a Public Defender for you."

"Public Defender?"

"Yep, you have a right to be represented by an attorney, and the court will appoint one for you if you can't afford it. But we getting ahead of ourselves. We don't even know what's gonna happen."

Right then, Johnny could hear angry voices outside the police office. Sid Hatfield and Johnny walked over and looked out the front window. Twenty-five or thirty men was standing around, talking to each other, and yelling Johnny's name. Then they started waving their arms around and raising their fists in the air.

"What do they want?" Johnny asked.

"They want me to throw you out the door so they can string you up," Hatfield said. "They crazy as loons."

Hatfield walked over and took his gun belt off the rack on the wall and buckled it around his waist. Johnny recognized the hardware as Single Action Army revolvers, two of them with long barrels, the kind used by Wyatt Earp and Teddy Roosevelt. Hatfield had quite a reputation, and nobody outside would want to take him on with gun in hand. He stepped out the door and faced the angry mob.

Blam! Blam! Blam! Blam!

He fired four thunderous shots in the air. Johnny crept to the window and peeked out. The men looked at Hatfield with wide eyes and shock on their faces. One drunk off to the side didn't look fazed by the shooting and raised a jug of moonshine to his mouth. Hatfield took aim and shattered the jug out of his hands and all over the street.

"Now listen up you fools," Hatfield said. "You come to the wrong place to make trouble."

"We want McCarthy," one of them shouted. "He murdered Big Jake."

Others joined in, yelling their demands. Hatfield fired two more shots into the air, shutting everybody up.

"I am the police chief of Matewan, and as police chief I am here to enforce the law. And the law says that if a man is accused of a crime, he has a right to a fair trial, and if charges are brought against him, that's what I will do. Make sure he gets a fair trial."

"But we know he's guilty," someone called out. "Let's just get on with it."

"You don't know nothing!" Hatfield yelled. "But I'll tell you this. Anybody try to take away anybody I got in my custody, take him out of my jail by force, I will send that man home in a pine box!"

The men was silent, and just looked around like they didn't know what to say.

"Now anybody want me to make an example out of him?" Hatfield called out. "Anybody? Then git! And don't come back here unless you got legitimate business."

Hatfield stayed out there and continued to watch as the men began to walk away.

"Now!" Hatfield yelled again. "Get out of here and go home!"

The men cleared the street and Hatfield came back inside.

"You be all right," the police chief said. "But we got to figure out where you sleep tonight."

"We want to sleep at our house," Johnny said, his arm around his wife.

"You might not make it there without trouble," Hatfield said.

"But our son is at home," Kate said. "We can't just leave him alone."

"All right, listen to me," Hatfield said. "Neither one of you is under arrest yet. You been detained for questioning and that's about it. If I let you go home and you run, that will cause me a lot of problems, do you understand me?"

"Yes, we do," Johnny said.

"If I have to come after you, or send a deputized posse after you, that ain't gonna make me happy and you ain't gonna be happy with the results, do you understand?"

"Yes," both Johnny and Kate answered.

"You both stay in Matewan, you get it? You still got a job in the mine, so you can go to work. And you can stay at the house or go to the company store if you need to. But if you run, you be in a whole lot of trouble and you just make yourself look guilty. Do you understand me?"

"Yes," they both answered again.

"I got to talk to the County Prosecutor out of Williamson to see how he wants to handle this, and that might take a few days or a week or two, so you have to work with us, okay? It's easier for both of us if I can trust you and you take care of yourselves at home than if I have to keep you here, okay?"

"Thank you, Sid," Johnny said. "You won't have any trouble from us."

Just then, a sharp wrapping on the door. Hatfield pulled both guns in a flash. He motioned for Johnny to get behind the door and open it.

"We looking for Johnny and Kate," Jim said. "They're friends of ours and we wanted to see if they was coming home tonight."

"You know these people?" Hatfield asked.

Johnny and Kate was glad to see friendly faces, and especially Corey. Jim introduced Caleb and Matthew.

"I'll tell you what," Hatfield said. "It's a good thing your friends come by. Why don't you all walk home together, and I'll follow along just a little behind you and I don't think you'll have no trouble."

Corey walked arm in arm with his ma, and the men walked just ahead. The group was slow because of Kate limping a bit. Sid Hatfield brought up the rear, just as he said.

"We had some trouble in town," Jim said to Johnny. "Some men saw Corey and knowed he was your son and they was blaming him as being part of Big Jake's death. So it broke out into a fight. Whole bunch of men got involved."

"Everybody all right?" Johnny asked.

"Yeah, we all did our part, but Caleb and Matthew sure held up their end."

"Really, the niggers helped out?"

"Mr. Johnny, I have just helped save your son from a beating, maybe even worse," Caleb said. "Do you think you could possibly stop calling me a nigger?"

"But that's what you are," Johnny said. "Ain't it? I mean, Gino here is a Dago, I am an Irishman, and you are a nigger."

"Let me wake you up to something, Mr. Johnny," Caleb said. "It is true I am of the Negro race, but the word *nigger* is a baser word, saying that I am of poor character and not to be trusted. And I must tell you that is not who I am. I am a husband, and a father, and a hard worker. I am a man who is not afraid to stand up for what is right, and to fight when I need to. So I must demand that you stop calling me a nigger!"

Johnny looked at Caleb face to face, eyeball to eyeball.

"I'll give that some thought, Mr. Jackson." Johnny said. "I will for sure give that some thought. Now if you'll excuse us."

Chapter 32

Early morning rays of sunlight barely started peeking over the mountains. Teeming emotions flooded through Johnny's heart and tears filled his eyes as he stood at the grave of his daughter, Baby Elsie. If only he had been there when Big Jake called on Kate. If he'd been home, he would have been down the hole and there wouldn't have been no reason for Jake to call on Kate, would there? If only he had gotten back the same day as he'd planned. If only he'd stood up to Jake the day he come over to the house while he was in the tub. Maybe Jake would have thought twice about getting violent with his family. If only...

Johnny got to the back end of the Stone Mountain Housing Project and the scent of skunk smacked him right in the face. Heavy skunk. Most likely more than one. Probably out all night raiding for whatever they can find. Seemed to Johnny like just another family in coal country doing what they gotta do to get by.

Three days passed since their meeting with Police Chief Sid Hatfield, and many things was going on. Johnny liked the police chief and was glad he cared about their safety. He stood up for them and did his job. He was a man's man and nobody was gonna get in his face or put something over on him. No word from the County Prosecutor, though. Would Kate have to stand trial, or not? Would she have the strength to stand up to it? Could she get a fair trial since the dead man was a coal operator and the jury would be sure to be stacked against her? Only time would tell.

The time Kate spent being questioned by Sid Hatfield seemed to snap her out of her bad mood and being quiet all the time. It helped her to sort of bust out. It seemed good for her to tell the police chief what had happened, and the way it came out, Johnny himself was able to take it in. It also gave the two of them a chance to talk and Johnny was grateful for that. He knew that she still felt guilty, but he could see no reason for her to feel that way. There wasn't nothing she could do under the circumstances. Johnny felt proud of her, but at the same time, wished he could have been there, maybe stop all this from happening. Kate couldn't save Baby Elsie's life, but she saved her dignity and kept her from being disrespected like Jake was doing. He'd be damned if he let his family be treated that way again.

Things was moving along with Corey, too. Johnny had talked to one of the mine supervisors and about giving Corey a chance to try out as a mule driver. At first, they didn't want nothing to do with Johnny or his family, what with his connection to Big Jake's murder. But no charges had been filed yet, and they needed a kid to handle the mules real bad. So they gave Corey a chance. They gave him the braided black leather snake whip and he was practicing with it, putting out the flame on a candle from ten feet. He seemed happy, and it was good to have him home and see him all excited about maybe getting to work with the mules.

The occasion of Corey's getting the whip wasn't a happy one, however. On Monday, Black Maria, the horse-drawn hearse had dropped the body of a young man on his family's porch. The story was while standing behind a mule he was kicked in the seat of the pants and fell under the wheels of a two-ton coal car. Johnny had concerns for Corey too, but he knew Corey had to try himself and grow into a man. And he knew he had to let him, and be a better father and protector.

"You ready to go?" Corey called out.

"You bet! We got our lunches?"

"Yep, Ma packed them."

Johnny walked down the slope and put his arm around Corey's shoulders.

"You excited?" he asked his son.

"Yep."

"I guess I don't have to tell you to be careful," Johnny said.

"I'll be all right."

Johnny took the lunch pail from Kate and gave her a big kiss. They held on for a long embrace, while Corey watched.

"You know, I'm going with you today," Johnny said to Corey as they walked out of the Stone Mountain Housing.

"Why you doing that?"

"It's okay. I got the supervisor's permission. I just want to see how Bobby the stableman breaks you in, that's all."

The two got into the cage at the portal and went down over five hundred feet to the level of the mules. Johnny could smell the stables the minute the cage stopped. They was right next to the landing.

"You Bobby?" Johnny asked.

"Yep, you Corey?"

"Naw, this is my son, Corey."

"How ya doing, man?" Bobby asked, shaking both their hands.

"Good," Corey said.

"You ever worked with mules before?" Bobby asked.

"Yes sir. In a stable outside of Charleston."

"Okay, why don't you grab this brush and curry old Sparky over here," Bobby said. "Get him feeling all warm and friendly and ready for work."

Corey started brushing the mule and Johnny took Bobby aside.

"Is Sparky that mule that killed that kid earlier in the week?" he asked.

"Yeah, he's the mule we need a new driver for," Bobby said. "That's why your son got the chance to take his place."

"I know," said Johnny, "but couldn't you put a more experienced driver on this mule, and let my son start out on another mule, one that ain't just stomped a boy to death?"

"I'll show him what to do," Bobby said. "Your son will be all right."

Johnny stepped up to Bobby and grabbed him by the shirt.

"He better be all right," Johnny said. "Anything happens to him I'm coming down here and you'll wish all you had to worry about was a nasty mule."

"Hey, take it easy," Bobby said. "I'm gonna train him. You can watch."

Bobby walked over to Corey. Johnny stood within earshot to be sure his son would know how to stay safe.

"The currying you been doing helps a mule to feel good," Bobby said, "so it helps them like you and trust you. But their mood changes, and you gotta be careful." Corey was looking right at Bobby and was looking like he was paying attention.

"Here's some sugar lumps," Bobby said. "Shove a couple into his mouth."

Sparky chomped down on them, and bobbed his head up and down.

"He'll also want some chew," said Bobby. "Some tobacco. It'll make him trust you because he'll think you know all about him."

"I got some," Corey announced, and reached for it in his pocket.

"Skoal?" Bobby said.

"Yep!"

"Sparky only wants Peerless."

"You mean he can tell the brand?" Corey asked.

"Yeah, they pretty smart," Bobby said. "Now you stick the plug in his mouth like this. Give him the first bite. Then you can have the rest."

"Whoa!"

"Now here's where these mules can get you," Bobby said. "Sometimes a driver has abused him, like maybe twisted his ears, hit him with the whip, singed his belly with a match, or hit him with a sprag. The mule never forgets. He get you back. So *you* can't forget. He bite you, or kick you, or crush you up against the rib of the tunnel."

"How can you stop that?" Corey asked.

"That's a good question," Bobby said. "You don't give him the chance. You never stand with your head around his mouth without paying attention. He get you. And you don't stand around behind him, because even if you thinking about it, the mule is so fast with his hind legs, he get you when you think he can't. You see it coming and still can't get out of the way. He too fast."

"What about not getting crushed up against the rib?" Corey asked.

"Okay, let me show you," Bobby said. "You know what a sprag is?"

"I've heard of it," Corey said.

"It's these sticks. The spraggers stick these sticks into the spokes of the wheels of the mine cars to slow them down. They very strong. If you walk on the side of the mule between the mule and the rib of the mine, always carry two of these sprags. If the mule moves over on you, stand up against the rib and put a sprag on each side of you and up against the wall. Even if he tries to lean into you, he won't push too hard because the stick will be pushing back against his ribs. That's the best thing you can do.

"Now it will be a while before you drive a six-mule team, but you could walk past one in the mines," Bobby continued. "The mules, of course, are one behind the other in their harnesses, but they never stand exactly in a straight line. They stagger themselves, one sticking out this side, one on the other side. So when you walk past you have to be careful you don't get in front of one so he bites you, or behind another one so he kicks you. When it's six of them and one man, they act like it's their job to gang up on the man. So you have to always be on guard."

Johnny stuck close all morning and felt confident that Corey was getting good, useful teaching that would help keep him safe. But Johnny knew teaching was one thing, and experience was another. Corey would need several successful outings with the beasts before he gained a feel for how to handle them, and how to handle himself in their company. A whole string of experiences would lead to confidence, and Johnny would feel better when he knew he was at that level. He also knew he could not stay with his son through every minute of his training. It was time for trust and faith, and more unionizing tomorrow.

Chapter 33

Johnny rose up out of the mines Thursday evening about 6:00 P.M., having reached full coal. He'd worked a wide seam that was easy to get to and mostly pure, so the work moved fast. He was excited to take in the rally in the field to the north and west of the Matewan Community Church.

Fred Mooney he knew. He'd heard of Bill Blizzard, but never seen him before. Had a reputation as a real fireball. Johnny knew he was a union organizer from Kanawha County and a leader in the Paint Creek and Cabin Creek strikes of nearly a decade ago. He'd heard lots of people died with coal operators and union men alike being shot to death. He was sure he'd have some stories to tell. But first, he'd wait for Corey to come up out of the portal above the mule stables.

The rain was coming down pretty good as Johnny planted himself beneath the overhanging branches of a stout oak on the north side of the street out in front of the portal. The air smelt fresh 'cause the rain always washed the soot out and down into the gullies. Many men was in town now, heading towards the field where the rally was gonna be. Johnny knew most of the men was on strike in neighboring coal camps. That's why they was free to be away from their own coal mines, and come to Matewan. They had no work to do, and it was always good to be built up by the words of leaders in the union cause, good men who had worked in the mines themselves since they was boys, men who had a plan and knowed how to make life better in the mines. Johnny would travel like that himself to a nearby town to hear the likes of Bill Blizzard, or Fred Mooney, and of course Mother Jones. He'd never forget Mother Jones. And there was one more speaker he'd heard a lot about and that was Frank Keeney. He was president of the UMWA, District 17. Johnny figured since he was president he must know more than anybody in the whole Tug Valley.

He'd listen to him for sure. But he still had his doubts about how smart it was to go up against the coal company that put a roof over his head. Papa always said to be loyal to the company. That way you could take care of your family.

After a few minutes, Corey stepped out of the cage.

"Hey young man," Johnny called out.

"Hey!"

Corey carried his whip and walked with an extra skip in his step.

"How's the mule driver?"

"Good. Learned a lot today."

"What'd you learn?"

"I learned that a mule is like a goat," Corey said. "They'll eat anything they can find."

"What happened?"

"There was a new kid down at the stables. His ma gave him an extra shirt to bring down the mine, and he set it down near Sparky. He just come over and whoofed it right down."

"Oh man," Johnny said. "Didn't choke on it, or nothing?"

"Nope, just went down like a carrot."

"That is one tough animal," Johnny said. "They must have cast-iron stomachs. So what'd you learn from that?"

"Never to set my shirt down near him."

"Yeah, or your lunch," Johnny said. "Imagine if you put some real food where he could get it."

"Yeah, it'd be gone for sure," Corey said.

The two hurried home. Johnny knew he barely had time to get a bath, some supper, and get over to the field where the platforms was built for the speakers. After a short time in the tub, he sat at the table with his family and spooned down some fresh chicken soup Kate made this day. The biscuits she fixed seemed to warm the whole house and gave off that special aroma that made Johnny glad to be home.

"Great soup, Sweetie," Johnny said.

"Yeah, it *is* good Ma," Corey agreed.

"Glad you all like it," Kate said. "You both going to the union rally?"

Johnny looked at his son.

"Why don't you stay home with your ma?" Johnny said. "Looks like it's gonna be raining all night anyway."

"Okay. Can I show you something I learned today?"

"The thing about what a mule can eat?" Johnny asked.

"No, it's a little song. Goes like this."

> *My sweetheart's a mule in the mine,*
> *I drive her without rein or line.*
> *On the bumper I sit,*
> *And tobacco I spit,*
> *All over my sweetheart's behind.*

"Corey, you stop singing a disgusting song like that," Kate blurted out.

"Oh Ma!"

Johnny just grinned and shook his head.

"I declare, the only thing he learns in that mine is cussing and chewing."

. . . .

Johnny walked up to the rally with hobnail boots, a jacket, and his miner's cap. The rain came down harder now with no signs of letting up. He sought the shelter of a tree again, but not many spots was open. He saw Jim, Gino, Caleb, Matthew, Heinrich, and some other familiar faces. A couple thousand men was expected in Matewan to hear Fred Mooney and Bill Blizzard. All week men worked on the field where they held union meetings before. This time, they nailed planks together to build a speaker's platform, kind of like a stage, so Mooney and Blizzard could see above the crowd of men and the men could see them. A cone-shaped bullhorn, a new Thomas Edison invention, sat upside down on the stage so the men speaking could be heard.

The pitter-patter of raindrops falling on the leaves created a loud *tap-tap* background noise as men took to the platform. Lanterns hanging from poles lit up the scene, and the silhouettes of close to three thousand men standing in the field created an eerie sight. Fred Mooney picked up the megaphone and an unknown figure sheltered him with an umbrella.

"Can you all hear me all right?" Mooney said into the cone.

Scattered voices told him they could.

"Many of you know I'm Fred Mooney, Secretary/Treasurer of the United Mine Workers of America, District 17. We're on a campaign to unionize the southern part of this great state of West Virginia."

Cheers from the crowd of men.

"There have been significant increases in wages in the coal mines in Pennsylvania and Ohio, yet here in our own backyard, in Sprigg, there are rumors of wage reduction. When the United Mine Workers plans a strike, we do it from area to area, so we're organized and so we can support our members. We're announcing a strike for Red Jacket, just up the river. That strike will start tomorrow. We was over there yesterday for the final preparations, and we'll go back again after we're done here tonight.

"Now when the union organizes a strike, there are certain guidelines we want you to follow. Number one, we want all members to participate in the strike. No member breaks the strike. And we want all members to continue to obey all laws so no accusations can be brought against anyone. And we want all union miners to be subject to the duly elected and qualified officers of the law. But we want you to resist the private gunmen who operate outside the law, and prevent them from superseding the authority of duly sworn officers. They are hired thugs of the coal operators and are entitled to no legal jurisdiction over you."

Johnny was shocked to note that the group of men was dead silent listening to their leader.

"It has been the practice of the Baldwin-Felts Detectives, in other towns like Holly Grove and Stanaford Mountain, to evict families out of their housing after they join the union.

These gunmen have been unscrupulous, and evicted miners from coal company houses without due process of law. They framed and jailed miners who would not agree with their terms. These gunmen cracked heads, maimed, and in many instances killed miners outright because they would not renounce the union.

"We are appealing to the legitimate local law enforcement officers to be sure that any activities such as evictions are supported with proper court documents and are carried out in a humanitarian way. God bless you men, and God bless your families."

Men clapped their hands and cheered. Mooney exited to the left, and another man walked to the center of the platform from the right.

"My name is Bill Blizzard, and I was right in the middle of the Paint Creek and Cabin Creek strikes in Kanawha County in 1912 and 1913. I ain't gonna sugar-coat nothing for you. It was an all-out war.

"The forty-one mines on Paint Creek was all unionized, but the miners was paid two and a half cents less per ton than other union miners in the area. Fifty-five mines on Cabin Creek did not have the union, so we wanted those mines to come under the union.

"What we was asking for would have cost the coal companies about fifteen cents a day, per miner. But do you think they could go along with that? Hell no! There was evictions, tent cities, beatings, sniper attacks, explosions, three hundred Baldwin-Felts gun thugs, and finally martial law with twelve hundred State Troopers marching right through town. You've heard of that armored train, the *Bull Moose Special* that put more than a hundred machine-gun bullets through the cabin of one miner, Cesco Estep, and killed him.

"One banker estimated the strike cost about a hundred million dollars, all because the coal companies didn't want to pay fifteen cents a day. So a strike ain't easy, but I ain't saying it will be as hard as Paint Creek either. The union is more established today and has more support, so we may not encounter that kind of violence and resistance.

"The thing to remember is our long-term goals. To get better wages and better working conditions, we may have to put up with some hardship for a little while, but we believe it will be worth it in the end. We are miners. We are union, and we are our own protectors."

Chapter 34

Sunday afternoon, and Johnny and Jim sat at an outside boardwalk table in front of a new restaurant in town known as Lively's.

"What'll it be?" the middle-aged man wearing an apron asked.

"Just a couple of coffees," Johnny said. "Black."

"You got it," the man said. "C. E. Lively's the name and this here is my establishment."

"Oh, okay," said both men.

C. E. extended his hand and officially welcomed both Johnny and Jim.

"You men was at the union rally earlier in the week?" Lively asked.

"Yep, we was there," Johnny said.

"Really something, ain't it?" Lively said.

"What do you mean?" Jim asked.

"Well, you know," Lively said. "The idea of standing up to the coal operators. Take a lot of guts, that's all. I'll be right back with your coffee."

"So what do you think?" Jim asked.

"I don't know," Johnny said. "I just ain't convinced making an enemy of your boss is the right thing to do. Papa always said it was acting like a barbarian to go out on strike against the company that paid you."

"You suppose things are different in West Virginia than they was back in the old country?" Jim asked.

"Maybe. Papa said the coal company paid them sometimes when they wasn't making much money. Just to help the men get through."

"You ever hear of the coal operators doing that for us?" Jim asked. "I mean, the way I see it, there ain't much to lose. They take all they want anyway. I'm joining."

"You joining the union?"

"Damn right I'm joining the union. Only way to go. By the way, how's Kate doing? You still bringing her daisies every Sunday?"

Johnny dropped his face to the ground.

"Yeah, I been meaning to tell you about Kate," he said. "You know the other day when we was at the police chief's office? Well, she talked a lot to Hatfield when we was over there, and it's like she cleared her head. She's able to think right now and she talks normal, like she used to."

"That's great to hear!" Jim said. "What'd she tell Hatfield?"

"Well, here's the thing," Johnny said. "She told him what happened that day that Elsie was killed."

"And what happened, Johnny?"

"Oh, man!" sobbed Johnny. "You ain't gonna believe this."

Jim fixed his gaze on Johnny and held it there.

"What happened was that Big Jake roughed up Kate that day. Slapped her a couple times, and with all of it, he throwed Baby Elsie up against the wall."

"Oh God!" Jim said. "Is that what killed her?"

Johnny nodded, tears dropping out of his eyes.

"Here you go gentlemen," C. E. Lively said. "Two black coffees."

"There's more," Johnny said. "When Kate tried to pick up Elsie's body, Jake threw her to the floor and grabbed Elsie by one leg, hanging her upside down."

Jim hung his head and shook it back and forth.

"Big Jake run out of the house, holding our baby that way," Johnny said. "Then when he took off walking so fast on that back path, Kate knew he was heading towards that old closed-down backhouse. He was gonna throw our baby in that shit! Kept saying, 'I'll take care of it. I'll take care of it.'"

"Oh my God!"

"Kate took off after him with the ax. Couldn't save Elsie no more, but wasn't gonna let him treat her like that!"

"Oh my God!" Jim said. "So Kate killed Jake with the ax?"

"Yep, that's how it happened."

"Oh my God!" Jim said shaking his head. "I wouldn't of figured that in a thousand years!"

"I know," Johnny said, hanging his head.

"Oh, I get it," Jim said. "So you're feeling guilty 'cause you wasn't able to protect your family."

"Yeah, I guess I'm feeling some of that."

"Well, you should feel proud of Kate. Sounds to me like nobody could have stopped Big Jake, but at least she got him!"

"Yeah, but here's the shit of it," Johnny said. "Kate might get charged with murder. We don't know yet."

"Murder? After what Big Jake did?"

"If people believe it. We don't know."

"How could they not believe it?" Jim asked. "If they know Kate at all, that's the only way it could have happened."

"Which *they* you talking about?"

"You know, the jury I guess."

"Yeah, the jury," Johnny said. "The man who died was a coal operator, and I wonder who's gonna be on the jury. Probably lots of coal company people, if they don't try to force things beforehand."

"What do you mean?"

"Well, before you got over to the jail the other night, there was a crowd of people out there calling for my head when they thought I did it."

"Oh my God!" Jim said. "What if she can't get a fair trial and she gets convicted? I can't remember a woman ever getting hanged in the State of West Virginia."

"Don't talk like that," Johnny said.

"I know. Just saying."

Chapter 35

Johnny, Jim, and a number of others including Gino, Matthew, and Caleb, along with a couple laborers stepped into the cage to be lowered into the mine. Hank, one of the operation supervisors, walked over to the box.

"McCarthy, you're working in the number four quadrant today, down to level five, chamber eight."

"Ain't that all mined out by now?" Johnny asked.

"Nope, some good coal left in there."

"Pillars?"

"Yep."

"There timbers down there?"

"Props was put in there when they was carving out the chamber," Hank said. "Should be just fine."

"If we gonna rob the pillars, we need fresh props to replace what we're taking out," said Johnny. "You know that."

"I'll see what I can do."

"Yeah, see what you can do," Johnny said. "And we'll need a good cross-cut saw, some wedges, a sledge hammer, and a timber-dog. Don't forget the timber-dog. We gotta grab hold of them logs. Can't do much mining without the right tools."

"Another shit assignment," Jim said as the cage descended. "This time they sticking it to you 'cause they think you killed Big Jake."

"Yep, probably so," Johnny said. "Probably so."

Johnny and Jim both knew that robbing the pillars was one of the most dangerous ways to pull coal out of the mine. When a large chamber was carved out, rock and coal was taken out and hauled away. The only thing left in the cavernous opening was the pillars they worked around to hold up the roof of the chamber, but they held a lot of coal too. The coal operators didn't want to leave nothing behind. They wanted their cake and eat it too. Can't have everything, he thought. But since they wasn't the ones down the hole, they didn't care.

"How deep we gonna be?" Jim asked.

"Seven hundred, maybe seven hundred twenty feet," Johnny answered.

The men stepped out of the cage, and stood in silence. Only the pressing weight of the massive granite down upon them could be heard, an eerie groaning in the distance as if the mountain was complaining about their invasion into its belly. A creak here and there as the tonnage settled, a trickle of water, marked by the occasional squeak of a rat.

The men turned to their left and walked down the gangway, the only light coming from the carbide lamps on their hats, and the lanterns carried by their sides. Johnny thought back to his first experience with total choking darkness years ago as a teen when he worked as a nipper, before the days of calcium carbide lights on their hats. Back then, the only light came from his lantern, and it ran out of oil. The darkness was suffocating. It was as if blackness was all that there was. That, and the rats, of course. They made their presence known. Squeak, squeak. Scratch, scratch. If he'd been much younger, Johnny didn't know if he could have handled it.

As a nipper, his job was to keep the big doors across the tracks in the gangway closed so air forced into the mine from large fans above would go into the airways and into the chambers where the men was working. The air also forced dangerous gases out of the mine. Then when a mule pulling coal cars approached, he had to open the doors. It was a boring job in some ways with long times of sitting, but important to the safety of the men and working of the mine. The thing that held him together in the darkness was knowing that one more coal car was due down the track and the mule driver would carry a lantern with him.

Johnny and the men approached two heavy wooden doors with a nipper sitting on a bench right there beside them.

"Howdy doo," Johnny greeted the young man. "No snoozing now."

"No sir."

"Chamber eight down this way?"

"Yes sir, right down this tunnel to the right."

When Johnny and his team entered the chamber, they trained their headlamps to the center of the room and then all around to survey the scene. The ceiling was propped at about nine or ten feet. Johnny checked the piece of slate initialed by the fire boss, which meant he had been there in the wee hours of the morning to check for fire damp or black damp, the heavy combination of carbon dioxide and nitrogen that settles at the bottom after a blast. The fire boss left a clean slate.

"Look at them timbers," said Jim. "Dry as matchsticks."

"Yeah, and bent over from the weight bearing down on them," Johnny said. "We ain't gonna be messing with anything over there."

"What's that over in the corner?" Caleb asked.

"Some fresh timbers, just laying there," Jim said. "And over there, some tools!"

"Yeah, we better use what we find," Johnny said. "They ain't gonna send nothing else."

Johnny could see that the spare timbers was wetter, greener than those that had been in place for so long. He was glad because that meant they was stronger and not brittle like the others.

"Look how rusty these tools are," Caleb said.

"Yeah, they been left behind for sure," Johnny said. "What are we gonna do with this rusty old saw?"

"I got some of this," Gino said. He held up a little can of 3-In-One Oil."

"You brought that? You a life saver! Squirt a little oil on the blade there and wipe it down so we can use it. The sledgehammer's rusty too, and the wedges, but they still work so it don't matter."

Johnny eye-balled the distance from the floor to the ceiling and paced it off against one of the timbers.

"Here, cut this off about here," Johnny said. "We'd rather be a little long at first and cut it again, than cut it too short."

The laborers made the cut and tried to place the timber in position, but it was still too long.

"Cut it again here, about four more inches."

They did, and the log stood straight up in place.

"A wedge here, and a wedge here," he said, pointing. "Make it real tight."

"Twelve pillars in this chamber," Caleb said, "but we only got maybe eight or ten timbers."

"Yeah, that ain't enough for all twelve pillars, that's for sure," Johnny said. "We'll have to do the best we can."

Johnny knew that the tricky part in putting up the props was putting them in the most needed positions. After taking out a pillar, what area of the ceiling needed to replace the support that the pillar supplied? Hard to tell, and can't always be right. Most of the pillars in this chamber was about fifteen feet square, smaller than some, but still they was important and supported a lot. A few timbers here and there might make up for tearing down the pillar, might not. That's what made robbing the pillars so dangerous.

One good thing was they usually took down a pillar with their pickaxes, not a powder blast. So the worst thing that could happen would generally be a small cave-in limited to the area of the pillar. You never knew about a blast. Could be way bigger, sealing miners in a chamber with no way out.

"Let's put one more timber over here on this side," said Johnny. "That should do it."

As Johnny and Jim moved to the next pillar, Gino, Matthew, and two of the laborers began digging their pickaxes deep into the black column. Chunks began breaking off and falling on the floor of the chamber. It didn't take long to hack down the structure. All of the men was watching and listening for movement and splitting off of the pillar.

Johnny and the other men sized up the next pillar. Without the timber-dog which would have helped them set up a metal handhold on the log, the men had to wrestle it into position and bear-hug it vertically into an area next to the pillar. They cut it like before, estimating the length, but leaving it a bit long so as not to make it useless in the chamber. Sure enough, a second cut was necessary. Just like before, three of them split apart the pillar with pickaxes and filled two more cars with coal.

"Let's break for lunch," Johnny called out.

The men seemed eager to dive into their food and gathered over by some of the standing pillars. They sat a bit scattered out each in their own area. They all opened their lunch pails and began gulping down sandwiches, apples, pie, and cake. Some brought goat milk in their canteen, others water. A chattery group was somehow silent as they ate. All at once, Johnny jumped to his feet.

"I gotta piss," he said.

He walked over to the far corner where the tools had been dropped. When he returned, his lunch pail was turned on its side.

"God damn it," he said. "Anybody see a rat over here by my lunch pail?"

"Yep," Matthew said. "But he was a big-ass rat and I tried to find a rock, but it was too late!"

"Shit!" Johnny said. "I should of knowed better than that!"

"He leave you anything?" Caleb asked.

"He left me an apple," Johnny said. "I wanted the rest of my sandwich. Had ham and even some cheese!"

"Well," Caleb said. "Looks like your lucky day. Seems like my wife packed me two sandwiches today, so I'm giving one to you. Now it ain't ham and cheese. It's hash and eggs, a little messy, but it makes a damn good sandwich, and unless you got another way to go..."

Johnny come up out of the hole that day grateful to see the light of day and breathe the fresh air, grateful for his wife and son, and grateful for friends like Jim and the others who shared the burden of the day. The men chopped down half of the twelve pillars with no trouble, and he hoped somebody else would finish out the chamber. But if it was him, he would be sure to have the extra timbers he needed, along with a timber-dog.

As he trudged out of the portal, Hank, the supervisor, came up quick.

"Police chief's looking for you," he said. "Wants to see you right away."

Chapter 36

Johnny walked through the front door of the police office and jail. He was black as the coal he'd been mining all day. The only white he showed was in his eyes and his teeth if he might smile, and he wasn't sure he'd be doing that for a while. He was unwashed and felt grimy and smudgy. He wanted to bathe before talking to Hatfield, but the situation seemed like it couldn't wait.

"Kate, what are you doing here, Sweetheart?"

She looked at him with sad eyes and stayed in her seat.

"What's going on?" Johnny asked, looking back and forth between the police chief and his wife.

"Have a seat, McCarthy," Hatfield said. "The County Prosecutor has decided to charge your wife with the murder of Big Jake."

"Oh no!" Johnny said.

He moved over next to his wife and placed his sooty hand on hers.

"He feels like there's too many unanswered questions about this to let it go, and I suspect Jake's position with the coal company has a lot to do with it. Because of who he was it could be a bad idea to just ignore his death like it never happened. Too much backlash."

"So what we do now?" Johnny asked.

"Well, the County Prosecutor wants to move on this. He's not gonna waste any time. So you're gonna have to get with your attorney so he can prepare your case."

"We don't have an attorney," Johnny said.

"We don't even know an attorney," Kate said.

"I know your situation," Hatfield said. "There's a Public Defender from Williamson who has been assigned to your case, and he's gonna be here Tuesday and Wednesday of next week. You'll have to be available to see him at that time."

"Could I work those days and see him at night?" Johnny asked.

"No, I think you better plan on taking those days off," Hatfield said. "And Mrs. McCarthy, I'm still willing to let you just keep living at your house as long as you assure me that you will be cooperative and available whenever you're needed to move this trial along."

"Yes, I will be," Kate said.

Johnny walked arm in arm with his wife up Mate Street on their way to the northeast of town, heading towards the Stone Mountain Housing. On the way, the men he'd worked with today was waiting, and they too was unwashed.

"What's going on with the police?" Jim asked.

Gino, Caleb, and Matthew gathered around.

"Kate's gonna have to stand trial for the murder of Big Jake," Johnny said.

Everyone gasped.

"How could they figure your wife could have killed Big Jake?" Caleb asked.

"Well, she did," Johnny said, "and she admitted to it, but it was after Big Jake killed our baby."

"What?" Matthew said.

Johnny noticed that others was gathering around, listening, and calling out jabs and questions.

"Look, it's Bitch McCarthy," one shouted out. "The murderer of Big Jake!"

"Now you tell me how a little bitch like that could get over on a man the size of Big Jake!" another called out.

Johnny bristled and took a step towards the rabble-rousers. His friends formed a wall between him and the gathering crowd.

"My wife done nothing wrong!" Johnny yelled to the growing crowd.

"The charges against her say different!" a voice shouted from the mob.

"In this country we got a policy of innocent until proven guilty," Jim called out. "Anyone accused of a crime gets a fair trial."

"Oh, we'll give her a fair trial all right," another voice called out. "How 'bout right now in the streets."

"Work your way back to Hatfield's office and get some help," Jim said to Gino. "This is gonna get ugly."

Johnny, Kate and their friends moved up on the boardwalk in front of C.E. Lively's restaurant. Johnny figured that way at least they had a building to their back and wasn't surrounded on all sides.

"So how you fixing to get out of this, McCarthy?" someone yelled. "Even if you get home, we know where you live."

"Yeah, and it don't make no sense that a woman could of killed Big Jake," another called out. "So that probably means you did it, McCarthy, and you trying to have your wife take the rap. That makes you a coward, boy!"

Johnny stood at the front of the boardwalk and looked out into the faces of thirty to forty angry men. Some he recognized like Max, the operations supervisor, and Hank, the area supervisor he dealt with today. It didn't feel good to him that a man who assigns him work and locations in the mine had so much anger stored up against him. How could he trust the man with his safety? How could he know that an operations supervisor even cared if he came back up out of the mine alive?

Other faces he did not recognize, but figured all had been friends with Big Jake. Some, he knew, would line up with Big Jake because they was part of the coal operators, even if they never met the man. Others he believed to be part of the volunteer militia that served at the pleasure of the mining company. Seemed like they always had the fire power to make things work like they wanted.

Just then, Johnny saw three men on horseback ride up from behind the mob. It looked like Police Chief Hatfield and two of his deputies. The three set themselves up, one to the rear and one to each side of the trouble-makers. Sid fired three shots in the air. All anyone could hear was the thunderclap of the chief's rapid fire revolver.

Everybody turned to face him. A bird chirped, but after that, everything was dead silent.

"Now all you men listen to me!" Hatfield called out. "Some of you had this conversation with me a few days ago when you got together outside my jail calling for Johnny McCarthy. I told you then that anyone who tries to take a prisoner of mine and harm them would be sent home in a pine box! Does anybody think I don't still mean that?"

Quiet all around, but the mob itself put out a nervous fidgety feel.

"Anybody? Now you know that the charges have been shifted to Mrs. McCarthy, and the law says that any accused, be it a man or a woman, is entitled to a fair trial, and by God, that's what's gonna happen. We also have an ordinance in Matewan that forbids a man from carrying a sidearm in town. How many of you are carrying a sidearm right now?"

One man on the right side of the crowd held up his hand.

"Come out to the front," Hatfield said. "Come out right now."

He motioned to one of his deputies to step down and disarm the man. The deputy placed the gun in his saddlebag and handcuffed the man with his hands behind his back.

"This side of this little gathering, you walk past my deputy on horseback over here. One at a time. Single-file. You let him see your beltline and your pockets, and if you're clear and not armed, you go home. And don't let me find any of you gathering together like some kind of lynch mob again or I'll be making a lot of arrests. Other side, do the same thing. Single file!"

The men was passing by the deputies on both sides of the crowd, and breaking off into town.

"Hold up!" one deputy yelled. "What's that bulge in your pocket?"

The man stood still and did not move. The deputy jumped off his horse and reached into the man's pocket.

"Thirty-eight special!" he called out to the chief.

Hatfield remained in the saddle and walked his horse over to the man.

"How come you didn't come clean when I asked for anyone carrying a sidearm to step up?" Hatfield asked.

"Didn't want to have a problem," the man answered.

"Well, you got a big problem now," Hatfield said. "Take these two back to the jail and book them for violation of 1402, and book this one for lying to law enforcement. Confiscate the guns for evidence, and then cut them loose. I'll be along in a few minutes."

Hatfield dismounted and walked over to Johnny, Kate, and their friends.

"Johnny, Mrs. McCarthy," he said. "Listen, you two ain't done nothing wrong regarding cooperation with law enforcement in this matter. But the fact is there's folks in town who would kill you just because of the charges against you. For that reason, I'm gonna have to take you into custody just so I can protect you."

"But can't I stay at my house?" Kate asked.

"I can't protect you at your house," Hatfield said. "But it is my duty to protect you, and the only way I can do that is to take you into custody, and my deputies and me will protect you at the jail."

"Wait a minute," Johnny said as he pulled Hatfield aside. "You ever had a woman in your jail before? How you gonna protect her from the other prisoners? You get some lowlife scum in there and..."

"Now hold on," Hatfield said. "You think I know how to do my job?"

"Yep, I figure that you do."

"Then you just gonna have to trust me."

"But what about using the toilet, or needing a bath, or having other prisoners yelling at her?"

"I got ways to make prisoners shut up, and we'll be real careful about her personal things. Nobody get near her for the toilet or a bath."

"She ain't gonna feel comfortable with this."

"She might not feel comfortable, but she be safe. Nobody be putting a hand on her, that I can say for sure."

"So I have to go to jail?" Kate asked, stepping over to where they was talking.

"Look at it this way," the police chief said. "you gonna take some time out from your normal chores. We gonna fix your food, feed you, clean your sheets, make it so you got nothing to worry about. And your family and friends can visit you any time you want to see them. All you gotta do is relax and let me do my job."

"You make it sound like it be hard to say no," Kate said.

"Yeah, that's right," Hatfield said. "It be really hard to say no."

Chapter 37

"Let me fix you some eggs and warm up some bread, son," Johnny said.

Corey remained silent and continued to lace his hobnailed boots.

"You hear me, son?"

"Yeah."

"I'm glad things are going so good for you with the mules," Johnny said. "Been about a week now."

"Yep."

"You learn anything new?"

"Yep. Sparky knowed when it was time to quit and he didn't want to work overtime, so he laid down right where he was. Wouldn't get up for nothing."

"What? So what did you do?"

"I took my canteen and poured some water in his ear," Corey said. "Got up right fast!"

"Ha, ha, ha. That's a good trick," Johnny said. "You still gotta always be careful with them, though."

"Yeah, I know," Corey said. "I remember not to trust them too much, just like you can't trust some people too much."

"What do you mean?"

"Nothing. Ma gonna be all right?"

"Of course she is, son."

"What if the jury don't believe her about what happened?"

"Well, I think they gonna believe her," Johnny said. "We gonna have an attorney and everything, a real smart man about the law, talking up for her in the courtroom."

"And he'll know how to say things to the jury?"

"Yep, your ma and me will be meeting with him today, and maybe tomorrow too," Johnny said. "Come in from Williamson on the train. Real smart man."

"Okay."

"I don't want you worrying about nothing," Johnny said, wrapping his arm around Corey's shoulders. "Come on, I'll walk you down to the portal."

. . . .

Johnny got back to their house and it was still dark. Once they got Corey used to reporting to the stable around six in the morning like a regular mine worker, now they want him to start at four o'clock, like most mule-drivers. Takes time to curry the mules, they said, and give them the attention they need to warm up for a full day's work. Johnny thought that made sense. He felt proud of Corey. He was so happy to have him back. Just wished Corey would warm up a little more. Sometimes he seemed kind of distant. Maybe not to his ma, but to him anyway. He would talk openly and share what was happening, but only if Johnny asked. Maybe he would share more openly with his ma.

Johnny was glad Corey was doing well as a mule-driver. Seemed like a real natural, and enjoyed his work. But he knew right now he carried a burden about his ma. He was worried about her. Couldn't imagine her facing people being mad at her and violence, and God forbid, punishment if things didn't go her way. She didn't deserve any of that, and Corey knew it. Johnny wished Corey could just have a happy, simpler life, without the worries of an adult. He's just a kid, for God's sake. But these days, there was many children working in a man's world. Johnny wondered what Mother Jones would have to say about this kind of situation. Come to think of it, he knew exactly what she would say, only she would say it with fire and brimstone, and better than he could.

Kate had been housed at the jail now for five days, since last Thursday night. So far, so good. Only problem she told him about was a loud drunk who had been arrested and locked up two cells down from her. He was yelling a lot 'til Hatfield knocked him out. After that he slept the rest of the night. Probably didn't know where he was, anyway.

Johnny felt an emptiness inside that she wasn't around. He missed her in a lot of ways. Liked laying beside her on the bed, holding her and kissing her, squeezing her breast, even though she still couldn't have relations. That tear she suffered in childbirth. Johnny hoped she'd heal up from that soon. He missed her being his wife. He had suffered pain in his life like everyone, but he knew he ain't never suffered nothing like the pain of childbirth.

Right now he missed her because of all the chores he was trying to keep up with. He wasn't complaining. He knew she would rather be home with him and Corey than where she was. Just that it was a lot to do. Made him appreciate all that she did do for him and Corey, and all that she did to make their home comfortable and nice. Laundry in the tub and the washboard had to be done every second day, and he had to do it for himself and Corey. Knew he was gonna have to pick up a few things at the company store soon. Chop some wood. Chop some wood? Have to borrow an ax to chop some wood. Don't have my ax right now. The list seemed endless. It's true. A woman's work is never done.

At about 7:30 Johnny thought of making some eggs for Kate, along with some warm bread, and maybe an apple. He knew the jail had to feed prisoners and people in custody. He didn't like to think of Kate as a prisoner, but she sure was in custody. But he also knew that Sid Hatfield was an awful busy man, and even if he asked one of his deputies to do it, he wasn't sure just how good they was at cooking, or how soon they would do it. He wasn't gonna worry about coffee, though. He figured Hatfield and his deputies must have a pot of coffee brewing somewhere over there.

Johnny fixed up a wooden bowl of scrambled eggs, a couple of torn-off chunks of bread along with some butter, and a sliced up apple. This he covered with a sheet of waxed paper and wrapped it tight so the warm things would stay warm, and the cold things would stay in the bowl. He knew it might not be the best-cooked breakfast in town, but it sure was done with love, and he wanted Kate to feel that.

....

"Howdy Chief," Johnny said as he entered the jail house. "How's Kate holding up?"

"She's doing all right," Hatfield said. "You brought her some breakfast?"

"Yeah, is that okay?"

"Yeah, it's okay. But Jim's wife, Mrs. Mullins already come by with breakfast about a half hour ago. And some of the other townswomen been bringing meals over which lightens the load for everybody. It's a good thing."

"What time's our attorney supposed to meet with us?" Johnny asked.

"Should be here any...uh, here he is now."

The door swung open and in stepped a young man dressed in coat and tie.

"Chief Hatfield," he said as he shook his hand. "Jeremiah Tucker. Pleasure to see you."

"Glad you're here," Hatfield said. "This here is Johnny McCarthy, the husband of the defendant. Your Public Defender, Mr. Tucker."

The two men shook hands. Johnny was struck by how young the attorney looked. How could he be an attorney, he wondered. Did he have experience in the courtroom? Did he know the law? Would he be able to stand up for his wife?

"So, um..." Johnny stammered, looking down and avoiding eye contact.

"I'm older than I look," Tucker said. "Been in the courtroom about ten years. Good record of acquittals."

"He's an excellent Public Defender," Hatfield jumped in. "Picked him myself 'cause I knowed you was gonna need a good one."

"Oh, I didn't mean…"

"Don't worry about it," Tucker said. "Let's go meet your wife and get on with it. I've heard a lot about her case, but I'm anxious to talk with her. Sid, you mind if we just bring her out here and use this table?"

"Works for me," Hatfield said. "But I'll be sitting at my desk doing some paperwork."

Kate walked out and Johnny gave her a big hug. After everybody swapped names, she sat at the table and stared at the Public Defender, looking very shy and withdrawn.

"Mrs. McCarthy, I've read the report," Tucker said. "So Jake killed your baby, and then tried to leave with her body."

"Yes."

"And you believed he was going to throw her in the muck behind the backhouse?"

"Yes."

"And what made you think that?"

"He was looking around and over his shoulder at first," Kate said. "Then he started hurrying really fast down that pathway that led to the backhouse, and I just knew what he was gonna do. 'Cause he kept saying, 'I'll take care of it. I'll take care of it.'"

"Why did he come to your house in the first place?" Tucker asked.

"Johnny missed work that day," Kate said. "He said he was looking for him."

"Did you invite him into your house?"

"No, he busted open the door."

"And he was angry at you?" the attorney asked.

"Yes, said I needed to learn some respect. That this was company housing and he could come in any time he wanted."

"And then he attacked you, or just your baby?"

Kate looked down and to the left, staring at the edge of the table. Tears welled up in her eyes.

"He attacked me too," she said. "But he threw my baby against the wall first, and she stopped crying right then."

"What was the nature of his attack on you?" Tucker asked. "What did he actually do?"

"He slapped me a couple times," Kate said.

She started crying and Johnny moved closer and put his arm around his wife.

"Could you give us a few minutes?" Johnny asked.

"Of course," the Public Defender said. "Why don't you just go back to the cell and take all the time you need."

Johnny walked his wife back to the cell, inside the interior door and just off the front office area. As Johnny held his wife in his arms and rocked her gently, Matewan's Mayor, Cabell Testerman walked in.

"Sid, you ain't gonna believe what just happened," the mayor said.

"Okay, surprise me," Hatfield said.

"These Baldwin-Felts fellows come in on the train today. They fixing to do some evictions tomorrow morning. So Albert Felts comes up to me and asks me if the town of Matewan will welcome them so they can use it as a base of operation for the work they got to do, meaning the evictions. I told them yes, they welcome to use our hotels and eat in our restaurants, whatever they need.

"Now these guys don't travel light, you know? They take a couple horses off the train so they can mount up. They even got three automobiles on flatbed cars so they can drive out to Stone Mountain Housing. Then they got their side-arms, their Winchesters, and they got these heavy grips, these big bulky satchels, and you know damn well what's in there."

"Yeah," Hatfield said. "Thompson sub-machine guns."

"Thompson sub-machine guns?" Tucker said.

"Yeah, we both seen them before," the mayor said. "So Felts asks my permission to set up these machine guns on the roof of several of our buildings off Mate Street."

Johnny continued comforting his wife, but couldn't believe what he was hearing.

"What?" Hatfield said.

"So I asked him what in the world he would want to do that for?" Testerman said. "And he said that Matewan was a nice, peaceful community, and they wanted to maintain that peace, and to preserve the security of the operation they was here to carry out, namely the evictions. He said they wanted to use Matewan as their headquarters and command the surrounding community. And I told them they was welcome to stay in the town, and eat here, and come and go, but they was absolutely not authorized to set up no machine guns.

"So Albert Felts tells me they could make it worth my while if I would have a change in attitude. I said how do you mean? Then the bastard offered me a bribe of a thousand dollars for me to look the other way and let them mount them machine guns. I told them I was not for sale, and that as long as I was mayor, there would be no machine guns. He said that maybe I wouldn't be mayor very long."

"Those sonsabitches," Hatfield said. "They try any shit like that, we'll kill them all before they get out of town!"

Chapter 38

The next day, Johnny hurried through the door of Sid Hatfield's office, trying to get out of the steady drizzle. He didn't own an umbrella, but held a tarp overhead most of the walk to the jail.

"Morning Sid," he said. "I'll just go in and visit with Kate for a little while before Mr. Tucker gets here."

"Here's the keys," Hatfield said. "Kinda wet out there, huh?"

"Hi Sweetheart, how you feeling today?" Johnny asked.

"Okay, I'm feeling okay."

"After I left, did Mr. Tucker ask you some more questions?"

"Yeah, we talked a while longer."

"You feel good about him, like he can help us?"

"Yeah, I think he's a real smart man," Kate said. "I think he knows what he's doing."

"What's this?" Johnny asked, pointing to a plate with some leftovers on it.

"Oh, Harriet Jackson brought me by some food last night. Real nice of her."

"Oh, Caleb's wife? What'd she bring?"

"Well, it was some chicken and boiled potatoes. It was real good."

"What's them greens you left there on the side. Is that spinach?"

"She called them collard greens, kind of like spinach, but real bitter."

"Hmm, I ain't never been around colored people a lot," Johnny said. "Don't know much what they do."

"Mr. and Mrs. McCarthy, good morning!" Tucker said.

The volume of his voice and level of enthusiasm surprised Johnny, but he was glad to see it. Kate needed someone in her corner who cared and would spend the energy to show the jurors what really happened. Tucker picked up his questioning.

"Now had Jake ever been out to your house before the day in question?" he asked.

"Yes, he was out some weeks earlier," Kate said.

"And what was the occasion for that visit?"

"He come out to talk to me about my buddee, a boy named Gilbert, who was killed in a cave-in," Johnny said. "Wanted to know what work he did for me, how he helped, 'cause they needed to replace him."

"Did he have the same demeanor at that time?"

Kate and Johnny looked at each other.

"What?"

"Was he angry and aggressive on this visit like he was this last time?"

"Yeah, I'd say he was," Johnny said. "Angry and yelling. Said I needed to learn some respect."

"Pushed his way in, too," Kate said. "Just like last time."

Johnny sat by Kate giving the support he intended for his wife. His thoughts was in and out of focus on what they was talking about 'cause his mind wandered to the evictions that was planned in the Stone Mountain Coal Camp today. The clock said it was about half past noon, and Johnny was tired of sitting.

"I have an idea," he said. "Chief Hatfield gave me some money for lunch for all of us. Why don't I go down to Lively's Restaurant and bring back some food?"

They both agreed, and Johnny made the trip. He returned to the office just about the time Chief Hatfield and Mayor Testerman came back from the housing camp. He never before seen the chief or the mayor so worked up and angry about something. The chief picked up the phone.

"Mae, connect me with Sheriff Blankenship's office in Williamson, please."

"Yeah, this is Sid Hatfield, police chief of Matewan. I need to talk to the sheriff.

"I see. And who is this?

"Deputy Tony Webb, and you're the office manager? Well Deputy Webb, I've got a situation here in Matewan about what I believe to be some illegal evictions done by the Baldwin-Felts Detective Agency. Yeah. Okay, thanks."

Johnny delivered the food to Kate and Mr. Tucker, but continued listening to Hatfield's conversation.

"Mr. Bronson, Wade Bronson. Yes sir, you're the County Prosecutor. Well sir, I've got a situation up here in Matewan where we've just had some Baldwin-Felts detectives evict some families from company housing, and as they was about to do this in the rain and everything, I asked them if they had legal authority and they said they did. I asked them what authority they had, and they said the Circuit Court Judge in Williamson give approval for it, but they could not produce a written court order. I told them they had to have that for it to be legal, but they said they didn't need it.

"Yes sir, that's what we thought. Mayor Testerman and I told them not to pull anything like that around here, and Albert Felts just ordered his men to go ahead. He offered me three hundred dollars a month to change sides and kind of look the other way."

Just then, Johnny saw Charlie Kelly, one of the evicted miners, stagger through the front door in tears over what they done.

"So you say them evictions was illegal, and we should get warrants issued against the detectives and place them in custody...Well you know, we got a miner right here who was evicted just now, and he can testify to what was done...So if we get him on the next train to Williamson, you can have someone pick him up, he can swear out the warrants, and be back here on the 5:15?...Yes, his name is Charlie Kelly."

"Charlie, what happened?" Testerman asked the miner.

"Mayor, I couldn't believe it," Charlie said. "Them bastards was like animals. Half of them gunmen stood around and held everybody at gunpoint, and the other half tossed their furniture out in the rain, their pots and pans, their food, their clothes. I saw one of them no good devils throw out a little child, about a three-year old little boy. Tossed him like a piece of garbage."

Johnny teared up when he heard those words.

"And they enjoyed what they was doing," Charlie said. "They was laughing and carrying on. And with their fire power, a man couldn't even protect his own family. There was one family where the wife was fixing to have a baby real soon. I mean she was big, and one of them bastards throwed her out in the rain and kicked her right in the stomach like he was playing football or something. Knocked her back and she begged for mercy, but nobody could do nothing. What's wrong with these people?"

"We gonna take care of it, Charlie," Hatfield said. "But you gotta get on the Norfolk-Western to Williamson right away, okay? Here's the fare. They'll pick you up at the station and take you to the County Prosecutor's office. They'll have the paperwork ready. You just sign your part of it, they'll sign and stamp it, and you bring it back here, okay? You'll get back here when the 5:15 rolls in."

Looks like something's really gonna get done about these thugs, Johnny thought.

"You know, Mayor," Hatfield said. "the operator I got for that call was Mae Chafin, and you know she was listening in on that call."

"Ain't she Don Chafin's sister or cousin, or something?"

"Yeah, cousin, I think," said Hatfield. "And with Don Chafin, the Sheriff of Logan County, the biggest enemy of the UMWA there ever was, you know he's gonna hear all about it and fill in his buddies at Baldwin-Felts. They all in one pot together!"

"Yeah, and they think they're gonna be on the 6:15 to Bluefield," Testerman said. "You gonna need some backup. Let me make a call…Mae, get me Hugh Combs over at the union office… Hugh? Yeah, this is Cabell Testerman. Listen, we bracing for trouble with the Baldwin-Felts bunch. I want you to find a dozen or so sober-minded men. Tell them to get their guns. We gonna swear them in as special officers to back up our police chief. We'll be down to the office in a half hour. Thanks."

"McCarthy, can you handle a sidearm?" Hatfield yelled.

"Uh, no, I ain't never used one," Johnny said.

"How about a rifle?"

"Yeah, I've shot a rifle."

"All right, grab yourself a Winchester off the rack. Let's get downtown."

Chapter 39

About 4:00 P.M., Johnny, Hatfield, and Testerman walked up to the Union Headquarters on Mate Street, right across from the Urias Hotel. The place was owned by Anse Hatfield, a cousin of Sid's and a man who sided with the coal operators and their hired gunmen. Johnny knew when the Baldwin-Felts thugs was in town, they was always hosted by Anse Hatfield and stayed right there.

Hugh Combs greeted the three, and indeed had a few more volunteers than the mayor had asked for armed and ready to back up Hatfield and the townspeople. They was sitting around cleaning their guns and checking their ammunition. Sid himself had brought a .44 Smith & Wesson for one hand, and .45 Service Colt for the other. In addition, there was fifty or sixty people standing around down the street outside the Old Matewan National Bank. They, no doubt, had heard what was going on and wanted to see what was gonna happen. Johnny saw many of the Baldwin-Felts gunmen walk into the hotel across the street where they was housed.

"Sid, I been watching these Baldwin fellows going into the hotel over there," Johnny said. "You suppose they gonna come out of there armed to the teeth and ready to fight?"

"McCarthy, I figure they know they gonna have to deal with me and the mayor," Hatfield said. "Now there's thirteen of them fellas in town today, and I figure most of them ain't licensed to carry a sidearm in this town. The only ones I know of for sure that are licensed are Lee Felts, Albert Felts, and C. B. Cunningham. There may be others, but I ain't sure. So it might just be that the ones that ain't licensed are breaking down their guns and packing them away in their satchels so as not to give us one more excuse to arrest them.

"Men, gather around here and listen up... Thank you for coming out at our request to be deputized as special officers... Raise your right hands and repeat after me. I... say your name... promise to uphold the laws and ordinances... of the town of Matewan... and to serve as a special officer... to the best of my ability... under the direction of Police Chief Sid Hatfield.

"Now listen to me, men. I am going to attempt to serve a warrant on all the Baldwin-Felts detectives that took part in the evictions today. The idea is to arrest them and take them into custody because their evictions was not according to law. What happens next will depend on how they react. I don't know how many of them will be armed, but if they start shooting, we gonna be shooting back a ton, and we gonna be shooting to kill. Everybody understand me? Any questions?"

"Chief, they be wearing any protection of any kind?" a miner called out.

"They might be wearing coats o'nails. Head shots be best. Stand by. We'll be out talking to them in a few minutes."

Johnny saw Jim Mullins checking his rifle and walked over.

"How you doing, Jim?"

"Okay, considering," Jim said. "You know we got evicted today?"

"Because you joined the union?"

"Yeah, it's pretty rough," Jim said. "Your wife, your children, all your belongings, and there ain't nothing you can do about it! They put their hands on your family and rough them up. Take your property. Ain't right, man. It just ain't right!"

"All right, men," Hatfield cried out. "They out there on Mate Street down by the railroad station, so let's move out. Me and the mayor will confront them, and the rest of you just be close by and spread out. Keep your eye on what's happening and stay ready."

Johnny was flanked to the right as the group of special officers formed a blanket of support to back up the police chief. Hatfield and Mayor Testerman led the way and Albert and Lee Felts led the Baldwin detectives as the two groups came together on Mate Street right in front of Chambers Hardware Store. When they stopped walking, they was probably no more than five feet apart.

"I'm gonna arrest you and your men," Hatfield said to Albert Felts.

Felts' face spread out wide with a big grin.

"For what?"

"Because them evictions was illegal, and your warrants be arriving on the train in a few minutes."

"You a funny man, Hatfield," Felts said. "Actually, I'm gonna be arresting you. Be taking you back to Bluefield."

"For what?"

"Interfering with the law," Felts said.

"What are you talking about?" Mayor Testerman said. "He's the police chief of Matewan. I can't afford to have him taken to Bluefield."

"Got the warrant right here," Felts said.

"Well then I'll post bond," the mayor said, "but I can't let you take him out of the county. Let me see that warrant."

Hatfield turned and walked the few steps through the front door of Chambers Hardware Store. Johnny stood right there and watched Hatfield move past him. Testerman studied the warrant. He read it for about a minute.

"Ha! Took a prisoner away from a local constable! This is bogus," he said. "Bogus!"

Johnny's eyes was trained on the exact spot on Mate Street where the confrontation was taking place. They was laughing at each other one second, and the next they was arguing, and in a sudden moment it seemed to Johnny they all run out of things to say.

In a flash, Albert Felts pulled his sidearm out of his belt and plugged the mayor right in the belly. He fell to the ground, unable to fire back or defend himself in any way. The gun was loud and ferocious, and belched a puff of gray smoke into the air.

Sid Hatfield burst out of the hardware store, guns in hand and fire in his eyes, blasting away with both hands. One of his shots hit

Albert Felts right in the head. The roar of gunfire and the smell of smoke filled the air. People started running in all directions—men, women, and children. Men with guns—men without guns.

Johnny stood frozen on the boardwalk in front of Chambers' Hardware Store. He wanted to help, but where to run and who to shoot? He had shot deer more than once, but never a man. It felt kind of final, like being deeper in up to his neck than he wanted to be.

In the middle of the street, two men stood ten feet apart, firing at each other with their revolvers. One was a deputized miner, the other a Baldwin hired hand, maybe Lee Felts. Johnny couldn't be sure. The crazy thing was that each man emptied his cylinder and missed with every shot. The Baldwin man finally threw his gun at the miner and run off.

C. B. Cunningham was a Baldwin bully who was armed. Almost every miner recognized him because he was a cruel and brutal man. Dogs slunk out of the way when he passed by, and everybody gave him a wide berth. Johnny saw him raise his pistol and begin to fire at the miners and townspeople. Such was their venom towards this big man that the miners cut him down in haste, blowing up his face and nearly taking off his head. Johnny couldn't count the shots that riddled his body after he hit the ground.

Another one of the Baldwin gang, who Johnny found out later was named A. J. Boohrer, either carried his weapon against the town ordinance, or picked up a gun lying in the street. He aimed at Jim Mullins, and shot him from the side right through his midsection below the rib cage. Mullins went down right away, and began gasping for breath.

"Oh Lord, I been shot," Mullins said over and over best he could.

Johnny dropped his Winchester, ran to his side, put his arm around him, and supported his head and shoulders. The life was fading from his face, and his eyes was rolling back in his head.

"No!" Johnny yelled. "No! No!"

Just then Johnny noticed that Boohrer, Jim's killer, was fixing to shoot at *him*. He rolled to the side, snatching the rifle Mullins had dropped. He cocked the gun, loading a round in the chamber, took aim, and fired. Blood squirted from Boohrer's chest, and he fell straightway on his back.

Johnny leaned back down to tend to Mullins, but he was gone. He stood up and started walking down Mate Street in the direction the gunmen had run. Many armed townspeople and special officers was already after them, and Baldwin thugs lay slaughtered in the streets all around. Johnny brought up the rear, one of the last miners to continue to march in that direction. He stood silently and surveyed the street before him. All at once, a mine guard sprang up out of a garbage can along the side of the street, and sprinted towards the Tug Fork River. He eked out a panicky squeal as he ran. Johnny had him in his sights for a second, but the homes in the background kept him from firing. When the man reached the river, he jumped in for a frantic swim to the safety of the Kentucky banks.

Johnny continued to march forward, ready with his rifle. Up ahead, he saw Sid Hatfield standing outside the post office, guns drawn. "Come out and fight like a man!" Hatfield yelled. Just then, Lee Felts came out shooting at Sid, but Sid cut him down with both guns blazing.

Johnny guessed the whole gunfight lasted maybe fifteen minutes. Seven of the Baldwin lot lay dead in the streets, along with two miners—Jim Mullins, Johnny's friend, and another miner Johnny didn't know. Johnny, Hatfield, and some others loaded Cabell Testerman onto a stretcher and set him on a train to Welch.

"What'd they have to shoot me for?" Testerman kept asking.

Seven Baldwin gunmen died that day in Matewan, and their bodies was left where they lay so Mingo County Sheriff George T. Blankenship could arrive that night and see right where things ended up.

Chapter 40

Johnny made his way, as quick as he could, to Sid Hatfield's office and the jail where Kate waited. There was certain things he needed to do, but he had to let Kate see him in the flesh to know that he was all right. On the way to the jail, people was coming out of their hiding places and asking questions.

"Is everybody all right?"

That seemed the most foolish question to Johnny. Even if they wasn't there, they heard the thunderous rounds of bullets, hundreds of them. No, everybody ain't all right. Others knew that people must have got hurt and wanted to know about it.

"How many got killed? How many was wounded?" Or they'd think of a name of somebody, and ask if they was okay. Johnny told them the truth when he knew the answer, but he didn't always know.

He burst through the door of the local jail and found Kate sitting near Hatfield's desk, along with the Public Defender. She rushed into his arms.

"Oh, dear God, you're okay," she said.

Johnny held on in silence for a long time.

"Is Hatfield okay?" Tucker asked.

"He is," Johnny said. "Sid Hatfield is okay. But Jim Mullins was shot and killed by a Baldwin gunman."

"Oh, no!" Kate cried.

"Yeah, I got to go out and try to find Stella," Johnny said. "They was evicted this morning in the rain and everything. I got to tell her how brave her husband was, and how much he loved his family."

. . . .

Johnny walked down Mate Street, past the Community Church, and out towards Stone Mountain Housing. The rain died down to a drizzle, and everything he walked on was soaked. The air had that freshness that comes after a hard rain, kind of like washing out a moldy ice box.

Johnny first showed up at the Mullins' old house on Shamrock Road a few doors down from his own. Just as Jim said, they wasn't there no more. A giant padlock made sure no one would fill the space until the Stone Mountain Housing Company opened it for new business. A few scraps of their belongings was scattered out in the dirt—a little boy's shirt, a shoe, a couple of hand cloths for bathing, and some forks and spoons. He collected the items and wrapped them in the washing cloths.

"Excuse me," he called out to a neighbor. "Do you know where the Mullins family is?"

"They was evicted this morning," the old man replied.

"I know," Johnny said. "Just trying to find them."

"They might be at the tent city, in the meadow a couple of hundred yards northeast of here. I think Jim went into town sometime after they was thrown out."

. . . .

Johnny never seed a coal town tent city before. Looked like about fifty families might live here. He didn't know so many was evicted out of company housing. Seemed far off when you heard about it. Five families here, six from over there. Even if you only know about it as numbers, they still people, and they still have to go someplace. Johnny could see that the people add up after a while.

This was not set up like any military camp Johnny ever heard of. There was no straight lines, no crispness to the order of things, nothing to where everything was the same. The tents was all different. Some was union-issue tents. Some was old union-issue, some new. Some was bought from Sears-Roebuck, some was borrowed from somewhere else. Some stood up straight, some was leaning. Some held the family's belongings. For others, they was scattered all around outside.

"Excuse me," Johnny said to a man who looked like he might be in charge. "I'm looking for the Mullins family. They got thrown out of company housing today."

"And who are you?" the man asked.

"I'm Johnny McCarthy, a miner, and a friend."

"Yeah, I know them," the man said. "I think only the wife and two kids are here. Let's walk over this way. You hear about the shootout today?"

"Yeah, I heard about it," Johnny said.

"I think that's where Jim was going," the man said.

Stella saw Johnny approaching and ran up to him, searching his eyes. Johnny maintained eye contact, but knew he couldn't hide the truth. Stella broke down and fell into his arms.

"He was a brave man," Johnny said. "He believed in the union cause and he fought to give you and the kids a better life."

Stella continued to weep in his arms.

"He hated what happened today," Johnny said. "He wanted to protect you and felt like he couldn't. But he loved you and your kids very much."

. . . .

Johnny made his way to the portal where Corey would be coming back from a day of work with the mules. Deep in the earth, Johnny knew that Corey would not have heard the thunderous shots that filled the air.

"Pa, what's going on?"

"What do you mean?" Johnny asked.

"There's talk in the mines about evictions," Corey said, "and shootings, and people getting killed. What's going on?"

"Yeah, that's what happened today," Johnny said. "I didn't know you knowed nothing about it."

"People was talking," Corey said. "Every time you'd pass a nipper, or a spragger, or a miner, they been talking to somebody who knew something was going on."

"Yeah son, there was evictions today. And they was pretty bad. And at the end of the day Chief Hatfield took up for the miners and their families. Ended up in a big shootout near the railroad station. Seven Baldwin-Felts detectives was killed, along with two miners. Jim Mullins was one of them."

Corey dropped his head and cried.

"Yeah, and Mayor Testerman was shot and sent on a train to Welch to get doctor's help."

"So now what do we do?" Corey asked.

"We just keep doing our jobs," Johnny said. "You keep working with the mules, and I'll keep knocking the coal out of the mountain. I believe the union will be getting stronger, and our lives will be getting better."

"You gonna be joining the union now, Pa?"

"Yes, I am," Johnny said. "But that's nothing to worry about now. Tonight, you need to get yourself cleaned up, get something to eat, and go visit your ma."

"What you gonna do, Pa?"

"I'm gonna go downtown, down by the union office, Chambers Hardware Store, Urias Hotel, you know, over there. Gotta talk to the people. Find out what's going on."

. . . .

The streets was filled with people. Johnny strolled among them and listened more than he talked. Seemed like everybody had questions, or a story to tell.

"This one old boy," a woman started to tell, "he was shot and he sat in the rocking chair on my porch. Next thing I know, there's more bullets flying and my chair's got all these holes in it. The detective is on my porch, dead as a squirrel!"

Johnny overheard another woman telling a friend that this boy she knew was hiding in a doctor's office off Mate Street. "A Baldwin-Felts man come in there looking for cover and firing his gun. The boy got scared and clobbered the detective with a jug of chloroform, and that was it."

"Did you see the mayor get shot?" one man asked another.

"It happened so fast, you couldn't see nothing," his friend said.

"That's 'cause Felts was wearing a raincoat and he shot him right through the coat," said another. "Couldn't see it coming!"

"I ain't never seen nothing like this," a miner said.

"Yeah, maybe next time they think twice before they go and toss people out of their homes in the rain," another said.

A couple of men tied some Winchesters together to form a litter, put the body of a dead Baldwin man on it, and paraded through town.

"Yep, they brought the guns in here," one bystander said. "Now they going out on them."

Mingo County Sheriff George T. Blankenship had just arrived by train from Williamson. He walked to the site of each fallen coal company gunman. When he saw the men showing off the body on the litter of Winchesters, he called them out for that.

"I got no use for thugs," the Sheriff said, "but we ain't gonna make a spectacle of them, neither."

He ordered that each bullet-riddled body be placed in a pine box, and loaded on the train back to Williamson.

Word spread on the street that more Baldwin-Felts detectives might be on their way from Bluefield, so the Sheriff deputized all the men he could to stave off further violence. Johnny was signed up as a special officer twice on the same day.

Johnny learned that evening that six of the hired gunmen found their way out of town. Some hid in the woods, or under a porch, or in a garbage can, and made their escape when nobody was looking. Two swam the Tug for greener pastures, but Johnny knew that none of them who lived through the shootout would soon forget the fury of a people squeezed to the breaking point in bloody Mingo County.

Chapter 41

This day was the second Sunday of the month in June, twenty-five days past the Matewan shootout—a rough time for every resident of the town.

It was a welcome day off for Johnny. He just returned to the house after visiting Baby Elsie's gravesite. He laid down a freshly plucked bouquet of daisies he gathered from the field. It was now over two months since Big Jake had dashed the life out of his daughter, and tears still filled his eyes and rolled down his cheeks when he thought of it, especially when he stood beside her grave. He wondered if he would ever get used to it so that he would not shed tears. He hoped not.

He felt bad that Kate had to witness Elsie's killing and that she had been roughed up by Big Jake. But he was so proud that she chased after the killer as he tried to get away and stood up for the dignity of their precious little baby. And to think she had to stand trial for that! Jake was cut down to size by a woman and got what he deserved. How dare they charge his wife with murder! Just another thing to get through. He believed in Mr. Tucker and could see no way they could convict Kate of murder, because that ain't what happened.

"Corey, you ready to go out to tent city?" Johnny called out.

"Yeah Pa," Corey answered from inside the house. "Just adding some bread and eggs to the grocery bag. Can Pete come along?"

"Don't see why not. This is a good thing we're doing," Johnny said as they walked down the path to the east meadow. "Stella ain't had much since Jim was killed. Least we can do is bring her some food."

"Yeah, I suppose so."

"Taking care of widows and orphans is the Lord's work," Johnny said. "Hi Pete. Corey tells me you're out of the breaker house now, working in the mine."

"Yep, working as an assistant."

"You pretty young to be working like that."

"Yeah, they like me 'cause I can climb into small places," Pete said, "and I'm fast."

"Pa, can I ask you a question? How come Ma's got to be on trial for killing Big Jake when all she done was try to protect Baby Elsie, and nobody has to go on trial for killing Jim Mullins?"

"Well, that's a good question, son. For one thing, the man who shot Jim was killed in the gunfight."

"He was? Who killed him?"

"Well, I never heard nobody say," Johnny said. "There was so much general shooting, maybe nobody knows."

"Are any of those Baldwin-Felts men gonna stand trial?" Corey asked.

"Well, we'll find out," Johnny said. "They got a grand jury working on it."

"What's that?"

"It's a group of people the community picks out to look into something big, like the Matewan shootout."

"Then what happens?" Corey asked.

"Well, they might recommend that people stand trial," Johnny said. "Look, there's Stella and the kids!"

Corey and Pete ran up ahead and hugged the Mullins kids.

"Let's go throw some rocks," Pete said.

"Yeah, or find some turtles," said Corey.

The kids ran off to the open field. Johnny sat down on a rock by the fire circle, and Stella brought out a little milking stool for herself.

"How you doing?" Johnny asked.

"Doing okay, thanks to friends like you bringing us food."

"Least we could do."

"How's Kate?" she asked. "They still holding her in jail?"

"Yeah, just to be safe," Johnny said. "Never know if somebody might want to kill her before the trial."

"This is so hard to believe. Is the trial gonna happen soon?"

"This week. We'll be taking the train to Williamson tomorrow, then we'll see where it goes."

"What's this I hear about a grand jury?" Stella asked.

"Yeah, the County Prosecutor ordered a grand jury to try to figure out what happened in the shootout. Lots of people being asked questions, but it's hard to figure out."

"Why's that?"

"Everything happened so fast," Johnny said. "People could have looked away when somebody got shot, and he got shot, but nobody knowed how it happened!"

"You think they'll do the right thing?" Stella asked.

"Who knows?" Johnny said. "But I hope so. I really hope so.

. . . .

Johnny and Corey walked through Stone Mountain Housing as Pete split off to go to his house.

"Could I go and play ball with Pete?" Corey asked.

"All right," Johnny said, "but you need to save some time to see your ma today, okay?"

Johnny entered Sid Hatfield's office, greeted the lawman, and walked into the back room. Kate lay on her bunk looking like she was asleep, facing the wall with her back to the bars.

"Hey Sweetie, you okay?" Johnny said.

Kate rolled over, looking sleepy but apparently glad to see her husband. She rocked herself out of the bunk with some effort and looked uncomfortable.

"You sure you're okay?" Johnny asked again.

"Yeah, just a little queasy."

"Where you hurting, Sweetheart?"

"Kind of in the stomach," Kate said.

"You need something to eat?"

"Oh no, no, no," she said, extending her left hand.

"How long you been feeling bad?"

"Since right after breakfast," she said.

"Was the food okay?" Johnny asked.

"Yeah, there was nothing wrong with the food," Kate said. "But as soon as I finished it, I just felt stuck, like it wasn't going up and it wasn't going down. And now I'm feeling..."

Just then Kate jumped to her feet and ran to the commode. Her retching was loud and deep, and she emptied the contents of her stomach faster than a tick could draw blood from a mule's ear.

"Sid, can you give me the key?"

"What's going on?" Hatfield asked. "She okay?"

"She's throwing up hard," Johnny said. "Can we get Dr. Barnes to come over?"

"Well, it's Sunday, but I'll see what I can do."

Kate stopped throwing up, but seemed exhausted, and needed to lie down. She held her stomach and moaned faintly. Johnny brought her a glass of water, but kept an ear on the police chief out there on the phone.

"Dr. Barnes, this is Sid Hatfield, Police Chief. We got a prisoner over here who's throwing up, and we'd like you to come over...yes, today! Shouldn't matter who it is. She needs help now!...Yes, it's a woman...You don't call her that!...Listen you son of a bitch, I know it's Sunday and the mines ain't working today, but you're the company doctor, and people need doctors when they need them!

"The good doctor said he'd be happy to come right over," Hatfield said with a smile.

"Right!" said Johnny. "Well, willing or not, as long as he gets here, I guess that'll be a good thing."

One hour passed, and the doc still did not show. Johnny was getting anxious. Kate slept, but it was a restless sleep with groaning and tossing around. Johnny didn't think she looked comfortable and knew she was still sick.

"Sid, would you mind calling the doctor again?" Johnny asked.

Hatfield tried the doc again, but no answer.

"Probably on his way," the chief said.

Johnny sat right next to Kate and gently rubbed her back. Another hour passed and still no doc. Corey walked in and took alarm right away.

"What's wrong with Ma?" he asked.

"Her stomach's all upset," Johnny said. "Threw up her breakfast."

"We got the doc on his way," Hatfield said.

"I just walked past the saloon on the way over here," Corey said, "and I think I saw the doc standing around in front of the saloon. Had a glass in his hand."

"That son of a bitch," Hatfield said. "I'll go get him, and he better be able to act like a doc when he gets here."

Johnny and Corey sat quietly in the jail cell, trying to calm Kate and make her comfortable. She continued to twitch around on the bunk, and make those unsettled noises. Just then, she started the dry heaves. She rushed to the commode, but evidently her stomach had nothing to give up. For a full five minutes, she couldn't stop heaving. They finally helped her back to the bunk, but she wanted to sit in the chair. Half an hour passed, and Hatfield burst through the door with the doc in his clutches.

"So there's the fine company doctor, huh?" Johnny said.

"I'm all right, I'm all right," he said.

"How much you had to drink?" Johnny asked. "I'll never forget what you did to Kate's pa."

"Don't you worry about it. Just got waylaid a little bit," the doc said. "Good enough for what you got here."

"What you mean by that?" Johnny said.

"Well, it's Bitch McCarthy, ain't it? Killed a good coal company man?"

Johnny grabbed the doc by the shirt and cocked his right fist.

"Hold on there," Hatfield said. "I do the beating around here."

"You want me to treat the prisoner, or don't you?"

"Get on with it," Johnny said. "And then get out of here!"

"Okay, you say she's throwing up?" the doc said.

"Yep, that's what's going on."

"Well here, give her some of this stuff," the doc said. "A new-fangled medicine just invented by a doctor."

The bottle was dark brown, like all medicine bottles, but when Johnny poured the liquid out on a spoon, he was surprised.

"But it's bright pink!" Johnny said.

"What do you care what color it is?" the doc asked.

"What is this stuff?"

"Called Pepto-Bismol," the doc said. "Should stop her from throwing up."

"All right, we'll try it," Johnny said. "Now get out of my sight."

"Yeah, I'll get out of your sight," the doc said. "'Cause when I'm out of your sight, you'll be out of *my* sight. Company doctors got to treat all kinds of lowlifes and scum..."

The doc's voice trailed off as he stumbled out the door.

"Hope this'll help," Johnny said. "She gotta get better. Trial starts this week."

Chapter 42

Johnny arrived early at the jail to tend to Kate and help Sid Hatfield prepare her to get to Williamson.

"You have some breakfast today?" Johnny asked.

"No, I don't feel like it, but I'm okay," she said.

"You sure?" Johnny said. "I'll get you whatever you want."

"No, I don't need nothing, Sweetheart."

"That pink stuff do you any good?" he asked.

"Maybe," she said. "Maybe that's what it is."

"Now Mrs. McCarthy," Sid said, "I know you're no threat to me and no risk of trying to escape, but regulation says a prisoner being transported to trial has to be cuffed, so that's what I got to do."

"I understand," Kate said. "You know, Chief, you been so good to me and Johnny, but you don't have to apologize just for doing what you gotta do!"

"Ha! Just want to be sure you get into town safe and sound, that's all."

"You going with us, Chief?" Johnny asked.

"Yep, me and two deputies," Hatfield said.

"Two deputies?" Johnny said. "You expecting trouble?"

"No special reason to," Hatfield said. "But in a situation like this, you got to expect it anyway. Hank! Josh! You ready to move out?"

The five moved out the front door of the police chief's office. Sid Hatfield wore a gun belt with his two high-caliber sidearms. One deputy wore another two sidearms, and the other a sidearm on his waist and a Winchester in his hand. The two deputies walked on either side of Kate, Sid walked a little ways behind her, and Johnny found his way right next to Sid. Johnny was not allowed to be armed under the circumstances, but he felt pretty good walking right beside the police chief. With his skills and determination, Johnny knew Kate couldn't be in better hands.

They all walked up on the platform beside the waiting train. Johnny saw some passengers standing around farther down the platform waiting for the okay to board. He also noticed a handful of men standing back from the platform at ground level, maybe twenty feet away.

"Bitch!" one them yelled.

"Bitch McCarthy, ain't it?" another called out.

"Hope she gets what's coming to her," another one said.

"Yeah, hope she swings at the end of a rope, just like a man."

"Bitch!" The catcalls and insults didn't stop.

Johnny moved towards the edge of the platform and prepared to jump off to face up to the men. Hatfield grabbed him by the arm and started talking close into his ear.

"Listen to me a minute," Hatfield said. "Your job as this woman's husband is to stand up for her honor, and I can see you're ready to do that. My job as police chief is to get her to Williamson safely and deliver her to a locked cell where she will be protected by sworn law enforcement."

Johnny stood looking directly into Hatfield's eyes.

"Now, the only time you don't get to enforce your job to stand up for her honor, is if it gets in the way of me doing my job."

"What you talking about?" Johnny asked.

"You run out there and take on those four idiots," Hatfield said, "and you either get in trouble where one or more of us got to go out there and help you, or even if we just get distracted 'cause you're kicking their asses so good, she could get shot or hurt just because our security ain't what it should be, you know what I mean? Now I know you don't want to do something stupid that gets your wife hurt."

"Well, of course not!"

"Then come on back over here with us," Hatfield said. "Your wife's honor is intact. She ain't done nothing wrong. Once the court clears her, you won't have to defend her honor. Her honor speaks for itself. So just come over here. The more people we got around her, the more protection she's got."

"All aboard," the conductor called out from the lowest step on the car.

Kate and Johnny, along with Hatfield and his deputies, climbed the steps that led up into the car. The passengers was all scattered out in the car, and about half the seats was filled. Johnny could see that there would be no way for all of them to sit together unless the chief moved everyone around. The people sat and stared as the party moved towards the back of the car. Johnny figured they either heard of the case and knew why Kate was cuffed, or the sight of a woman in custody wearing manacles was so unusual and riveting they just couldn't help but be stunned.

Hatfield led the way and moved from the car they entered to the next car to the rear. As they all got back there, Johnny could see there was only about six or eight passengers.

"Listen up," Hatfield said as he held up his badge. "I'm Police Chief Hatfield and we're transporting a prisoner, so we need you all to move forward to the next car and find a seat there. Plenty of room."

A woman and a child, and a man traveling alone, stood and moved out of the car as Hatfield had asked. Then a few others got up and carried their stuff to the next car, except for one man who sat rigidly like a fixture, like he was deaf.

"Excuse me sir," Hatfield said. "Maybe you didn't hear me, but I'm asking you to move into the next car."

"Why?" the grizzly middle-aged man asked.

"Cause I asked you real nice."

"Don't have to," the man said. "I paid for my ticket and I can sit where I want."

"When a police officer asks you to do something," Hatfield said into the man's ear, "and there's a police reason for you to do it, you got to do it. Else you in violation of the law."

"Why can't I sit here?"

"Because we transporting a prisoner, and if you don't follow my orders, you jeopardizing the safety of my prisoner."

"I don't give a shit!" the man said.

With that, Hatfield lifted the man up by his beard and walked him towards the door to the next car.

"Now listen to me," Hatfield said. "You interfering with the law and you could be arrested, but I don't want the distraction of having to keep an eye on you. But if you make me, I will cuff your hands behind your back, tie your feet and hogtie your ass, and carry you off this train like a suitcase. Or you can just move into the next car and sit there like a gentleman. Which suits you best?"

"Well, I'd say the next car would be all right," the man said. "Yeah, I could do that."

"I was hoping you'd see it that way," said Hatfield.

With the car to themselves, Johnny and Kate sat in one seat together. Hatfield and his deputies sat one man to a seat, surrounding the couple. The train started out of Matewan and Johnny was relieved. He felt that everyone was starting to relax, when all at once, a good-sized rock shattered a window near where they sat. The sound of the impact shot through Johnny like he'd been stabbed with a red-hot poker. He jumped up and kneeled over Kate to shelter her from anything that might come flying through the space inside the car. Hatfield also rose to his knees on the seat, watching, but not moving towards a window.

"Bastards!" he said.

"What should we do?" one of the deputies asked.

"Just ride the train out of town, boys," he said. "Just get on out of town."

The short ride to Williamson was easy the rest of the way. Johnny's eyes closed a couple times and his body wanted to slumber, but he would fight it. Every time his head wanted to nod, his body jerked straight up. It was almost as if to fall asleep was to abandon Kate, and that fought against every desire in his body. When the train squealed to a stop, Hatfield led the couple off the train with the deputies bringing up the rear. A car out of the sheriff's office had been assigned to pick them up and bring them to the courthouse, where an empty jail cell waited for Kate.

State Police stood in doorways, along corridors, and at the entrance to the jail. Hatfield showed his credentials and moved to the heart of the system with his prisoner. He uncuffed Kate and smiled warmly.

"Of all the prisoners I have delivered to jail," he said, "I ain't worried about you. You gonna be just fine."

Kate smiled.

"You gonna be staying some place close by?" Johnny asked.

"No, I have to go back to Matewan," Hatfield said. "But you be in good hands. The State Police working around the courthouse be taking good care of you. You'll be back home in no time. But get some good rest tonight. They get you up pretty early. You got jury selection tomorrow."

Chapter 43

"All rise," the bailiff cried out.

"The Eighth Circuit Court of Mingo County is now in session. The honorable James Damron presiding. You may be seated."

"Ladies and gentlemen," the judge started in, "thank you for being here today. We are here for jury selection in the case of the State of West Virginia vs. Kate McCarthy, charged with capital murder in the killing of Jake Moskowitz. I want to thank the men and women who are here for the jury pool. You will be called to the stand one at a time and questioned by the attorneys involved in the case. I want to also thank attorney Jacob Smith of the Mingo County Prosecutor's Office, and Public Defender Jeremiah Tucker, representing the defendant in this case. Will the bailiff call the first potential juror to the stand, please?"

"Isaiah Tillman, come to the witness chair please."

Johnny sat in the first row of the general audience. He was not allowed to sit next to his wife. He could not put his arm around her and comfort her. He was probably only ten feet from her, but it felt like ten miles. In this courtroom, she sat there by herself, and looked alone and defenseless. Johnny wished there was more he could do.

"Mr. Tillman, place your left hand on the Bible, raise your right hand, and repeat after me. *I, Isaiah Tillman… promise to tell the truth… the whole truth… and nothing but the truth… so help me God.*"

"You may be seated," instructed the bailiff. "For the record, please state your name."

"Isaiah Tillman," the man said.

Mr. Jacob Smith of the Mingo County Prosecutor's Office approached the stand.

"Mr. Tillman, what is your occupation?"

"I'm a supervisor with the Red Jacket Coal Company," the man replied.

"So you're a coal operator?"

"Yes sir."

"And how long have you worked for the coal company?"

"I've worked for Red Jacket for about twenty years," Tillman said.

"And what is your age, sir?"

"I'm thirty-four years old."

"So you started working in the mines when you were about fourteen years old?"

"Yes sir."

"In what capacity did you work at the age of fourteen?"

"I started out as a breaker boy," Tillman said. "Then I was a nipper, and then a spragger."

"So you've worked in the mines," Smith said. "And when did you start working in management for the coal company?"

"I was about twenty," Tillman said. "There was an opportunity to become a supervisor, so I took it."

"And are you a resident of Mingo County?"

"Yes sir."

"How long have you lived in Mingo County?"

"All my life," Tillman said.

"Where were you born?" Smith asked.

"Red Jacket."

"And Mr. Tillman, what is your interest in being part of the jury in this case?"

"To see that justice is done," Tillman replied.

"And do you feel that you could be a fair and impartial juror in this case?"

"Yes sir. Absolutely."

"That's all the questions I have your honor," Smith said.

Mr. Tucker approached the stand.

"So Mr. Tillman, you have worked both sides of the fence," Tucker said. "You have worked as a coal miner, and you have worked as a coal operator."

"That's right, sir."

"And if my math is correct," Tucker continued, "you worked in the mines for the first six years of your working life, from the age of fourteen to about the age of twenty."

"That's right."

"And then for the next fourteen years, you worked as a supervisor for the coal company."

"Yes sir."

"And after this twenty some odd years of employment, where would you say your loyalty lies, with the miners or with the coal operators?"

"I object, your honor!" Jacob Smith called out. "That is not a fair question, what with the last fourteen years being in the employ of management in the coal company."

"You saying his loyalty is most obviously with the coal operators?" the judge asked.

"Well, uh, no sir. I'm just saying it's an unfair question, that's all."

"The prospective juror is directed to answer the question," the judge said.

"Well sir, when I was with the coal miners, I was very young, just a boy, and I tried to live up to what everybody expected of me. And for the last fourteen years, I tried to do my job to suit my employer. So I'd have to say that now, my loyalty is with the coal company."

"I appreciate your honesty, Mr. Tillman," Judge Damron said.

"And have you ever, in your time working with the miners, experienced what it's like to be evicted from company housing?" the Public Defender asked.

"No sir."

"And have you ever harassed any of the miners under your supervision?"

"No sir."

"Do you have children, Mr. Tillman?"

"Yes sir."

"And have any of your children ever been harassed or abused by coal operators?"

"Your honor, I object to this line of questioning!" Smith called out.

"Sustained! What are you trying to prove, Mr. Tucker?"

"Just that with a bias towards the coal operators, a juror is not likely to understand the position of the defendant."

The debate continued like this into the third day. Johnny was growing tired of the arguments, the debates, the positioning. Couldn't they just find honest men who would live by the courage of who they was and what they believed? And what about women? There was women in the jury pool, but none had been taken seriously. None appeared to have a real chance of being called into service. Johnny thought he'd heard something about being judged by a jury of your peers. What about that? In Kate's case, wouldn't that include having women on the jury? He didn't feel good about how this trial was shaping up.

Johnny knew that Mother Jones was speaking at a rally in town on Friday. It was now Thursday night. He felt sure she must be in town already.

. . . .

Johnny walked down Main Street to the Panorama Hotel. He had been told the Panorama had a large meeting hall and stage big enough for a convention. It was the largest hotel in town. If Mother Jones was speaking, she'd be speaking to a lot of miners, and he figured there was a good chance this would be her location. He searched the restaurant but she wasn't there. He walked through the bar but didn't expect that she would be in there. He walked through the open patio areas and the parlors and sitting rooms of the hotel and could not find her. Finally, he went to the registration desk.

"Excuse me," he said to the clerk. "Is Mother Jones speaking here tomorrow?"

"Yes, she is," he said. "She'll be in the Ambassador Room at seven o'clock."

"Can you tell me where she's staying tonight?" Johnny asked.

"Lose my job if I did that," the clerk said.

Johnny turned away and walked through the huge lobby. Just then, through the east door came a bunch of men in suits, led by a white-haired woman in black with white lace.

"Mother Jones!" Johnny called out.

Two of the men rushed to block Johnny while the others whisked her away from the intruder.

"Mother Jones, it's me, Johnny McCarthy!"

Mother Jones turned and looked at him.

"I'm the guy who gave you..."

"I know who you are," she replied. "Got it right here."

She pulled the blarney stone out from her garments and let it dangle from its leather cord.

"Mother Jones, I've got to talk to you."

"What's wrong, son?"

"Mother Jones, please," he said. "Can we just sit for a minute?"

Johnny took her by the hand and led her over to an ornate Victorian couch. The men walking along with her looked puzzled, but was not about to overrule her.

"Mother Jones, my wife is on trial for murder this week here in Williamson," he said. "She killed a coal operator who just killed our baby. He was about to toss our baby into the pit behind an abandoned backhouse. So to save her from this horrible treatment, my wife cracked him on the back of the head with an axe."

Mother Jones looked at Johnny like she didn't understand.

"I'm sorry for your loss," she said. "But it sounds like the bastard had it coming!"

"He did," Johnny said. "But here's the problem. They've been picking jurors for three days now, and they're about to announce the jury."

"So what's the problem?"

"I don't think there's gonna be one woman on the jury," Johnny said, "and most of the men they're picking are coal operators. She could hang by the neck!"

Chapter 44

The courtroom was full of possible jurors and spectators, people who just couldn't stay away because the stakes was high and the happenings was about to get real interesting. As Johnny walked in he could hear the buzz. He spotted the empty seat in the front row saved just for him, so he could sit near his wife, though not with her. As he moved towards this up front position, the buzz elevated to an awestruck racket as the woman who had pierced the hearts of management and labor alike all over the country walked through the door, Mother Jones! Johnny was proud that she agreed to attend, but didn't know how she would speak up in court or make a difference with the judge. He waved for Mother Jones to come to the front row and take her seat. Then he moved to a place on the back wall.

"All rise!" the bailiff called out. "The Eighth Circuit Court of Mingo County is now in session. The Honorable James Damron presiding. You may be seated."

"I want to thank the residents of Mingo County who have come out to be considered for jury service in this case," Judge Damron started in. "Prosecuting Attorney Jacob Smith and Public Defender Jeremiah Tucker have submitted to the court a list of the twelve jurors they have proposed to serve in this action. Nine of the names are the same. Nine they have agreed on. They find nothing lacking in the nine. Nor do I. So there are three names that we have to work on.

"First, "the judge continued, "it has been discovered that one of the selected jurors on the prosecutor's approved list, a Mr. Isaiah Turner, is a convicted felon as of six years ago, in a case up in Boone County."

"On what charges?" Mr. Smith asked.

"Mr. Smith," the judge responded, "the case is a matter of public record, of course, and you can check on that later. But so as to save Mr. Turner any unnecessary embarrassment, we'll not reveal that at this time. Mr. Turner, you are dismissed from jury service."

The man rose to his feet and walked out of the courtroom.

"Another juror candidate," continued the judge, "submitted by the Public Defender, is the only woman candidate to make the list, though several have been interviewed, Mrs. Rosalie Johns. Prosecutor Smith, I'll allow you to make your arguments before the court."

"Thank you, your honor," Jacob Smith said, rising to his feet. "While it is commendable of the Public Defender to want to have a woman on the jury, after interviewing the several women who have been considered here these last few days, I would submit to the court that those in the jury pool are women of no special qualification, that they do not have an education, do not have experience in the world of business, do not understand how things work in the courtroom. These are simple-minded women whose life experiences have been limited to household chores like raising children, doing laundry, cooking, and providing for the needs of their family. And while that is certainly commendable, it does not qualify such a woman to make judgments on weighty court matters."

"I object, your honor!" Jeremiah Tucker called out.

"Mr. Tucker, these were Mr. Smith's thoughts on the matter," the judge said. "You can't object to his thoughts, but you can present the other side. Mr. Smith, do you have any further comment?"

"No, your honor."

"Mr. Tucker, you may now proceed."

"Well, your honor," Tucker said. "It just seems to me that if these are the best and most qualified women we've got in these parts, then they ought to be considered for service on the jury."

"That's it, Mr. Tucker?"

"Uh, yes your honor."

"All right," the judge continued. "Let me summarize the last two objections to jury service. On Mr. Smith's list, there are two names, Elias Miller, and James Taggert. Mr. Smith, my understanding is that you oppose Mr. Miller because at the age of twenty-six, he continues to live on the family farm and has never been engaged in coal mining, even though coal mining is the dominant industry in Mingo County, and in fact is the industry the parties to this court case have been engaged in, and although he does live in Mingo County, the only work he has ever done is farming, is that essentially correct, Mr. Smith?"

"Yes, your honor."

"And your objection to Mr. Taggert is essentially the same, though an issue a little bit different," the judge continued. "Mr. Taggert is a resident of Mingo County but has worked all of his life in the stables, shoeing horses, grooming, tending to the animals in their various needs, but never embracing the coal miner's lifestyle. Is that essentially correct, Mr. Smith?"

"Yes, your honor."

"The two juror candidates that our Public Defender, Mr. Tucker objects to are Kenneth Robertson, who is a mine supervisor at the Red Jacket Coal Mine, and Ernest Johansen, an operations foreman, also of the Red Jacket Coal Mine. Your objection, Mr. Tucker, if I understand you correctly, is first of all that these two men work for the same company and know each other, and that they are part of management, and therefore may be biased against a coal miner's wife, is that essentially correct?"

"Yes sir."

"Now there are other coal operators who have been submitted for the jury that you have not objected to. Why do these two stand out as objectionable to you, Mr. Tucker?"

"They just seem more deeply entrenched to me," Mr. Tucker said, "and less likely to give the defendant a fair trial."

"Do you have anything to say Mr. Smith?"

"Yes, your honor," Smith said. "I would like to say that these are good and honest men, that they are business-savvy men who understand how things work, that they are intelligent enough to know when a crime has been committed. I believe they are a valuable part of a jury that can get at the truth in a case like this."

"Thank you Mr. Smith," the judge said. "I'm going to call for a thirty-minute recess and consider the arguments that have been made in this phase of the trial. I will make a decision and also select an alternate for the juror who has been dismissed. Court is in recess until 11:30 A.M."

Johnny's heart was in his throat. He had brought Mother Jones into the courtroom for moments such as this. He couldn't understand why, in the discussion of women jurors, she didn't jump into the conversation. Was she just going to sit there? Maybe she didn't want to be out of order, but Johnny didn't think that would bother her with so much at stake. And the Public Defender! Couldn't his arguments be stronger? Couldn't he make a better stand for his beloved Kate? He didn't want to think what could happen in the event of a loss in this court case. Johnny was working his way towards the front of the room when he heard Mother Jones engaging his wife.

"Hello dear," Mother Jones said to Kate. "I've heard so much about you. You must believe things are going to work out. You're going to be okay. The truth is on your side."

"I hope so," Kate said.

Mother Jones picked up Kate's hand.

"You don't seem well, dear," Mother Jones said. "Are you feeling all right?"

Johnny placed his arms around his wife. She gently started to cry.

"You're gonna be all right," he said.

"It doesn't seem like it." Kate said. "What will I do if I can't be there for you and Corey?"

Johnny and Kate cried in each other's arms and comforted one another best they could. Before they could believe it, the bailiff called the court to order and Judge Damron sat back down on the bench.

"Ladies and gentlemen," he started in, "in considering the arguments put forth regarding the juror candidates, I am going to allow Kenneth Robertson and Ernest Johansen to be part of the jury, and I'm going to replace Isaiah Turner, as well as Rosalie Johns as the one woman candidate, with alternate jurors."

Mother Jones stood at her chair. Judge Damron started to continue his instruction to the court, but when he looked out at the audience, Johnny noticed that he saw Mother Jones standing. He almost flinched back like he'd run into a tree.

"Your honor," she said.

"Madam, you are out of order," the judge said.

"Your honor, I am Mother Jones."

"I know who you are, madam. But this is not a parlor somewhere in a rooming house, nor is it a rabblerousing platform where you can stir things up. It is a court of law!"

"Your honor, I come to you in the deepest respect for the law," Mother Jones said. "Please just hear me for one minute. One minute is all that I ask."

"And why should I give you any time at all?" the judge asked.

"Because I am interested only in justice, your honor. I only want what is right to prevail, and there is so much at stake here."

"And if I deny your request, is it your intention to go into a disruption and turn my courtroom into a circus?"

"Oh no, your honor. I am on good behavior. Everywhere I go I am followed by an ample contingent of the press. Half the men at the back wall are reporters. And even if you cleared the courtroom, they would talk to me outside."

"Very well, madam. Your clock is ticking!"

"Thank you, your honor," she said. "To have a fair trial for the accused, is she not entitled to a jury of her peers?"

"Madam, the sixth amendment to the constitution calls for a fair cross-section of the community to sit in judgment. It is to be a jury without bias."

"Yes sir, but is it not true that with so many coal operators on the jury there is a high likelihood of bias in favor of the deceased and against the defendant?"

"We have both miners and coal operators," the judge said. "It is a fair cross-section of the community."

"But your honor, how can it be fair if not one woman is on the jury?"

"Women don't even have the right to vote," Damron said. "How can we put them on a jury?"

"Your honor, I have never had the vote, and I have raised hell all over this country. I have given my voice to issues that mattered. I have made a difference in the affairs of men. The case before this court is an issue that matters because an individual's life is at stake. Should she not have one woman on the jury to share her perspective?"

"It becomes an issue of qualification," Damron said. "What woman among us would be qualified to sit on a jury?"

"Would you consider me qualified, your honor?"

"Yes, but you are the exception. You are an educated, articulate woman. But you are not qualified because you are not a resident of Mingo County."

"Your honor, have you heard of the poet William Ross Wallace?"

"I believe I have," Damron said. "Nineteenth century. A contemporary of Edgar Allan Poe."

"Your honor, his most famous poem was *The Hand that Rocks the Cradle, is the Hand that Rules the World*. He talks about the value of a woman's influence, her nurturing, her wisdom, her understanding of life. Because a woman devotes herself to her family does not mean she is not intelligent, that she cannot understand the issues in a court case."

The judge sat, reflecting on what had been said.

"Very well, madam," the judge said. "You may be seated. I would like to recall Rosalie Johns to the stand. I would remind you, Mrs. Johns, that you are still under oath."

"Yes sir."

The woman sat at the witness stand and looked at the judge.

"Mrs. Johns, what is your family situation?"

"I have been married to my husband for sixteen years," she said. "He has been a coal miner that whole time. We have three children, two boys and one girl. Our oldest boy is fourteen and he works as a nipper in the mine. The other boy is twelve, and he works in the breaker house."

"And this is the Red Jacket mine?"

"No sir, this is at Chattaroy."

"And what is the age of your daughter?"

"She's five."

"Mrs. Johns, what do you think about a woman's right to vote?"

"Well sir, I believe women *should* have the right to vote. We make a difference in life, and I believe we should have a say in how things go."

"And do you think women *will* get the right to vote?"

"Yes sir, I do. I believe Congress votes on that later this year."

Mother Jones turned around and caught Johnny's eye. She broke into a big smile with that answer to the judge's question.

"Mrs. Johns, do you know who the president of the United States is?"

"Yes sir, it's Woodrow Wilson."

"And the governor of West Virginia?"

"Yes sir. It's John Cornwell."

"And how would you feel about serving on this jury?" the judge asked.

"I would welcome it," she said. "I would just want to have a part in seeing the right thing is done."

"And you feel you could be impartial, that you wouldn't be siding with the defendant just because she is a woman?"

"No sir, I wouldn't do that," she said. "I just want to see the right decision being made."

"And the defendant is not personally known to you? You are not friends or acquaintances?"

"No sir."

"Mrs. Johns, you may step down."

Mother Jones looked back again at Johnny.

"It is the decision of the court," the judge said, "that Rosalie Johns will sit on this jury. The court will recess until Monday morning, June 21st. Arguments will begin at 8:00 A.M."

"Your honor," the Public Defender called out. "Could I have a continuance until July 12th to prepare my case?"

"Mr. Tucker," the judge said, "you have been assigned to this case for several weeks. With all that's been happening in Mingo County, and all that's on the court calendar, there will be no continuance. Arguments begin at 8:00 A.M. on Monday, June 21st.

"Court is adjourned!"

Chapter 45

"All rise!" the bailiff called out. "The Eighth Circuit Court of Mingo County is now in session. The honorable James Damron presiding. You may be seated."

"Members of the jury," the judge started in, "Prosecuting Attorney, Mr. Jacob Smith, Public Defender, Mr. Jeremiah Tucker, witnesses, and spectators, this court is in session to try case number 682870, the case of the State of West Virginia vs. Kate McCarthy.

"We will hear the evidence, and witnesses from both sides, and the jury will be asked to determine whether Mrs. McCarthy is guilty of the crime of capital murder in the killing of Jake Moskowitz. Mr. Smith, as Prosecuting Attorney and representing the state, will you please give your opening statement to the court."

"Thank you, your honor. Members of the jury, we shall present testimony from those who knew the victim in this senseless murder, that Mr. Moskowitz was a kind and gentle soul who bore no animosity to anyone, much less the wife of another man. We shall establish that when he visited the McCarthy residence on the day in question, April 5th of this year, he did so out of concern for Mr. McCarthy's well-being because he did not report to work that day. Mr. McCarthy's work record was without blemish and he never missed a day of work, period. We shall establish beyond a shadow of a doubt that the defendant is guilty of the senseless and vicious crime of capital murder, and should suffer the consequences."

Johnny sat just a few feet behind his wife in the courtroom, the same chair that Mother Jones occupied during the jury selection. Hearing this attorney spout these words as if they was true was infuriating. He wanted to defend Kate. He wanted to jump to his feet and take this man to the ground. How could he say these things? Anyone who knew Jake knew that was not the picture of this man—a kind and gentle soul? He was very near the point of at least shouting out to defend her with his words, but knew if he did, he would be kicked out of the courtroom and that would be worse. In his place, he wondered what Mother Jones would do. For now, he would hold his peace.

"Very well, Mr. Smith," the judge said. "Mr. Tucker, as Public Defender for the accused, you may make your opening statement."

"Thank you, your honor," Tucker said. "Ladies and gentlemen of the jury, well, uh, lady that is. My client, Kate McCarthy, has already admitted that she killed Jake Moskowitz, but in this case, it is the circumstances that will vindicate her of the charges of capital murder. We will establish through the defendant's own testimony that Mr. Moskowitz was hostile and violent when he came to the McCarthy house, that he barged in uninvited, that he slapped Mrs. McCarthy several times, and that he threw her baby against the wall, killing her instantly. When she defended the honor of her baby is when Mr. Moskowitz was killed. In the interest of justice, you will know without a doubt that you need to return a verdict of *Not Guilty*."

"Thank you, Mr. Tucker," the judge said. "Now we will turn again to the prosecution. Mr. Smith, do you have witnesses you'd like to bring before the court?"

"Yes, your honor. I'd like to call Max Thornberry to the stand."

After swearing to tell the truth, Mr. Thornberry settled into the witness box.

"Mr. Thornberry," Smith started in, "were you acquainted with Mr. Moskowitz, the deceased in this case?"

"Yes sir, I knew him for about fifteen years."

"And how is it that you knew him?"

"We both worked for the coal company," Thornberry said. "He was a foreman, and I was a supervisor."

"And over that fifteen years," Smith said, "do you feel like you got to know Mr. Moskowitz fairly well?"

"Yes, I'd say so."

"Did you know him as an even-tempered man, or one that was prone to violence?"

"I'd say he was even-tempered, calm, and most of the time, even cheerful."

"You never knew him to drown kittens, or kick puppies across the street, or throw babies against the wall?"

Laughter rippled through the courtroom. Johnny bristled again, but just then, Jeremiah Tucker sprang to his feet.

"Objection, your honor! The prosecutor should not trivialize what we shall present as facts in this case."

"Sustained!" the judge said. "Mr. Smith, try to be a bit more sensitive as you phrase your questions."

"Yes your honor. Let me rephrase that. Uh, would you say that Mr. Moskowitz was a decent man, one who respected the person and the property of others?"

"Yes, that's the way he was," Thornberry said.

"And on the day in question," Smith continued, "do you know what the occasion was of his visit to the McCarthy house?"

"Yes, he was going to find out if Mr. McCarthy was sick or something worse happened to him."

"So it was strictly a check on the welfare of the miner?"

"Yes sir, that's what it was."

"And can you think of any reason why violence might occur out at the McCarthy residence on such a visit?"

"Objection, your honor!" Tucker shouted out. "Calls for speculation on the part of the witness!"

"Sustained!" said the judge. "Mr. Smith, do you have any more questions for this witness?"

"Uh, no, your honor."

"Mr. Tucker, you may cross-examine."

"Mr. Thornberry, have you ever known of a history of trouble that Mr. Moskowitz might have had with the McCarthy family?

"No, I'm not aware of any run-ins or nothing like that," the supervisor said.

For two days it went back and forth like this, with the Prosecuting Attorney calling one witness after another testifying to the sainthood of Big Jake Moskowitz, and the Public Defender cross-examining, trying to call into doubt such an affectionate assessment of the foreman. Since there was no actual eyewitnesses to the action, the only witnesses that could be called on behalf of the deceased was character witnesses. Johnny was tiring of all the lies, but he could handle it because he understood the reason behind it. As long as Tucker didn't lose sight of the truth and continued to plant seeds of doubt in the testimony of the prosecution's witnesses, Johnny remained hopeful. His concern was for Kate, whom he felt must be taking every comment so personally because she knew the truth. He felt it must be so frustrating to Kate to hear the constant lies favoring Big Jake when she knew who he actually was.

Wednesday morning, the third day of the trial, it was finally Jeremiah Tucker's turn to call witnesses. Tucker had warned Johnny of his first call.

"Corey McCarthy, please take the stand."

After getting sworn in, Corey was ready to answer questions.

"Corey, you are the son of the defendant, Kate McCarthy and your father is Johnny McCarthy, is that correct?" Tucker asked.

"Yes sir."

"And you work as a mule-driver in the coal mine, is that correct?"

"Yes sir."

"Was there a time, maybe a few months ago, when this man known as Big Jake stopped by your house when you were at home?"

"Yes sir. I remember that visit."

"What stands out about that visit in your mind that you would remember it?"

"Big Jake busted down the door, and yelled a lot at my pa."

"What did he say to him?"

"He told him that this was company housing, and he could come in any time he wanted. And I remember he told my pa he needed to learn some respect."

"Did your pa have a response for him?

"Not much of anything," Corey said.

"Why not?"

"Well, first of all he was standing in the bathtub fumbling with his towel, dripping water all over the floor."

Laughter spread throughout the courtroom.

"And my pa was always careful about not making coal operators mad at him 'cause he wanted to keep his job."

"Did you have any other encounters with Big Jake?"

"Yes sir, once in the colliery," Corey said. "He roughed me up a little bit."

"You mean he actually struck you?"

"Yes sir."

"Why did he do that?"

"He heard that some of us broke up a beating that Old Man Morgan was giving to one of our friends, but he didn't know the whole story."

"Were you afraid of Big Jake?"

"Yes sir."

"In your experience, do you think of Big Jake as a good man?"

"No sir."

"Objection!" shouted Jacob Smith. "Calls for a conclusion."

"Overruled!" the judge yelled. "The boy can state his opinion based on his own experience!"

Johnny noticed the frustration on the prosecutor's face.

"Do you have any more questions for your witness, Mr. Tucker?" the judge asked.

"No, your honor."

"Cross-examination, Mr. Smith?"

"No, your honor."

"Court is in recess. We will reassemble after lunch at one o'clock."

Chapter 46

Lunch was a needed break for Johnny. Hearing witnesses sing the praises of Big Jake Moskowitz was becoming way too heavy. At least today, Corey presented some facts about the big man, though not without embarrassment to Johnny. Yeah, he just stood there dripping water. It was awkward and he didn't know what else to do, but at least the mean side of Big Jake was made known to the jury. That was the main thing.

Johnny thought about Mother Jones. He was thankful for the support she had been, and how she influenced the judge to allow that woman to sit on the jury. He felt it was important. Mother Jones was so busy yet so giving of her time. She was in Charleston in meetings this week, but had told Johnny she wanted to come back for the verdict. So Johnny sent a telegram to her hotel telling her that the case was wrapping up and would likely be in the jury's hands tomorrow. Least that's what people was saying, and it seemed right to Johnny.

He knew that court was about to start, but Johnny hopped the barrier separating the defendant's table and the audience, and embraced his wife one more time before court started up again. He leaned down and kissed his wife on the forehead with his arm around her shoulders. She looked tired and a bit down, but her testimony was coming up and he knew she'd feel better after this was over. He couldn't help but notice her skin was a bit warm and she didn't look comfortable. This would all soon be in the past, though.

"All rise!" the bailiff called out.

After the court was called to order, the judge asked Mr. Tucker to call his next witness.

"I call Brian Cooper to the stand," Tucker called out.

Cooper got sworn in and settled himself in the witness box.

"Now Mr. Cooper," Tucker started in, "where do you live and work?"

"I live in company housing just outside of Matewan, and I work in the mines."

"And are you a miner?"

"No sir, I'm a laborer."

"You're a laborer," Tucker restated. "Could you explain to the court exactly what it is that you do?"

"Yes sir. I install timbers and shore up the roofs and the ribs of the mines."

"Very well," Tucker said. "And in the course of your living and working around Matewan, did you have occasion to encounter Jake Moskowitz?"

"Yes sir. What happened was we had a puppy and he was out on the street, and Big Jake come walking along outside and he kicked the puppy, sent him flying in the air."

"Did you actually see him do this?"

"No sir, I was in my house, but I heard the yelp of the pup, and my son seen it, and he come and told me what happened."

"And then what happened?"

"I come outside and saw that the puppy was thrashing around on the ground and couldn't walk. My son pointed out Big Jake to me and I called out to him."

"And then what happened?"

"He come over and grabbed me by the shirt. Told me this was company housing and he was a foreman for the coal company, and he could come in here any time he wanted and do whatever he wanted."

"How tall are you, Mr. Cooper?"

"About five-seven on a good day."

"And how big was Mr. Moskowitz?"

"I don't know," Cooper responded. "Big man, for sure. Towered over me."

"Was it your impression that Mr. Moskowitz was a kind and a good man?"

"No sir, he was a mean son of a bitch!"

Judge Damron pounded the gavel. "Mr. Cooper, this is a court of law! You must keep your language to a civil tone!"

"Sorry, your honor."

In cross examination, Mr. Smith went right on the attack.

"Mr. Cooper, when you refer to Mr. Moskowitz kicking the puppy, isn't it true that you got that idea from the question I asked a previous witness about Mr. Moskowitz not drowning kittens or kicking puppies across the street?"

"I object, your honor!" Tucker called out.

"I'll allow the question," the judge said.

"No sir, it really happened. The puppy died that night."

"No further questions!"

After a brief recess, it was Kate's turn to take the stand. As she sat there before all, she looked only at the Public Defender. The setting seemed almost too big for her, like it would swallow her up, but she remained steady and calm, and Johnny knew she would present the truth the best she could.

"Mrs. McCarthy," Tucker started in, "would you relate the circumstances of your encounter with Jake Moskowitz on April 5th?"

"I was at home, taking care of my baby."

"You were inside the house?"

"Yes sir, and I heard some heavy stepping on my porch and then a loud rapping on the door. And then silence, and I was scared."

"Did you go to answer the door, or call out?" Tucker asked.

"No, I knew something wasn't right, so I just stayed quiet."

"And why did you remain quiet, Mrs. McCarthy?"

"Cause I was hoping whoever it was would just go away."

"So you didn't know who it was, and you were not looking for a confrontation. You just wanted this person to go away."

"That's right."

"And then what happened?"

"Big Jake started yelling and then I knew who it was, 'cause I heard his voice before. And I was scared because we had some bad run-ins before and I was alone with my baby."

"Then what did you do next?"

"I was trying to just stay quiet so he wouldn't know we was there, but Baby Elsie started crying at that point."

"Then what?"

"Then he broke down the door and come in, looking for Johnny. I told him to get out, that Johnny would talk to him about missing work when he got back. And that's when Big Jake got real mad and things started coming apart."

"And what happened next?"

"He told me I needed a lesson of respect, and that's when he tried to hit me, but I was holding Baby Elsie and I guess she was in the way, so that's when he grabbed her and threw her up against the wall."

Johnny sat still, tears welling up in his eyes.

"And then what happened?"

"I was just trying to find my baby," Kate said. "I kept calling her name, but there was no sound from her. She was just quiet. Jake slapped me a couple of times and I couldn't see much with the tears and being hit and everything. So I got up and ran across the floor looking for my baby, and Jake pushed me away and said he'd take care of it."

Johnny hung his head, hearing almost more than he could bear.

"Do you know what he meant when he said he'd take care of it?"

"There was a dead baby laying on the floor," Kate said. "That's what he was gonna take care of. He picked her up by the leg and was fixing to walk out the door with her. I charged at him one more time trying to get my baby. That's when he pushed me down on the floor."

Kate sobbed with her face in her hands. Mr. Tucker handed her a handkerchief.

"Did he say anything else to you?"

"He just told me I better keep quiet about this if I wanted my husband to keep his job."

"And then what happened?"

"He walked out the door, carrying my baby. So I ran to the doorway, and I saw where he was going. He was going down the pathway that led to that backhouse, the one that was closed now 'cause it was too close to the river. And I knew what he was fixing to do. He was gonna throw my baby into the filth of that pit at the backhouse."

The courtroom was dead silent listening to Kate's testimony, marked by her choking, fitful sobs. This was almost more than Johnny could bear.

"So what did you do?"

"He already killed my baby, but I couldn't let him throw her away like a piece of trash, so I grabbed our ax and ran after him."

"And you struck him with the ax?"

"Yes sir," Kate sobbed. "God forgive me, but that's what I done."

"No further questions, your honor."

The judge called for a ten-minute recess. Johnny held his wife and comforted her during that time, assuring her she had done a great job, and this would all soon be over. In the blink of an eye, court was back in session.

"Cross examine?" the judge asked.

Jacob Smith rose to his feet and drifted over near the witness stand, close to Kate.

"Mrs. McCarthy, as you were giving your testimony about what allegedly happened in your encounter with Mr. Moskowitz, you said that you got up and ran across the floor looking for your baby. Got up from what, Mrs. McCarthy?"

"Uh, well, I got up from my bed."

"So you were lying on your bed as you were talking to Mr. Moskowitz?"

"Yes sir."

"Isn't it true that you were lying on your bed *with* Mr. Moskowitz, that you were carrying on secret relations with Mr. Moskowitz, and when he threatened to make this known, you killed him with your ax?"

The courtroom broke into an uproar and Johnny had to be restrained by two of the State Police. Kate was hysterical in her crying and sobbing.

"No, no, no!" she cried out.

Judge Damron pounded the gavel and called for order in his court.

"Mrs. McCarthy," the judge said. "The prosecuting attorney has just asked a question. I understand it may be a question that is upsetting to you under the circumstances, but because he asks a question doesn't mean the answer is the affirmative. Just try to answer the question truthfully to the best of your ability."

"The answer is no, I was not having relations with that disgusting man! I have always been faithful to my husband!"

Tears was streaming from Johnny's face.

"More cross examination?" the judge asked.

"No, your honor."

"Any further witnesses, Mr. Tucker?"

"No, your honor."

"As there are no more witnesses, and no more questions for witnesses, tomorrow morning I will give instructions to the jury, and turn the case over to them.

"Court is adjourned!"

Chapter 47

This day Kate is set free, Johnny thought to himself. This day the nightmare is over. People will know his wife is a good woman and they can go home together and live in peace with their son.

Johnny moved towards the front of the courtroom, getting set up at his regular seat, right near to Kate. She and her attorney had not yet come into the room, but Johnny knew it wouldn't be long. As he was about to sit down, who walks up but Stella Mullins, Jim's widow. Seeing her and knowing she cared enough to take the train up here to Williamson filled Johnny's heart with gladness. He sure did like that. Then, just as he was about to sit down, Caleb Jackson and his wife Harriet walked in.

"We understand this is the big day," Caleb said as he patted Johnny on the shoulder. Harriet smiled at him and they sat down nearby. Then Corey surprised his father by walking into the courtroom.

"I didn't know you was coming today," Johnny said as he hugged his son.

"Thought it was pretty important," Corey said. "Wanted to be here to ride home with Ma."

Kate and her attorney walked out and took their seats at the table near the front. Kate shared a loving smile with her husband and son.

"All rise!" the bailiff called out. "The Eighth Circuit Court of Mingo County is now in session. The honorable James Damron presiding. You may be seated."

"Ladies and gentlemen of the jury," the judge began, "in the capital murder case of the state of West Virginia vs. Kate McCarthy, you have heard the witnesses, and you have heard the testimony, and it is your job to deliberate and arrive at a unanimous verdict, guilty or not guilty. If, based on the evidence, you believe without a shadow of a doubt, that the defendant maliciously and with premeditation killed the victim, Jake Moskowitz, then you should find her guilty. If you find that the death of Jake Moskowitz was not premeditated or malicious, then you shall find the defendant not guilty of the crime of capital murder. The bailiff will lead you to the jury deliberation room."

The jury walked out of the courtroom in single file, and the judge continued speaking.

"The defendant will be kept in the holding cell under protective custody until a verdict is rendered. Friends and family members of the victim or the defendant, as well as all spectators, will vacate this courtroom and wait in the hallways or at the front of this building until called to reassemble. Court is adjourned!"

Johnny was grateful for the presence of friends, especially his son, but he still kept an eye out for Mother Jones. He knew she was a woman of her word, and even though she was busy, and even though he hadn't yet seen her, he had confidence that she'd arrive as soon as she could. The people emptied the courtroom and stood around out front.

"How long you figure this'll take?" Caleb asked Johnny.

"Shouldn't take long," he said. "Pretty obvious what happened."

"You joining the union?"

"Yep," answered Johnny.

"They got a strike scheduled for July 1st," Caleb said. "You know what that means."

"Yeah, I know," Johnny said. "We be living in tents."

"Yep, and winter is coming."

"Yep. Gotta stand up, though."

Just then, a parade of people walked right up the courthouse steps, and in the lead was Mother Jones.

"Johnny, my boy, how you be this fine day?"

Johnny burst into a big smile and embraced the woman who had adopted him in her heart.

"They send the jury out today?" she asked.

"Yeah, they're talking about things right now," he said. "How long you think this should take?"

"I've learned to never predict a jury," Mother Jones said.

"Well, you made all the difference," Johnny said. "Can't thank you enough."

"It just had to be done."

At about 2:00 P.M., word came out that the jury had reached a verdict. Not bad. Just a few hours, he thought. Everyone hurried back into the courtroom—friends, foes, spectators—one and all. Kate sat next to her attorney at the defendant's table. Mother Jones sat at Johnny's immediate right, Corey to his left. The bailiff called the people to order and the judge asked the jury foreman to read the verdict.

"We the jury, in this case of the state of West Virginia vs. Kate McCarthy, find the defendant *guilty* of the crime of capital murder."

The reaction in the courtroom was like an explosion, but divided. Evidently there was more people liking the coal company than Johnny knew who didn't want to see the killing of a coal operator go without payback. They actually cheered. Others accepted what Kate had to say, and believed her and wanted her found not guilty. There was still others who knew Kate personally, and knew positively that she was not and could never be guilty of capital murder. Their reaction was disappointment and anger. Judge Damron nearly broke his gavel bringing the court to order. Stella Mullins cried openly, and tears fell from Corey's face but he bowed his head and remained silent. Mother Jones clutched onto Johnny's arm and looked at him with horror on her face.

Just then, Johnny noticed that the bailiff approached the judge up behind the bench and whispered in his ear.

"I'm going to call a ten-minute recess," the judge said, "but I want everyone to stay seated and remain exactly where you are in this courtroom. State Police and deputies that are on duty here are to see that no one leaves the courtroom and that no one enters. Does everyone understand me?"

The ten-minute recess seemed more like two hours to Johnny. He tried to move forward and comfort Kate, but the deputies would not allow it. He was in agony having to remain separated from her, unable to comfort her, unable to help in any way. And what did this verdict mean for the future? For Kate's future, and Corey's, and their future together as a family? There was an awkward silence in the courtroom. It was as if people wasn't sure if they could speak to one another or not. The judge had called a recess, but not really because people was not free to move around. Johnny put his arm around his son and encouraged him the best he could.

"All rise!" the bailiff shouted out. "Court is now in session."

"Mrs. Rosalie Johns," the judge began, "I need you to come and sit up here next to me on the witness stand."

As she approached the stand, Mrs. Johns looked haggard and beaten, like she'd been through a war. She also seemed afraid. When she settled in, Judge Damron began talking to her.

"Mrs. Johns, I want to remind you that you're still under oath," he said. "So it's very important that you tell me the truth, do you understand?"

"Yes sir."

"Mrs. Johns, in the jury room, when it came time to cast your verdict, how did you see it? Did you believe the defendant was guilty, or not guilty?"

"Not guilty, your honor."

"Then how is it that your jury foreman read a verdict of guilty?"

"Well sir, they tried to talk me into changing my mind, but I just couldn't see it."

"So you stuck with your verdict of not guilty?"

"Yes sir, I did."

"Mrs. Johns," the judge continued, "thank you very much for your service. You may step down now. Bailiff, what is the jury foreman's name again? That's right, Harry Grucker. Mr. Grucker, would you please come up here and sit on the witness stand."

Mr. Grucker took his seat, looking a bit nervous and scared himself.

"Mr. Grucker, you are still under oath, and I need to hear the truth from you as well. Do you understand me?"

"Yes, your honor."

"One of your jurors, Mrs. Rosalie Johns told me under oath that she cast a verdict of not guilty in this case. Is that the truth?"

Mr. Grucker fidgeted in his seat.

"Well, I guess."

"You guess?" the judge said. "You are the jury foreman. You're supposed to be a little more certain than just guessing."

"Well, she didn't seem real sure about it," Grucker said, "so I wasn't sure what she meant."

"Well, did she say *not guilty,* or did she not?"

"Um, yeah, I guess she did."

"You back to guessing again?"

"No, she did," Grucker said. "She said *not guilty.*"

"And everyone else said guilty?"

"Yes sir."

"And so you as the jury foreman just decided to ignore the vote of one of your jurors and go with the majority?"

"Well, no your honor. That ain't what I did."

"That's *exactly* what you did, Mr. Grucker. Bailiff, I want this man placed under arrest and taken to a holding cell. He will be charged with jury tampering, obstruction of justice, and interference with the law. In the case of the state of West Virginia vs. Kate McCarthy, I hereby declare a hung jury! The defendant is free to go!

"Court is adjourned!"

Chapter 48

The train from Williamson to Matewan was packed with happy people, at least the car Johnny was riding in. Each reacted differently to the turnabout in the courtroom. Smiles was everywhere.

"Did you see the look on the face of that jury foreman when they put the cuffs on him?" Caleb Jackson said. "Whooey! He didn't expect nothing like that!"

"That judge done did his job today," Harriet Jackson said. "He sure enough did."

Kate looked exhausted. Her face was all smiles, but she had nothing to say and leaned on her husband's shoulder through much of the journey back. She would raise her head up once in a while and favor everybody with a smile, and close her eyes and soak up the victory. Corey sat on the other side of her and stroked his ma's head with tears in his eyes.

"Mother Jones," Johnny said, "tell us again what you found out about what happened in that jury room."

"Well, it goes like this," Mother Jones said. "One of the deputies was in charge of guarding the safety of the jury and making sure no one tried to interfere with them, and he was sitting in this little alcove by the door. So he was in the same room as the jury but on the other side of this wall, and it seems like the jury, and especially the foreman, forgot that he was there.

"So they were just carrying on their business, and talking about the trial, and talking about Kate, and especially what a good man Big Jake was, and the foreman decided to take a vote and see what everybody thought. And eleven of the jurors voted *guilty*, but Mrs. Rosalie Johns, she voted *not guilty.* And the deputy said the discussion got really heated with the coal operators even threatening her and telling her if she knew what was good for her she would just go along."

"So they even threatened her?" Stella Mullins asked.

"That's what the deputy told me," Mother Jones said. "So then after all this and that, they decided to take another vote, and again all eleven voted *guilty*, but Mrs. Rosalie Johns. She stuck to her guns and said *not guilty.*"

"And the jury foreman just decided to lie about the vote, and say that all twelve of them agreed that Kate was guilty?" Stella said.

"Just like the judge said, that's exactly what he did."

"Lord, have mercy!" Harriet Jackson said.

"So after the jury foreman lied in court about the verdict," Mother Jones continued, "the deputy wasted no time in telling the judge right away, even before anyone could get up out of their chair and leave the room."

"Well, I'll say!" Caleb Jackson said.

Johnny noticed Mother Jones looking over at Kate with concern on her face. She got up and looked at Johnny like she was feeling sorry for Kate. She put her hand on Kate's forehead, and Kate opened her eyes and smiled.

"Dear, you don't look like you feel well," Mother Jones said as she placed her hand on Kate's forehead. "Seems like you may have a fever."

"Oh, I'll be all right," Kate said.

"Johnny, I think she needs to see a doctor," Mother Jones said.

"Ain't no doctor around here that I want to see," Kate said.

"That's for sure," Johnny said. "That company doctor as worthless as a dead mule."

"I know a doctor in Charleston," Mother Jones said. "Very fine doctor. I think we should go in there tomorrow morning."

"Don't know how I'd pay him," Johnny said.

"He's a friend of mine," Mother Jones said. "We'll work something out."

. . . .

The next morning, Johnny walked into the union office on Mate Street, right across from the Urias Hotel. While he signed the papers to join the union and took the oath of allegiance, Kate crossed the street to look for Mother Jones at the hotel.

In no time, the three of them boarded the Norfolk & Western and headed for Charleston. Johnny felt relieved that the trial was over and that they was doing something good for Kate's health. Kate had been through so much lately and Johnny knew she wasn't feeling good. Maybe a new doctor, this time a very fine doctor like Mother Jones said he was, could do Kate some good.

"What'd you say the doctor's name was?" Johnny asked.

"Dr. Davidson," she said. "Dr. Vincent Davidson."

"How you make his acquaintance?"

"Couple of years ago I was speaking at a union rally in Charleston," she said. "There was a collapse in a mine off of Quarrier Street and he personally came out there. A little ten-year old boy got his foot crushed. Ended up losing his leg below the knee. Dr. Davidson jumped right in, dress-white shirt and all. He didn't care. All he cared about was helping that little boy and I credit him with saving his life that night. He's a good man, and a fine doctor."

Johnny felt very satisfied as the train rolled down the track towards Charleston, towards new discoveries and new people. He felt hope for a better future. He just knew Kate was gonna get better. He valued Mother Jones in his life now. He found it hard to believe she was actually a personal friend now, one who had already made a big difference in their lives. He appreciated her life and work even before he knew her personally, but now as a presence in his and Kate's life, he knew the effect of her influence and the power of her will.

It was a pleasant ride into Charleston. For some reason, Johnny was able to see the beauty of the mountains and the richness of the trees as an outsider would, detached for a brief time from the struggles and challenges of life in the mines. A visitor to these parts would see nature at its finest—a lovely place, even peaceful.

The train pulled into the Charleston depot and they took a cab down Kanawha Blvd to a bridge that spanned the river of the same name. Across to McCorkle Blvd and they found the office of Dr. Vincent Davidson. His nurse brought him out to greet the travelers.

"Mother Jones," the doctor said. "So good to see you!"

He embraced her and held on for a long time.

"I knew you were in the area," he said, "but I can't keep up with you."

"These are two friends of mine," Mother Jones said. "This is Johnny McCarthy, and his wife, Kate."

"Pleased to meet you," the doctor said. "What can I do for you today?"

"We wanted you to take a look at Kate," Mother Jones said. "She's been through a lot lately and hasn't been feeling well."

"All right, well we can use the examination room down the hall," the doctor said. "Let's see, Mother Jones, would you like to accompany me with Mrs. McCarthy, and my nurse, and Mr. McCarthy, you can wait here in the lobby? Is that all right?"

"Yeah, that's fine," Johnny said.

Truth be told, Johnny actually felt relieved. He wanted Kate to get the help she needed, but he wasn't all that good with the hands-on stuff, and he was glad Mother Jones was there to keep company with Kate and make her feel good. He was really glad Mother Jones knew this doctor so well and had so much confidence in him. Johnny was feeling very good about the whole situation.

He picked up a magazine sitting on a lamp table, *Field and Stream*. It had a picture on the cover of a man bringing in a smallmouth bass out of some river. Wow, thought Johnny. He hadn't been fishing in a while. Reminded him of some tricks Leonard and Conan showed him out on the Tug. He looked at every page of the magazine, read some of the words, and enjoyed all the photos. In what seemed like only a moment, Dr. Davidson's nurse stood in front of him.

"Mr. McCarthy," she said. "The doctor would like you to come in now."

When Johnny walked into the doctor's office, Kate was crumpled in a chair, hiding her face, unwilling to make eye contact. Mother Jones had one arm wrapped around her, and would barely look at him. What could be so bad?

"Kate, what's the matter?" Johnny asked.

"Mr. McCarthy, have a seat right here next to your wife," Dr. Davidson said. "I'll explain what's going on."

"Yeah, what is it?" Johnny said. "Coming here was supposed to be a good thing."

"And it is," the doctor said. "First, I've given your wife a thorough gynecological exam, that is, her private, reproductive parts, and I've discovered some injuries. From childbirth, back in February, she's had some tears to muscle and one ligament. This has caused her a lot of discomfort. But I'm about seventy-five percent sure I can fix that through surgery so she'll be out of pain and can function more normally, which will be good for both of you. I think I can schedule that with the hospital in the next few weeks."

"Okay," Johnny said.

"The second issue," the doctor continued, "is more sensitive, I understand, due to the circumstances. But please, hear me out.

"Your wife is pregnant!"

Chapter 49

Johnny jumped to his feet.

"No, that ain't possible," he said. "You see, we ain't..."

Johnny started to turn in an angry fashion towards Kate and reached for her with his hands. Mother Jones jumped between them, as did Dr. Davidson.

"Johnny, listen to me," Mother Jones said. "It's not what you think. Doctor, is there a room where I can talk to Johnny?

"Yes, nurse would you show them to the examining room down the hall? I'll stay with Mrs. McCarthy."

In the very short time it took them to enter the room, Johnny's anger had got stronger. He was ready to punch someone. He remained standing when Mother Jones faced him. He did not want to sit. He did not want to calm down.

"Johnny, promise me that you'll hear me out before you run out of here," she said.

"Kate's telling me all these months that she's hurting down there so she can't have relations with me," Johnny said. "So she was lying and found somebody else?"

"Johnny, Kate loves you. She would never carry on with somebody else."

"Well, how else could you explain it?" Johnny said. "She ain't the virgin Mary!"

With that remark, Mother Jones looked down for a moment and then looked him in the eye in a most serious way. She put her hands on his arms and kept her gaze fixed into his eyes.

"No, you're not saying..."

Mother Jones pursed her lips.

"No, you don't mean that Big Jake..."

Her slight nod drove Johnny to the floor.

"Why didn't she tell me?" he said through sobs and tears.

"You had already lost Baby Elsie to Big Jake," she said. "You already knew that the bastard slapped her and threw her to the floor. She didn't want to hurt you even more."

"So she's been keeping this to herself all this time?"

Mother Jones grabbed his face and made him look right into her eyes.

"He raped her, Johnny. That she knew and that she has lived with for almost three months. But she didn't know she was pregnant!"

Johnny lowered his head and sobbed.

"Now what?" he said through his tears. "Don't I ever catch a break? What am I supposed to do now?"

"Well, for one thing," Mother Jones said, "you could start thinking about Kate and not so much about yourself. She's the one who was raped by this bastard. And she's the one who suffered injuries at his hand. You know, the tearing and damage that was done in childbirth was made worse by his attack."

"How bad does this have to get?"

"That's a question that depends on how you look at it," Mother Jones said.

Johnny continued to hang his head.

"Look at me," Mother Jones said. "*Look* at me!"

Johnny looked into her eyes.

"I can tell you this. Life is not fair, and bad things do happen. When I was a young woman, I was married to a wonderful man named George Jones. He was an iron molder. He was a strong man in the labor movement and he taught me a lot.

"We had four children and we lived in Memphis at the time. In one week, my husband and all four of my children got sick with the yellow fever and died. *In one week!*"

Mother Jones held up the single digit to throw attention on her loss. Johnny looked at her, stunned.

"For a few days," she continued, "I didn't know what to do. I used to live in Chicago, so I went back there. I was trained as a school teacher, and as a seamstress, and I guess I preferred sewing to bossing little children. I'd be working inside the home of a wealthy Chicago family and look through the plate glass window and see the poor and hungry walking by the frozen lake. I was all warm and comfortable, but they worked in a factory or a mill, and they couldn't *ever* earn enough to be comfortable.

"I was doing well. Had a nice house. In 1871, that all changed with the Chicago fire. Lost my house and all my belongings in the fire. So now what? No husband. No children. No house, and no belongings. All I had was my beliefs and my commitment to the working man. My address is now like my shoes. It travels with me. My home is wherever there is a fight against wrong."

Johnny hung his head.

"I feel so ashamed," he said. "I don't know what to say."

"No reason to feel ashamed," Mother Jones said. "Coal miner's life is a hard life. Ain't nothing easy about it. The thing is to make it the best life it can be, or get out."

"And do what? Mining's all I know."

"Exactly! And you're good at it, right? Most days you make full coal, don't you?"

"Yep."

"No matter where you go or what you do," Mother Jones said, "you got problems."

"That's the truth."

"The thing to do is be real good at what you do," she said. "Know your assets, and figure out how you can give to other people. Do that, and you can create a good life wherever you are."

Johnny looked at Mother Jones and didn't know what to say.

"See, one thing you've got on your side is a faithful woman who loves you very much," she continued. "I didn't have that. My husband was gone. Now you talked about feeling ashamed. Don't waste pity on yourself! Kate is the one who feels ashamed! She feels like she let you down, and she didn't do anything wrong! She needs somebody in her life to stand by her side and love her, and be her rock-solid strength, and let her know she's a wonderful wife and mother. That's what she needs! I wish to God I knew where I could find a man like that for Kate. That's what I wish!"

Johnny smiled, but couldn't stop the tears from falling just yet.

"I see why they call you Mother Jones."

"Yes, you and all the young men and children who go into the mines, and the factories, and the mills, wherever they are, are my children."

"I gotta go get my wife."

Chapter 50

Johnny awoke early this Monday morning, the first day of work in a week that he knew called for a strike. That would be Thursday, July 1st. He was new to the union, and this would be the first strike he had ever been through. The work stoppage had been talked about so much among the miners, he couldn't believe the coal operators didn't know about it. Seemed like common knowledge to him.

Kate began to stir.

"How you feeling, Sweetheart?" Johnny asked her.

"Pretty good," she said. "Slept really good. Let me get some breakfast going for you."

Kate seemed like she was gaining strength, though still a bit stooped over. Johnny figured with the trial over, the secrets out, and Mother Jones helping with her health problems, a lot of weight must be lifted from her shoulders. He figured that when the doc could get her in for surgery, things would get even better. Johnny finished getting dressed and ran out the door for the new backhouse at the end of the street. He got back and threw some dry wood chips over the embers from the night.

"You know, the strike starts on Thursday," Johnny said.

"Yeah, I know."

"I feel bad," Johnny said. "I mean if I'd of known, well, you know..."

"That I'm pregnant?"

Johnny hung his head.

"If you want me to go away, you just tell me," Kate said.

"No, no, no," Johnny said. "You are my wife and I love you. This is not your fault and I am with you every step of the way."

"How you gonna feel about this baby when it's born?"

"This baby's part of you, ain't it?" Johnny said. "Growing inside your belly. I'm gonna love it like it's my own."

Kate smiled.

"You a good man, Johnny McCarthy."

"It's just that if I'd of known, I could of waited a while before joining the union. At least we could of had a house for a little while longer."

"I'll be okay," she said. "Long as I got you to lean on."

Johnny walked out of the house eager to start the day. He knew he had three days to earn all he could before the strike. His pay wouldn't come in 'til after the strike had started, and if it was scrip, he didn't know if they'd let him shop at the company store. He didn't know how that would work. He'd have to ask somebody.

The air hung heavy over the Stone Mountain Coal Camp this Monday morning, what with the coal dust mixing with the dust from the dirt roads and the smoke from fires belching out of chimneys and rising off the bone piles and refuse in the streets. It kind of stuck to your clothes and lay heavy over your skin, not to mention burn your eyes and coat the inside of your mouth.

Mate Street was filled with miners and breaker boys headed for the colliery. Corey was already down the hole 'cause mule-drivers had to roust their beasts early and get them in the mood to pull coal cars. Johnny heard a few voices, men greeting one another, but mostly the men was silent as they trudged towards their entrance to the deep.

Johnny walked past the Urias Hotel, then the pool hall, then the drug store. On the way to the portals, he liked to walk past the drug store because they usually had a few left-over pieces of yesterday's Charleston Gazette, and he could check the headlines. Later, after he was down the hole, the Norfolk-Western would deliver the latest edition, and he'd start all over again the next day. He picked up the front page of the paper sitting there and held it up to the street lamp.

"GRAND JURY INVESTIGATES MATEWAN MASSACRE!"

Yeah, Johnny knew about that. The shootout was more than a month ago, and Judge Damron, the same judge who sat on the bench in Kate's trial, convened a grand jury to find out what the hell happened. Johnny was there, and the action took place so fast, he had a hard time remembering exactly the way things was. As he looked back on it, seemed like ten thousand shots was fired in about five minutes. Anybody who was there was caught up in the action, just swallowed up in the crazy things happening around them. Johnny couldn't see how nobody could make sense of it. Maybe the grand jury could.

Johnny walked up to the main portal and checked the clipboard. He was going down to level five to expand a new chamber they just opened up two weeks ago. That would mean low ceilings and cramped space. It was conditions he'd dealt with before, and he'd get through it.

"Hey Johnny," Caleb said as he reached for the clipboard. "Where you working today?"

"Level five, new chamber with a low ceiling."

"Looks like I'm going there too," Caleb said. "How's your wife doing?"

"She's glad to be home," Johnny said. "Not that that'll mean much in a few days."

"You mean 'cause of the strike?"

"Yep," Johnny said. "We'll be getting evicted just like all them other folks."

"Wonder when they be doing it," Caleb said.

"I don't know, but I'd like to already be gone when they do!" Johnny said.

"I hear you!"

Johnny knew that level five was below the bedrock of the Tug Fork River, and that water was likely to find its way into the tunnels and chambers. Water flowed down to its own level. Everybody knew that, and gravity sped up the process. They'd just have to figure out the conditions when they got there.

Johnny and Caleb stepped out of the man-cage at level five and moved down the gangway to their right. The new chamber wasn't far, and Johnny could see that the height of the excavation was no more than thirty-two inches or so. Barely rose up to their belts. The miners who worked here before, however, did get some width going for the new chamber. The seam appeared to be maybe twenty feet wide and the miners had carved out just under that for the opening. In depth, the chamber extended maybe fifteen to eighteen feet into the mountain. Coal mines, when you're down deep, was eerily quiet. The only sounds Johnny could hear was the leaking of water, and once in a while the squeak of a rat. Johnny knelt down and shined his headlamp into the depths.

"Whooo!" he cried out.

It wasn't for what he saw that he called out, but for the stench that almost knocked him on the seat of his pants. The tunnel was damp and puddles lined the floor of the new chamber. Johnny knew that no coal operators put backhouses inside the mine, and miners did their business where they could. The little chamber had become the toilet for the miners who worked the area. Unfortunately for him and Caleb, it looked like a lot of miners took advantage of the privacy of the new chamber, and the two of them would have to deal with it.

In addition, the ceiling in this new excavation was not high enough to roll in a coal car. All they had available was large buckets, about the size of what a miner would bathe in at the end of the day. They would have to knock coal off the ceiling with their pickaxes and then load it into buckets. Then they'd have to slide the full buckets the fifteen feet or so out of the chamber, and dump the coal into the cars sitting in the gangway.

"This is gonna be a lot of work for not much coal," Johnny said.

"Yep, looks like it's gonna be one of them types of days," Caleb agreed.

As Johnny set himself up under the low-hung ceiling, his dilemma became clear. Do I sit in a squat position and try to swing my pickax in an underhand lob, or do I kneel and give myself some room to swing with more leverage, or do I lay on my back in the water and the pee and the shit where I can barely take a swipe at the ceiling and glance off of it? Caleb could see Johnny's predicament and started laughing. Johnny, at first shocked, started laughing too.

In the end, the two of them did the best they could, trying all those positions and more. One of the real challenges was sliding a fully loaded bucket out of the low-hung chamber. The bucket would slide all right because of the slippery surface of the rock floor, but Johnny soon realized that he and Caleb had to use the same surface for traction to gain a footing to push on the bucket. Their hobnailed boots would not hold up to the task. By lunchtime, the men's clothes was saturated with water and pee, and smeared in human shit.

Johnny and Caleb posted up at the mouth of the chamber, out of the stench and facing into the main tunnel. A rat squeaked out of the darkness. They sat on a narrow bench wedged against the rib of the gangway. Johnny poured some water from his canteen over his hands so he could touch his food without throwing up. He realized he left his satchel just inside the chamber and stepped away from the bench, leaving his lunch pail behind. Caleb was sitting right there, but out of the corner of his eye, Johnny saw a giant rat come scurrying out of the darkness and leap up on the bench. In one fluid motion he spun around, hooked the handle of Johnny's lunch bucket with his tail, and streaked into the blackness. Caleb jumped up trying to help, but before Johnny could shout a warning, he saw another brute of a rat dash out of the darkness on the other side of the bench and make off with Caleb's lunch. He stood there with his hands out to his side and his mouth open.

At the end of the day, Johnny knew that he and Caleb hadn't put more than three tons of coal between them into the cars. Pretty sad for two grown men. Two skilled, certified coal miners, actually. Dear God, give me something good, Johnny cried out in his head. Give me something good for Kate, make her smile in her heart!

Chapter 51

Three days of work flew by, and at the same time crawled as Johnny looked ahead to the big day, the day he and more than a thousand miners refused to go down the hole. He didn't know what the day had to offer, but he found out that Fred Mooney, the secretary-treasurer of District 17 would be speaking to the men, as well as Frank Keeney, the District 17 president. That should be pretty special, he thought. With the big day finally here, Johnny kissed Kate good-bye and started walking out of the Stone Mountain Coal Camp towards the Matewan Community Church. Same open field as last time to the north and west of the church.

The sun was just filling the air. As Johnny walked past a green storage building on the outskirts of the church property, he noticed a huge spider web clinging to a corner of the little house. The other side of the web grabbed onto a nearby, mostly straight up tree branch.

The silk strands of the web shone bright in the new light and cradled dew drops here and there along the way. The web looked strong, and had lines that went side to side, up and down, and off at different angles. In the night, the web had done its work and ensnared a couple moths and a big horsefly. Of all God's creatures, even a spider casts out his net and gathers what he needs.

Johnny saw the usual faces in Caleb, Gino, Matthew, Sean and some others. Today their faces looked different. They carried a certain resolve, like they was preparing for a period of hardship for their families. In a way, they was all scared, Johnny thought, 'cause nobody knew what to expect. They all stepping out and putting it on their shoulders. No turning back now. They knew who they was, and they knew what they wanted, and that included Johnny. They'd just have to see how strong their will was, and how strong the coal operators' was.

Thursday, July 1st, 1920. Johnny figured would be a day he'd never forget as long as he lived.

Fred Mooney stepped up on the platform first.

"Hello men," he said. "Most of you know I'm Fred Mooney, secretary-treasurer of the UMWA, District 17. We are striking beginning today all the mines of Matewan owned and operated by the Stone Mountain Coal Company. We have about seventeen hundred union members in Matewan, and all members are expected to participate in the strike. If any union members refused to strike and reported to work, that makes them a scab, and that ain't gonna work out too good.

"Our objective in this work stoppage is to get a higher wage for you hard working men, and to get safer conditions in the mines. West Virginia has the highest number of fatalities in the coal mines in the country, and we need more support and prevention. I could go on and tell you more about what's gonna be happening today, but we have a special guest here this morning who will fill you in, the president of the United Mine Workers of America for District 17, Mr. Frank Keeney."

Johnny heard enthusiastic cheers and applause from men all over the meadow.

"Good morning men," Keeney said. "I appreciate the courage of every one of you, first to be a mine worker, and second, to step up and take a stand and demand the wages and the protection that you deserve."

"Yeah!" a bunch of men called out over the meadow. "That's right," others said.

"With seventeen hundred men going on strike in an area like this," Keeney continued, "this is a major operation. It will take a while for all of the evictions, but the Baldwin-Felts men are already in town. Come in on the Norfolk-Western bright and early."

The crowd of men went eerily silent.

"Now after what happened here in May, we expect that they'll have their paperwork in order."

A few cheers and catcalls arose from the crowd.

"But they also come with more firepower," Keeney said. "And they brought more manpower. From what we can tell, there's over a hundred of them, and they got high-powered rifles and some Thompson submachine guns."

A low murmur spread out over the meadow.

"But all we want you men to do is follow the law," he said. "Just like they supposed to. If we all do that, this is nothing more than an orderly transition to a tent city. Behind you, we got some flatbed wagons pulled by those horses loaded with tents and cots. More will be coming every day until everyone is moved out. Now let me ask you a question. How many of you men have a wife at home who is with child? Raise your hands up high. Okay, we want you men to move out of the crowd right now and go over to the wagons, and pick up your tent and your cots. The rest can report every day to the same area over there and pick up a tent as they come in. We'll be shipping up to four hundred tents a day, so it won't take long to get everybody covered. So you men with a wife expecting a child, go ahead and move out and get your tent. And I got some other things I got to say to the rest of you."

Johnny started moving out, glad that he could set up right away and provide housing for Kate. Maybe *housing* wasn't the right word, he thought, but at least it was shelter and cover, and he'd be there to take care of her. He could hear Mr. Keeney going on with his speech, talking about how they was going to negotiate with the coal company owners and management, who they was bringing in to help, like some big shot politicians and stuff like that. Johnny didn't care too much about the details of all that, just so they looked out for the safety and interests of the families. He did feel a bit sorry for his son because Corey was too young to join the union, but would be evicted like the rest of the family just because he was part of us. He figured Corey would still be able to work because of not being part of the union or the strike, and they needed all the mule drivers they had.

A canvas tent big enough to shelter a whole family was a big tent, and heavy. No way Johnny could carry it half a mile or whatever it was to the open meadow near where Stella had her tent. After Johnny signed for the tent, he was glad that Matthew and Caleb was right there to help. They each grabbed one end of the folded tent with the poles and ropes. Johnny carried the three cots stacked up on his arms. Even with that, it was a long walk, all the way down Mate Street, then down and out of town and on to the Stone Mountain Coal Camp, and on past into the meadow.

As the three men carrying their burdens came up to company housing, Johnny could see that armed Baldwin-Felts men was already at the houses doing their work. It looked to Johnny that they was already at *his* house. He dropped the cots and ran as fast as he could. As he got closer, he saw Kate standing off to the side, crying.

"What's the matter," Johnny said. "Are you okay?"

Kate threw herself into his arms and poured out her tears.

"Are you all right Sweetheart?" Johnny said. "Are you hurt?"

Kate shook her head.

"Just upset," she said. "We knowed we would have to move out. They could have just asked us to leave and not come in and throw our stuff out."

Johnny looked down at the ground and saw broken glass.

"What's that?" he asked.

"Yeah, that's my mama's crystal vase," she said. "They tossed it out and broke it up against that rock."

Johnny ran over to one of the detectives who looked like he was in charge. He grabbed him by his shirt and spun him around.

"What the hell you breaking our stuff for?"

With that the lawman tried to get out of Johnny's grip, but Johnny took him to the ground. He was about to punch him in the face, but two Baldwin-Felts gunmen rushed to his side and grabbed his arms. Two others pointed guns right at Johnny's head.

"Johnny," Kate called out. "Stop it! I need you!"

Johnny released his hold on the man on the ground, but before he could get up one of the thugs hit him in the head with the butt of his rifle. The other stomped him in the ribs with his hobnailed boot. Caleb and Matthew started to rush them, but before they could help, two more gunmen joined in and all the miners had guns pointed at their heads.

"All right, all right," said Johnny. "You win. We'll get out of your way."

He started to get up, but they pushed him to the ground one more time.

"Come on, let's go," Johnny said to Kate. "You can sit with Stella while I set up our tent"

Caleb and Matthew looked very upset. Johnny figured they all thought they could handle the situation, except for them guns. He was just glad the hired thugs held back a little and didn't try to get revenge for the shootout downtown. Had to be on their mind. They might have had strict orders.

The men picked up the tent and the cots, and walked probably a quarter of a mile to the area where others who had been evicted set up their tents. Stella offered Kate a cot where she could stretch out, and Johnny and the others continued on a hundred yards to an open space in the meadow. They set up the tent and then walked back to the house Johnny and Kate was just forced out of and picked up the few personal belongings they could still find. Johnny thanked Matthew and Caleb for their help. He knew he couldn't have carried everything by himself.

When Johnny got everything set up just like he wanted, he returned to Stella's tent and picked up Kate. Corey had been there for about an hour. He figured out what happened and decided to check with Stella. The three walked back to the new tent house. Corey started to go in, but Johnny held him back.

"Ladies first," he said.

He opened the flap and escorted Kate through the front door. There, against the back wall of the tent and between the two main cots, stood a small wooden table. On the table was a Mason jar filled with water and a handful of daisies, freshly picked.

"Aw," said Kate, tears flowing freely.

She put her face in her hands and continued to cry.

"Aw, you know, daisies are always beautiful," she said, "but this is the first time I seen a Mason jar that's more beautiful than a crystal vase."

Chapter 52

Johnny sat on a stool outside the tent in the meadow northwest of Matewan. So much going on. It was mid-July now, about two weeks after the strike and the eviction. Kate lay stretched out on a cot in the tent, jug of water nearby.

Johnny talked to some of the boys to pick up on what was happening, especially in labor and the strike. So far, the two sides not even talking, far as anybody could tell. He knew the strike would take a while, but he hoped they'd be back to work and back in housing before the baby came. Should, he thought. That would give it six months.

Johnny got notified the other day that he, along with twenty-one other miners and Sid Hatfield had been indicted to stand trial for murder in the Matewan shootout. Price you gotta pay, Johnny thought. Murder is a serious charge, for sure, but under the circumstances, with all the general fighting that went on, he thought it might be hard to know exactly who did what to who. The newspaper said with all the manpower it would take to work the cases, the authorities didn't see how trials could start before the end of the year.

Just then, several bullets crashed into some branches in a tree overhead, twenty feet away. The branches split open, showing the white pulp beneath. Never get used to that. He knew by now it was snipers and sharpshooters with high-powered rifles shooting from Kentucky across the Tug. They was probably stationed in little platforms up in the trees, like deer blinds. Gave them leverage and angle to fire across the river and direct some rounds down low enough to do some damage. A man got hit with a round last week. Seems like he'll be all right, though.

Johnny and Kate talked about getting her out of here, but they figured they needed to be around these parts for Corey. Couldn't leave him alone. Besides, the union wanted a lot from their strikers. Can't just run out of the area. Kate crawled out of the tent and sat on a log next to Johnny.

Just then, Caleb ran up with a copy of the Charleston Gazette.

"You see this headline, Johnny?"

"What headline?"

"A little girl went missing. Name was Janet Johns, daughter of Rosalie Johns."

"Rosalie Johns," Kate said. "Why does that name sound like I heard it before?"

"That was the woman who served on your jury," Caleb said.

"Oh my God!" said Kate. "Something happen to her daughter?"

"According to the paper," Caleb said, "body was found in the culm banks there in Chattaroy. She was shot to death."

"Oh my God," said Johnny. "That poor child!"

"And that poor woman," said Kate. "That's the price she paid to stand up for me!"

"What's wrong with people, they could do something like that?" Johnny said. "There a service listed there in the paper?"

"Noon tomorrow in Chattaroy."

. . . .

The Norfolk-Western pulled into the Chattaroy depot just before 11:00 A.M. Kate and Johnny stepped off the train and began asking where the child's service was gonna be held. "Don't right know," one man said, looking the visitors up and down. Another just stared at them and walked away.

Johnny knew for sure that everybody in a small town like this would know about the murder and where the service was. Could it be that they knew who they were, that some of them remembered the trial? Did they blame Kate for causing the little girl's death because the girl's mother sat on the jury? It was very possible. But he knew they was in town for the right reasons, to give comfort to these grief-stricken parents. They would keep looking.

Johnny and Kate walked down Main Street and saw the same kinds of businesses they had in Matewan—drug store, hotel, café. They stopped in at the café.

"Could you tell us where the service is at for that little girl that was killed?" Johnny asked the clerk behind the counter.

The man stared an icy gaze right through him.

"Anybody?" Johnny asked. "Anybody know where the Janet Johns service is being held?

People turned around on their stools and looked at them like they was snubbing them. Least that's what it felt like to Johnny. Seemed like all the people in the town was either blaming Kate for the little girl's death, or they was on the side of the coal company. Maybe they was just unfriendly folk to everybody. Whichever way it was, they had no regard for their guests. As they was about to turn and walk out the door, a woman stood up.

"Go down Main Street a couple more blocks to Tenth Street," she said. "Make a left and you come to Boone's Funeral Home. They be able to tell you where the gravesite is."

Johnny was happy to escort Kate out of the café. They walked through the front doors of the mortuary and stood in the lobby. Nobody around, but they eased through the next doors into a little chapel. A handful of people was scattered about seated on benches just like church. To the right, near the front, a man and woman sitting close together and hunched over. Kate and Johnny walked down the far aisle and came up next to them. The man and woman both raised up their heads and looked at Johnny and Kate. They knew right away who they was.

"Oh, thank you for coming!" Rosalie said.

As she stood up, Kate embraced her. Johnny shook hands with Rosalie's husband.

"I am so sorry," Kate said. "I don't even know what to say."

"There's some bad people in this world," Rosalie said. "Can't tell what they gonna do sometimes."

"But if you wasn't on that jury…"

"Don't go blaming nothing on yourself," Rosalie said. "I was on that jury 'cause the Good Lord wanted me on that jury. That's all. What happened to our daughter ain't on your head. It's on the ones that did it, and one day they answer for it."

"But I feel so bad for you," Kate said.

"Yeah, I ain't taking this too kindly," Rosalie said. "But you lost a daughter too, and both our girls, well, they in better places. That's all we can say."

The two women embraced and held on for a long time. Johnny and Rosalie's husband hugged briefly. Johnny felt awkward, but he wanted to break the ice and say something to the man.

"Is the gravesite nearby?" he asked.

"Yes, and by the way, my name is Bill. Sorry."

"No, no, no apology needed," Johnny said.

"They be loading the coffin on a wagon outside and we be walking along behind out to the gravesite. Not too far. You wanna come?"

"Sure do," Johnny said. "We come up here to be with you for this, and to tell you how sorry we was."

The man who drove the wagon kept the horse under control and they was moving slow. The women was the slowest walkers, so Johnny thought this was the way it should be so they could keep up. At the beginning, there was just the two couples walking behind the wagon, the driver, and the company preacher, a pipsqueak of a man with a nasal whine, who talked a lot and rode on the seat up front. Then, as they was getting just outside of town, Johnny looked around and saw many people streaming out of the streets of Chattaroy. A few wagons was rolling up too, carrying a dozen or so people. A few was on horseback, and others on foot, rushing to catch up. Maybe the people of Chattaroy had more love in their hearts than Johnny thought at first.

When they got to the gravesite, two men lifted the coffin off the wagon and set it next to the hole that was dug. The mound of dirt was on the other side. The company preacher stood at the end of the oblong hole, and a couple hundred people spread out around the other side.

"Welcome all. I am Brother Josiah Moffitt, preacher of the Ebenezer Apostolic Church of the Most High God in Christ Jesus, also known as the Community Church in Chattaroy, West Virginia.

"The Bible says that life is short upon the earth," Brother Josiah said. "It is like a vapor that appears for a little time and then vanishes away. When a man lives three score and ten years, that seems like a short time when the time of departure comes. But this time on the earth for this little girl was really short, only five years."

Johnny didn't like the sound of the opening remarks. He was no preacher, but he believed that a preacher, if he truly had compassion, should say some comforting things and try to make the loved ones feel a bit better when they left than when they come in.

"The Lord giveth, and the Lord taketh away," the preacher said. "And this time it sure looks like He tooketh away."

He continued on with words that was anything but comforting. Johnny glanced over at Bill and Rosalie and could see the pain on their faces. Rosalie was sobbing and dripping tears onto the ground.

"Children are given to us for a little while," he continued, "and we have the responsibility to look after them to see that no harm comes."

With these words, Johnny looked over at the grieving parents of Janet Johns and could take no more. He stepped over next to the preacher and asked to see his Bible.

"What are you doing?" Brother Josiah said.

"I just want to see something," Johnny said.

He took the book out of the preacher's hands. Kate stood next to Rosalie with wide eyes and shock on her face. Bill and Rosalie was also riveted on Johnny.

"Excuse me," Brother Josiah said firmly. "I'm not finished."

"Oh, you finished all right," said Johnny.

With that, Johnny hip-checked the preacher right down into the hole. It was deep, and the ground like to swallowed him up. Kate's mouth popped open and Rosalie held back a smirk.

"We gonna close the service today with a reading from the 23rd Psalm," Johnny said. "The Lord is my shepherd; I shall not want. He maketh me to lie down in green pastures; he leadeth me beside the still waters. He restoreth my soul; he leadeth me in the paths of righteousness for his name's sake. Yea, though I walk through the valley of the shadow of death, I will fear no evil, for thou art with me; thy rod and thy staff they comfort me. Thou preparest a table before me in the presence of mine enemies; thou anointest my head with oil; my cup runneth over. Surely goodness and mercy shall follow me all the days of my life, and I will dwell in the house of the Lord forever."

Johnny looked up and saw scores of smiling faces.

"May God bless this family," he said.

Chapter 53

It was a week after the Janet Johns funeral service. Johnny was bringing back about sixty pounds of venison from a doe he had shot and dressed in the field. If she had a fawn stashed in brush somewhere, he never saw it. Hoped it would survive somehow, but life goes on. More important that Johnny and his family survive. Jim Mullins' Winchester had been real handy to use, and he would see to it that Stella got all the meat she needed.

Johnny knew there was lots of deer around the Tug Fork, but with all the commotion, shooting and everything, they headed for greener pastures, and he knew he'd have to cross to the other side of the ridge to the north and east of the meadow. First time he'd slept under the stars in a long time.

Gave him time to sort things out. He found that life seemed to go better when he thought about the things he was thankful for, rather than the things he wished was different. Even though, by joining the union and going on strike, he was moving towards changing something. At least he was taking action in that direction. Gave him some control and didn't feel so helpless. He sure was thankful for Kate, and for Corey, and for the miracle of Baby Elsie and the time they had her. And even though he was thankful for his job, he felt it was time to take a stand so his family could enjoy a better life. It was hard to be a coal miner's wife. Not a lot of soft, pretty things going on for her. Nothing easy come her way.

Johnny knew this deer would really help out. No way to store the meat so they'd have to use it up right away, but he'd share it with his friends like Stella, and Gino, and Matthew and Caleb. Caleb especially had really been there for him. He had become a good friend.

Johnny knew he could probably trade his venison for some other food, like eggs, and bread. People be happy to get some venison steaks. Another thing he was happy for was the bit of money paid by the union while they was on strike. Johnny got five dollars a week since he was the union man on strike, and two dollars a week for Kate. Corey, as a child in the family would get a dollar a week, but the union said since he was a mule driver in the mines and still working, he couldn't have that dollar.

Thing was, since they was out on strike, they wasn't allowed to shop at the company store. Except for Corey, 'cause he was still working down the hole. But he wasn't making a lot, being a kid and all, even though he was now up to two mules. Once you could handle six mules at a time, you made a full man's wage. But Corey helped out a lot. Most families didn't have the advantage of a son bringing in any kind of wage. But still they had these men buying food in Charleston and shipping it by train out to Matewan. Something come in every day. So they was piecing it together.

Johnny was lugging the venison in two canvas bags with handles that he held in each hand with the rifle strapped over his back. Those bags was usually used to haul bits of coal out of the culm bank. He figured he carried about thirty pounds in each bag. The weight was starting to bear down on him, but he could think of no other way to manage the load. If there was just one bag, yes, he could do other things. He could put it on a shoulder and steady it with the other hand, or hold it out in front for a while, or maybe even carry it on his back like a backpack. But with both of them, the only way to go was with one bag in each hand. Even if he switched bags, made no difference. Each weighed the same. His shoulders started to ache.

The trail ahead started to rise in a long, gradual upward slope. That added to the challenge of walking and carrying at the same time. Good thing was, Johnny knew that the top of the slope was the ridge that was the gateway to the Tug River Valley. On the other side was home. He couldn't wait to see Kate. He wasn't worried about her because Stella, Emma, and some other friends was looking after her.

Johnny could feel his pace slowing down. There was plenty of daylight left, but it would take him longer to cover the distance. To his right, maybe ten feet off the path, he saw a mother grouse covering her brood with spread out wings. The grouse reminded him of a plump chicken round of breast and belly. Would be delicious to eat, but his Winchester was not the right weapon. Too hard to hit and probably destroy most of the meat if he made a lucky shot.

Top of the ridge now, and nothing but a downhill slope all the way home. With the trees and the distance Johnny couldn't see the tents, but he knew they was out there. Cottontail rabbits scurried here and there, moving from their cover in the grasses and behind brush to their nests in the ground and under rocks. He always said that the cottontail was the easiest animal to name. Exactly what it looked like. Rabbit meat was good, too. Trick is to get it.

Kablaam!

A thunderous blast from a shotgun stopped Johnny in his tracks. He peered through the trees to the east to see what this was about. He set the two bags of venison down and started walking in that direction, rifle at the ready. Then he saw him. A man about six feet tall, dark skin. He bent over and was picking something up. He turned around and it was Caleb!

"I didn't know you had one of those," Johnny said.

"Oh, you scared me half to death," Caleb said. "Got me a cottontail for dinner. Now I just need one more."

"Yeah, well if you come up short," Johnny said, "I got me some venison steaks over on the trail."

"Venison steaks!" Caleb couldn't believe it.

"Yeah, I was out over night across the ridge. Ain't no deer gonna stick around close by with all the shooting going on."

"You right about that," Caleb said. "How often you get a deer?"

"It depends," said Johnny. "I can get 'em if I can see 'em, but sometimes they just spooked and you don't even know they around."

"That's what I like about this," Caleb said. "I ain't gonna get me nothing as big as a deer, but at least I get something small any day I want."

"Let me see that," Johnny asked.

"You ever hunted with a shotgun before?" Caleb wanted to know.

"I ain't never even fired a shotgun," Johnny answered.

He held the gun pointed at the mountain.

"This is a double-barrel shotgun, as you can see. Two triggers down here, a front one, and a back one. A twelve-gauge."

"I'll be damned," Johnny said.

He held the gun up by his eyes like he was aiming a rifle.

"Now you notice with this here shotgun, the barrel is shorter," Caleb said. "It's been sawed off. So you don't aim it like a rifle. You just point it and shoot it down here from the hip."

"Where'd you get something like this?"

"A friend of mine had it in the Great War," Caleb said. "He was wounded and couldn't do nothing with it, so he give it to me."

"Man oh man! And you say you get a rabbit or a dove or something any time you want?"

"Around here, yeah," said Caleb. "No reason not to."

"Can I try it?" Johnny wanted to know.

Caleb pulled a couple of shells out of his pocket.

"Here, you break open the barrel like this, put in your shells and close it back up. Now again, you shoot from the hip. Point the gun right at what you want to hit. The shell sends out buckshot like in a spray, so it's good for small game. But it's got a bit of a kick, so you gotta get used to that."

Kablaam!

"Man, it *does* have a kick!" Johnny said. "Let me try it again."

Kablaam!

"I like it," Johnny said. "How close you gotta be to hit a rabbit?"

"Twenty feet should do it," Caleb said. "And by the time you see them, you already that close. But you don't have to worry about anything. Hell, you got all this venison!"

"Well, it's not all for me," Johnny said. "Stella gonna get some."

"Yeah, and who else?"

"Probably Gino, I guess."

"Yeah, and who else?"

"Probably Matthew."

"Oh man." Caleb said. "Yeah, and who *else*?"

"Well, I guess maybe you and Harriet could have a steak or two."

"Man, I thought you forgot who brought you to the party," Caleb said.

"So can I keep this shotgun for a little while?" Johnny asked. "I'd like to practice with it."

"You gonna need some shells to do some shooting," Caleb said. "How about I give you a box of shells, and you give me four steaks?"

"That sounds good to me," Johnny said. "Course I probably would have gived you four steaks anyway."

Caleb laughed.

"That's okay with me," he said. "Could I borrow your Winchester, I mean since we both got so much to eat and everything."

"Yeah, that sounds all right," Johnny said.

"You wanna do some practicing right now?"

"Nah, I gotta get home and see Kate."

Chapter 54

Over the next week, Johnny practiced his shotgun skills a lot. He had Corey buy him a box of shells from the company store. Took it out of his scrip. Cost about fifty cents. They was able to offset the cost with the food they was able to grow and shoot, so they was doing okay. Johnny liked the idea of being able to shoot something to eat the day he wanted to eat it. Never thought much about that before. Counted too much on the company store. Figured he get himself a shotgun somewhere down the line. Didn't know how, but figured he would. While Johnny was out with the shotgun, Corey was out with his slingshot. Made it out of an elm tree. He shot up in the trees, and out in the field. Looked like he was having a lot of fun.

It was early morning, with the sun just peeking over the eastern ridge. Johnny walked out to Elsie's gravesite to lay some daisies in front of her tombstone. He carried Caleb's shotgun with him just in case he come upon a cottontail he could use for dinner. Didn't think he would, what with all the shooting he'd already done in the area. He figured all the cottontails either dead or run off. But he knew where to find some more. That venison helped a lot of people. Johnny felt good about being able to give something like that to his friends. All of them really needed it, especially Stella. She just living on the good will of other people, and with giving him Jim's Winchester, he thought she felt better about receiving something that was made possible with his rifle.

Baby Elsie. What a sweet thing she was. What a beautiful gift from God. Still hard to understand how all this happen. Hard to figure how a mean son of a bitch like Big Jake could do what he done. God sort it out in time, he supposed. One thing he worried about. As much as he loved Baby Elsie, he wanted to be able to love this new baby just as much, even though it come from Jake. Not the baby's fault. Baby had nothing to do with it. He prayed God would give him the strength to be the man he should be.

Later in the week Johnny would take Kate into Charleston by train. Mother Jones sent word by telegram that Dr. Davidson was ready to do Kate's surgery, and if she could get there in the next few days, that would all work out. Today, Johnny had to meet with other union members and greet the train at 9:00 A.M. that was rolling in from Charleston. There was a load of strikebreakers coming, and they thought they was gonna waltz into Matewan and take all the miners' jobs. Up to the strikers to have a little talk with them. Johnny picked some daisies for Kate, and headed back to the tent.

"How are you, Sweetie?" Johnny asked his wife.

Kate was still stretched out on the cot. She rolled over to face him and lit up with a smile. "Ooh, fresh daisies!" she said. "You're up bright and early today."

"Yeah, let me set these up for you," he said.

Kate started to sit up and let out a groan, grabbing her low back.

"What's the matter?" Johnny said. He immediately put his hands on the area above her hips. "You really tight in here," he said. "Guess these cots ain't so good for a pregnant woman."

"They're okay," Kate said.

"Wish I could do better for you."

Kate smiled and touched the side of Johnny's face.

"Here, lay down on your belly. I'll rub your back for a little while."

"Ain't you got stuff you gotta do?

"Nothing as important as this."

"Aw, well when you finished here, what you doing today?"

"Gotta get me some breakfast and head out to a meeting. We got a lot of strike breakers coming in today."

"You supposed to do something about that?" Kate asked.

"Yeah, we supposed to let them know this is a union coal town," Johnny said. "These companies recruit workers and send them out here, and they think they just coming into a big welcoming situation and that nobody is out of a job. And it just ain't that way."

Johnny unloaded the shotgun and stashed it under his cot behind a duffle bag.

He walked over to the field west of the church and saw all the familiar faces—Gino, Sean, Caleb, Matthew, Heinrich, and many others. Everybody seemed pumped up for the day. Johnny knew there could be trouble, but all the men seemed ready. Ed Chambers led the meeting.

"All right, men. The train from Charleston is set to get here in about thirty minutes. We are told it will have a whole shit load of strikebreakers on it. Now some of you carrying rifles and sidearms, and that's fine. We don't want you to fire on nobody unless they fire on you first. And since they coming into a strange town and a coal company they don't know about, we don't expect they gonna be looking for trouble, or that they gonna be looking to shoot nobody. I don't think many of them will even be armed. But it's good if you are 'cause it shows strength and lets them know we mean business. Make them think twice about starting anything.

"Now some of you should grab a sign and hold it up in the crowd as these strikebreakers pull into the depot and take their first look outside. They gonna see a welcoming committee that is strong and dug in."

"What do the signs say?" one man called out.

"Oh, one of them says *Go Home, Scabs,* another one says, *Go Home Strikebreakers,* and I think another one says *This is a Union Town.* We want them to know that we care about our jobs and we ain't moving over just to let them in.

"Now when they start to get off the train," Chambers continued, "if there's a mass of men, like fifty or more in one group, you got to split them up to be able to talk to them. Move through them and kind of cut them in half or in quarters and surround them to get their attention. It's not as good if you stand there and talk to fifty or a hundred in one group. They feel like they the stronger group. But if you can cut them off and surround a group of, let's say ten or less, then you got the advantage and they'll see it that way."

"What do you want us to tell them?" another miner called out.

"Good question," Chambers said. "The first thing we gonna do is explain to them that we are certified miners, we have jobs here, and we care about those jobs. Just 'cause we on strike don't mean we don't have jobs. And we gonna offer real nice to pay their train fare back to Charleston. And if they do that, we got no problem with them."

"And what if they won't do that?" one worker wanted to know.

"Then you can put the squeeze on them by insulting their ancestry. Call them any name you can think of. Tell them what happens to people who interfere with a man supporting his family. And tighten the circle around them so they get the feeling that we mean business. We real serious about this."

"Un-ion! Un-ion! Un-ion!" The men started cheering, and Johnny felt a lot of determination coming from the meeting.

"Those of you who want to carry a sign, grab one," Chambers said. "The rest of you get on out to the landing at the depot. That train'll be here in a few minutes."

Johnny guessed maybe a couple hundred men was at the meeting. They moved together about a hundred yards over to the train depot and got set up on the platform. Johnny knew he didn't want to be one of the sign-holders, so he left that to others. He wanted to be one of the talkers, one who had a *come-to-Jesus* meeting with these scabs.

One thing Johnny saw on the platform that he didn't expect was about a dozen sheriff's deputies. He knew that West Virginia didn't have a national guard like Kentucky. They used to, but a couple years ago, it got federalized to help with the Great War. After the war ended, the governor never got around to putting the guard back in place. So to keep the peace, the counties was left to the sheriff and whatever deputies he had. Most sheriffs took the side of the coal companies 'cause they was on their payroll, and the miners didn't have a chance. Here's where Mingo County was different. Sheriff

Blankenship favored the miners, so when you saw a sheriff's deputy in Mingo County, there was nothing to be afraid of if you was a miner on strike.

The train pulled into the station and the cars was so crowded all the spaces was filled. Men was sitting in the seats, and men was standing in the aisles. The men inside the train was staring straight at the men standing on the platform, and the men standing on the platform was staring straight at the men inside the train. Seemed like neither side was sure of what they was gonna say to the other.

As the train jerked to a stop, a couple of deputies boarded each car before anybody could get off. The last deputy on board turned towards the strikers and motioned to be quiet and to be patient. Johnny figured it was Sheriff Blankenship's attempt to cool things off and get the strikebreakers to head back home. The men inside the cars was quiet and was paying attention to the deputies. Johnny couldn't hear what they was saying, but he knew they was trying to keep the peace. In about five minutes, most of the deputies stepped off the cars and spoke to the miners.

"Listen up, men," the lead deputy called out. "You know that the men on the train are strikebreakers, and they know that all of you are miners on strike. We don't want any bloodshed. When they come off the train, we want you to talk it out and that's it. Anybody who breaks the law will go to jail. Does everybody get that?"

With that, the deputies got out of the way, and the strikebreakers poured out of the train. The mingling of the two groups was like two ferocious hunting dogs meeting each other for the first time. Each is so eager to sniff the other out, a fight could break out in a second.

"What you doing here?" Johnny said to the man in front of him.

"Come here to work," the man said.

"You know these jobs was taken?" Johnny asked.

Matthew, and Caleb, and Sean, and Gino stood right close to Johnny.

"We was told that the coal ain't coming out of the ground no more," he said. "We just looking to feed our families, too."

"This ain't the place to do it," Johnny said. "Fact is, this a really bad idea."

"Why is that?" another of the scabs asked.

"They didn't tell you what's already happened to strikebreakers down here?" Johnny asked. "Mostly they get shot or beat up, sometimes killed. Coal mining's dangerous enough without trying to do it in a place where men trying to kill you."

"We didn't hear all that," the first strikebreaker said.

Down the platform to the south, Johnny thought he could hear a commotion breaking out, maybe a fist fight or some general fighting, but he didn't take his eye off the man he was talking to.

"Tell you what we're willing to do," he said. "You all sit back over here behind the station and wait for the train going the other way, back to Charleston, and we'll pay your fare for you. How's that sound?"

"I didn't come here to turn tail and run!" one of the scabs called out.

A couple of the miners moved quickly to the man's side and stared him down, pointblank.

"Let me explain something a little bit better," Johnny said. "We don't want you here. We offering you a chance to go back to Charleston with your fare paid and in one piece, or you could go back in a pine box."

"I'll take the fare," one man called out.

"Me too!" another said.

"Now we making some sense," Johnny said.

Just then a fist fight broke out between the strikebreaker who wouldn't turn tail and run and those trying to talk some sense to him. More fights broke out farther down the platform. Others did as Johnny said and found a seat by the station waiting for the 10:40 to Charleston. Some of the scabs who chose to fight was put down. Others ran off through the town or into the woods. Sheriff deputies made some arrests, just like they said. And Johnny could see that things was pretty much the same in Matewan as they always was.

Chapter 55

Johnny stepped off the last train of the day in the Matewan depot. He wasn't sure the exact time, but it was heavy dusk and he felt like he just had time to get to the tent before dark. As he walked down Mate Street, he saw Heinrich Mueller standing on the walkway with about half a dozen suitcases at his feet.

"How's your wife?" Heinrich called out. "Heard you got on the train with her for Charleston this morning."

"She be all right," Johnny said. "Gonna have surgery in a couple days. You going on a trip?"

"Ha! I wish," Heinrich said.

"What's all those suitcases for?"

"Remember them scabs we talked to about going home?" Heinrich said. "Well, some of them was in such a hurry they forgot to take them."

"Ooh! Guess we scared the shit out of them," Johnny said. He picked up the pace and hurried into tent city. He stopped by Stella's tent first.

"Hey Stella, how you doing?"

"Oh, I'm good Johnny," she said. "How about you and Kate?"

"Yeah, you know I dropped Kate off at the doc's today."

"What doc?" she asked. "Can't see the company doc no more."

"No, wouldn't want to neither," Johnny said. "The surgeon that's gonna operate on her is in Charleston. Real good doctor. Mother Jones is in town and she's rented a flat. Kate be staying with her for a while. You need anything?"

"I'm all right," Stella said. "But, I wouldn't mind a couple more of them venison steaks, you get a hankering to go out again."

"Been thinking about that," Johnny said as he walked toward his own tent.

"Hey, I hope that surgery does the trick for Kate," she called out.

Johnny smiled and gave a thumbs up. As he walked up to his own tent, Corey was stoking the fire. A couple of plucked birds sat on the log.

"Hey, where'd you get them doves?" Johnny asked.

"Slingshot."

"Whoa! You kidding me? I didn't know you could handle that thing like that."

Corey burst into a wide grin.

"You take Ma into Charleston today?"

"Yeah."

"Think she's gonna be okay?"

"Yeah, I think this surgeon's gonna do her a whole lot of good," Johnny said. "I think it be the best thing to happen to your ma in a long time."

"How come one doctor can be so bad, you know, drinking on the job, not caring about his people, and another one is so good?"

"That's a good question, son. I guess some people care about helping others through their work, and others are just in it for themselves. If you a doctor and you really want to help people, you gonna work hard to become the best doctor you can be. Seems like that's what this Dr. Davidson done. Seems like he really cares about the people he sees, and he's really good at doctoring."

"That be nice for Ma to finally find a doctor who cares about his people and knows what he's doing. When she be home?"

"Don't know exactly," Johnny said. "She'll have surgery in a couple days, then stay in the hospital for a week or more. Mother Jones is in town and gonna be looking in on her. Your ma might stay with her for a little while."

Johnny sat on the stool, while Corey sat on the log. Johnny thought the supper was especially good—each ate the tender meat of a dove roasted on a stick over the open fire, a cob of corn, and a couple small potatoes buried in the embers and cooked just right. The warm bread and pot of coffee capped the perfect meal.

"Your Ma would have loved this supper," Johnny said. "You gonna have to get some more of them doves."

"What's that out there?" Corey said.

"Way out there through the trees?" Johnny said. "Looks like a fire."

"That ain't no campfire," Corey said.

"Sure ain't," Johnny said. "That's gotta be a half mile away."

Johnny darted into the tent and grabbed Caleb's shotgun.

"Grab your slingshot," Johnny cried. "Heinrich! Gino! Caleb! Matthew! Sean!"

The friends came running.

"Where's Caleb and Matthew?" Johnny called out.

"Ain't seen them in a while," Heinrich answered.

"Grab your guns," Johnny said. "We gotta get out to that fire."

"What's going on?" Gino said.

"Don't know, but it ain't good," Johnny said. "Ain't no good reason for a fire that big out there."

Johnny jammed two shells into the chambers, snapped the breech closed, and stuffed the rest of the shells into his pockets. He held the shotgun by the base of the barrel and began running toward the blaze. Corey stayed with him, slingshot in hand.

"You got some ammo for that bad boy?" Johnny asked.

"Big marbles," Corey said.

Johnny glanced at his son and smiled. The other friends was running alongside or right behind Johnny. He could see that Heinrich carried his Winchester. He forgot what guns the others had, but they was armed and all them could shoot. They was West Virginians, wasn't they?

The night was moonlit, but cloudy, so the moonlight was filtered, not as bright as if it was a clear night. Johnny knew this would help him and his friends arrive at the fire with a bit of surprise on whoever was there 'cause it would be harder for anybody to see them coming. The other side of it was that it was harder for Johnny and his friends to see all the debris that covered the ground, just natural stuff like stumps and logs and rocks.

Just then, someone tripped and fell, sprawling face first on the ground with a loud crash. Johnny turned and saw it was Gino. Tangled up in a dead branch. They helped him up, and the band of friends continued on and was getting close to the fire. Johnny could see there was timbers or logs piled up and leaning against one another. The fire was streaming high into the sky with a full draft of air flowing up through the space at the bottom of the mountain of wood. The bright orange of the fire set a stark contrast to the night sky.

Off to the side, someone had set up a big wooden cross. Looked like it was whitewashed. Johnny saw a man dressed in white on horseback with a white mask holding a flaming torch and moving towards the cross. *Oh my God!* Johnny realized he was witnessing a KKK rally. Men was hooting and hollering. Must have been five or six of them on horseback, three of them holding torches, all of them armed. Johnny and his friends was thirty feet away, and it appeared the men on horseback was so busy playing with the fire, they didn't notice they had visitors.

Then he saw it. This wasn't just a KKK rally. This was a lynching. Matthew and Caleb was off to the side under a spreading oak. Each sat on a horse with his hands tied behind his back and a rope around his neck stretched up to the stout limbs overhead. Johnny and his friends walked into the breech.

"Well howdy boys!" called one of the horsemen. "Looks like you just in time."

"For what?" Johnny said.

"We about to hang ourselves a couple niggers," the man said.

Johnny stood about fifteen feet from Caleb and looked him in the face. He'd obviously been roughed up. Same with Matthew. The way them boys fought, he figured they was outnumbered and surprised to be overtaken by these cockroaches on horseback. Johnny read the look on Caleb's face as angry but sad and defeated, resigned to his fate. Giving up his hopes, giving up his family. But something about this outraged Johnny. These good-for-nothings was cowards. They had to be to gang up like this. And they was about to kill two really good men. For what? Caleb and Matthew was always there for him and his family. Johnny *knew* they was good men.

"You boys want to join in on the festivities?" the man on the horse asked.

"You gonna hang the niggers?" Johnny asked.

"Yep, that's what we fixing to do," the man said. "Then go get some moonshine."

"That's funny," Johnny said. "The only niggers I see are you cowards dressed in damn bed sheets and afraid to show your faces!"

With that, Johnny pointed the shotgun over Caleb's head.

Kablaam!

The rope was severed. In two seconds he fired at the rope above Matthew's head.

Kablaam!

Again, the rope snapped. Both horses bolted, but Caleb and Matthew fell to the ground before their mounts could move away. Johnny flipped open the breech and shoved two more shells into the gun. He was real good at this now, but it seemed to him that he was not. It seemed like hours before he could get the chambers to receive his offering. But Johnny was learning about time. The amount of time it took for the cowards to react was greater than the time it took for him to reload. Their horses wanted to flee, and the rogues wanted to turn and fire. It was as if they was stuck in time, floating over their horses and their horses floating over the ground.

During that time Gino and Heinrich took aim and dropped two horsemen to the ground. Sean untied Caleb and Matthew. Corey stretched the band on his slingshot and just missed his target, but reloaded with a direct hit on his next try. Johnny couldn't believe how fast that shot was. The man cried out with a painful yelp and hit the ground the same as if he'd been shot with a gun. Johnny patted Corey on the back.

"What took you so long?" asked Caleb.

Chapter 56

Green leaves turned to red, orange, and yellows as the months passed. Drizzles of rain became sprinkles of snow flakes, and wind out of the north brought a chill to the bones.

It was January 2nd of the new year, 1921. Johnny stood beside Kate's hospital bed rubbing her belly, while Mother Jones stood at her feet.

"I know you feel bad about not being with Kate," Mother Jones said, "but don't you feel bad about her being here with me. Been my pleasure to help out. Charleston's been a good base of operations for me. They're gonna bring her down to the delivery room soon. I'm gonna step out and give you two a few moments alone."

"I'm sorry," Johnny said. "One month you getting over your surgery. Then there ain't no money. Then the union need me real bad. Then it's getting colder and colder, and all the time you getting bigger and bigger with child."

"No need to be sorry," Kate said. "You taken real good care of me by letting me stay here with Mother Jones. Got me off them cots and out of that tent city away from the shooting."

"I know. Just wish I could of been by your side more."

"You here now, and you taking real good care of me."

"You know," Johnny said, "this baby couldn't be more mine than if, well, you know. And looks like he's gonna be a big boy, your belly's so big."

"You a good man, Johnny McCarthy."

. . . .

Johnny found a chair in the room for friends and family members who was waiting for their loved ones to be treated by the doctors.

Kate was taken to that special room where they delivered the babies. Dr. Davidson was in there running the show, with the help of a nurse, a midwife, and Mother Jones. She sure did have a lot of people looking after her. Johnny felt real good about this doctor. Kate did good on his surgery last summer. Said she could stand up straight again and not have no pain, at least not much, he thought. She and Johnny still ain't had relations for a long time, what with healing from the surgery and being apart like they was. But then with her being so big with child and all he supposed nothing could of happened anyway. But Johnny still had hope that everything was gonna get back to normal.

Johnny was glad he didn't have to be in that room where Kate was having that baby. Not much he could do anyway. It's a woman's world in there, except for the doctor, of course. Johnny knew he didn't like being around medical stuff, and blood, and all that. He could never forget when the company doctor operated on Kate's pa a few years ago. Had him all opened up, deep into his guts and everything, when he called Johnny and Kate into the room where he was doing the surgery.

"Here's your pa, Mrs. McCarthy" he says. "Big problems. I wanted you to see what I was up against."

Johnny almost retched when he saw it. Kate cried.

"Is he gonna die?" she asked.

"Well, of course he's gonna die," the doc said. "You can't survive something like this."

"But..."

"Don't worry about it," the doc said. "Your father is how old now, let's see, yeah right here. He's fifty-four. That's a good long life."

Johnny never could forget that last sight of Kate's pa laying on that table all spread out, all opened up, and blood, and inside parts he never knew was there. He never seen nothing like that, and he could never get that picture out of his mind. A terrible thing, and he knew he didn't like to be around hospitals and doctors, even though he was grateful for a good doctor like Dr. Davidson.

A day old copy of the Charleston Gazette sat right there on the table next to him. Since it was a day old, it was for the first day of the year and it highlighted some of the big things that happened in 1920. Starting at the beginning, the first thing they talked about was what they called Prohibition, the Eighteenth Amendment to the Constitution. Didn't affect Johnny a lot. He didn't drink much anyway, not like some. And he figured that those who wanted the booze would find it no matter what the law said. His Papa was like that. In the old country, Papa drank all day every day he had off. By the time the sun was ready to go down, he was so stinking drunk he either passed out or somebody knocked him out, no two ways about it. Johnny never understood why his Papa did that. Made no sense to him. Sometimes drinking made him mean. Sometimes drinking made him gone. Johnny knew he didn't need to drink like that.

Other things on the list. Hmm, silver reached $1.37 an ounce. So an ounce of silver worth more than a dollar. Make no difference to him. He figured he'd never see no silver no how.

Let's see, League of Nations, whatever that is. Arabs attack Jews in Jerusalem. Pancho Villa surrenders. Ah, here's something, he thought. Babe Ruth hit his first Yankee homerun. And the first colored baseball league got established. Hmm. Called it the National Negro Baseball League. All right. Yeah that could be good. If they had players as strong and quick as Caleb, that would probably be *real* good.

Oh, and women got the right to vote, the Nineteenth Amendment. Lots of amendments to the Constitution in 1920. Well, he'd heard of it and didn't think it would do no harm. Long as they was thinking right, but he figured they would.

Oh, here's a big one that hit close to home. Governor Cornwell requested Federal Troops be sent to West Virginia to put down the violence. So on August 28th, 1920, Woodrow Wilson did just that. Even with the troops, though, they didn't declare martial law. Governor Cornwell said as long as the two sides, the coal operators and the miners, could work together in a spirit of cooperation, he wouldn't declare martial law. So it was more like the soldiers just being there kept everybody in line.

Was odd, though, seeing all them armed with high-powered rifles walking around town. No wonder both sides got along. Ain't nobody want no trouble from Federal Troops.

Johnny could see why Governor Cornwell needed some help from the feds. He thought back at some of the things that went on last year after them strikebreakers landed in Matewan. Some of them things Johnny did not agree with and would not do. He had a son who was watching him, after all.

One of the things they did was toss logs on the tracks of them coal cars. When men run over to throw off the logs, they'd fire at them with their rifles. Johnny thought that was chicken-shit. Face a man straight up, eye to eye, and talk about things. Let him know where he stands. Even threaten a strikebreaker to get him to go back home. All that's okay. But to set him up for ambush?

Another thing some of them union miners did was shoot at men while they was working, while they was at the tipple, standing by the coal cars, dumping the coal into the breaker house. Same as an ambush to Johnny's way of thinking. Cowardly and chicken-shit. At those times when the union officials was ordering the men to do things like that, Johnny just kind of made himself scarce. He'd fade into the woods and hunt for deer or rabbit, or he'd throw a line in the river and try to snag a smallmouth bass. Wished he could have sat with Kate in those times as she got more pregnant. More pregnant? Johnny laughed to himself. Wondered if that was the way to say it. Well, bigger anyway.

He was asked by the union officials about where he was a time or two, but he just said he might not have been right there, but he was out working for the strike effort as much as any of them. They seemed to accept it, and he felt better in his conscience that he done the right thing.

Now that January got here, Johnny knew that trials was gonna start about the Matewan shootout. Wouldn't be long now. He'd be back at the courthouse in Williamson, same place Kate had to stand trial. Johnny thought about it. All they do is work and try to take care of their family, and they both be standing trial for murder within less than a year between them. Hard to figure.

It was cold and blustery outside with snowflakes flying around in the wind and chilling people deep down. Johnny didn't know how cold it got. All he knew was that in the morning any standing water was frozen hard over the top, and sometimes through and through. Tent city was real uncomfortable. You had to keep your tent poles straight and your guy lines taut, else your tent would be blowed over in the wind. Then the cold would come in more than it already was. And you had to have enough wood to keep that fire going. But the fire was outside. No way to have it inside, all the smoke and everything. Johnny saw little children outside crying without the kind of clothes they needed—no socks or shoes, no long pants, no coats or hats. It was a sad thing to see. He tried to help by bringing firewood and something to eat when he could.

Tent city was no place for a baby to be born, that's for sure. Especially in the winter. They thought that's what they was gonna have to do, but Mother Jones talked to Dr. Davidson and they somehow worked it out that Dr. Davidson would be in charge at the birth and it would be at the hospital just to be safe. Most babies wasn't born in a hospital—Johnny knew that. They thought maybe they could get one of them colored midwives to help out. He knew others who had did that, but Mother Jones said that would be very hard in a tent and a snowstorm, and she worked something out with Dr. Davidson. She said doctors was more and more active at helping in childbirth, so Johnny and Kate felt real lucky.

Johnny looked at the clock on the wall—three o'clock. He had been sitting there reading the newspaper, remembering last year, thinking and hoping, talking to himself, and wondering about the future for almost five hours! Where did the time go? And how long does it take to have a baby? He never heard of any other births taking this long. He wondered if everything was okay.

Just then, the door to his room opened, and there stood Mother Jones. He could not read the look on her face. At one glance, she seemed very serious. Another moment, like she didn't know what to say.

"Is everything all right?" Johnny asked.

"Yes, Kate is doing well."

"And the baby?"

"Follow me," said the wiggling finger. They walked into the room where Kate lay holding a baby boy in one arm, and a baby girl in the other.

"You have twins!"

Mother Jones placed the baby boy in Johnny's arms. The nurse handed him the baby girl. As he stood there holding both his babies and looking down at Kate's weary smile, tears flushed out of his eyes and drenched his shirt. He cried for a long time and could not stop gushing with joy and good cheer.

Chapter 57

The date was January 26th, 1921. Johnny was herded into the Williamson Courthouse. As a murder defendant, he was handcuffed behind his back, along with twenty-one others, plus the one celebrity defendant, the one at the heart of it all, former Matewan Police Chief, Sid Hatfield.

Journalists swarmed all over Hatfield, and Sid seemed to eat it up. He posed for pictures outside in the streets before the trial got started, flashing his Colt .45s. He gave interviews, downplaying the charges against him, and smiling ear to ear. In fact, he was dubbed *Smiling Sid*. Johnny couldn't figure how he looked so calm under the pressure. Seemed to Johnny, Sid didn't feel no pressure at all. Johnny didn't think he'd feel like he was under pressure neither, but now that the time had come, now that he sat in court shackled with twenty-one others, the reality had sunk in and he couldn't help but worry about the outcome.

What if he was convicted? What then? What would Kate do with two new babies? Just a few months earlier, their roles was turned around. He was glad that Mother Jones had rented herself a flat in Charleston where Kate recovered from surgery and now the babies could stay for a few months and get through the snowy season. With Johnny in jail and at the courthouse for what could be a long trial, he couldn't imagine Kate at the tent city with two little babies through the dead of winter. He couldn't see how she'd make it. Mother Jones was truly a good friend, and she actually became a life saver.

It brought a grin to his face when Johnny thought of how Kate came up with names for the two babies. "I think we call baby boy here James, after your good friend Jim Mullins," she said. "And our little baby girl here we call Stella, after Jim's wife. What you think about that?" How could he not agree? He had been so busy with things he didn't even think about names. He felt lucky to have two healthy new babies, and more than lucky to have a good woman like Kate as his wife.

Federal Troops surrounded the courthouse and lined the walls of the courtroom. This trial got national attention, and the governor and local authorities was not willing to take no chances with the lives of witnesses or defendants.

"All rise!" the bailiff called out. "The Eighth Circuit Court is now in session. The Honorable R. D. Bailey presiding. You may be seated."

Johnny looked around and knew right away that this trial was different from Kate's. At the defendant's table sat three attorneys, along with the star defendant. Aside from Sid, Johnny didn't know none of them. At the prosecutor's table sat four attorneys. Johnny knew one of them only because he was James Damron, the judge at Kate's trial. He had resigned his position on the bench and taken a place on the prosecutor's team to try to prove that Johnny and twenty-one others and Hatfield was guilty. Johnny liked him as the judge in Kate's trial, but wasn't too sure about him now.

Judge Bailey was a fat man with a red face, but he showed himself to have a kindly heart when he ordered the bailiffs to unshackle the defendants. Johnny couldn't imagine what it would be like to sit there all day with hands pinned behind his back. No reason for it neither, what with all the firepower in the room.

Jury selection went on for more than two weeks. More than a hundred men was called, and none was chosen. Seemed like it was such a small venue, as they called it, that practically nobody wasn't good friends with one of the defendants, or had some kind of conflict of interest about the whole matter, or was a blood relative of somebody else. Opposing attorneys passed objections around like a plate of cookies. Finally, outside of the coal industry twelve men was picked—common laborers, teachers, and farmers.

The judge called for brief opening statements from each side. A man by the name of Joseph M. Sanders stood and spoke for the prosecution.

"The prosecution shall show that the root cause of the Matewan massacre lies in the black heart of one of the defendants, Sid Hatfield, who with murderous intent walked out on that downtown street, backed up with dozens of armed miners, and cut down in cold blood and in violation of the law sworn officers of the law and employees of the Baldwin- Felts Detective Agency."

With these and many other words did Mr. Sanders exhort the jurors. Finally, it became the turn of a man who identified himself as John J. Conniff, leading the defense.

"Men of the jury, the defense shall show any murderous intent on that bloody day in the town of Matewan, was on the part of Tom Felts, head of the Baldwin-Felts Detective Agency, and that by his orders his men brutally and illegally evicted men, women, and children from company housing at the Stone Mountain Coal Camp."

With these and many other words did Mr. Conniff exhort the jurors. After a lunch recess, the prosecution took the floor.

"Your honor," Mr. Sanders said, "We'd like to call Sid Hatfield to the stand."

After swearing in on the Bible, Hatfield took his seat.

"Mr. Hatfield," Sanders said. "Do you serve as the Police Chief of the town of Matewan here in Mingo County?"

"No sir," Hatfield said. "I used to, but after the death of Mayor Testerman, I have not been the Police Chief of Matewan."

"What is the nature of your employment now?" the attorney asked.

"Now I serve as constable of the Magnolia District," he said.

"So you serve as constable of the Magnolia District?"

"Yes sir."

"And are you married, Mr. Hatfield?"

"Yes sir."

"And how long have you been married?"

"Uh, well into last year," Hatfield said.

"Well into last year," Sanders reiterated. "And what date did you marry?"

"Uh, it was June 1st of last year," Hatfield said.

"June 1st, you say?"

"Yes sir."

"And what was the date of the infamous Matewan shootout that brings us to court today?"

"Uh, that was May 19th," he said. "Last year."

"So you married the woman who was to be your bride less than two weeks after the Matewan shootout?"

"Yes, that's right," Hatfield said.

"And what was your bride's name prior to becoming your wife?" Sanders wanted to know.

"Her name was Jessie," Sid replied, breaking into a wide grin.

"What was her full name?" Sanders asked.

"Her name was Jessie Testerman," Hatfield said.

"Testerman, Testerman," Sanders repeated. "Wasn't that the name of the mayor of Matewan who was killed in the shootout on May 19th?"

"Yes sir."

"So are you saying, Mr. Hatfield, that less than two weeks after the Matewan massacre where Mayor Testerman was shot to death, his widow married you and became your wife?"

"Yes, that's what happened."

"Don't you find that a bit strange, Mr. Hatfield?"

"Objection!" shouted Harold Houston, general counsel for the UMW. "The defendant established the veracity of his actions. The appropriateness of his actions calls for a conclusion and should not be expected of my client."

"Sustained!" yelled the judge.

"And isn't it true, Mr. Hatfield, that before the dead man's widow became your wife, that you and Jessie Testerman were arrested in the town of Huntington on the charge of improper relations?"

"Yeah, but that don't prove nothing," Hatfield said. "We was there to get married, not do nothing improper."

"And isn't it true, Mr. Hatfield, that you were actually the one to shoot Cabell Testerman so that you could have his wife, and the entire purpose of lining up on Mate Street was to have the presence of guns so you would have the opportunity to act on your murderous intent and that you shot Mayor Testerman yourself, in cold blood?"

"No, that ain't true at all," Hatfield said. "Albert Felts is the one who shot the mayor and that started all the general fighting."

And so it was that Johnny heard attorneys on both sides question Sid Hatfield. He was questioned, cross examined, redirected, and generally asked questions every which way that was possible. He remained in good humor while on the stand, and sometimes seemed amused by the attorneys. At one point in the trial, Tom Felts apparently noticed the bulge in Hatfield's pockets and sent word to the judge that Hatfield may be armed. The guns was removed, and Hatfield was soundly dressed down for bringing guns into the courtroom.

Anse Hatfield, owner of the Urias Hotel, where the Baldwin-Felts thugs was catered to when they was in town, and a cousin to Sid, was shot to death outside his hotel late last summer. The prosecution tried to blame that on Sid because of Anse's coziness with the Baldwin-Felts group and his testimony to the grand jury. Everyone knew his testimony would support the cause of the private police bunch, but his untimely death prevented that. Although the allegations was made, that's all they was, allegations. No solid proof could link Sid Hatfield to his cousin's murder.

Other witnesses was put on the stand. Phone operators Elsie Chambers and Mae Chafin claimed they overheard Sid Hatfield tell Sheriff Deputy Toney Webb, when he was trying to get warrants, "We'll kill those sons-a-bitches before they get out of town." Webb was put on the stand by the defense and denied ever hearing Sid Hatfield say any such thing.

A coal company guard, Joe Jack, claimed just before the shootout that he heard Sid Hatfield, Reece Chambers, Ed's father, and Sheriff Deputy Hugh Combs say they was gonna kill every last one of them, referring to the Baldwin-Felts men. Jack also claimed he had been threatened that if he testified to this, he would be did the way Anse Hatfield was did. He said a woman from Matewan, a Mrs. Stella Scales gave him that message and the message was from Sid Hatfield. When Mrs. Scales was put on the stand by the defense, she claimed she didn't even know Hatfield, but she'd be very interested in meeting him. Laughter rippled through the courtroom. As she stepped down, she walked right over to Hatfield and shook his hand.

Another witness called by the prosecution was Isaac Brewer, one of the twenty-two coal miners and conspirators on trial for the murder of the Baldwin-Felts gang. Brewer flip-flopped and decided to testify for the state. On the stand, he claimed he saw Hatfield shoot Albert Felts. He also claimed that Hatfield voiced threats, saying he and his men would kill every last one of them, and that Hatfield claimed he shot Testerman. Johnny couldn't believe that. He was glad the attorney asked Brewer what Hatfield said the reason was that he would shoot the mayor. He claimed Hatfield said that Testerman was getting too close to the Baldwin-Felts bunch and he didn't want any interference.

Serious allegations against Hatfield, to be sure. The defense would now cross examine.

Chapter 58

John J. Conniff approached the stand.

"Mr. Brewer, you are a coal miner, is that correct?"

"Yes sir."

"And you are employed by the Stone Mountain Coal Company in Matewan, is that correct?

"Yes sir."

"And you were present on May 19th, 1920 in Matewan at the event that has come to be known as the Matewan massacre, is that correct?"

"Yes sir."

"And what side were you lined up on that day?"

"I was with the coal miners," Brewer said.

"And what made you become a turncoat in this trial?" Conniff asked.

"Objection!" Damron shouted out. "Demeans the witness!"

"Sustained!" yelled the judge. "Rephrase your question, Mr. Conniff."

"Yes, your honor. Um, what caused you to change sides and testify for the prosecution?" he asked.

"I was interested in the truth coming out," Brewer said, "and I wanted justice to happen in this trial."

"So that was the sum total of your reasons for testifying for the prosecution?" Conniff said. "You felt that the things you had seen and heard, being embedded amongst the miners, if they were known, would help the truth to come out?"

"Yes sir, that was it."

"So you didn't stand to gain anything personally by switching sides?"

"No sir."

"Mr. Brewer, isn't it true that the prosecution offered you one thousand dollars to change sides and testify for them?"

"Well, uh, yes," Brewer said.

Gasps could be heard throughout the courtroom.

"And isn't it true that it was offered to you that all charges would be dropped against you for your testimony against the defendants in this case?"

"Um, uh, yeah, I think I heard something about that," Brewer said.

Moans and murmurs roamed the courtroom.

"You think you heard something about that?" Conniff said. "Yeah?"

Johnny was impressed. He was very glad this attorney represented him too.

"And one more thing, Mr. Brewer," Conniff said. "Isn't it true that you are related by blood to a member of the prosecutorial team, Mr. James Damron?"

"Well um, uh, yes sir."

"And isn't it true that the same can be said for another member of the prosecutorial team, John Marcum? You are a blood relative of Mr. Marcum, are you not?"

"Oh boy. Yes sir, I am."

"No further questions, your honor."

Johnny sat there with a big grin on his face. Goes to show in some ways you can knock a man to the ground without laying a hand on him. Pretty powerful.

Johnny didn't exactly feel like they was in prison the whole time the trial went on. The jailer treated them pretty good, better than he expected. The food was good, most time better than what they could scrounge up in the tent city. The men was housed in a separate jail house behind the courthouse where they was not confined to a small cell. The jailer allowed the cell doors to stay unlocked so the men could move about freely, set up card tables, play dominoes, and visit with their families if they was in town. Some of the men felt like it was a country club like they'd heard about in rich parts of the country. Johnny wasn't sure if the coal operators or the Baldwin-Felts boys knew about it, but he was pretty sure if they did, they wouldn't like it. The jailer even brought in brand new mattresses. No stains. No smells. Johnny couldn't believe it. Good as those mattresses was, he would sure rather be sleeping on the ground next to Kate. He missed her so much, and hoped that some day soon he and his wife would get their married life back together. It had been a long time.

As he stretched out with his hands clasped behind his head, Johnny thought about Kate with little James and Stella in the flat rented by Mother Jones in Charleston. Little Jimmy, he figured he'd call his boy. He was so thankful that's where they was. He knew that Mother Jones had a busy schedule and was in and out of town, but he hoped she was home more than she was gone, just so she could help out with Kate. He was sure she would be if she had anything to say about it.

The days started mixing together in Johnny's mind as so many witnesses had been called, but one day stuck out so that he could not forget it. It was the day C. E. Lively was called to testify. He had all kinds of allegations against Sid Hatfield and a number of the miners on trial. *C. E. Lively, C. E. Lively*, Johnny thought. He knew the name but hadn't seen the man in a number of months. But now he remembered. This was the man who opened up the little restaurant in downtown Matewan. The man who was so friendly, glad-handing people left and right. The man always volunteering to help at union rallies and sign people up. Harold W. Houston, of the defense team, was about to have at him.

"Mr. Lively, what is your role in the big scheme of things out in Matewan?" Houston asked.

"I'm a businessman," he answered. "I opened up a little restaurant in town, right there on Mate Street."

"So you're a businessman," Houston repeated.

"Yes sir, that's what I am."

"And does your restaurant do pretty well, Mr. Lively?"

"Yes, I make ends meet," Lively said.

"And how long have you had your restaurant open there in Matewan?"

"Oh, almost a year," Lively said. "Yeah, just about a year."

"So you opened your restaurant right about the time the United Mine Workers started making inroads into establishing the union right there in Mingo County, is that right?"

"Well, coincidentally I guess that would be about right," he said. "Yeah, but just by coincidence."

"Just by coincidence," Houston said. "Is your restaurant your only source of income, Mr. Lively?"

"Well, I have other business interests throughout the state of West Virginia," he answered.

"Like what, Mr. Lively?"

"Well, um…"

"Mr. Lively, can you name any other business interest or source of income you might have in the state of West Virginia?"

"Well, uh, no, I guess the restaurant is about it," he said.

"Mr. Lively, I would remind you that you are still under oath in this courtroom," Houston said.

"Yeah, I know that," Lively said.

"Well then, let me refresh your memory," Houston said. "Are you on the payroll of the Baldwin-Felts Detective Agency?"

Lively's lily-white skin turned another shade of pale, and he nervously swished his hand over his mouth.

"Mr. Lively?"

"Uh, well, uh yes, I am on the payroll."

"And in what capacity do you work for them?" Houston asked.

"Well, um, I'm not really at liberty to say nothing about that," Lively said.

"Answer the question!" Judge Bailey screeched.

"Well, your honor, it's like I'm in the secret service," he said. "I'm under cover, and I can't really talk about it."

"Are you saying you're a spy, Mr. Lively?" Houston asked.

"Well, in a manner of speaking, yes!"

Gasps and shouts exploded from the gallery in the courtroom.

"So are you telling this court that when you were serving food and drink to these miners, and when you were helping sign men up for the union at these union rallies, and shaking men's hands and looking them in the eye, that you really were just gathering information to turn over to the Baldwin-Felts boys?"

"Well, that was my job, yes."

Boos and rants poured out of the gallery and a number of men stood, outraged by what they heard.

"Order in the court," Judge Bailey wailed, pounding his gavel.

"Now Judas Iscariot betrayed our Lord for thirty pieces of silver," Houston said. "How much did *you* get for betraying these good men, Mr. Lively?"

"Well I never thought of it that way!" he said.

"How much were you paid?" Houston barked.

"Two hundred and fifty dollars a month," Lively said.

"Two hundred fifty dollars a month!" Houston repeated. "And the miners you were ratting out are working six days a week, risking their lives down the hole, and they're barely making eighty, ninety dollars a month. Yet you come into this court and tell us that for spying on these good men, you were paid two hundred and fifty dollars, every month?"

Tom Felts sat there with a red face, frozen to his chair, while all the miners jumped to their feet shouting their outrage. It looked to Johnny that the judge would break his gavel trying to restore order.

"Order in the court!" he squawked. "Order in the court!"

"Yeah, that's what I made," Lively said.

"How do you sleep at night, Mr. Lively?" Houston asked.

"Objection!" snorted Damron.

"Sustained!" croaked the judge.

"Let me put it this way," Houston said. "You come into this courtroom and acknowledge pretending to be a friend and ally to these hard working men, yet through deception you get information about them and give it to the Baldwin-Felts outfit. How do you expect that any honest, hard-working man on the jury is supposed to believe your testimony against them?"

For the first time, Johnny saw that C. E. Lively had nothing to say.

"And besides that," Houston continued, "where were you on the day of the shootout, May 19th, 1920?"

"Uh, I was in Charleston, sir."

"You were in Charleston brownnosing with the leaders of the UMW, weren't you sir!"

"Objection!" boomed Damron.

"Sustained!" howled the judge.

"So all these allegations," Houston went on, "he did this, she did that, he said, she said, all of this is based on nothing but hearsay. You didn't see or hear any of this!"

For the second time on the same day, C. E. Lively had nothing to say.

"No further questions, your honor."

Wow. Another man destroyed with the power of the tongue.

Over the next several weeks, many witnesses was brought forth that talked about Sid Hatfield and the twenty-two miners on trial. People talked about what they heard, and what they thought, and who they was related to. Very little of the testimony was eyewitness action accounts of what somebody did, and much of it was different from what somebody else said. All of it was very confusing to Johnny. When his name was mentioned, he was not asked to take the stand, and all a couple witnesses could testify to was that he was there that day of the bloody shootout.

The jury was sent to deliberate on Friday, March 18th, 1921, and decide the fate of Sid Hatfield, along with the twenty-two. On Monday, March 21st, they marched back into the courtroom. After forty-six days in court, the bailiff called out the jury's findings as they applied to all defendants.

NOT GUILTY!

Chapter 59

The miners came back home to Matewan with a sense of being believed. They stood up and fought back, and even the law found nothing wrong with that. Sid Hatfield was the toast of the town, a nationwide celebrity and a true hero to the miners. Johnny admired him as well, and had gotten pretty friendly with him. But the sense of wellbeing among the miners did not last long as forces working against the union always seemed to be boiling just beneath the surface, and lurking behind the next bush.

"What you say we go find some game today?" Johnny said to Caleb.

"Big game or little game?" Caleb asked.

"Well, let's see what we find," Johnny said. "You're the one taught me you can't get a deer every day, but you can get a rabbit."

"All right, where you want to go?"

"Let's walk north up along the Tug," Johnny said. "There some seams up there along the canyons that lead into some open fields. We might snag us a deer right in there."

"All right," said Caleb. "You bring your Winchester, and I'll bring my shotgun, and we'll see what we find."

The two walked along a pathway that was greening up with buds, blossoms, and leaves. It was springtime and the woods was alive with new life. Clumps of daisies appeared everywhere and Johnny wished he could bring some to Kate.

"How's Harriett holding up?" Johnny asked.

"She's hanging in," Caleb said. "She'd be right there supporting me if I was in a coal mine or a cotton field. Don't make no difference to her."

"Yeah, that's the way Kate is. Guess we lucky men to have women like that."

"You bet," Caleb said. "But you notice there seems to be more shooting and fighting than we ever seen before?"

"Federal Troops pulled out now," Johnny said. "Been gone a month or two. I wonder if it's gonna get as bad as about ten years ago in the Paint Creek and Cabin Creek strikes."

"Yeah, Bill Blizzard talked about that," Caleb said. "He said it was all out war."

"You hear about the other day some of them militia, and them coal guards, you know the ones propped up by the coal operators, they roam around and ambushed some strikers out by the culm field? Beat the shit out of them."

"Yeah, they always doing stuff like that," Caleb added. "Long as it's five against one."

Johnny shook his head in dismay.

"But you know, our own men been crossing the line too. You hear about that strike breaker they killed last week?" Johnny asked. "Cut his balls off and let him bleed to death right there by the tracks."

"Yeah, I don't get that," Caleb said. "Uh huh, that ain't right, no how."

"Couple cottontails right over there," Johnny pointed out.

"Yeah, but I don't want to take them this early in the day," Caleb said. "Let's see if you get us a deer first."

"Oh, that's right. I forgot," said Johnny. "You can get a rabbit any time you want."

Caleb broke into a wide smile.

A train could be heard chugging down the track heading into Matewan. Johnny and Caleb stopped to look at it.

"Full of strikebreakers, looks like," Caleb said.

"Boy, they don't know what they getting themselves into," Johnny said.

Just then, the crack of a rifle pierced the heavy air and smashed a train window. More shots followed. The strikebreakers, sitting and standing in the aisles, disappeared, diving to the floor. More glass exploded as the train rumbled down the track.

"Can you believe that?" Caleb said.

When the train passed by more gunfire sounded from the other side of the Tug. Johnny could feel bullets whiz overhead and just past his ear.

"Duck down," Johnny yelled.

The two hit the ground with no special cover except for being low to the ground. More fire passed overhead from the other direction.

"We caught in a crossfire," Caleb shouted.

Several big logs sat just ahead lying the same way as the path.

"We got to get down by them logs," Johnny cried out. "Just crawl! Keep low to the ground!"

Gunfire continued overhead, but neither Johnny nor Caleb was about to raise up to see where it was coming from. After a few long seconds, the two men reached the cover of the logs.

"Stay down!" Johnny yelled.

"How you even know who's shooting at who?" Caleb asked.

"The ones on our side of the river got to be union," Johnny said. "They shot at the strikebreakers."

"Guess you're right," Caleb said.

"And the ones shooting from the other side of the Tug has got to be State Police, or militia, or strikebreakers, or coal company guards," said Johnny. "There a whole lot of people against us right now."

"Yeah, every time you turn around somebody's deputizing somebody else to go take some shots at the union miners," Caleb said.

More shots ripped overhead and tore bark and limbs off nearby trees. After what seemed like about an hour, the shots died off. Maybe no more than two or three every ten minutes or so.

"You know," Johnny said. "We can't see who's shooting at us, so we can't shoot back. But if we stood up, they probably could see us. Best thing we can do is stay put and crawl out of here after dark."

"Yeah, if we really want to get out of here without getting shot," Caleb said.

"Well, that's the way I'd like to get out of here," Johnny said. "How about you?"

"You know, the other thing is this is like war," Caleb said, "but we ain't wearing no uniforms or nothing. We could just as easy be shot by some union man who don't know us as by some strikebreaker. Wish we had some way to show what side we on."

"Yeah," Johnny said. "And I wish we had them cottontails you decided not to shoot a while ago."

"And I suppose you'd like a nice campfire and a spit to grill them on too," Caleb said.

Johnny laughed, while staying down below the logs. The day crawled by with here and there gunfire messing up the natural beauty of the woods and the lazy flow of the Tug Fork. Finally the sun dropped in the western sky and the light was dim.

"What you say?" Caleb said. "Time to go?"

"Not yet," Johnny said. "The moon ain't gonna be but a sliver. We best wait 'til it's really dark."

. . . .

Three days later, right about in the middle of May, 1921, the open warfare stopped. Johnny and Caleb walked downtown to pick up the latest copy of the Charleston Gazette. Find out what all happened.

On the corner of Mate Street and where the bank was, a small group was gathered listening to a man dressed in church clothes who was standing on a chair or something to make him taller than the crowd. As they got closer, Johnny could hear that he was talking about the *Battle of the Tug.*

"Some people calling this the *Three Day War*," the man said. "Started up in Merrimac where strikers blew up the White Star Mining Company power plant. They fired from the hills at the strikebreakers and cut telegraph lines and phone lines. But the strikebreakers fired back. Coal company fixed the damage and kept operating."

"Yeah, that's all those bastards would care about is keeping the coal coming out of the ground!" a voice from the crowd yelled.

"Most of the trouble was on the other side of the bend," the speaker kept on, "down around Sprigg. and Blackberry City, and Rawl. But it could have been anywhere."

"Ain't no way to live," another voice called out.

"One strikebreaker was shot on the railroad bridge at dawn, but the shooting was so heavy nobody could get to him. He lay there all day until dark 'til they could pull him off of there. Died two days later."

"Union thugs in the middle of it," someone yelled.

Johnny bristled at that statement.

"Oh, and listen to this. Harry Staton testified against Hatfield at the trial in Williamson. He was found shot dead along the railroad tracks not far from where he lived. Calvin McCoy was arrested for his killing. It's like Hatfield and his henchmen use the union and the strike to help themselves out."

"What do you know about it?" Johnny called out.

"I'm just saying this ain't good for nobody," the speaker shouted back. "Some twenty men killed, maybe more. State Police and deputized militia still pulling dead bodies out of the woods. No way to know if they got them all."

"So what are you thinking we should do about it?" another voice shouted.

"Forget about the union and go back to work," the man said. "Make a good living and keep your family safe. You care about your family, don't you?"

"What are you, some kind of coal operator hack?" Johnny yelled. "Some anti-union man? How much they paying you to be out here?"

"That ain't the issue," the speaker shouted. "And you, your family ain't even here where all the shooting is. Your murdering wife and them two bastard kids of yours in Charleston, ain't they?"

With that, Johnny walked into the crowd and headed towards the speaker. The clump of men had grown, but parted like the Red Sea as Johnny stepped forward. Close up, he could see that the tub-thumper was dressed in fancy city duds and stood on a sitting bench that had been pulled from the wall out to the edge of the boardwalk. His eyes grew wide as Johnny closed in with Caleb right behind him.

With one hand Johnny clamped onto the man's balls like the jaws of a starving dog on a T-bone. With the other, he grabbed a handful of shirt and heaved him from his perch onto his back in the muddy street. With two quick punches, the man was out, but the action was just beginning.

General fighting broke out all around with about ten men siding with the rabble-rouser. It didn't take long for the miners to make their point, and the coal company sympathizers to take off. Johnny and Caleb walked down Mate Street back towards the tent city, dabbing the blood off their faces.

"Where you learn to fight like that?" Caleb asked.

"I just been hanging out with you."

Chapter 60

This day was Thursday, May 19th, and State Police came by early in the morning rousting people from their sleep. They strode through the tent city on horseback—even fired some shots into the air. Johnny thought that was a dumb thing to do. Most of the people was armed and that's a good way to get fired on, even if they was just shooting to wake people up. Nobody in the mood for that neither.

A stocky man in full military dress-up sat on a tall horse and leveled a megaphone in front of his mouth.

"Tent dwellers of Matewan," he called out. "My name is Captain Brockus of the State Police, and I am here to inform you that Governor Morgan of the great State of West Virginia has declared martial law in Mingo County, starting immediately."

Everybody looked around at their neighbor. People was just waking up, crawling out of their tents, stretching and letting the rising sun light up their day. Johnny was glad Kate and baby Jimmy and little Stella was still in Charleston.

"I'll be leaving this pile of flyers here with you in case any of you can read," Brockus called out. "But right now I'm gonna tell you what some of the rules are. First of all, nobody is to walk around with no guns. As of right now, if you have guns you can keep them in your tent, but nobody walks around town armed. If you do, you'll be arrested and your gun will be confiscated. If you think having a permit to carry your gun is all you need, you would be wrong. Under martial law, it don't matter!

"No meetings will be allowed. A meeting means two or more people together talking. No public assemblies. No processions. If you go into town, you go alone or you walk in single file. If you violate any of these edicts of martial law, you will be arrested and held without bail. Does everyone understand?"

Everyone just looked around in stunned silence.

"One more thing," Brockus said. "It's very important that you do not put out any publication, or pamphlet, or flyer, or any written information that finds fault with the U.S. government or the government of the State of West Virginia, or any of its officials. Trying to influence public sentiment in this way could incite riot and disorder and will not be tolerated. In like manner, anyone who is found in possession of literature that promotes the union, contrary to the peace and stability of the land, will be found to be in violation of the martial law edict."

With that, the horsemen was gone, with a few trampled tents left behind. Johnny figured they was on to the next tent city, anywhere striking miners and their families could be found. A few of Johnny's friends wandered over.

"I knowed some big shit was gonna happen," Caleb said.

"Hey, ain't this May 19th, one year to the day after the shootout?" Heinrich said.

"I think it is," said Johnny.

"Been a hell of a year," said Gino. "Did he just call us *tent dwellers*?"

Matthew stared at one of the flyers.

"Says here you can't even speak out against the martial law," he said. "And if you get arrested, you don't even get a hearing."

"Ain't that illegal?"

"Don't think nobody cares."

"Hey, ain't this a meeting?" Caleb asked with a twinkle in his eye.

"Guess it is," Johnny said, "but ain't nobody knowing about it."

"So what we gonna do now?" Gino asked.

"Keep surviving," Johnny said. "One day at a time. Take care of your families and we take care of each other."

"Yeah. This will be over before you know it," Matthew said. "Everything will work out."

Five days crawled by with Johnny and his friends trying to stay out of the way and attract nobody's attention. They took their guns and went hunting 'cause they knew their families was always gonna need food and the coal operators and authorities wasn't gonna see to it they got fed. Plus it would help them stay out of town and out of trouble. Johnny made sure Corey just kept working in the mine and kept his head down low.

The next morning, gunshots woke them up again, this time followed by the calling of names.

"Matthew Washington!" the trooper yelled out. "Caleb Jackson! Johnny McCarthy! Gino Antonnucci, Heinrich Mueller!"

"What's this about?" Johnny asked as he walked up to the trooper.

"You're coming with us," he said.

"For what? We ain't done nothing."

"It's nothing to worry about," the trooper said. "It's just a roundup. Turn around."

Before he had time to think Johnny and his friends was handcuffed behind their backs.

"A roundup?" Caleb said. "What are we being charged with?"

"They'll tell you when we get down to the jail."

The men was marched into town, single file, and lined up at the train depot. Johnny was struck by the cold, unyielding stiffness of the town. Never warm and welcoming, the streets was now lined by State Troopers, sworn citizen militia with high-powered rifles and striped arm bands, sheriff's deputies, and mine guards. Here and there State Police watched over the entire operation carrying Thompson submachine guns. Two of them guns was mounted on the top of buildings overlooking the depot area, with vigilant rooftop troopers watching every movement below.

"Would you look at that?" Johnny said under his breath.

"I thought we was going to the jail." Heinrich said to the trooper in charge.

"Matewan jail's all filled up," he said. "You taking the train to Williamson."

The Norfolk-Western rolled in and the men was loaded like so many cattle onto a car. They took their seats and sheriff's deputies boxed them in by standing in the aisle before them and behind them. The handcuffs was left in place and no attempt was made to make them comfortable. Johnny felt that something wasn't right about all this. He was no lawyer, but always before he knew that things had to be explained to a person being held so they knew what was happening. This didn't feel like the same thing.

The ride was long, and when the train jerked to a stop in the county seat, State Troopers grabbed each of the union miners by the arm and forced them off the train. As Johnny's feet hit the ground, he couldn't help notice an officer who looked like he was in charge. He was a brick shithouse of a man sitting on a high horse looking down on his subjects. Least that's what it looked like to Johnny.

"Get them in the jail," he called out to the troopers.

"Yes, Major Davis," the officer in charge of the prisoners called back.

Major Thomas B. Davis? Lord have mercy.

The five miners was marched to a cell that looked like a ten by ten room, like it should hold about two prisoners, four at the most. But Johnny counted ten men already standing around. After they took off the cuffs, Johnny and his friends was pushed in there with them. Must have been a holding cell. Not even any bunks.

"How long you guys been here?" Johnny asked.

"Brought in yesterday," one of them said.

"What you here for?"

"Nobody never told us."

"Where you from?"

"Lick Creek."

"That ain't far from Matewan," Heinrich said.

All the men exchanged names and was trading stories.

"We'll probably get a hearing in the morning," Nate, from Lick Creek said.

"Not with this guy in charge," Johnny said. "He's a little emperor. History goes all the way back to Paint Creek and Cabin Creek. And with martial law, he be doing whatever he wants."

"Who farted?" somebody yelled.

Johnny smelled it too, but when his boots started getting wet, he knew the problem was bigger than cut gas.

"What the hell?" Caleb said.

"It's sewage water!" yelled Gino.

In an hour, the water rose ankle deep on the men's hobnail boots.

"Hey, get us out of here!" the men yelled.

They banged on the steel bars with tin cups and continued to shout until they got the jailer's attention. He walked in and pinched his nose, motioning with his other hand that he'd be right back. In a half hour he did return and offered chicken and potatoes in wooden bowls for dinner.

"Hey, we can't stay in here!" Johnny yelled.

"No place else to put you!" he said

Then he tiptoed out and closed the door.

Chapter 61

Some of the men kept shouting and clanging on the bars with their cups. Others yelled and struggled against the iron as if their anger could tear down the barriers that kept them in place, but nobody came. The men was left on their own.

"Try to stay calm," Johnny told the men. "They get us out in the morning. Right now, this is the way it is. Try to help each other get through this."

One young man from Lick Creek threw up right in the middle of the stinking pool. When he finished, he started tearing around the cell, splashing everything up, and screaming as loud as he could.

"God damn you sons-a-bitches! I'm gonna kill every last one of you!"

"Hey," Johnny said. "What's your name?"

"What the hell you care what my name is?"

"His name's Bobby," Nate said. "Hothead in the group."

"Bobby, listen to me," Johnny said. "Ain't none of us like what's happening. If we stay calm, we get through this better, and they feel our anger when it counts."

"I shoot them right between the eyes!" Bobby shouted.

"Well, maybe so," Johnny said. "But right now all we can do is help each other. Let me show you something."

Bobby started to turn towards Johnny in anger.

"Listen to this man," Nate jumped in. "He's on our side!"

"Look at this," Johnny said. "All of you, look at this. If you stand at the bars facing out, and run your arms through the bars and cross your hands over towards your elbows, your arms kind of lock in place and hold you up. And breathe the fresher air outside the bars. It ain't rising straight up from the water we standing in. Then you feel better and rest a little bit. You might not sleep, but at least you can rest and get through the night."

"He's right, this could work," Nate said.

"And it's a tight fit," Caleb said. "If we get in right up against each other shoulder to shoulder, we can all do this."

Nate was pressed right in against Johnny.

"That was a good job," Nate said. "Help Bobby get through the night. Help all of us get through."

"Yeah, he'll be all right," Johnny said. "Learn something from it. Grow up to be a fine man."

Nate chuckled.

"Well, let's not go *too* far," he said.

"No, he will," Johnny said. "When a young man starts to use his anger in the right way, he can do good things with his life. So how's things in Lick Creek?"

"Well, it's tough," Nate said. "Like everywhere, I guess. But there's a lot of us, and sometimes it seems like there just ain't enough food to go around."

"You all have gardens?"

"Yeah, lot of people have gardens."

"Ever get a deer?"

"Not so much," Nate said. "Once in a while. Once in a *great* while."

"I'll bring you a deer sometime," Johnny said.

"Yeah?" Nate said.

"Yeah, I get them once in a while. You just think about a nice venison steak on your plate with some carrots and potatoes. Hmm, hmmm. That be a nice way to end the day."

Nate looked at Johnny with a grin on his face, and shook his head.

The night was long and cruel. Johnny never spent a night like that. The sewage water stayed right at ankle level. Didn't get no deeper. He was grateful for that. But the stink seemed to get deeper. It coated the inside of his mouth and nose, and seemed to reach all the way down into his gullet. Throughout the night, men had to pee and shit. Tried not to, but there was no stopping it. They had no choice but to empty themselves into the middle of the cesspool at their feet. It added to the freshness and muscle of it all.

In the early morning, as sunlight was just beginning to peek through the outside windows of the jailhouse, a couple of the older men from Lick Creek was down in the water. Their legs gave out. Couldn't hold themselves up no more. Matthew Washington helped one of them up and let him lean into him. Helped support him. Caleb did the same. Some of the men started banging the bars again. Others shouted in anger. It felt to Johnny as if they'd been left behind like rats in a cage, rats you don't want to see no more, rats you want dead the hard way.

There was no windows in the jail cell room, but light filtered in from the outside through cracks and seams in the building. Johnny guessed it was mid-morning, at least nine o'clock, maybe ten. Who walked through the door, but Sid Hatfield.

"What the hell is going on here?" he shouted out.

"Sid!" Johnny called out.

"Whooey!" he yelled. "God, this stinks. What you men doing here in this filth?"

"How'd you find us?" Johnny asked.

"I come in on the train to make an appearance in court," he said.

"How'd you know we was here?" Caleb asked.

"You just gotta get within a hundred feet of this building to know something's going on," Hatfield said.

"Can you get us outta here?" Johnny asked.

"Oh, I'll get you out, all right," he said. "I'll come back in thirty minutes with some authority to get you out, or I'll shoot the damn locks out the door."

"You think he'll come back?" Nate asked.

"Pack your suitcase!" Johnny said.

Johnny knew Sid Hatfield was a man of his word and stood up for right, and he would have bet the farm that the former police chief would return. And he did not disappoint. All the men broke into smiles and cheers when Hatfield and Public Defender Jeremiah Tucker walked through the door.

"Oh my God!" said Tucker. "How long you men been here like this?"

"Some of us come in yesterday," Johnny said. "These boys from Lick Creek come in the day before."

"This sewage water backed up last night," Nate said. "Just before dinner."

"All right, listen to me," the Public Defender said. "Constable Hatfield told me and Judge Bailey what was going on. The judge is writing a release for you boys to get out of here and I'm authorized to let you out now if the conditions are what the constable described, and they certainly are.

"But listen up! We're going over to the toilet facilities by the courthouse and let you clean up, but then the judge wants to see you in the courtroom right away. Don't anybody try to escape, or you'll be arrested and taken back into custody. Does everybody understand?"

. . . .

"All rise," the bailiff cried out. "The Eighth Circuit Court is now in session. The Honorable R. D. Bailey presiding. You may be seated."

"Gentlemen, this is an emergency session of the court due to the conditions in which you were found," the judge said. "I would like to call one of you to the stand to speak for the group. Is there a man who would so volunteer?"

The men looked around at each other, and everybody chose Johnny.

"Do you swear to tell the truth, the whole truth, and nothing but the truth, so help you God?"

"I do," Johnny said.

"State your name for the record."

"Johnny McCarthy."

"Mr. McCarthy, where do you reside?"

"In the tent city just outside Matewan."

"And what is your occupation?"

"I'm a coal miner," he said.

"And why were you arrested and brought to jail here in the county seat?"

"They told us the jail in Matewan was full."

"But I mean why were you arrested in the first place?"

"Nobody never told us," Johnny said. "They just said it was a roundup."

"A roundup?" the judge said.

"Yes sir."

"Were any of you men who were in this lockup presented with any charges that were being filed against you? No one?"

The judge looked bothered about that real bad.

"Mr. McCarthy, you are excused," the judge said. "In this country, everyone has the right of habeas corpus. That means you are entitled to have a hearing where you are told the charges against you, so that no man can be imprisoned at the whim of another. Your rights of habeas corpus have not been suspended in this time of martial law. It appears that your rights in this regard were violated. Let the record show that these men are released by the order of this court. I'll have a warrant prepared for the arrest of the jailer who abandoned his charges in these conditions. Bailiff, see that these men get some food. You are free to go."

. . . .

"You know what I heard?" Nate said to Johnny. "When Hatfield come into town this morning, Major Davis, Captain Brockus, and a dozen armed vigilantes, the kind with them arm bands, was waiting for him to get off that train so they could grab him and put the hurt on him while they was bringing him to court."

"Yeah…" said Johnny.

"So what does he do but gets off the other side of the train and slips away into town so's he can get welcomed by all them people that really love him."

"Yeah, kind of make Davis and them look like fools," Johnny said. "But that's the way he is. That's how he come by here and got us out of our mess."

"Yeah, he something else," Nate said.

"Yep, nobody ever get over on Sid Hatfield," Johnny said. "Nobody!"

Chapter 62

Almost three weeks had passed since Johnny and his friends was locked up in the Williamson jail. He knew he would never forget that, but it sure made him happy for his friends and the freedom to come and go in the tent city, even if they *was* still under martial law. He missed Kate more than he could say, but he was very glad she had the chance to stay in Mother Jones' rented flat in Charleston. Couldn't imagine trying to care for two young babies in a tent, plus dealing with all the hardship and violence. He wondered what little Jimmy and baby Stella was doing now. He knew they wasn't running around yet or talking. They was about six months old now, and he tried to remember how old Corey was when he started crawling around and pulling himself up on things. He figured they was doing some of them same things too.

Johnny did not forget his promise to bring Nate and his folks a deer. He knew that Lick Creek was the biggest tent city around, and that means there was a lot of mouths to feed. He figured it was also hard to keep track of your garden. Lots of folks stealing things, he imagined, just to survive. So he thought Nate and his family would be real excited when he showed up with a deer.

He was lucky enough to get one yesterday and dress it down. Ed Chambers said he'd drive Johnny over there with his pickup truck and they could deliver the meat.

"Nice of you to do this, Ed," Johnny said.

"Hey, no problem at all," Chambers said. "Nice of you to think of these people."

"Yeah, they was good enough guys, and with what we went through together in that jail, I know they could use it."

Chambers drove his truck the twelve miles or so southbound along the winding road next to the Tug Fork River. They pulled into a dirt road that led up to Lick Creek and the tent city sprawled out almost as far as you could see in this big wide holler. Chambers stopped at the first man looking like he could give them directions.

"We looking for a guy named Nate," Chambers said.

"Yeah, Nate Wheeler's his name," Johnny yelled out the truck.

"Oh, you bringing him this here meat?" the man asked.

"Yep. You know where he's at?"

"He gonna have some good company tonight," the man said. "So yeah, go down here straight ahead keeping the creek to your left," the man said, "and you come to this strong smell of hog shit and you make a right."

Johnny and Ed looked at each other.

"Well, it be about two hundred feet before you go to the right," he said. "Then you go back in there 'til you get to the crags and the rocks. His tent's right there near the boulders leading up to the mountain."

Johnny figured the man was just about right with the smell of the hog manure.

"Can you believe that?" Johnny said. "A man keeping a pig pen all the way back here under these conditions?"

"Is what it is," Chambers said. "You do what you gotta do."

As they come to the foothills of the mountains with the crags and the boulders, half a dozen hillbillies showed themselves and their Winchesters. Johnny felt they was in good shape with them bringing meat and all, but anyone with bad intentions would be thinking twice.

"Hey, you guys know Nate Wheeler?" Johnny called out.

"Who's wanting to know?" one of the gunmen shouted back.

"Friend of his from Matewan," Johnny said. "Johnny McCarthy."

"You ain't vigilantes looking for trouble?"

"No, me and Nate ended up in jail together a few weeks back in Williamson," Johnny said. "Told him I'd bring him some meat."

All of the gunmen lowered their rifles and looked around. Nate popped out of a tent over against a large boulder.

"Johnny McCarthy, you gotta be kidding me," Nate called. "You a man of your word."

"Never forget a promise or a good friend," Johnny said. "Look what we got."

Nate walked to the back of the pickup.

"Oh," he sighed. "That is the most beautiful thing I ever seen."

"Yeah, except for daylight and sunshine," Johnny laughed.

"Yeah, except for that," Nate agreed.

Howdies was said all around and the men sat down around the fire pit next to Nate's tent. Moonshine was poured into tin cups and passed around.

"How come you got so many guards out?" Johnny asked.

"They always leaning on us," Nate said. "About a week ago Sheriff Pinson come out here with Captain Brockus and lots of thugs looking to arrest a man. One of our men fired a shot and they didn't take too kindly to that. They arrested a bunch of men. Said if there was any more shooting, men be in jail for a long time."

Just then, three cars sped up next to Chamber's truck. Captain Brockus jumped out, along with Major Davis himself. Lots of troopers and vigilantes backed them up.

"We looking for Breedlove," Davis called out. "Alex Breedlove."

Right then a shot was fired that broke the windshield of Davis' car. Then other shots rang out from the hills with snipers popping out from behind rocks. Davis signaled to one of his troopers to spray the rocks and the hills with machine gun fire, and spray he did. When he finished, not even a bird peeped.

All the lawmen jumped back in their cars and made quick turn-arounds, leaving tread marks in the dirt.

"That's really something," Johnny said. "We don't shoot it out as much with sheriffs and militia and whatnot in Matewan."

"Well, out here they deserve it," Nate said. "Shooting up the woods like that."

"They gone for the day, you think?"

"I don't know," Nate said. "The Emperor of the Tug didn't get his man so he likely be back."

Nate's wife and kids threw some wood in the fire pit and got ready to cook dinner. Some men come out of nowhere with a fiddle, a harmonica, and a banjo and started playing some old mountain tunes. One of the older men was shuffling to the beat and having a good old time. Everybody was clapping and grinning, and passing the moonshine. A feast was shared by all with Johnny's doe the centerpiece. They also found some onions, corn, potatoes, carrots, and tomatoes. And somehow some fresh warm bread was passed around with butter to melt on top. A few hours went by and everybody seemed real happy.

Just then, the sound of yelling up the mountain. Then shots was fired. Johnny looked up and saw a line of men working their way down the mountain, shooting at anybody they saw. Then a whole lot of yelling and lots of shots, maybe seventy-five or a hundred. People was getting shot up. Turned out Captain Brockus himself was shot through the shoulder, and who did it but one of his own troopers.

The captain was none too happy and took his wrath out on the miners and their families as he worked his way down the hill. He ordered his men to slash the tents, just cut right through the canvas and tear up everything inside and out. They broke legs off of stools and chairs, and smashed lamps and dishes and all that they could. Turns out they blocked all the get-away roads out of the colony from the side out of Sycamore Creek so the people was trapped. Marched them all the way out to the road and arrested more than forty men. Johnny wasn't shooting, and neither was Nate, but a lot of them hillbillies was.

"Where's Breedlove?" Nate called out.

Johnny ran up the hill with Nate and the others to see what damage had been done. Several wounded men was found laying on the ground, and next to one of them, a body that was not moving. Nate rolled it over and it was Alex Breedlove. He'd been shot through the chest.

"They shot him in cold blood," the wounded man nearby said. "Asked him if he had any last words to say. Then they plugged him."

Chapter 63

The date was August 2nd, 1921.

Johnny stood on Mate Street by the train depot in the drizzling rain. Looked to him like a couple thousand other people was standing around too, waiting for the train to pull in. He usually didn't pay attention to the date, but he knew today was the 2nd because yesterday, August 1st, Sid Hatfield was gunned down in cold blood on the steps of the courthouse in the town of Welch, McDowell County. A date he would never forget. Ed Chambers was by his side, and he was gunned down too.

The train would be dropping off two pine boxes holding the bodies of these young men, patriots and heroes as regarded by the people in these parts, bringing them back to their hometown of Matewan. A crowd this big usually pretty noisy, but Johnny figured most people was deep in their own thoughts. He knew he was. His close friends was standing right nearby, but everybody was stunned and thinking to themselves.

It had been about six weeks since the violence at Lick Creek, since a man was executed by a State Trooper who decided it was time for him to die. In the meantime, Hatfield and other players in the conflict was called to Washington to testify before the Senate. After that, Hatfield was supposed to show up in court in McDowell County, a nest of anti-union hotheads. Johnny wondered if Sid was in danger going up there.

After Sid got back from Washington a couple weeks ago, Johnny stopped him and asked him point blank. "Sid, you worried something might happen when you go up to McDowell County?"

"You know," Sid said, "I was a little, until I talked to one of them union attorneys back in D.C., Sam Montgomery. He told me not to carry no guns into the courthouse in Welch like I done at the trial in

Williamson. Just show respect for the law and everything, and walk in there like a respectable citizen, and people would treat me the same way. So that's what I'm gonna do."

Johnny could hear Sid's words hanging right there in the moist air just like when he said them a couple weeks ago. Made it awful hard to believe Sid was on his way back to Matewan in a pine box. Caleb Jackson stepped over and spoke quietly into Johnny's ear.

"What did Hatfield go to court in Welch for?" Caleb said. "What was that about?"

"Oh, the charges was something about conspiracy to blow up a tipple in the Mohawk Coal Camp," Johnny said. "But they was trumped up charges. Happened about a year ago. Anybody cared about it they'd a moved on it right away. I think they just set him up for an ambush."

"Who set him up?"

"The Baldwin-Felts gang," Johnny said. "Tom Felts was probably behind it. Remember, his two brothers was killed in the Matewan shootout, and he blamed Sid for it."

Caleb shook his head. The mood among the people was somber, and a few umbrellas popped up here and there. Some sought the overhangs along the boardwalk. Others didn't care about the rain. Over yonder, it sounded like some had broken out singing a hymn, but Johnny couldn't quite make out the tune.

"You think he really did that?" Caleb asked. "You know, blow up the tipple?"

"Sometimes it seemed like Sid was on both sides of the law," Johnny said. "But I never knowed him not to do what he thought was the right thing at the time. He sure was there for us when we needed him."

The train was heard rumbling down the track. Seemed slower than usual, almost like it knew it was in a funeral procession, being respectful of the dead. It came to a stop in front of the Matewan station and released the built-up pressure from the coal-driven engine, almost like a sigh of relief. For a moment there was silence, then an occasional sob heard in the crowd. All eyes was looking at nothing but the train.

"Do they know who did the shooting?" Caleb asked quietly.

"Their wives was with them," Johnny said, "so they was the perfect witnesses. It was C. E. Lively."

"The one with the restaurant in town last year?"

"Yeah, you know he was just a spy for the coal company?"

"Yeah, I heard about that," Caleb said. "And the wives was right there with them?"

"Yep."

"And they wasn't hurt?"

"Not a scratch."

"Anybody else do the shooting?"

"Yeah, there was this guy, Billy Salter," Johnny said. "He was one of them Baldwin-Felts thugs in Matewan the day of the shootout. He was the one that hid in the garbage can 'til he made a run for the river. Had him in my sights for a while."

"Why didn't you plug him?"

"If I'd a knowed what he was gonna do, I'd a found a way," Johnny said. "Then there was a guy named George Pence. Don't know much about him."

"So, the three of them just come up and shoot them?"

"Yeah, they must have knowed they wasn't armed," Johnny said. "Ain't too many men who knowed Hatfield would come out and face him knowing he had a gun."

"So they just shoot them in cold blood?"

"That's what the paper says. As they was walking up the steps to the court house with their wives, these bastards jumped out of the bushes and started firing. Now Jessie and Sallie say it seemed like there was a whole lot more of those men shooting, but these was the only names they could both remember."

"Yeah, it's hard to remember what happened in the middle of a fight," Caleb said.

"We both know that, don't we?"

Men started jumping off the side of the train and opening it up. A conductor lowered the little stairs on the passenger cars, and a few people began to step off. Everyone was quiet and respectful, apparently mindful of how serious the occasion was. The third car was an enclosed flat bed. From the inside, a man slid open the side door, and another fixed a ramp to the floor of the opening. Johnny could see the pine boxes inside the car.

Four men climbed up the ramp and set themselves around the first coffin. They each lifted a corner of the box to their shoulders and walked down the ramp into the gray drizzle. Sobs was heard from all over, deep and heartfelt.

"We love you, Sid!" somebody called out.

This seemed to fire up the emotions, and the sobbing and weeping was louder and all over the place. The men brought the second box off the train and set it some ten feet from the first, right out on Mate Street. Johnny didn't know which coffin held which body, but figured it didn't matter. Both men was loved. Both gave all they could to help the miners. Both was sacrificed on the altar of greed at the hands of the coal operators.

People started filing past the coffins, lingering for a few moments with their hands touching the pine, saying a prayer or offering good wishes. The sobbing and weeping was loud, but it seemed that people tried to pull themselves together when they touched the boxes.

"I almost hate to ask this," Caleb said. "But did they arrest the bastards?"

"Nothing yet. They claiming self-defense."

"How can they do that when the wives was right there?"

"You know how it works, Caleb. Don't matter what the truth is. Don't matter what the wives say. They staged it to make it look like self-defense."

"What they do?"

"They had somebody fire bullets into the stone wall that was behind the gunmen," Johnny said. "Make it look like Sid and Ed had fired at them. Then they planted guns on both of them when they wasn't carrying nothing."

Caleb didn't respond. Johnny figured he just didn't know what to say. But as Johnny looked at him, he could see a resolve, a focus, an anger building up in Caleb that he had not seen before. Johnny felt that way, too, and he figured all miners did.

Johnny looked down to the end of the street and saw Sheriff Pinson, and Captain Brockus, arm in a sling, both sitting on tall, dark steeds, along with several State Troopers armed with high-powered rifles and one Thompson submachine gun. They was staying back today, which was real smart. On this wet, gray morning, the people was having *their* way.

Chapter 64

A few weeks passed, but the outrage never did. Johnny read things in the paper, like men was grouping together in Charleston. They was arming themselves and having meetings. Some was patrolling the streets in towns all over southern West Virginia and sending strangers on their way. Friends, and men he didn't even know in town, talked. Couldn't stop it. Rage was building inside every one of them.

"You notice how we still under martial law?" Heinrich said. "So we not supposed to carry no guns in town. But you notice the strikebreakers carry them?"

"Yep," said Johnny. "Seems like it's martial law only against the miners."

"Yeah, well I hear in Charleston they bringing in Springfields like they used in the Great War," Gino said. "Stockpiling them to give to miners."

"What we doing staying around here?" said Caleb. "Ain't much we can do here. Why don't we go to Charleston?"

"They ain't gonna just let us go to Charleston," Johnny said. "We'd have to stow away on the train and sneak out of town."

"So what are we waiting for?" Heinrich said. "Least maybe we could help out some way."

Johnny had even more reason to go. He'd received a letter from Kate. Mother Jones would be giving up the flat at the end of the month. Time to move. No choice. Johnny was grateful for the time she was able to stay there, circumstances what they was. Violence had actually died down in Matewan and the surrounding area. Kate would probably do all right in the tent city, even with Jimmy and Stella being seven, eight months old. Least no shots been fired overhead in a couple months.

. . . .

"How's work today, Corey?"

"It was all right," Corey said. "Working with three mules ain't that hard, and it makes the time go faster."

"They still dangerous animals," Johnny said. "How can you keep your eye on all of them?"

"I might not always be able to watch all of them at the same time," Corey said, "but I never take my eye off of one of them for too long."

"You're doing real good, son. I'm proud of you."

"You hear from Ma?"

"Yeah, I wanted to talk to you about that. Your ma will be coming home by the end of the month, maybe sooner."

"Really? She's been gone a long time. How's she doing?"

"Sounds like she's feeling better and ready to get outta there. I'll be going in to see her tomorrow. Actually, leaving tonight."

. . . .

Johnny and his friends Gino, Matthew, Heinrich, and Caleb was creeping in the bushes on the outer side of the railroad tracks right around dusk. All the guards was on the other side near the town buildings and the depot. Johnny figured they didn't post guards to the outside of the tracks because the slope was steep on this side and there wasn't no good place to stand. Besides, the bushes was right there, thick and gnarly. Johnny got the idea for using the other side of the tracks when he heard about Sid doing it to get off the train in Williamson.

At just the right moment the five friends slid the side cargo door open and hopped aboard. They closed it slowly, careful not to slam it. They got some shut-eye and in the early morning hours, arrived in Charleston.

"Get something to eat?" Caleb said as they slipped away from the train depot.

"Sounds good to me," Johnny said. "I want to get over to Kate's real soon, but I'll let her sleep a little more first. Awful early."

"Yeah, we gotta talk to some people and find out what's going on," Gino said.

"Pick up a Gazette, too," Johnny said.

The men was seated in Tom's café. Opened at 5:00 A.M. Bacon and eggs was ordered all around, along with steaming black coffee. Johnny paid a nickel for the paper.

"Oh, listen to this," Johnny said. "Mother Jones spoke to a rally of union miners and called the coal operators sewer rats with reptilian brains."

"Ooh, that's tough!" said Gino.

"Even railed against Keeney and Mooney. Said they lost their nerve, not pushing for an all out march. Says here the coal operators and the politicians calling us Bolsheviks."

The server came over and apparently heard what the men was talking about.

"Thing is," he said, "Keeney and Mooney met with the governor and gave him a petition of union demands. You know, the usual stuff about the eight-hour day, the check weighmen, and the joint commission of management and labor. But he come back and rejected all of it."

"That's the problem right there," Caleb said. "The governor don't think there's a real problem, only unreasonable demands and agitators on the coal miners' side."

"Yeah," the server said. "And Keeney and Mooney been going around trying to get the miners to go home, like they running scared."

"So who's gonna lead this thing?" Heinrich asked.

"Bill Blizzard is stepping up," the server said.

"Remember we heard him at Matewan one time?" Johnny added.

"We got thousands of men camping all around here," the server said. "They over at Lens Creek near Marmet. They armed to the teeth and mad like a drenched cat. No mood to negotiate."

"What's the plan?" Johnny asked.

"Word is they gonna march into Logan County and hang Don Chafin," the server said. "Then they march right into Mingo County and free all the jailed union organizers, and overthrow martial law."

"That's some pretty big stuff," Caleb said.

"Yeah, they're real serious about it," the server said. "Ain't gonna just arrest people and put them in jail."

The server walked back to the kitchen, and the five friends searched each other's eyes.

"I'm gonna have to get Kate and the kids out of here," Johnny said.

"How you gonna do it?" Gino asked.

"Gotta take the train," Johnny said. "No other way."

"Yeah, but with martial law, you suppose they'll just let her into Mingo County?" Heinrich asked.

"I'm wondering if she had a medical letter if it would help," Johnny said.

"Yeah, well I'm wondering if people might recognize who she is," Caleb said, "traveling with two babies and everything. Might not be safe."

"Besides, you as a striking miner ain't gonna be able to just sit by her side and bring her home," Gino said.

"Maybe I'll have to get her back like we got here," Johnny said.

"Well, we got some practice at it," Caleb said. "You wanna do that, I'll go with you. When we get her to Matewan, we come back and stir things up."

....

Johnny got up and walked out the door so he could go see his wife. Felt a little guilty for waiting, but had to get the lay of the land. Find out what's going on. Work up a plan. He climbed the staircase and knocked on the door.

"Who is it?" a voice called out.

Johnny knew this to be the voice of Mother Jones.

"It's me, Johnny," he shouted.

He could hear footsteps running towards him. When the door was pulled open, there she stood, his beloved Kate. She smiled and patted the back of her head to straighten her bun. She looked refreshed, and younger than she had in a long time. Even stood a little straighter. But the best thing was the natural smile on her face and the brightness of her eyes.

"Kate!"

"Oh," she said, throwing her arms around his neck.

"Oh, Kate, I've missed you so much."

"And I've missed you…"

Just then a great rumble of gunfire invaded the peace, like a dark thunderstorm pelting hale onto flimsy roofs. It felt to Johnny like all the buildings was coming down. Jimmy and Stella started to cry. Kate picked up one, and Mother Jones the other.

"Ah, let me see them," Johnny said. "A little over seven months old, huh?"

"Oh, listen to that," Mother Jones said. "Any man who remembers that well deserves a prize."

"Yeah, that's pretty good, Sweetheart."

Kate came over and gave Johnny a kiss.

"So what's going on out there?" Johnny asked. "Why all the gunfire?"

"The striking miners are worked up to a fever pitch," Mother Jones said. "After Sid Hatfield and Ed Chambers were shot down in cold blood, they know the only talking in West Virginia that gets heard is with bullets. And they aim to do some talking of their own."

"This sort of thing happen every day?"

"There's thousands of miners camped all around Charleston," Mother Jones said. "They been looting stores for guns and ammo. They've taken over cars, and trucks, and trains. We're all scared to death they're gonna come into town here and shoot the place up and loot these stores for whatever they can get."

"Kate, we gotta get you and the kids out of town," Johnny said. "Mother Jones, what are your plans?"

"End of the month, I'm going to Ohio," she said. "Doing some UMW work over there."

"All right," Johnny said. "Kate, you be ready to go tonight. Get you back to Matewan. Lot safer there."

"With martial law and everything, how we gonna do that?"

"Trust me Sweetheart," Johnny said. "We gonna get it done!"

Chapter 65

Johnny and Kate stole away in the darkness, each carrying a baby in one arm. Johnny figured little Jimmy was weighing about twenty pounds, and Stella didn't look much less. With all the wiggling and fidgeting, neither Johnny nor Kate could manage much more than the one child. Caleb led the way, loaded down with most of the bags and satchels. They all walked naturally because there was no need to sneak or hide. Charleston, after all, was not under martial law. But as they neared the train depot, Johnny saw several armed guards watching the comings and goings of people as they got near the tracks. It was obvious that any major means of transportation was a focus of concern as feelings of war was in the air.

Johnny and Caleb led Kate out of the main roadway, to the side and behind a train that was parked on the track, pointed in a southerly direction towards Matewan. Johnny knew it was scheduled to depart at midnight and arrive at Williamson in the early morning hours, stopping at all depots along the way.

As they did before, Johnny and Caleb slid open a side cargo door and carefully helped Kate onboard. Caleb quietly closed the door, and the three adults settled in towards the back, left corner of the car. The floor in that area was covered with straw, and several animal crates was setting in front of the corner.

"Sounds like goats," Caleb said.

"Hope they don't mind we ride with them," Johnny said.

The goats was mostly quiet, but every now and then they'd get restless and stir in their cages, bleating out when they was feeling finicky.

"When's this horse set to get rolling?" Caleb asked.

"Should be any time," Johnny said. "It's close to midnight."

They sat there in the dark and in the quiet, ready to leave. Soon a locomotive engine started. It was hard to know if it was attached to this train, but Johnny heard movement outside, men yelling and running on the ground near the tracks. He believed the noise of the engine was from the locomotive that would pull this train to Matewan. Little Jimmy was asleep in Johnny's arms, but baby Stella started to whimper and fidget.

Just then, a latch on the sliding cargo door facing the depot was flipped and the door slid open. The goats stirred. Kate gently covered Stella's mouth with her hand and rocked her in her arms.

"Get up in there and check it out," a man said.

"I ain't climbing up in there," the other said. "You do it."

"For Christ's sake," the first man said. "I can hear something."

At the first sound of the latch, Johnny, Kate, and Caleb made themselves small in the straw behind the goat crates. Least as much as possible holding two twenty-pound fidgeting babies. Just then, baby Stella strained and grunted in the blackness.

"Step up on that foothold and shine the light in," the second man said. The light bathed the animal crates and the back walls of the car. Johnny held his breath.

"Just some damn goats in the cages," he said.

"See, I told you nobody needed to climb up in there."

"What do you know about anything?"

The door slammed shut and sealed the aloneness that rode with them the rest of the way home. Johnny counted the stops and knew when the train pulled into Matewan. They quietly opened the same door that gave them entrance and slipped into the early morning air. Caleb walked to his own tent where his wife Harriet slept. Johnny woke Corey, got Kate settled in the tent, and made sure Jimmy and Stella had what they needed. By the time Johnny and Caleb made the return trip to Charleston, Mother Jones was speaking to the men.

. . . .

The date was August 24th, 1921. Mother Jones stood on a wooden platform set up right there on Kanawha Boulevard. Johnny guessed at least a thousand men, most of them armed, was standing there listening to the crusader. He expected to be lifted up and inspired for the coming battle.

"I have in my hands a telegram from President Warren G. Harding," she said as she waved the paper around. "The president wants all of you to go home, and wants me to encourage you to do that. He says fighting is not worth the price you will pay."

"What's going on?" Caleb asked Johnny. "Ain't that different from what she said before?"

"I guess so," Johnny answered.

"The president promises that if you go home he will use the powers of his office to get rid of the private police system that has been so hard on all of you."

"Boo!" a shout was heard coming from the crowd.

"We ain't come here to quit!" another called out.

The men started to turn and walk away.

"Wait," she called out. "The president promises to get all these problems resolved…"

"Too late for politicians' promises!" someone shouted.

"We take care of this ourselves!" another yelled.

Johnny didn't know what to think of Mother Jones' change of heart. He tried to find her after the rally, but the crowds was such that he never could lay eyes on her. Then he got swept up in getting ready for battle. Bill Blizzard spoke to a smaller group of men.

"Chafin has got two fortified lines of defense to keep us out of Logan," he said. "He's got a trench dug out at Spruce Fork Ridge on the border of Logan and Boone Counties. About fifteen miles long. Most of that was dug out a few years ago when we rolled out back then.

"Then there is a gap between the two peaks of Blair Mountain," he said. "It's a natural well-beaten path to get past the mountain on into Logan. We think he almost for sure will have that defended.

"Now we got more men than he does," Blizzard went on. "We got men pouring into town from all over—the Upper Kanawha Valley, Boone County, Fayette, Raleigh. We even got men supporting us from out of state, God bless 'em. We think by now we got close to ten thousand men!"

"Whooey!" someone shouted.

"But here's the thing," Blizzard said. "He's got the weaponry. He's got Gatling guns, Thompson submachine guns, high powered rifles. And he's got the advantage of the upper ground. He's got fortified positions higher up in the mountain. And he knows we're serious and he knows we're coming. And we ain't coming to sit down and talk. We're coming to kill him, and he knows it. And we gonna piss on his grave!"

Johnny felt that all the men was caught off guard with that statement. *He* was, but to him it made him feel good and the men cheered and shouted at the idea. Johnny felt it was a release from the tension that had been building. It made the men strong for battle.

"Mr. Blizzard," a man called out. "When we out there in the woods and we run into another man, how we know if he one of us or one of them?"

"That's a good question," Blizzard answered. "We gonna be wearing these."

He held up a red bandanna.

"We tie these around our necks, and then we know we can be recognized by our own."

"So we see the red neck, and we know he's on our side," a young fella said.

"But what if somebody lost their bandanna somehow?" another asked. "Or what if one of the other side got hold of a red bandanna and used it to fool us?"

"Good thinking," Blizzard said. "We also got secret passwords. You think you dealing with a man who ain't one of us, you ask him *where you going?* The right answer is *to Mingo.* Or you ask him *how you coming?* The right answer is *come a creeping.* Now you got that? There ain't no more important words for you to know than these."

"Mr. Blizzard, what if we're talking to a man who don't give the right answers?"

"You shoot to kill, son," he said. "That's why I say these are the most important words for you to know. 'Cause if you can't answer right, you'll be the one taking the bullet."

"They wearing anything to show they with the coal operators?" another called out.

"Some of them might be wearing white armbands," Blizzard said. "You see that, you shoot just to the right or left of that, right through the heart. We ain't looking to take nobody back to jail.

"Now before you leave here, you pick up your rifle and ammunition, your bandanna, a helmet if you want. We got some regular army uniforms, or you can wear overalls, whatever you want. Long as you got your red bandanna on your neck. We get everybody shipped out in the morning.

Chapter 66

Governor Morgan shut down the railroad, but the miners opened it back up. Johnny and his company was getting ready to board the train. The engineer and his crew was standing at the back of the locomotive.

"Get this train moving towards Blair Mountain," said one of Blizzard's deputies.

"The governor shut the trains down," the engineer said. "We ain't going nowhere."

The deputy raised his rifle and pointed it right at the engineer's face. "We ain't asking you to fight, and we ain't asking you to stand guard nowhere. We asking you to do what you know how to do, and run this train over towards Blair Mountain. So you got a choice to make. You can run the train, or you can die. Which will it be?"

The engineer's face turned pale and his cheeks seemed to drop straight down to his chin. "Stoke the firebox," he told the fireman. "And see that we got enough water in the boiler. The rest of you take to your stations."

Johnny and Caleb boarded the train, which was filled with armed miners and red bandannas. The two friends sat next to each other. Heinrich, Gino, and Matthew was somewhere in the crowd. As men was finding a seat, one with a long gray beard turned to look at where he was gonna sit. His and Johnny's eyes connected for just a moment. Johnny stood.

"Hey, ain't you…" he said.

"Conan's the name," the man said as they shook hands.

"You taught me to fish in the river last spring," Johnny said.

"I remember you," Conan said. "You was looking for your son."

"Yep, found him too," Johnny said. "Your friend's name was Leonard? How's he doing?"

"Leonard got wounded in the Battle of the Tug."

"Oh, real sorry to hear that."

"Yeah, messed up his shoulder real bad," Conan said. "So he's back minding the store at the holler."

Johnny felt good to see Conan again and know that he was standing up for the miners, even though he got out of the mines years ago.

"You got your ammo?" Johnny asked Caleb

"Well, of course I got my ammo. What you think?"

"How many rounds you got?"

"About two hundred."

"Two hundred? Where you got two hundred rounds?"

"Right here in this ammo box."

"Ammo box? How you gonna carry that up the mountain?"

"I'll carry it," Caleb said. "What you think I want to run out of ammo and hit them upside the head with the butt of my rifle?"

"The mountain's almost two thousand feet high!"

"Yeah, but the seam that passes through ain't all the way at the top!"

"Damn near!" Johnny said.

"Well, how many rounds *you* got?" Caleb asked.

"Don't know exactly," Johnny said.

"Well, where you got 'em?"

"In these pockets in my overalls," Johnny said. "Jerky and biscuits in my trouser pockets."

Caleb shook his head. Blair Mountain sat about thirty-five miles south of Charleston and it didn't take long for the train with a full head of steam to roll out in front of it. This was not the depot in Logan or any other town. This was just a place on the tracks near the mountain where Bill Blizzard's deputies made sure the train came to a stop. The men jumped off.

"Put on your bandannas!" a deputy yelled. "And stick to the trails leading up the mountain. They'll bring you to the seam that gets you to the other side."

"On to Logan!" someone yelled.

"Supper tonight in Logan!" another called out.

"And remember the passwords!" a deputy shouted.

Johnny could see that the grade of the slope towards the mountain was gradual enough at the beginning, and the trainload of men spread out on the trail seemed to handle it easy enough. But as they got closer to the mountain, the slope got steeper and the men slowed down. Caleb was just ahead and Johnny noticed he kept shifting his ammo box from hand to hand.

"You still glad you got all that ammo?" Johnny called out.

"You just wait," Caleb said. "I'll be loaning some out to you!"

Halfway up the mountain, with men scattered out on the trails, Johnny heard a loud buzzing noise overhead. "What the hell?" he said.

All the men stopped to look at it. A plane with two wings on each side, one atop the other with enough space for a man to stand between them fluttered in the sky above like a giant butterfly. After it passed over, it turned in the sky and flew back again, this time a bit lower.

Johnny could see two people aboard. The first, he figured, was the pilot flying the contraption. The second, a passenger seated behind the first seemed to be along for the crazy ride. Just then, the man in the rear stood and dropped something out of the plane. It landed probably thirty feet from the nearest miner, and then *boom!* A deafening roar. The explosion rocked the ground.

Johnny ran over to where the thing fell. There in the ground, a hole big enough to hold a man's coffin. "They bombing us!" he yelled.

In the time it took for Johnny to see the crater, the plane made a second pass over the men and dropped another missile. By now, Caleb set his ammo case down and took aim. *Pow! Pow! Pow!* The high-powered Springfield sent three rounds into the side of the plane.

Johnny couldn't tell what damage was done, but the plane took off and disappeared from sight. The second bomb never exploded.

"Let's get the hell up the mountain!" one of the deputies yelled.

Johnny needed no further convincing, and it seemed that everyone picked up the pace. As they was closing in on the top of the mountain, Johnny could see that dense laurel and honeysuckle made a thicket it looked like nobody could crawl into, clustered along the sides of the rock. The soil was rich and deep, and held up broad-leafed evergreens like holly and larch. Sugar maples and yellow birch dotted the landscape, and the table mountain pine towered over all.

As they approached the lower region between the twin peaks, Johnny could see that the seam contained a wide dirt road, a well-worn path to guide travelers through the pass. He knew it would not be so easy for these men. Several of the rednecks stepped right out onto the clear path. Conan rushed to grab a young man and pull him into the bushes, but right then machine gun fire tore up the dirt.

The Gatling gun must have been set up on an overhead ridge and had a bead on the open roadway. The rapid firing of the gun was deafening and each bullet came with a loud explosion pushing it through the air. The noise made such a racket it confused the senses and made it hard to think. In a few brief moments of pause from firing, Johnny saw that all the men who had been in the open was down. Only Conan appeared to be alive, but his arm was ripped open, blood pouring into the dark soil. Johnny dove to his side and right away grabbed Conan's red bandanna off his neck and tied it tightly around his arm above the elbow. Just then a single rifle shot pierced the fleshy part of Johnny's right arm. He rolled off to the side under cover and saw that the shot missed the bone and passed through the upper part of his bicep, a solid flesh wound. He then reached out for Conan and dragged him into the thick laurel and honeysuckle.

"Over here!" Caleb called out.

In the thicket he had found an outcropping of rock that offered protection from punishing machine gun bullets. Johnny crawled into position, dragging Conan behind him.

"Well, leave it to you," Johnny said.

"Hey, my momma didn't raise no fools."

Just then, the Gatling gun roared again, tearing up the tamped dirt of the open area and turning away any would-be invaders along this troubled patch of roadway. The long afternoon turned to night. Conan finally stirred from an hour-long nap.

"Here, take a drink," Johnny said, offering his canteen.

"Thanks."

"Some jerky and a biscuit?"

"Oh, that's what I need," said Conan. "That help me out a lot."

Johnny, Caleb, and Conan ate in silence, keeping their ears tuned to movement in the brush. Crickets chirped, but not much else stirred. After some time, Johnny turned to look Conan in the eye."

"Can I ask you a question?" Johnny asked.

"Shoot."

"When you guys gave me them fish to take home, but you made me carry them in a pickle jar because of them bears, was you serious or was you just messing with me?"

Conan laughed.

"You thought about that, did you?"

"Yep, I did."

"Well, I guess we was messing with you a little bit," Conan said. "But the other side of it was, at night, by the river, who's to say when a bear ain't gonna come down from the mountain to take a bath or get a drink? Bears are where they find you, man. Bears are where they find you."

Chapter 67

It was the second day pinned down behind the rock overlay. They couldn't move, and the brush was so thick they couldn't see who to shoot at. But at least the rock protected them.

"Don't know how we supposed to do any good stuck in here like this," Caleb said.

"Chafin knows we out to kill him," Johnny said. "He ain't taking no chances."

Johnny's arm was getting stiff. He looked at the wound more closely and could see the hole made by the bullet as it passed through his bicep. The hole was near the top of the muscle and not close to the bone, but still took a chunk of flesh with it. He knew he couldn't handle a rifle like this.

He reached over and shook Conan. "Hey, you all right?" he said. Conan appeared to be asleep, but was cold and clammy.

"Conan, wake up!" He shook him again with no response.

"I'm gonna have to get him down the mountain," Johnny said. "Get him to a doctor."

"You gonna have a hard time with that arm," Caleb said. "I'll help you down part way."

As the two friends moved from their position, the snipers must have been watching the rustling in the brush. A thunderous volley of shots rang out from above, and the men flattened themselves against the mountain. Tree branches splintered and debris hung in the air. In a few moments Johnny and Caleb kept moving on down the mountain on their bellies, dragging their wounded companion with them. In minutes they was around the curve of the slope and out of reach of the monster gun.

"Can you take it from here?" Caleb asked.

"Yep," Johnny said. "What you gonna do?"

"I'm gonna creep back up and see if I can get a shot at that Gatling gun."

Johnny threw Conan over his back bent at the waist and walked him off the mountain.

. . . .

Conan got sent to a hospital in Charleston. Johnny was kept back in a medic's tent. They cleaned his wound, bandaged his arm, and gave him a cot. Told him to rest. After a couple days, leaflets was passed around with a proclamation from President Warren G. Harding. He ordered all persons engaged in unlawful and insurrectionary proceedings to cease and desist, and retire peaceably.

That's the first they'd heard from the president. But the miners wasn't having none of it. They was gonna march into Logan, free the miners jailed illegally, force the union on the coal companies, and fix the whole damned system.

"Ain't there somewhere I can go and be useful in the battle?" Johnny asked one of Blizzard's deputies.

"Your arm okay?" the deputy asked. "Can you use it?"

"Use it good enough," he said. "I'll be okay."

"All right," the deputy said. "We'll get you back up into Blair Mountain, but not where you was. We'll get you into Blair. You find the schoolhouse. Behind the schoolhouse is a little holler and you climb up the mountain through there.

"There's a group from Blair led by a miner turned preacher, John Wilburn," the deputy said. "Good man. Got about seventy-five men with him. They on a ridge up there on Blair Mountain. I think you could help them."

. . . .

It took Johnny most of the day to get to Blair, find the schoolhouse, and make the climb up the mountain. Just as the sun was starting to set, he came upon a group he thought was Wilburn and his men. Not a red bandanna among them. His own red bandanna had long since been lost, used as a tourniquet, rag, whatever. They turned towards him, rifles ready. Johnny kept his Springfield slung over his shoulder. The password was his lifeline.

"Where you going?" they said.

"Going to Mingo," Johnny answered.

"How you coming?" another asked.

"I come a creeping," Johnny said.

It was the first time Johnny had been asked for the passwords at the business end of a rifle. A sobering thing to happen to a man. John Wilburn stepped to the fore.

"Where you from?"

"From Matewan," he said.

"What you doing here?"

"I was over at the seam between the twin peaks," he explained. "We was pinned down something awful with machine gun fire. Took a bullet through the arm. They fixed me up and I got tired of laying around the medic's tent, so they sent me up here."

Wilburn's group welcomed Johnny and camped for the night high on the ridge above the town of Blair. In the morning, as they was pulling things together, some shots was heard nearby. Wilburn headed up a patrol to check it out and asked Johnny to be part of it. The rest of the men was to follow along directly.

As they walked towards where they heard the shots, they came upon three men riding in a Tin Lizzie. One of the men who seemed to be the leader spoke for the group. "What are you men doing here?" he asked. "Who are you?"

"That's what we want to know out of you," Wilburn said. "What's the password?"

"Amen!" they shouted.

Wilburn and his men leveled their rifles at the Model-T and fired away. The three in the car got off a few shots in defense, but came out on the short end. The thunderous roar of rapid gunfire racked

Johnny's ears and reminded him of Matewan. His rifle was at the ready, but Wilburn and his men fired so fast that Johnny's bullets was not needed. He was not sorry he didn't have to kill another man.

"That's for Sid," one of Wilburn's men called out.

As the day wore on, word came that Federal Troops had arrived and was calling for the surrender of both sides. General Harry Hill Bandholtz, at the behest of President Warren G. Harding, declared a cease fire. Word spread that rednecks was to lay down their rifles and report to the town of Blair. Chafin's troops was to report to Logan.

"We can't fight Uncle Sam," John Wilburn declared. "But I ain't laying down my arms 'til I know I'm safe in the custody of the U. S. Army."

"That's the way I see it too," Johnny said.

All the men agreed, and began their trek down the mountainside. When they walked into town, they was greeted by the 19th Infantry under the command of Colonel C. A. Martin. Johnny saw that Bill Blizzard was engaged in a discussion with one of the officers. The captain had searched Blizzard and found a revolver, but also discovered a carry permit for the gun.

"So I can keep my gun?" Blizzard asked.

"Yep, you got a permit."

"What about the other side?"

"They can keep theirs too, if they got a permit," the captain said. "Or if they sworn law enforcement, of course they can keep their guns."

"So the police thugs still gonna be coming around shooting us down where we live," said Blizzard.

"I'm just following orders, sir."

"When you men lay down your rifles," Blizzard called out, "you better remember where you can find them!"

Bill Blizzard was feisty, all right. Good man to have on your side. Take no shit from nobody. Here he was standing in front of the 19th Infantry, giving a captain a hard time. The army division spread out on the main street of the town looked to be no less than a thousand men. Officers on horseback, infantrymen with high-powered rifles, side arms, Howitzers, black leather combat boots. They meant business, and Johnny knew no redneck would buck their authority. Nor did they want to. A platoon of about a hundred soldiers marched to surround the group of miners.

"Lay down your weapons," an officer commanded.

They did, down to the last man, and boarded the train back to Madison. Johnny looked, but found none of his friends on the train, at least not in the car he rode in. He hoped they was already in Madison, safe and warm, and well-fed. Ah yes, well-fed would be real good.

He thought of Kate and her courage, living in a tent with little Jimmy and baby Stella to nurse and care for. What a good woman he had. Oh, how he would love her when he got home. Could the shooting really be over? All he wanted was to love and provide for his family. Shooting didn't seem to fit the picture, unless it was shooting a deer. Just leave me alone, he thought, and let me be the husband and father God wants me to be.

Chapter 68

The next morning, Johnny boarded the train for Matewan. All his friends from home had been found, and they was all excited to get back to their families.

"You okay?" Johnny asked.

"Yeah," Gino said. "Glad it's over."

"Wish they didn't stop us when they did," Heinrich said.

"Where was you at?"

"I was with some boys at Craddock Fork, and we was doing all right. We had that Gatling gun they stole from the company store in Gallagher. After a while, one of them machine guns from the Chafin boys jammed, and we was able to move them back pretty good."

"Was you on that outlaw train, where they brought you in on flatbeds at night?"

"Yeah, it was crazy," Heinrich said. "They got us as far as Madison, and we grabbed some autos from there."

"So they was able to stop you?" Caleb asked.

"Yeah, they had lots of Thompsons. Lots of fire power. Plus, they had the higher ground. They could just bear right down on us. But we got to within about four miles of Logan."

"Probably made Chafin shit his pants," Caleb said.

"Where was *you* at?" Johnny asked Matthew.

"I was in this attack on the Bluefield Boys at Blair Mountain," he said. "We tried to blow up that bridge to keep the Norfolk & Western from bringing in reinforcements. We wasn't able to explode the dynamite, but we set the bridge on fire. But they had guards who put it out."

"So you get in a gun battle?"

"Yeah, we was moving against them pretty good and they was going the other way," Matthew said. "At one point, we drove them out of these trenches they used for cover, and we moved right in. But it turned out to be an ambush. They had machine guns trained right on us and a lot of guys got hit."

"Anybody have pipe bombs dropped on them?" Gino asked.

"Yeah, we saw them at Blair Mountain," Johnny said.

"Is that crazy, or what?"

"Yeah, I heard they was made of oil well casings and when you took them apart, they had black powder, and nuts and bolts, and nails. Shit like that."

"Can you believe that?"

"I heard women and children was being shot at Blair," Johnny said.

"Yeah, that's part of what got us all going," Caleb said. "But turned out not to be true."

"What about Keeney and Mooney in all this?" Heinrich asked. "Where was they at?"

"Guess they high-tailed it out of town when the fighting started."

"Yeah, they was doing nothing but trying to get us all to turn back and go home," Johnny said. "I heard that General Bandholtz held them accountable for what we all did, and they didn't want no part of it. They was already charged with several killings in the Three Day War."

"I'll just be glad to get home," Caleb said.

"Yeah, me too," Johnny said. "Put all this behind us and just settle down with our families."

Lots of the miners slept a deep slumber, snoring louder than the rumbling of the train down the track. Johnny slumped down and closed his eyes, but continued to think of the happenings of the last few days. He was relieved to be going home to Kate. He thought most of the men felt the same way about going home. There was a few, though, who wasn't happy with being turned back. They wanted nothing but to hang Chafin and set the union men free. It didn't happen that way.

The train slowed and squeaked to a halt at the Matewan depot. Cheering, waving women and children lined the walkway beside the tracks. The men jumped up and grabbed their satchels, shirts, jackets, and hats and bounded off the train. In a moment, Kate was in Johnny's arms, but he sensed something was wrong.

"The siren went off," Kate said. "The one that tells you there's been some kind of accident? But then they turned it off, and they won't answer no questions."

Johnny walked over to the portal. A foreman stood by the bulletin board with the assignment clipboards.

"Where's the cave-in?" Johnny asked.

"What cave-in?"

"Siren went off a while ago. Where's the cave-in?"

"No cave-in I know about."

Johnny grabbed the foreman by the shirt.

"Look, we just trying to hit full coal today," the foreman said. "You know, trying to make up for lost production because of the strike."

"Where's the cave-in?" Johnny asked again.

"Level four, north quadrant."

Johnny let loose of the man, jumped in the cage, and lowered himself down. At that level, the gangway was busy with mules and coal cars, nippers and spraggers. Everybody doing something.

"Where's the cave-in?" he asked a supervisor.

"Who's asking? Who are you?" he said.

"I'm a miner."

"You on strike, ain't you?"

"Don't really matter. Where's the cave-in?"

"What cave-in?"

Johnny stepped real close to the man, eyeball to eyeball.

"Where's the cave-in?"

"About two hundred feet down the gangway, on the right there's a chute. About fifty feet in, that's where the cave-in is. Sealed off a chamber."

"Why ain't there rescue work going on?"

"We got to bring the coal out," the man said. "As long as the gangway ain't blocked, coal company says we gotta keep loading the coal."

Johnny ran the two hundred feet down the gangway and made a right into the chute. Miners and laborers, all the workers—everybody turned to look at him as he ran by. Carbide lanterns along the gangway rib splashed a shadowy, uneven light on the walls and the rock floor. He came to the site where the collapse was. Rocks the size of tub basins and loaves of bread. Rocks that could be tossed out of the way if people had a mind to. Johnny placed his hands on the rocks and moved to the side where he could touch the rib of the chamber wall. *Tap, tap, tap.* Somebody was tapping from inside the chamber! *Tap, tap, tap.* Somebody was alive, wanting to get out. He turned around to call for help, but nobody was in the chute. He looked and found a rock the size of a baseball and started tapping with it. *Tap, tap*—pause— *tap.* The man on the other side got it.

Johnny ran to the end of the chute and into the gangway.

"Help," he shouted. "We need some help over here."

Men looked, but nobody came his way. He ran up to a miner with a full tool belt and asked him to come down to the chute and help out. The miner just stared at him like he was a crazy man. Johnny grabbed a small pickax out of the miner's belt and ran back towards the chute.

"Hey!" the miner called out.

The chase was on. When Johnny got back to the site of the cave-in, he listened and felt for the sound of the tapping, and returned a message of hope. *Tap, tap, tap.* He turned around and there was the miner whose pickax he borrowed, along with six of his buddies.

"We got somebody trapped in here," Johnny said. "Maybe more than one. We gotta throw these rocks off."

Johnny didn't know none of these men, but he knew most of them was strikebreakers. As he looked into their eyes, he knew they wasn't listening to him. Seven pairs of icy cold eyes are what glared back at him.

"You a union man?" one of them asked.

Johnny nodded.

"You one of them rednecks been out there firing on the State Police and sheriff deputies?"

Johnny just looked straight ahead.

"You being on strike and going to war against the state is the main reason they fell behind bringing the coal out of the ground," another said.

Johnny looked at them from face to face. Cold, dank stares.

"You probably one of them boys that fired shots into our houses, practically killing our women and children," another said.

"Maybe you one of them that cut the balls off our friend and let him to bleed to death out on the tracks."

The men started pulling pickaxes and hammers out of their tool belts, smacking them against the palms of their hands.

"Looks like you gonna have to pay a price for all this trouble you caused, Mr. union man."

"Let's get him!"

Chapter 69

"Whoa!" Johnny shouted as he raised a clenched fist in the air.

"So seven armed miners hack to death one man who is not armed. What does that prove?"

His words stopped their advance.

"If you do that, you're cowards, and I seen how you come in here and fought for the chance to work, and we didn't make it easy on you. So I don't believe you're cowards. I believe you love your families and want to provide for them, just like I do. Like *all* miners do."

The miners was looking at each other, not saying nothing, but thinking. Just then, Corey stood behind them, dirty and ragged looking, holding a sprag in his hand, a look of determination on his face. At the sight of his son, tears welled up in his eyes and Johnny almost lost his way of thinking.

"Which is more important," he kept on, "bringing in full coal today, or living to bring it in again tomorrow? And the next day, and the next? Setting up something where your children can keep working in the mines and have a better life. That's why we stood up.

"Got to think for yourself. The coal company don't want you thinking for yourself. Just want you to step over the dead bodies and keep working. Get the coal out. That's all they care about. If anybody's gonna care about the miners it's us who are down here in the hole.

"Now you got somebody tapping from inside, asking for help. They begging for their life. This is about life and death. So either kill me, or put your pickaxes away and let's start moving rocks."

"I'm getting out of here," one of the scabs said.

"Yeah, me too. Let's get back to work."

"No, that ain't your choice," Johnny said. "Your choice is life or death. What you gonna do? You can't just walk away. If you do you are killing the miners behind this pile of rocks. Are we so messed up we don't care about people no more? Anybody know who's behind here? We don't know, but sure as hell it's somebody's son, or father, or brother. What if it was yours? Can you just walk away and leave him in there to die? You men are better than that. I *know* you're better than that."

"I want to say something," one of the miners spoke up. "I'm not a strikebreaker or nothing. Just a miner who didn't join the union. And I just want to say to everybody here that this man who's trying to get us to save some lives here, this is a good man. A family man. A hard worker. He's been through the wars. And I think we ought to listen to him."

Johnny pressed his lips together and nodded in appreciation towards the man.

"You want to hit full coal," Johnny said. "I know. And lots of days I did that. That's important. But a man's life is important too. And his family. His family wants to see him again. That's what it's all about. We stop caring about each other and our lives, what we got? A dark shit hole in the ground with rats and cockroaches? That what we working for?"

The faces softened a bit. They was thinking.

"We don't know who's trapped behind this pile of rocks," Johnny continued. "But one thing I can tell you. Whoever it is, he still alive. Come over here."

Johnny motioned for the men to come forward. He put one hand on the wall of the chute and tapped with a small pickax. He placed his ear against the rock. *Tap, tap, tap.* The men could hear it too, the way they reacted.

"This man's alive back in there. Now he might not be alive in an hour. He could be injured, he could be out of water. His air could be running low. But right now, he's alive, God damn it! What we gonna do about it?"

Johnny picked up a rock from the pile and pushed it into the belly of the worker next to him. The man grabbed the rock and passed it on to the next man.

"Let's do this!" one of the men called out.

"Yep, worry about the coal tomorrow," one said. "Coal don't care when it come out of the mountain."

"Make two lines," another said. "We get this done twice as fast."

The men started hustling. Small and medium rocks was moving down the line handed from one worker to the next. Corey joined the men. Working like this, they quickly uncovered a large boulder that sat up over waist-high on the other rocks. Take more manpower than they had to lift it out of its resting place. They'd have to pry it loose and let it fall. Some men came over with some timbers and poked and prodded to find a leverage point. *Crack!* One of the timbers busted in two.

"Too dry," the miner said. "Need a greener piece."

"Let's get some of these smaller rocks out around here, and here," Johnny said. "Give us some more space."

Men lugged smaller rocks out of the wall, and another walked up with a new timber, less splintered and gray. Just then, a piercing voice from behind.

"What the hell's going on here?"

The men turned to see a company supervisor standing with hands on hips. "Why ain't the coal cars moving down the gangway?"

"We digging somebody out right now," one miner said.

"I don't give a shit what you're doing. Get your asses out in the gangway and start moving the coal!"

The men glanced at him for a moment, but kept hustling rocks. Corey kept working in the line. Two of the miners brought in shovels and was clearing the floor of stones and debris. The one with the timber found an opening where he could leverage his strength and wobble the stubborn boulder.

"You have trouble hearing me?" the supervisor shouted. "I want to see nothing but your Goddamn asses hustling out to the gangway, loading them cars, and hitting full coal today. Do you hear me?"

The men kept working. The supervisor walked up quickly, with great energy, and got in the miners' faces.

"If any of you hillbillies are interested in keeping your jobs, you will stop throwing rocks around in here, and get your Goddamn asses out there in the gangway!"

Just then, the stubborn crag gave way. The supervisor was standing nearby, veins throbbing in his neck that all the men could see, concentrating on his angry message and not paying attention to what was going on around him. Johnny lunged forward and pushed him out of the way. The man landed on his back but in the clear. With a loud rumble the great rock toppled from its perch and landed with a thud on the granite floor right close to where the supervisor had been standing. Thankfully, it wasn't round and did not roll down the floor.

"What the hell?" the supervisor shouted, picking himself up off his back. "Who the hell are you?"

"Johnny McCarthy. You okay?"

"I don't give a shit what your name is, God damn it! I don't recognize you. You don't work here. What are you doing down here?"

"We digging somebody out right now," Johnny said.

"You one of them striking miners, the ones that been killing people around here and fighting Federal Troops?"

"We never fired on Federal Troops," Johnny said.

"I'll have you arrested for trespassing and interfering with company business, and I'll have the rest of you fired!"

The man's face was red like a beet, and his neck pulsated like the throat of a bullfrog. One of the leaders walked over.

"Look, you ain't gonna fire us for digging somebody out of a cave-in, and no officer of the law is gonna arrest this man for saving somebody's life."

"Corey!" a small voice called out.

Pete crawled out of the dusty opening, dirty and scraped up, but with a big smile.

"Pete, you all right?"

The two embraced and held on for a long time. Johnny walked over and wrapped his arms around both of them. He held on tight with his eyes closed, savoring the lives of the two young boys. When he opened his eyes, he saw two miners and another boy not more than ten years old crawling out the opening. They gulped water from the rescuers' canteens. All looked wide-eyed and grateful.

The miners who pulled the rocks away stood around and watched the men and boys who had been freed, and actually clapped their hands in support. Then everyone foot-slogged down the gangway to the lift, rose to the portal, and shuffled out of the mine.

Chapter 70

Almost a week had passed since the boys returned home from the siege of Blair Mountain and the rescue in the mine. Lots of stories being told. Everybody feeling good. Caleb turned his rabbits on the fire, and Johnny danced around the outskirts flipping his venison steaks. Musicians came from all over the camp. Johnny never seen so many instruments in one place—two fiddles, three harmonicas, a banjo, even a guitar. They was having a good old time. Gino, Heinrich, and some others was passing the moonshine.

Corey and Pete sat on the log next to Johnny.

"Hey Mr. McCarthy, tell me again what you said to them miners when they was about to swing them pickaxes at you," Pete said.

"I told them you boys must have never seen me in a fight!" Johnny said.

Everybody laughed. The music hit a fever pitch and old man Jackson was doing his thing with the Appalachian shuffle.

"How he *do* that?" Johnny said.

"Harriet, here's a plate for you," Caleb said.

"Ooh, look at this," she said. "You outdid yourself this time. Grilled rabbit, warm rolls, collard greens, tomatoes, onions. What's this sauce on here? How you come up with that? You ought to open a restaurant!"

Caleb smiled as wide as the Tug River. Johnny saw what he did and brought a loaded up plate to Kate and to Stella, Jim's widow. Seemed like a good thing to do.

"Hey Mr. McCarthy," Pete said, "tell me again how you got them strikebreakers to start pulling off them rocks."

"I took off the first rock myself, handed to one of them, he passed it to someone else, and we was off and running," Johnny said.

"Say, not too many miners around here go tapping on the wall. How'd you know to keep doing that?"

"Corey told me," Pete said. "He tells me everything you say!"

"Oh, he does, does he?"

Corey had a bear grip on his dad's arm with his head lying on his shoulder, looking up with a smile.

"Well, best thing you did was keep tapping," Johnny said. "That's how I knowed you was in there."

"I'm gonna go play ball with Pete," Corey said.

Just then, a commotion over by the fire.

"Conan! When they let you out of the hospital?"

"They wanted to keep me, but I heard there was a celebration going on at Stone Mountain. Didn't want to miss nothing."

"Let's get you some food," Johnny said. "They didn't cut that beard off while you was in there?"

"They knowed they better not try!"

"That arm gonna be okay?"

"It be good enough to put meat on the table, that's all I need."

Just then, Kate and Stella came over, each carrying a cranky little babe.

"Hey Papa, time for you to take one of these little wigglies."

"Aw, look at this," Johnny said.

"Here, why don't you take my namesake," Stella said. "I got to do some things over at my tent."

Johnny held his daughter with both hands overhead, jostling her around a little bit. As he looked straight up at her, he didn't see the satisfying smile he hoped for, but a red face, a strain, and *urp!* A blast of white goop hit him on his forehead with some in the eyes. He pulled her down into his arms and tried to clear his face.

"Aw, look at that," he said. "Whooee! You never know."

Caleb tossed him a towel and gave him a cup of water. His eyes stung and he poured water in them to flush them out. Kate took baby Stella and had the twins sitting on her lap.

Kids was playing tag and hide'n'seek, and older boys was throwing the ball around. The music had folks dancing to the beat even if they wasn't right near the playing. Friends called out to one another and plates of food was passed around.

A soft breeze rustled the leaves on the trees and brightened the dying embers of the camp fire. The sun started to dip in the sky and seek a resting place on the other side of the western peaks.

Johnny noticed Kate walking some distance from the fire, looking back, and motioning for him to join her. He jumped to his feet, hustled off in her direction, and took her hand.

"What you doing?" he asked.

"Oh, just taking a little stroll before bedtime."

"What about the kids?"

"Stella's got them."

They strolled beyond the trees and into the lush meadow to the west. Tall granite peaks framed the peaceful field of daisies all around. Johnny suddenly flipped his head around and looked back at the tent city, now quite some distance behind.

"Where we going?" he said.

Kate looked at him, and motioned forward with her head. They walked another hundred yards.

"What's this?" Johnny asked.

A tent stood pitched in the gap between two white birch and a scattering of low-lying brush.

"A gift," Kate said.

In front of the tent was a fire pit dug out and loaded with fresh-chopped wood.

"Whose is this?"

"Ours."

"How..."

Kate placed a finger over his lips.

"Friends," she said.

Kate stood facing her husband and reached behind her head. She pulled off the rubber band that confined the ball of hair he called a bun. She shook her head, and hair fell down over her shoulders. The cool soft evening breeze kissed her radiant face. Johnny's eyes were fixed. He didn't know her hair was so long and beautiful.

Kate unbuttoned the top two buttons on her dress and loosened the fabric at her bosom. She stepped up to Johnny and unbuckled his belt and the button that kept his trousers tight, and plunged an eager hand into idle but unforgotten places. For a moment, Johnny couldn't see. He placed his hands on Kate's shoulders and their lips met in a soft wet kiss.

"Did you think I'd forgotten your touch?" Kate said. "Did you think I no longer wanted you?

Johnny sighed and wiped a tear from his cheek.

"I haven't forgotten about you, big boy…"

She pulled Johnny into the tent, and a canopy of love settled over the meadow. Squirrels snuggled into the ground and blue jays nestled in the trees. Chilly autumn winds began to blow but the little tent was protected by a blanket of warmth no gale could quench. Stars twinkled, the moon drifted across the black sky, and the night became a new day.

AUTHOR'S NOTE

Johnny and Kate McCarthy were fictional characters, but the suffering of the coal miners and their families in the early 20th century was very real. They were oppressed with violence and hardship, their civil rights were violated, and they were exploited. These good people endured it all in hopes that their children would have a better life.

No one was ever punished for the assassination of Sid Hatfield or Ed Chambers. The self-defense argument prevailed, despite the eyewitness accounts of the victims' wives.

The Battle of Blair Mountain is believed to be the biggest armed insurrection in the history of American labor. No one knows exactly how many men were involved, but estimates range from 9,000 to 20,000 miners, 5,000 mine guards, State Troopers, sheriff deputies, and volunteer militia, and 2,500 Federal Troops. It is estimated that upwards of 30 men were killed with many more wounded.

After the battle, the rank-and-file foot soldier was sent home, but leaders of the insurrection were arrested and held accountable for the actions of the many. Nearly 1,000 men were charged with various crimes ranging from murder, to insurrection, to treason. Bill Blizzard, regarded as the general in the Battle of Blair Mountain, was acquitted of murder and treason, and went on to serve the UMWA for many years. Frank Keeney and Fred Mooney were acquitted of murder and treason, but fell out of favor with UMWA President John L. Lewis, and were forced to retire. Preacher John Wilburn and his son of the same name were convicted of murder but were paroled by Governor Morgan in 1925. A miner named Walter Allen was convicted of treason, but during an appeal, disappeared into the night never to be heard from again.

Author's Note

In the ensuing years, unions lost their foothold in southern West Virginia, with declining membership and diminishing influence. It wasn't until Franklin Delano Roosevelt came into office in 1933 with his New Deal programs and Congress passed the National Industrial Recovery Act, that unions were accepted as a permanent fixture in the labor movement of southern West Virginia.

Made in the USA
Las Vegas, NV
14 March 2022

45631023R00203